THE
AMETHYST
TALISMAN

Also by Aerin Apeltun

The Cursed Weapons Trilogy
The Amethyst Talisman
The Malachite Quest
The Opal King

Crystal Bloods Series
Crystal Bloods

THE AMETHYST TALISMAN

THE CURSED WEAPONS: BOOK 1

AERIN APELTUN

Elsewhen Press

The Amethyst Talisman
This updated edition published in Great Britain by Elsewhen Press, 2026
An imprint of Alnpete Limited

This book was originally published by SmashBear Publishing, 2023.
This is a new updated edition.
Elsewhen Press, PO Box 757, Dartford, Kent DA2 7TQ
www.elsewhen.press

British Library Cataloguing in Publication Data.
A catalogue record for this book is available from the British Library.
ISBN 978-1-917507-23-3 Print edition
ISBN 978-1-917507-33-2 eBook edition

Designed and formatted by Elsewhen Press

To my husband and daughter,
for their never-ending support and love.

And to my sister, without whom there would be no Magic

CONTENTS

THE BLOOD RULE DECREE OF AERBA

1. There will be three Blood Classes – High Bloods, Middle Bloods, and Low Bloods
2. The High Bloods will consist of the Royal family and extended relations
3. The Middle Bloods will include other Nobles, high status citizens and Priests
4. The Low Bloods will include all other citizens
5. Sexual Relationships outside of Marriage are strictly forbidden
6. All Sexual and Romantic Relationships, including Marriage, between Blood Classes is strictly forbidden in order to keep the Blood Classes pure
7. Entering into Marriage or Relationships with citizens of other Lands of the same Blood Class will be permitted but are greatly discouraged and Royal Approval will be required
8. Entering into Marriage or Relationships with citizens of other Lands of a different Blood Class is strictly forbidden
9. Entering into Marriage or Relationships with members of the same sex whether in the same or different Blood Class are strictly forbidden whether Aerban or from another Land
10. All Citizens names will be taken from the Father's Family Line/Land
11. All Citizens Blood Classes will be taken from the Mother's Blood Class
12. Citizens born out of Wedlock will automatically be Low Bloods and their parents Demoted
13. The King has the power to Demote a Citizen from their birth Blood Class as he sees fit
14. The King has the power to enforce the Execution or Imprisonment or Demotion of any Citizen found to be disregarding any element of the Blood Rule Decree at his discretion

As laid out by King Cinquefoil in the year 3929.
Rules 7, 12 and 13 amended by King Finule the First in the year 5643

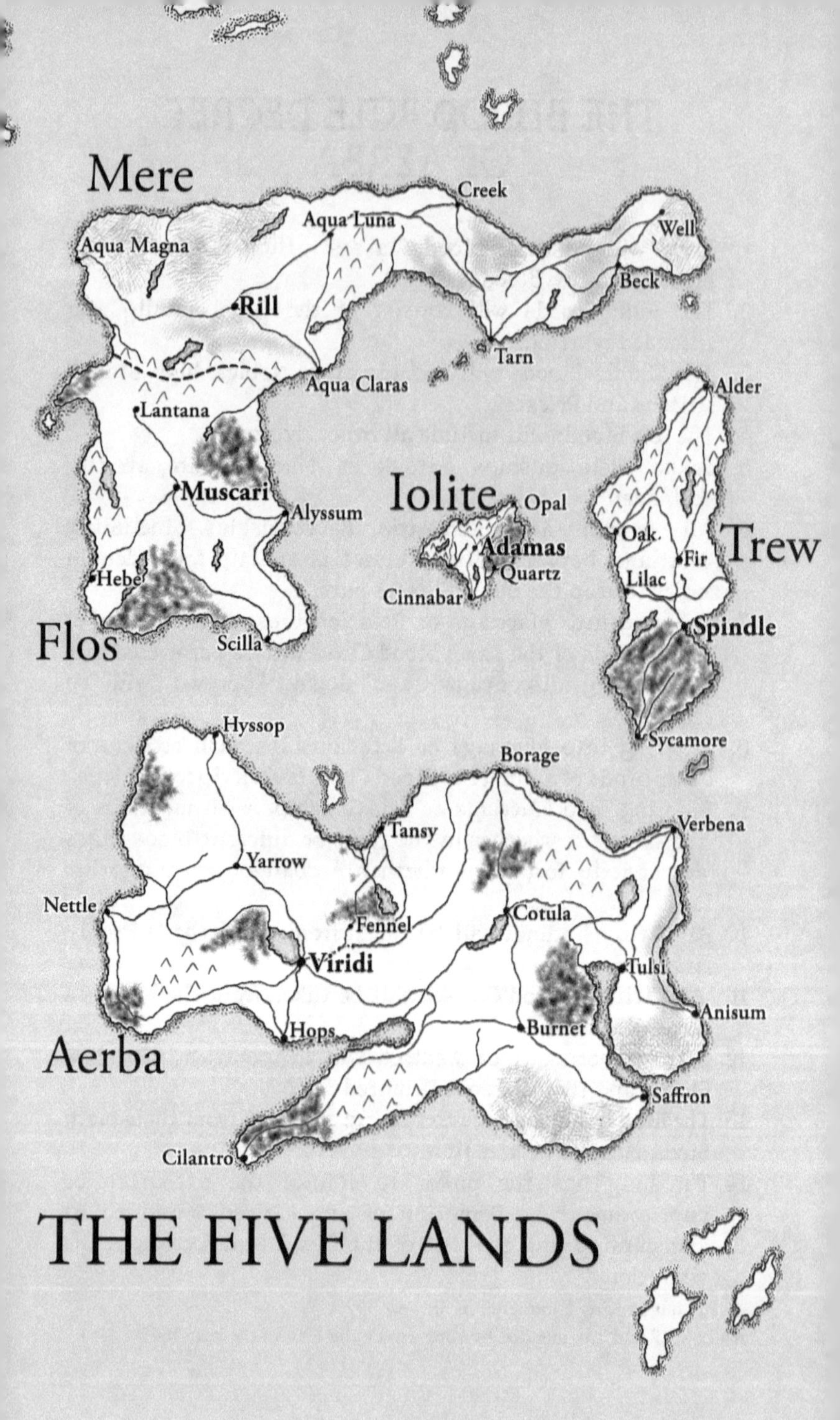

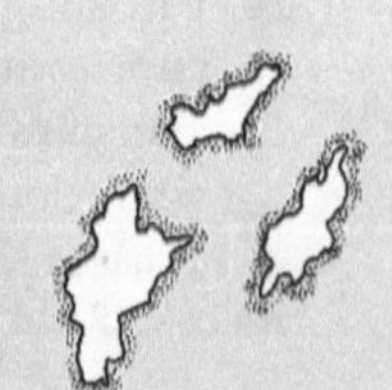

THE FIVE LANDS

CHAPTER ONE

Know your place, Amethyst, and don't you dare fail me.' Lady Juniper, Mistress of the Island of Iolite, sat in front of me on her "throne" in the vast hall at the centre of the Crimson Castle. Her customary long, yellow silk gown fell to the floor like a waterfall, matching the colour of her serpent eyes that pierced my soul. 'Complete your mission, or your sister will suffer, Daughter.'

I wanted to scream *I'm no daughter of yours* right in my stepmother's face, but I didn't dare, so I swallowed and nodded. I wiped my sweaty palms on the soft material of my suede tunic.

'I haven't failed you yet,' I said, determined to leave the castle with at least a modicum of self-respect still intact.

Juniper's eyes narrowed as she fiddled with her necklace of diamonds and agate which she wore for their alleged powers of protection. Her long, blonde hair fell over the golden skin of her shoulder. The pitch torches that illuminated the red granite walls sent grotesque shadows flying across the stone like bats, and set her diamonds alight with all the brilliance of the midday sun. The torches also left a smoky tinge to the air that tickled the back of my throat.

On the wall behind Juniper sat the Malachite Dagger. Its hilt and crossguard were of gold and silver, the quillons curving towards the malachite blade with its swirling shades of vibrant green. The Dagger had been passed down through my father's side of the family for generations, and it meant so much to him he'd even named my elder brother, Malachite, after it. It was to be Mal's on his twenty-first birthday. At least, that was what Father had promised him, but Father wasn't here anymore. *She* was in charge, and the Dagger may never be my brother's now.

'You have the poison?' Juniper asked.

I suppressed the desire to shudder. 'Yes, I collected it earlier.'

'The Crown Princess Angelica of the Land of Aerba must be dead by the end of next week. Those are the terms of the contract. Now, go.' She pointed to the door, her gown falling away from her wrist, exposing a small patch of freckles similar to something I had on my own wrist – but that was permanently covered these days.

I nodded and left.

I hated my life.

I hated that I'd been forced into being an assassin. I dreaded each new day, feared where I'd be sent, who I'd be expected to kill. I resented being in Juniper's control and my twin sister's life being in the balance every time I went off on one of these hideous commissions. Every night I went to bed with butterflies swarming in my stomach, only to find them replaced by a rising sensation of nausea each morning when I awoke.

My reluctance didn't go down well with my stepmother. She saw it as a sign of weakness.

As a member of the Iolite Coterie of Assassins, I'd achieved a kind of notoriety. Lady Merciless, they called me in certain quarters, for my cunning and skill. But she was a myth invented by Juniper to peddle my services. She'd built Lady Merciless from lies, spread rumours, and made her a myth beyond my seventeen years – one I could never hope to live up to. No one outside of the Coterie knew my real name, knew I was the daughter of the dead Master of Iolite. A constant stream of customers requested Lady Merciless for her deft work – if only they knew the truth.

Eleven days after leaving Iolite, I arrived at the Aerban capital, Viridi, which nestled close to the great Viridi Lake that sparkled like frost in the morning sunlight. I cast a wary glance out over the distant water, my heart skipping a beat. I knew exactly what creatures might be lurking there – powlers and lake morgens – although I'd never seen any. Powlers were legendary creatures, twice the height of a man; the beautiful morgens could be sea or lake-dwelling. They were both likely to be myths, too, just like Lady Merciless.

Viridi City had no need for walls, thanks to the wide, poisoned moat that encircled the buildings. Rumour had it you'd be dead in seconds if you tried to swim across, and from the colour of the moat, it was a rumour I chose to believe. A large archway of honey-coloured marble, carved with herb reliefs, marked the way into the city with its lowered wooden drawbridge where disinterested Gate Guards stood talking to each other in their red suede uniforms, spears in hand. I slipped through the gates with a crowd of merchants and citizens unhindered, making my way into the city.

During the rough sea voyage, I'd studied the map of the Aerban Palace that Lord Flint, Chief Assassin of the Coterie, had given me until I knew the place like the back of my proverbial hand. I could find the princess' apartments blindfolded. Enter through the back gate, make my way to the Throne Room, cross it to get to Princess Angelica's apartments, kill her, and get out.

I glanced around at the people as I moved swiftly along the streets. Their clothes signified their Blood Class, of which there were three: High, Middle and Low. The Blood Rule Decree governed the Blood Classes in all the Five Lands, and although everywhere had slight variations, it all amounted to the same thing – you kept to your Blood Class. The Aerban's version was the strictest, and they followed it to the letter.

Iolite was only a small island. Soon after coming into effect, it had altered its Decree to welcome incomers from the other Four Lands – Aerba, Flos, Mere, and Trew. The other Lands didn't welcome new blood. As we had no royalty, we had no High Bloods. Instead, we had a Middle Blood Master or Mistress who ruled the island. My stepmother, Juniper, was originally from the land of Trew. She'd married my widowed father, and now he was dead, she ruled.

I didn't altogether care for High Bloods. My experiences on my various travels had led me to believe they were all cruel and arrogant. Show me one that wasn't. I'd very nearly been trampled under a High Blood's horse in southern Flos once because he couldn't control the beast. He started whipping it, which of course made him lose control even more. He had the nerve to glare at *me* as if I'd got in *his* way. I'd even seen a High Blood deliberately barge a Low Blood girl out of the way in a coastal Merean marketplace a few months ago. He dropped his purchases, including an elaborately painted vase which shattered into a thousand pieces. All his own fault, but he'd screamed at her anyway. The last I saw of her, she was being dragged away by the Town Guard.

I pulled my cloak around me to cover a stolen Middle Blood's beige coat. I'd already removed the tie that usually held my unruly, curly hair back in a traditional Iolitian low ponytail, allowing it to fall loose. Many Aerban's wore their hair up in a high ponytail, but I didn't look out of place. Most of the people here had dark hair, but a few were redheads, so I fitted in well enough, although my pale skin was in contrast to their beautiful rose-beige, so I pulled my hood up and my sleeves down and tried to blend in with the city folk.

I moved through the unfamiliar streets of honey marble buildings, the homes of Middle and High Bloods, leaving the wooden houses of the less wealthy Low Bloods behind in the outer city as I hurried along, passing the vast Temple of Herbs with its moss-green marble intricately carved with herbs. People of all

Blood Classes came and went from its elaborate, open, wooden doors.

I made my way towards the white marble palace at the centre of the city. I dodged one of the King's Warriors in his burgundy outer coat – a tall, good-looking High Blood with his black silk headband embroidered with golden vines of thyme, Aerba's sacred herb. His sun-bleached, brown hair was in a high, slightly messy ponytail that swished as he walked. The twin swords on his back clanked gently, his golden-brown eyes taking in everything around him, but hopefully not me as I dived into the shadows at the edge of the street.

As he moved off, I sped into the market where the smell of dried herbs lingered in the air. I joined the throng of Middle Bloods in their red hemmed beige outer coats that fell halfway down their thighs. Low Bloods scurried about, their short, dark brown coats distinguishing them and their Blood Class from everyone else. There were few High Bloods about in their burgundy coats, and they did their best to avoid everyone else.

I had three days before the contract deadline, and I wanted to get this over with early. I never waited until the last day in case of any unexpected obstacles. Making my way into a quiet side alley near the back of the palace, I hid in a grain store until night fell. I slipped a small bag of oats into my pocket as I left, making my way to the palace's back entrance. The night air was cool and clear as I kept to the shadows. Two men stood guard next to the gate, chatting quietly beside a flaming brazier as I moved as close as I dared. I took the oat bag from my pocket and hurled it beyond the guarded gate and into a woodpile where it dislodged a few logs and sent an axe clattering to the ground. Both guards looked up, said something to each other, and went over to inspect the woodpile. I slipped out of the shadows and ran behind them through the gate, heading across a courtyard and into the palace before they could see me.

I entered through an open door into a passageway that took me past the kitchen storerooms, where the smell of rosemary and thyme filled the air, and headed for the Throne Room. Crown Princess Angelica's apartments lay on the other side of the great chamber.

I found a laundry store cupboard where I hid until after midnight, surrounded by the smell of clean linen. With nails suitably chewed, I made my way towards the princess' apartments. I didn't know much about her other than she was in her mid-twenties, heir to the throne of Aerba, and rather vain. I dodged a Palace Guard in his emerald-green coat, hiding in a shadowy alcove. My heart thudded in my chest and my hands turned clammy. Once he'd passed by, I continued, slipping into the Throne Room unnoticed.

Thankfully, the great chamber stood empty. A few pitch torches flickered on the walls, their flames sending odd shadows careering across the white marble walls and floor. A bright yellow-red glow from the far end of the room grabbed my attention; I couldn't help but investigate. As I moved silently towards it, I noticed flashes of purple and green at its heart.

The legendary Fire Opal of Aerba.

The faceted stone, about five inches across, sat at the top of the King of Aerba's Cedarwood Throne, which was expertly carved and covered in thyme reliefs and gold leaf. The Fire Opal glowed like a living thing with a fire burning at its heart, watching over the great chamber. I recalled an old story my father had told me about the Fire Opal being mined on Iolite and given as a gift from the first Master of Iolite to the King of Aerba some eighteen hundred years ago as a sign of friendship between the two countries. I shivered. I couldn't see the friendship that had endured for so long continuing after tonight.

A flash made me look down. My Amethyst Talisman had escaped my clothes. The purple, hexagonal, prism-shaped gemstone with its pointed ends twinkled in the torchlight as it swung on its silver chain, sending little purple sparks across the stone floor. The silver wires wrapped around it shone like the moon as they formed a kind of swirling metal cage to hold the stone secure. I quickly tucked it away.

Leaving the Throne Room, a wide carpeted staircase with bannisters elaborately carved with herbs, took me up to the princess' rooms. I entered quietly, glancing at a small oil lamp that burnt merrily in a corner of the luxurious sitting room, illuminating its plump silk cushions and tapestries of herbs and trees. The smell of lavender filled the room. My nose tickled and I desperately hoped I wouldn't sneeze. I moved over to the bedroom, slowly taking hold of the handle, praying the door wouldn't creak. It opened silently and, beyond the threshold, lit by the moonlight streaming in her window, lay the Crown Princess sprawled on her bed.

For a second I froze.

The hairs on the back of my neck stood to attention. Uneasiness wormed its way into the pit of my stomach as I took a couple of tentative steps forward on the soft carpet so I could see her more clearly. I stifled a gasp, my heart thundering against my ribcage. Her dead body lay on her bed, an empty teacup lying upside down beside her, its contents spilt over the silken sheets. Her face bore the mark of Blue Water Hemlock poison; her eyes wide open in horror, great pain etched into her features, and a wet trickle of blood running from the side of her mouth. The same poison I'd brought from Iolite, and the appearance of the princess' body indicated she hadn't been dead long.

Hell's teeth.

My shaking hands shot to my mouth.

Again – this had happened yet again.

Surely not. I tried to calm my erratic breathing, tried to stop my body from shaking. Thoughts raced through my mind, but in such a jumble that I could only focus on one.

Every time I went to kill, someone got there before me.

Despite my fearsome reputation, killing didn't come naturally to me. In fact, I'd never actually killed anyone. It was a line I didn't want to cross. I never had. And all because some mysterious assassin beat me to it; I just didn't know why, or how. Or who, for that matter. That still eluded me.

Yet again I'd avoided the thing that terrified me most – becoming a killer. A kind of calm began to wash through me as my shoulders sagged and I let out a long breath. I closed my eyes for a moment. Thank the Stars.

My eyes snapped open as a sudden chill swept through me. No, killing wasn't what scared me most. Juniper finding out I hadn't completed my mission *myself* scared me most. What would she do to me if she did? My immediate death was likely. So far, no one knew; each time I returned to the Crimson Castle in Adamas City the congratulations on my kill had started before I'd had the chance to say anything to the contrary. I'd built up quite a reputation for doing absolutely nothing. For killing no one. A reputation for an enigma far beyond my years. I'd trained hard, I could fight well, but whether I could kill in cold blood – that was another matter.

I'd kept up the pretence for my older brother's sake. For my sister's sake. For my own survival. If Juniper found out, it wouldn't just be my body parting company with my head – we'd all die, and the axe would be the least of my worries.

My dearest wish was to escape the Coterie with my brother and sister but, as my brother said, no one ever left the Coterie alive, and we had my twin to consider. She was constantly watched and escaping with her too would be nigh on impossible. So, I dreamt of escape whilst trying to survive.

I slowly backed out of the room. Escaping the palace didn't prove difficult. Because of the late hour, the High Bloods were all asleep and wouldn't find the Princess until the morning, giving me, as well as the real assassin, something of a head start.

I'd arranged to meet Lord Flint at Tansy, a few days north-east of Viridi, after the mission, to sail back to Iolite. The journey there was uneventful. When I arrived, I found the heavily-built man waiting in the little harbour.

'I hear you did well, my girl,' he said in his deep, grating voice as we set off in a small sailing boat.

'She's dead,' I said, looking out over the water as I took off my Aerban coat. 'Where's the ship?'

'A little further along the coast,' he replied, adjusting the plain white sails that fluttered in the wind.

The sun sank towards the horizon, sending little sparks off the waves, the water chattering against the side of the boat as we cut through the sea. Flint lit a small lantern on the mast as dusk settled over us, the yellow glow flickering on his pale skin. In the distance, the lights of a small fishing village twinkled like a constellation of stars as we hugged the Aerban coastline.

'You've been lying to us, haven't you, my girl?' Flint said after a while, shifting his black hair from his face.

'I'm sorry, what?' A chill ran down my spine.

'You haven't been killing anyone.'

I gulped. 'You know all my marks are dead, in exactly the way I was told.'

'But you haven't been doing the actual killing, have you?' Flint asked, turning towards me, his beady brown eyes shining in the last of the sunlight.

'I...'

'An assassin who doesn't kill is of no use to us,' he said, his knees creaking as he crouched down to rearrange the two oars lying on the far side of the boat.

'But it's not my fault; they were dead before I got there.'

'And you never told us.' He looked at me as the wind fluttered in the sails. 'Your brother, Mal, is dead, by the way. Killed by thieves on his way back across Flos after his recent commission.'

I shook my head in disbelief. Not Mal, please. My pulse pounded in my ears as I stared at him. 'What? No! What proof is there?'

'Carnelian was on a mission in Flos and found his body,' Flint said, picking something up from under the oars, 'and this.' He threw a sword at my feet, the steel glinting in the light from the lantern as it clattered to a halt. In its pommel, the normally vibrant green malachite stone tonight looked dead.

I gasped. Mal's sword. He never went anywhere without it. A shard of ice slammed into my heart. I struggled to breathe. This couldn't be true. How could this be true? But the sword was evidence enough.

'Don't worry, my girl, you're about to meet him,' Flint continued.

'You wouldn't dare! I'm the heir now.'

'We have a spare.'

'Beryl? She's too fragile.'

Flint barked a grating laugh. 'Fragile? She's been helping Juniper coordinate the Coterie for some time. She's up to her neck in Coterie business.'

'W-what? But Juniper always said she'd kill her if Mal and I didn't do what we were told. Beryl knows nothing of the Coterie.' I shook my head, refusing to believe what I was hearing.

Flint sneered, picking up one of the oars. 'Beryl's been working behind the scenes for years; her life has never been in any danger – she's too valuable. You, on the other hand, have outlived your usefulness.'

In one swift movement, Flint swiped the end of the oar right at my head. I had no time to dodge, nowhere to go. The last of the sun's light vanished into darkness.

The thumping in my head raged like a hot summer storm as something cold and sharp pressed against my throat, jolting me from my stupor. A knife? Salt filled the air. I looked up, squinting in the dawn sunlight, trying to make out the face staring down at me. The crouching silhouette shifted position, a burgundy and gold coat catching the light – a High Blood, and not just that, a member of the Royal House of Aerba. My heart decided to do an impression of the drums at an Iolitian folk dance. I squinted again in the bright light. A young man stared at me, his long, straight, maroon-coloured hair tied in a high ponytail, loose strands falling about his handsome rose-beige face. His deep amber eyes bore into me, full of hate. And yet, behind them there was a kindness – something I didn't associate with High Bloods.

His amber eyes were extremely rare in the Five Lands, rather like my amethyst ones, and the combination of amber eyes and maroon hair was even more so. I immediately recognised the young man from a conversation with Lord Flint before I'd left Iolite. I knew exactly who this was.

Prince Valerian.

Crown Princess Angelica's youngest brother.

'Give me one good reason why I shouldn't kill you right here, right now,' he said, menace filling his rich voice.

I swallowed. 'I didn't do it, Your Highness,' I said as confidently as I could.

He frowned at me, his eyes narrowing. 'What do you mean, you didn't do it?'

'Just what I said. It wasn't me that killed your sister.' I tried to move my head, but he held the blade of his knife too close to my neck.

'You're lying,' he said, the furrows in his forehead deepening.

I shivered, my cold, damp clothes clinging to me.

He reached out. A gold ring on his little finger with tiny diamonds and some sort of engraving caught the sunlight as he moved the hair from my temple. I flinched at the sudden pain. My heart stuttered at his touch, and a strand of my copper hair fell in front of my eyes. 'Someone gave you a good wallop,' he said.

'That "someone" was trying to kill me because I hadn't killed your sister as instructed,' I said.

By the look in his eyes, you'd have been forgiven for thinking he was making the biggest decision of his life. He reached out again, taking my Amethyst Talisman in his hand. His fingers were long, rather like mine, but the similarity ended there. His hands were smooth, with the odd callus from wielding a sword; mine were rough from my training, and dry from lack of fine soaps and lotions to heal them when injured and blistered. He let go. He pulled back, chewing his lip for a moment.

'All right, get up,' he said, standing.

I scrambled up from the marshy creek, my skin flecked with grey-brown mud. As I stood, the world tilted for a moment, and a sharp needle drilled into my head. I stumbled and landed on my knees. I didn't want to fall headfirst back into the muddy inlet where I'd washed up. The dizzy sensation passed, and I looked around at the salty marshland dotted with creeks full of brown water and green salt-tolerant plants. Grey rocks broke through the marsh like broken teeth, covered in clusters of green succulents with little umbels of tiny white-yellow flowers, as warm sunlight skittered off the distant sea.

'Where am I?' I asked, finally making it to my feet beside the prince. He was tall, probably a good six feet, although I was only three or four inches shorter.

'The Tansy Marshes,' he replied, his amber eyes narrowing as he looked at me.

'Oh,' I said, wincing as I gingerly touched my forehead.

He hesitated a moment, the soft smell of rich sandalwood swirling around him. 'You obviously know who I am?' he asked; his voice had a steely edge, but at the same time, it could probably melt glaciers.

I nodded. 'Prince Valerian,' I said, flinching as another sharp stab of pain shot through my head, making me stagger slightly.

'Then you know I'll be taking you back to Viridi City to face my father.'

Unfortunately, I did.

I looked more closely at him. He was impeccably dressed, but then, he was a prince. His burgundy suede coat fell to his knees, bordered by a deep golden hem embroidered with thyme, a world away from my tired, dark suede tunic. His black suede britches sat neatly tucked into his mud-covered leather boots. The black silk headband resting high across his forehead had gold embroidery similar to that on his coat, which marked him out as one of the King's Warriors.

I nodded to him.

'What's your name, girl?' he asked.

The rules of the Coterie firmly stated that if caught, you never gave up your name. Whether this actually applied to me now, after Flint's revelations, was a moot point, but I didn't feel inclined to divulge it just yet.

Valerian raised an eyebrow. 'You don't want to tell me? Then I'll call you Samphire, seeing as I found you surrounded by it,' he said, glancing at the tiny white-yellow flowers growing on the rocks around us. Of course, I now recognised the Aerban Rock Samphire.

I didn't know why he had to call me anything, but I preferred it to being called "girl".

'This way, Samphire,' he said, pointing his knife at my back and ushering me inland, his coat shifting in the wind, the twin swords on his back clanking softly as he walked behind me. 'And don't try anything clever because I won't hesitate to kill you if you do.'

I didn't doubt it, but the way my head hurt and the fact the world periodically tilted made the prospect of fighting him out of the question, at least for now. I squinted at the sunlit landscape, devoid of feature or structure, other than the grey rocks and the distant sea out beyond the muddy, marshy creeks.

'Where're we going?' I asked, wiping perspiration from my brow.

'To meet my friends,' he said.

For half an hour I stumbled along with the prince behind me, slipping in the mud, my damp clothes chafing me. At one point, a sharp pain shot through my hip and I glanced down to see my War Fan hanging from my belt. The silver of its outer cover shone in the sunlight as the semi-precious stones adorning it sparkled. My brother, Mal, had given it to me for my sixteenth birthday and I was never without it. The same year I'd given him a malachite ring for his nineteenth birthday – he'd worn it every day since. The thought of him made my nose tingle for a moment and my eyes sting, but this was no time for tears. The Fan may come in handy if the chance to escape presented itself.

Finally, the marsh turned to more solid ground where a small village came into view, set within oak and cedar trees, the buildings consisting of little log cabins with oak shingles. The villagers, Low Bloods from their clothes, moved between the buildings pausing to look curiously at us, some giving small bows as smoke drifted lazily from the chimneys of the dwellings, promising warmth. I shivered. Although my damp clothes had begun to dry, a chill had taken up residence in my bones.

'Rian! Over here,' a voice shouted. I turned to see a young man, attired similarly to the prince but with a black rather than gold edge to his coat, and a single silver earring in the shape of a sprig of thyme dangling from his right ear. Another High Blood, but not royalty. He wore the same embroidered headband over his long, straight, dark brown hair, caught in a high ponytail. Another King's Warrior.

'Sage,' Valerian nodded as he reached the young man.

Sage looked at me, his brown eyes narrowing, his earring jingling. 'Who is she?'

'Our quarry.'

'You found her? We wondered where you'd got to – Tarragon's gone off to look for you.'

'I decided to do my own little search while we were here and came across her in a creek.'

'So why is she still alive?' Sage asked, a hard edge to his voice, the scent of violet and lemon surrounding him, and his expression less than friendly.

'She says she's innocent,' Valerian replied, moving me over to three horses that stood not far from Sage. 'And that someone tried to kill her because she didn't follow through on her orders.'

'And you believed her?' Sage asked, glaring at me and tugging at his earring. 'You can't trust her, Rian – she's an assassin.' He continued to watch me closely as the prince stood beside him. Sage was nearer my height than Valerian's, his appearance neat, and his nails well-manicured.

'She has a wound to prove it,' Valerian said. 'I thought we'd take her to my father, see what he has to say.'

'You know what he'll say – you should have killed her when you found her. Those were our orders.'

'Maybe I can change his mind.'

'You've never managed it before.'

Valerian frowned at him.

The longer the conversation went on, the more my stomach tied itself in knots. I took a step back, right into someone. I spun around to find another young man dressed the same as Sage, but with lighter brown hair, bleached by the sun, and golden-brown eyes that bore into me. The same good-looking young man I'd seen in Viridi on my way to kill Angelica. His ponytail was still as messy as before. He obviously wasn't as particular as Sage in his appearance, but the dishevelled look suited him.

'Is this our assassin?' he asked, his voice deep and husky.

'It is, Tarragon,' Valerian said. 'Get some rope and tie her hands.' Valerian still had his knife out and I had no option but to let Tarragon bind my hands in front of me. 'Help her onto my horse; she's coming back with us to Viridi.'

'What's her name?'

'She won't say, so we're calling her Samphire for now.'

Tarragon nodded. 'Fine with me.' He was Valerian's height, lithe, and as I soon discovered, very strong. In one smooth movement, he had hold of my elbow, and before I knew it, I was sitting on one of the horses, the prince getting up behind me.

I'd landed in a heap of trouble with no obvious escape. Valerian urged our horse on and the smell of sandalwood wafted around me, which was strangely calming in the circumstances. I considered slipping off the horse and making a run for it, or better still, knocking Valerian from the horse and riding off without him, but with Sage and Tarragon present too, my chances were slim.

Valerian slipped a strong, warm arm around my waist and I tensed at his touch, realising I'd missed any chance I'd had to escape. On the other hand, his warm body resting against me helped to ease my shivering.

A sudden itch at my right wrist made me glance down. I wriggled my sleeve up a little to find the source of the tickle. I caught sight of the Coterie tattoo that covered the little area of freckles I had. The freckles couldn't be seen now – they were hidden the day Juniper took me into the Coterie and had me branded. A cold chill like the first snows of winter whistled through me. Yes, branded. This wasn't a tattoo of camaraderie. It was a mark of shame.

We rode out through the trees into the open Aerban countryside. Heading south we passed enclosures of animals, plantations of pine and spruce, and fields stuffed full of a plethora of herbs, many of which I recognised but couldn't name. We spent the day riding, only stopping at the edge of a small wood as dusk settled over the land, the sun slipping slowly from the horizon and flooding the sky with pinks and reds. The young men made camp just into the trees, lighting a small cooking fire. Before long, Sage had a stew bubbling away, the smell of herbs wafting across the little campsite.

The prince had found a log for me to sit on. He glared at me, resting his hand on his knife each time I tried to move. I looked at the well-tied rope binding my hands, ignoring the chewed nails on my fingers. Tarragon had done this before. I glanced at my Fan. Its highly-polished silver cover was embossed with the sun, moon, and stars, sitting proudly next to faceted stones of dusky rose, sky blue and spring green. They glittered in the firelight, but the large, exquisitely-cut amethyst set in the silver at its base sparkled most. I could probably open it with my hands tied like this, push the button to release the blades, but I'd never be able to twist it around and cut the ropes. In all likelihood, I'd only get one chance to escape, so I'd have to pick my moment carefully.

But maybe there was another way. I had nothing to go back to Iolite for, not with Mal gone and Beryl forsaking me. The Coterie thought I was dead. Perhaps I could prove my innocence to the King and find a new home, away from Juniper.

Valerian glanced at me, his hair appearing to catch light in the reflection of the firelight, before turning back to the others. The three young men sat on their own logs around the fire, preparing to eat. Tarragon looked like the eldest, maybe two years older than the prince, Sage in the middle and Valerian the youngest – probably just a couple of years older than me.

Sage presented me with a small bowl of stew and a spoon, scowling at me as he did so. I rested the bowl on my lap and took the spoon in my tied hands, my stomach growling, making me query when I'd last eaten. Eating like this wasn't easy, but I managed as the young men talked quietly amongst themselves while they ate, casting the occasional unfriendly glare in my direction. True High Bloods.

After the meal, Tarragon came over to me carrying a heap of blankets. 'Here, it gets cold out in the open at night, y'know,' he said, setting them out for me near the fire.

'Thank you,' I said gratefully, because although my clothes had dried out some hours ago, a chill still held me in its thrall.

'One of us will be keeping guard all night, so don't think about escaping, assassin,' Sage said, narrowing his eyes as he glowered at me.

Nodding, I crouched next to the flames and watched their mesmerising flickering as I warmed my tied hands. I listened to the crackles as the flames licked the wood, slowly devouring it, tendrils of smoke drifting into the air.

A humming whistle suddenly pierced my thoughts. I lunged towards Valerian who sat not far from me on a log, knocking him to the ground as an arrow skimmed over our heads.

CHAPTER TWO

What the...' Valerian started. Before he could finish, three dishevelled men appeared out of the darkness, wicked-looking knives in hand, yelling loudly. Valerian immediately rolled to his feet, drew his swords, and sped towards the men, Tarragon and Sage right behind him.

I made an instinctive grab for my hip, but my bound hands closed around thin air. No sword.

I'd trained back on Iolite until I was bruised and bleeding, practised fight moves until the movements were memories in my muscles, so ingrained I didn't have to think, didn't have to worry about what I would do next, my body just did it. The lack of weapons didn't bother me. I may have had to resort to elbows and knees in the end anyway, but there was no point starting there if I could help it. I quickly scanned the little camp. I grabbed a flaming branch from the fire. If the cutthroats came for me, I'd use this first.

For a few moments, I let the fight unfold. All three young men were excellent swordsmen, wielding their twin swords with grace and ease, but the three brigands matched their sword strokes, holding their own in a haphazard, brutal way.

With them all busy, I had a sudden chance to escape. I backed away into the darkness of the trees, glancing at Tarragon who fought closest to me. He sliced his swords towards his opponent's upper body, meeting him head on with every strike. Fool. It was an early lesson I'd learnt – outflank them, get around their back. Finish it from behind. Far easier way to end a fight, and far quicker than to string it out the way Tarragon was. The problem was the King's Warrior was having too much fun.

Tarragon stepped back, tripping on one of the logs around the fire. He fell backwards, hitting the ground, and dropping one of his swords.

I stopped.

Tarragon's opponent raised his sword over his head, preparing for the kill. I sighed. Took a deep breath. By the Stars, I knew I'd probably regret this later, but I sprang forward out of the shadows brandishing my flaming branch, jabbing it straight into the brigand's face. He yelled, stumbling backwards as I dropped the branch. I grabbed Tarragon's discarded sword, my heart pounding both from the exercise and the adrenaline. I drove the brigand back and away from Tarragon, who sat up, a confused expression on his face.

I lunged at the brigand. My bound hands made it an awkward attack. The brigand tried to parry, his momentum taking him to one side. I spun around behind him. Slammed the hilt of Tarragon's sword in the back of his neck and watched as he fell to the ground. I turned to see Sage running his man through, his swords scarlet, and Valerian standing staring at me, a slightly wild look in his eyes and his mouth open. A man lay at the prince's feet in a pool of blood.

I moved back to Tarragon and rammed the sword into the earth beside him.

He looked up at me, his eyes wide as he tried to get his breath back. 'Bugger me.'

'Idiot. Next time don't get carried away and prolong the fight, however much you're enjoying it. Finish it quickly, or one day, it'll finish you,' I said, holding my hands out to him to help him up.

He hesitated a moment, a little frown forming on his face, then took my hands, clambering to his feet. 'I'll remember that, Samphire. Thank you.'

'You're welcome.'

'How did you do that? I've never seen anything like it.'

His voice had a profound respect to it that caught me by surprise. I shrugged. 'Training,' I said, giving him a little smile.

'You didn't kill him,' Sage said, looking at my fallen opponent then back at me, his forehead wrinkled. 'Why not?'

'I don't kill,' I said, turning towards him and gritting my teeth.

'Really?' Sage asked, his earring swinging and catching the light. 'That's rich, coming from someone like you, assassin.'

'I'm not who you think I am,' I said, clenching my bound hands.

Valerian gave me a quizzical look, his head tilting to one side.

'I owe you my life,' Tarragon concluded, resheathing his swords before placing a hand on my shoulder. 'Thank you.'

'So do I, and I won't forget it,' Valerian said, a flicker of respect in his eyes even as he frowned. 'How did you know?'

'You didn't hear the loose fletching on the arrow?' I asked.

Valerian shook his head, his face losing all colour in the flicker of the firelight. 'No, I didn't. Lucky you were here, then, or I'd be dead.'

'We'd better move on; it isn't safe to stay here,' Sage said, looking into the dark shadows between the trees. 'Who knows if these three have any friends in the neighbourhood?'

Valerian nodded. 'We'll ride on until dawn, then rest.'

'You need your Father to get control of the local rabble down here,' Sage said. 'If they'd caught us when we were sleeping…'

'I'll have a word when we get back.'

They collected their things, put out the fire, and we were back in the saddle within minutes, riding out across the open, moonlit countryside. Valerian still had his arm around my waist as we rode. Why had I just done that? I should've left them to it during the fight but leaving someone to die when I could've helped them wasn't in my nature. I couldn't do something as callous as that.

As dawn broke, we found an old ramshackle barn out on the grasslands not far from a forest that loomed like a dark green curtain in the distance, and took the opportunity to rest for a while. Sage lit a small fire by the door and made up a tea which I sipped, glad of the chance to finally rest. The drink had an odd tang to it, but nothing unpleasant.

'So, you were sent to kill my sister, Lady Merciless,' Valerian said as he fed the fire with twigs.

Hell's teeth. I looked at him, heart thumping. 'You know who I am?' I asked, forcing the words out of my dry mouth.

The prince nodded, looking up. 'You're Lady Merciless of the Iolite Coterie of Assassins, Bane of the Five Lands – the murderer of my sister.'

I winced, swallowing hard as my palms became sweaty. 'I've told you already, Your Highness, I didn't kill her,' I said.

Sage snorted. 'Liar.'

'I didn't, truly,' I said.

'Who ordered her death?' Valerian asked, turning back to the fire.

'I don't know, we never do – they don't tell us who commissioned the assassination, just where to go and what we have to do.'

'Convenient,' Sage said, clearly not believing me.

'If you think I'm lying, why haven't you killed me?' I asked. They'd had plenty of chances.

'Because we want to know what you did with the Fire Opal.'

I looked sharply at Sage. 'The Fire Opal? The one in the Cedarwood Throne?'

'That's the one,' Tarragon said, staring intently at me with his golden brown eyes.

I frowned. 'It was still there when I left the palace.'

'So, you admit you were in the palace to kill my sister?' Valerian gave me a particularly unfriendly look.

'I'd been sent to kill her, yes, I admit it, but I didn't – she was already dead when I got there. It wasn't me, Prince Valerian, it never is.'

Valerian's forehead furrowed as he looked at me, his eyes searching mine. 'What do you mean?'

'Nothing, it doesn't matter.' What was the point in telling them? They'd never believe me. 'The Fire Opal was in the throne when I left. Are you saying it's been stolen?' I knew how much the Fire Opal meant to the Aerbans, how it symbolised their power, how myth said that it protected the Land and the King whilst it sat in the Cedarwood Throne. Now it was gone, there'd be hell to pay.

'Don't play the innocent with us, Lady Merciless,' Sage said, glaring at me.

Valerian held up his hand. 'Wait, Sage, I believe she's telling the truth about the Fire Opal.'

'What? You must know she's lying about your sister; why shouldn't she be lying about the Fire Opal?'

Valerian turned to me. I met his look, but his stare made me increasingly uncomfortable. 'Why would she take the Fire Opal? I want it back, believe me. It's my dearest wish, and I'll kill any man that gets in my way to retrieve it, but the Coterie has no interest in material things.'

Tarragon nodded. 'They've never stolen anything before, y'know. It's not their style. I don't see why they'd start now.'

'She probably left it on board the sailing boat with that man before she fell overboard,' Sage said.

'Wait, you've been watching me?' I asked. 'If that's true, you'll know I didn't fall. Flint attacked me. He was trying to kill me.'

Valerian's eyes narrowed at my words and he chewed his lip. 'You said that before; tell me more.'

'Why?'

'Because it might save your life,' he said.

I sighed. What did it matter if I told them or not? I was no longer beholden to the Coterie, and there was a small chance that perhaps they'd believe me after all. 'All right, his name's Lord Flint; he's the Chief Assassin of the Coterie. My stepmother, Mistress Juniper, the Leader of the Coterie, had discovered that despite my fearsome reputation as an assassin I've never killed a single person, so she sent Flint to kill me. An assassin who doesn't kill is apparently of no use to her.'

'You're Lady Amethyst?' Valerian asked, raising an eyebrow in surprise. 'Daughter of the late Master Peridot and Mistress Emerald of Iolite?'

I blinked. 'You've heard of me, Your Highness?'

'I've heard you were named for your vibrant amethyst eyes. Now

I see why,' he said, gazing at me once more, sending shivers down my spine.

'My father's idea, Mal always thought-' Mentioning Mal brought home his death, something I couldn't decide if I was suppressing or had chosen to deliberately sidestep. Perhaps I was just numb to it still.

'Mal?' Valerian asked.

'My brother.'

'Lord Malachite?' Tarragon asked suddenly. 'I met him once. Nice guy. Isn't he supposed to be taking over as Master of Iolite soon?'

I swallowed. 'He was supposed to take over on his twenty-first birthday in a few days' time, but he won't now. He's dead. Flint told me on the boat before he tried to kill me. That, and the fact my twin sister, Beryl, has been working for them all these years when I thought I was protecting her.'

'By carrying out the assassinations?' Valerian asked, his eyes softening ever so slightly as he began to understand.

I nodded.

'So, what happened to your brother?' Tarragon asked quietly.

'Killed by thieves in Flos,' I said, keeping my voice level.

'I'm sorry,' Tarragon said, bowing his head. The look on his face convinced me he was genuine. Maybe this High Blood had a heart.

'Really, you believe all this from an assassin sent to murder your sister?' Sage asked, shaking his head.

'She has no reason to lie about this, Sage,' Valerian said.

'She wants to save her skin, of course she's going to lie.'

'Rian's right, the Coterie have never gone in for theft,' Tarragon said. 'But killing their own because she hadn't been following through on her orders? Now that I do believe.'

'How did you get away with it for so long, then?' Sage asked, staring at me.

'Every time Juniper sent me on a mission, when I reached the person I was supposed to kill, they were already dead, killed in exactly the way I'd been told to do it,' I said. 'I don't know if it was the same person each time, or a different one, but whoever it was, they were skilled. They did it just before I arrived, so it would've appeared to anyone else that I'd done it, but I never saw them.'

'If they hadn't already been dead, would you have followed through on your orders?' Valerian asked intently.

I hesitated. 'I don't know. My sister's life was at stake, or I thought it was, so…' I paused, truly not knowing the answer. 'I'm not sure I could've lived with myself, though, taking a life. In a fight, in self-defence, that might be different, but in cold blood? I guess we'll never know now.' I bowed my head, suddenly feeling incredibly alone in the world. 'Are you going to kill me? Maybe you should.'

'If I was going to kill you, I'd have done it in that creek, just like I'd been ordered to,' Valerian said. 'But something told me you weren't everything we'd been led to believe.'

'You could say that,' I said. 'So, what are you going to do with me?'

Valerian looked directly into my eyes, searching. I held his gaze for a moment then looked down, my face flushed. 'We'll take you to my father and see what he decides to do with you,' he said.

'He'll kill her, y'know,' Tarragon murmured, scratching his chin.

'Not necessarily. If he believes in her innocence, he may decide to ransom her,' Valerian said.

Sage made a choking sound. 'You think so? I'd lay money on the fact he won't.'

'Then I'll have to persuade him otherwise,' Valerian said, a steely note to his voice.

'How? He never listens to you.'

'Maybe I can get him to this time.'

Tarragon sighed. 'I'm not sure he'll ever listen to you, Rian. He's never treated you like the other two. He's not going to suddenly change now.'

'You know we're right,' Sage said quietly, bowing his head. 'He'll never treat you the same.'

Valerian muttered something under his breath and glanced at me. 'I won't let him kill her if she's innocent, that would be a crime all of its own,' he said, fist clenched.

'I'd rather die than go back,' I said, my stomach tying itself in knots at the prospect of returning to Iolite.

'You don't want to go back home?' Valerian asked.

I shook my head. 'Iolite isn't home anymore. My parents have been dead for some time. My brother's dead. My twin sister knew what Flint was going to do and went along with it. The only thing left for me in Iolite is death, and Juniper won't make it pleasant – she has an executioner, Serpentine, who makes pain a speciality. Flint was under instructions to kill me, and now the Coterie thinks I'm dead. I'd like to keep it that way.' Nausea welled in my throat. 'If you're going to send me back, you might as well kill me now, get it over with.'

I thought a brief wisp of sympathy flickered in the prince's eyes, but it quickly vanished. I was doomed either way, but escaping, even if I could, didn't hold much appeal. I had nowhere to go, and they'd find me again quickly enough in this Land with my pale colouring. Maybe one person in the Coterie didn't want me dead. Onyx, but he'd never be able to help me. Maybe trying to escape was the right thing to do, but the look Valerian had given me and the fact he seemed to believe me caused a little spark of hope to flare inside. I'd take my chances with him and his friends, despite them being High Bloods – if I could prove my innocence to them and the King, maybe this would be my chance to escape the Coterie once and for all.

'Perhaps I can help you find the real assassin,' I said. Helping High Bloods didn't sit well with me, but as a means to an end, I'd live with it.

'And how would you do that?' Sage asked.

'Each one has their own style, methods, skills. I might be able to identify them for you if I know everything that happened.'

'What's *your* style, Lady Merciless?'

I gave Sage a long look. 'I don't have one. I've never killed.'

'We'll see what my father decides, Lady Amethyst,' Valerian said.

'Samphire,' I said, wanting to break free of the Coterie and Iolite forever.

'What?'

'Call me Samphire, it's a much better name than Amethyst.' And it didn't remind me of Mal.

Valerian frowned, turning to Tarragon.

'Don't look at me, Rian. You gave her the name, y'know,' Tarragon said, shrugging.

'Very well, we'll continue to call you Samphire.' Valerian nodded to me. 'You should get some sleep.'

I nodded and moved across the barn, lying down to rest in the blankets Tarragon had once again presented me with. My tattoo poked out from my sleeve and I quickly hid it. I closed my eyes, a sudden drowsiness engulfing me as the conversation unfolded.

'I still don't trust her,' Sage said softly from the other side of the barn. I didn't trust him, so it didn't matter much. 'Tarragon?'

Tarragon hesitated. 'I'm inclined to believe her.'

'What? You know what she did.'

'No, we don't, not for sure. All I know is she saved my life last night when she could've left me to die and run off, but she didn't.'

'Rian?' Sage asked.

'Tarragon has a point,' Valerian murmured.

'But your sister...'

'My sister had it coming.'

'You can't say that,' Sage said, a horrified note to his voice. 'She was the Crown Princess.'

'And not a very nice person,' Tarragon said.

'You know it's true,' Valerian said.

'For some reason she liked you, Sage, but she was a right bitch to me and Rian.'

'I never wished her ill,' Valerian said, 'but my sister had a knack for causing offense and raising hackles wherever she went because of her damn self-obsessed, spiteful nature.'

'That's an understatement,' Tarragon sniffed. 'Although perhaps it's where your brother gets it from.'

'Now he *is* difficult to get on with,' Sage said.

'That's putting it mildly,' Tarragon said, a laugh escaping his lips.

'I wonder who arranged Angelica's assassination, paid for it,' Valerian said.

'Y'know, I could hazard a few guesses.'

'And not only in Aerba – but it's also possible someone from one of the other Lands ordered it,' Sage said.

'The list is a little long and we may never know,' Valerian said.

'She definitely hasn't got the Fire Opal with her, though,' Tarragon said, stifling a yawn.

'She could've dumped it on the boat with Lord Flint,' Sage said.

'No, I don't think so,' Valerian said as the hypnotic crackling of the fire broke a sudden silence, beckoning me into darkness. 'As for Samphire...' Valerian's voice trailed off. 'We'll see. She saved my life, too.'

A black wave of oblivion rushed towards me.

'How much of that stuff did you give her, Sage?' Valerian asked suddenly.

'More than Anise would've,' Tarragon muttered. 'Do you even know what you're doing with it?'

'I gave her enough,' Sage muttered.

The wave hit.

When we started out again later in the day a fog hung in my head, and a stubborn drowsiness clung to my thoughts as a muffled voice somewhere on the distant edges of my mind muttered something about a sleeping draught. I shook my head, only succeeding in making the fog worse. My blurry eyes tried to focus as we rode along, grass and bushes on either side of our path, and although I squinted the vegetation remained indistinct green and brown smudges. My head pounded and I wobbled slightly, only regaining my balance as Valerian's arm tensed around my waist, steadying me.

He gave me a strange look, frowned, then turned and glared at Sage. 'By the Herbs, Sage,' he said.

'What?' Sage asked, his earring jingling as he gave a little shrug.

Valerian shook his head. 'Never mind.'

They'd obviously drugged me with some of their herbs in that drink. Typical High Bloods, didn't trust me to stay put.

We joined the main road, presumably to Viridi City, and now rode on in the late afternoon sun, riding through the forest I'd seen earlier in the day. Pine needles snapped under our horses' hooves, giving off a fresh, sharp sweetness into the air around us and slowly piercing the fog in my head. Birds called from the emerald canopy above, and squirrels scampered through the branches, leaping from tree to tree. The forest appeared never ending as the sun began to sink behind the trees, the skirts of twilight engulfing us. The last thin, golden shafts of sunlight reaching through the gently moving leaves like fingers. The snap of a dead branch blew any remaining fog from my head.

'What was that?' I asked, sitting up straight as my pulse quickened. Was that a shadow moving in the trees? Could that be a strange footprint by the side of the road? 'Are there any creatures here?'

Valerian laughed. 'No, they're mainly contained to the eastern forests, mountains, and deep lakes these days. We've eradicated them from most of the more populated areas. The odd one still lives in the depths of Viridi Lake, right out to the north-west. They all tend to leave us alone as long as we don't encroach on their territory, so you don't need to worry.'

He'd confirmed what I'd been told, but the sudden loud snap had shaken me, and I became alert to every sound, every bird's call, every gust of wind in the trees. I'd be glad when we got out of this wretched forest – I didn't like not being able to see very far; I blamed my assassin training.

'We haven't been riding long, but when do you want to stop, Rian?' Tarragon asked from behind us.

'I think we'll keep going until midnight, then camp,' Valerian said.

'We might make Fennel Town by then,' Tarragon said, a hopeful tinge to his voice.

'You never know.'

We rode on through the forest as night fell, the moon rising, casting its silver light through the trees, illuminating our way. Deep shadows nestled between the trees. Owls hooted, and foxes barked their chilling cry, making the horses shift restlessly. Gradually, as the evening wore on, the trees began to thin. Our path finally broke free of the forest and swept on over rolling countryside, lit by moonlight and fire.

'Damn,' Valerian murmured.

'What's happening?' Tarragon asked, his voice strained.

'Fennel Town's on fire,' Sage said, gathering his horse's reins in his hands.

'We'd better see if we can help,' Valerian said, urging our horse into a dead run, the others following in our wake. As we approached the town, great flames loomed out of the darkness, licking at the sides of buildings, devouring the wooden dwellings with ease. As we passed the gate, Tarragon slid from his horse, approaching one of the Town Guards in his yellow coat, who appeared to be directing operations. Tarragon quickly returned.

'They had a storm a couple of hours ago – lightning set light to several buildings, and they're having trouble getting water to the flames,' he reported.

'There's a river over there,' Sage said, pointing back the way we'd come.

'We need to get a chain of buckets going from the river,' Valerian said.

Tarragon nodded, moving back to the Town Guard as Sage tied his horse with Tarragon's and followed him. Valerian dismounted then helped me down, tying me to a post.

'You'll be safe here,' Valerian said.

'I can help,' I said, straining at the rope.

He hesitated a moment. 'No. Stay here.' He tied our horse up before disappearing through the smoke in the direction Tarragon and Sage had gone.

The houses here were Middle and Low Blood dwellings of wood, and of very little stone. They acted like tinder, burning with ease. The townsfolk ran back and forth, women screamed, men shouted, children cried. Pops and bangs filled the air as explosions punctuated the roar of the fire, and acrid smoke clawed at throats as orange-red flames illuminated the centre of the wooden town.

A cry to my left made me turn. At the end of a side street, fire started to consume another house, caressing the base of the building until the ground floor shimmered with flames and heat. Another cry sent a chill down my spine.

'Help!' screamed a child from the top floor window.

Nausea rose in my throat. Suddenly, a smaller figure appeared at the window beside the first, making my heart stutter. A woman plunged out of the building's front door, choking, beating out flames from her dress, then started screaming as she looked up at the two children. I looked around desperately for Valerian or one of the others, but I couldn't see them in the smoky confusion. I glanced back down the side street – the flames gorged themselves on the lower floor.

I had no choice.

I wouldn't let two children burn to death in front of their mother. I tugged at the rope attaching me to the post, but it didn't give. Valerian had tied it too well. He was forcing my hand, then. I twisted my bound wrists toward my hip and grabbed my War Fan. Although the ropes around my wrists hampered me, I managed to open it. Silver metal spokes reached up to the thin green Iolitian Malachite leaves, the semi-precious stone catching the light. I pressed the amethyst button. With an audible click, thirteen knife points emerged from the top of my Fan, one from each of the spokes, and one each from the two covers. I sliced through the rope attaching me to the post, but couldn't manoeuvre the Fan to cut my bonds, so I returned it to its clip and ran down the side street, hands still bound.

Flames illuminated the buildings on either side of me as I ran, along with a wood pile. Red light reflected off a metal surface. An axe. I skidded to a halt, returning to the wood and the axe. I rubbed my ropes against the sharp blade of the axe, glancing over at the house. The flames were getting higher all the time. I frantically moved my hands up and down the blade, and finally the ropes gave as the sound of the children's screams cut through the air.

I ran towards the building. The flaming ground floor made entering through the front door impossible; however, I'd noticed some of the houses had wooden skylights in the roof for summer days. I prayed this house did, too. I ran to the house next to the children's, scrambling onto a barrel before climbing up a rickety drainpipe, which for a heart-stopping minute creaked as though about to break, and up onto the roof. From my vantage point I could see half the town in flames, but it seemed a concerted effort now took place to battle the fire with two chains of buckets being passed along the main street by the desperate townsfolk. Whatever Valerian and the others were doing, it appeared to be working.

I scrambled across the oak shingles towards the burning house. Below me, the woman shrieked, the children screamed from their window, and the flames roared, continuing their steady progress up towards the trapped children. I didn't have much time. I looked at the gap between the houses – not much more than six feet, not a problem.

A barrel of some sort of alcohol exploded below me, sending splinters of wood in all directions. I fell to my knees, ducking the worst of it. The sides of both buildings now burnt, the fire reaching up towards the sky.

I took a couple of steps back then ran towards the flaming gap, launching myself into the air. I landed on the smoking shingle roof, desperately looking around for a skylight – there, on the left. I scrambled over the shingles and knelt next to the skylight, slipping my fingers around its edge. It didn't budge. *Hell's teeth*. I grabbed my Fan and opened it; the green malachite leaves with their cut-out design featuring stars allowing the golden flickering light of the flames to pass through them. I hoped the extra layer of resin the craftsmen had applied would give the stone the strength I needed, although being Iolitian Malachite, it was already far stronger than the usual stone. Using the metal knives as a lever, I heaved on it, forcing the skylight up. It worked. This time, I managed to slip my fingers under the edge of the skylight, prising it free. I threw it open. A surge of heat, smoke, and screams flew up at me, and I quickly dodged out of the way. I returned my Fan to my hip and dropped into the burning building, barely able to see in the smoke as it clutched at my throat and eyes.

'Children!' I yelled over the roar of the flames creeping up the stairs, heat grabbing at my face. 'Children!' I opened the door into the room at the front of the house where I'd seen them. They turned to me, their faces full of terror, tears streaking their smoke-stained faces. 'Quickly, this way,' I said, ushering them out of the room onto the landing. Grabbing a chair, I stood on it, helping the older child, a boy, out onto the roof.

'Come here, little one.' I reached out to the small girl and lifted her up towards the skylight, where her brother pulled her up onto the roof. I climbed on the back of the chair and pulled myself up to join them. 'Come with me,' I said, urging them over towards the gap between the buildings. The voracious flames in the space between the houses had intensified, and a little shiver crept down my spine.

'Samphire!'

Through the smoke and flames, Valerian and Tarragon stood waiting on the opposite roof.

'We need help,' I shouted over the crackle of the fire.

Valerian nodded as the flames between the buildings receded a little.

'Can you jump?' I asked the boy.

'Y-yes, I can jump it,' he said.

'They'll catch you,' I said, indicating Valerian and Tarragon.

The boy took a few steps back, then ran towards the gap, jumping into the air. He cleared the gap easily as Valerian and Tarragon reached for him, pulling him to safety on the far roof.

'Now it's our turn,' I said to the little girl, crouching down as she looked at me, her big brown eyes swimming in tears. 'Get on my back; we'll go together,' I said, and she climbed onto me, her fingers digging into my shoulders and neck. I caught Valerian exchanging worried looks with Tarragon.

'Are you ready?' I shouted to them, standing up. They nodded. 'Hang on,' I said to the girl.

I stepped back before running forward, leaping off the edge of the roof.

CHAPTER THREE

Despite the girl's slight weight, we fell faster than I'd anticipated. My foot caught the edge of the opposite roof and I slipped, slamming down, grabbing at the shingles, dangling from my fingertips. Then Tarragon appeared at the edge, lifting the little girl from my back even as Valerian grasped my wrists, yanking me up over the edge to the relative safety of the roof. I suddenly realised I stood with his arms around me, my heart thundering against my ribcage as the flames leapt up between the houses once more.

Valerian cleared his throat as he released me. 'You took a chance,' he muttered.

'I had no choice,' I said as he led me across the roof to the far side, where a ladder stood waiting for us. Tarragon reached it first, helped the boy down, then took the girl on his back and climbed down after him. I climbed down next, seeing Sage holding the ladder at the bottom, steadying it for us. Tarragon had already passed the children to their mother as I reached the ground, Valerian following right after me.

'Thank you,' the woman said, her face streaming with tears as she hugged her daughter. 'Thank you for saving my children,' she said, taking hold of the boy's hand.

'My pleasure,' I said, smiling at her. 'I'm just glad they're safe.'

She nodded, moving off into the town.

The enormity of what had just happened hit me. My arms and legs tingled, suddenly weak, as my body trembled, and my heart hammered from the exertion.

'I thought I tied you up,' Valerian said as we made our way back to the horses.

'You did,' I said, my mouth suddenly parched. 'But if I hadn't gone, those children would've burnt to death in front of me, and I wasn't going to let that happen.'

Valerian glanced at me, a frown covering his face. 'You could've been killed.'

'And that would have bothered you?'

He didn't answer.

'Is the fire under control now?' I asked.

'Yes,' Tarragon said. 'They're beginning to dampen it down, so it shouldn't spread any further. That little rescue of yours was quite impressive, y'know, Samphire.'

I couldn't help but smile at him as he grinned back. Perhaps all High Bloods weren't cruel, vindictive idiots after all.

'What do you want to do?' Sage asked Valerian as we arrived back at the horses.

'We'll go and camp down by the river,' Valerian said, 'get a few hours of sleep before dawn.'

We retrieved our horses and walked out of the town and down to the river, tethering them before setting out our blankets. After the thick smoke of the town, the open countryside smelt of starlight. I cast a glance back at the town, relieved to see the flames receding, the sky gradually returning to inky black.

I held my hands out to Valerian.

He hesitated a moment. 'Tarragon, tie her up.'

Tarragon looked questioningly at his friend. 'Are you sure?'

'Do it.'

Tarragon muttered something and wandered off to find some rope. He came back and tied my wrists, maybe not quite as tight as before, an apologetic look in his eyes.

The heat of the town now sat in stark contrast to the dampness hanging in the air around us, but it didn't bother my companions as we settled down to sleep, and within minutes Tarragon and Sage were snoring away merrily. After the terror and excitement, I couldn't settle. Despite my fatigue, my heart refused to calm as I lay there, and my body still trembled with the after-effects of my exploits. I got up, walked down to the river, and stood looking out over the gurgling water, taking deep breaths of sweet night air as I wiggled my hands to shift the ropes around my wrists into a more comfortable position. A strong hand gripped my arm.

'Where'd you think you're going?' Valerian asked.

'Nowhere. I just wanted some peace away from their snoring,' I said as the water bubbled past me.

'Why did you do that back there? You damn well could've been killed.'

'I couldn't let them die, could I?'

'They're nothing to you; they're only Low Bloods.' He pulled me around to face him.

Typical High Blood.

'They were children, whatever their Blood Class,' I said, clenching my fists as best I could with them tied.

He shook his head, his grip lessening ever so slightly. 'I'm surprised you didn't leave them.'

'You think because of my reputation, I'm a cold-hearted monster who would let children die without a second thought?' I challenged him as I railed at his cold, callous words. 'I'm not that person. I'm not Lady Merciless. She doesn't exist, never has.'

He looked down, letting go of my arm. 'I'm…'

'Surprised I have a heart?'

'No, I'm just having trouble making you out, that's all,' he said, a pinkish tinge high on his cheeks in the last of the pale moonlight.

'I've never killed anyone, Prince Valerian. Neither have I knowingly let anyone die, and I'm not going to start now.'

Valerian looked at me appraisingly. 'Fine principles if you can keep to them.'

'Well, so far I have,' I said, an edge to my voice I didn't try to hide. 'I don't have to be a High Blood like you to have principles.'

He frowned, then reached out once again, his lips parting slightly, resting his hands on my upper arms. He hesitated before speaking. 'I'm truly sorry, I didn't mean to upset you. You did a very brave thing tonight. A courageous thing.'

I looked into his eyes for a moment, wondering if I could drown in those amber pools. I took a sharp breath at the thought. 'I appreciate your apology, but I don't believe anyone will ever take my word as truth once they know who I am, and you're no different, Your Highness. I don't blame you for it; I guess I expect it.'

An almost sorrowful frown settled on his forehead. 'Give it time,' he said.

I snorted. 'As far as everyone is concerned, I'm Lady Merciless of the Coterie. No one will ever see me as anything else, even if the crimes I'm accused of aren't mine,' I said, gently pulling away.

'For my part, I've only seen Samphire up until now, not Lady Merciless.'

'That's because Lady Merciless is a phantom, made up by Juniper to suit her own ends,' I said bitterly, glancing towards the ground.

The prince reached out to my chin, his hand gently raising my face towards him as a flicker of sympathy flared in his eyes. 'Like I said, give it time,' he said, his irises dilating slightly, his voice suddenly like a warm summer breeze.

I gave him a wan smile.

'Do you really think you can work out who killed Angelica?' he asked.

'Maybe. Each assassin has their own methods and calling card.'

'Calling card?'

'Yes, something they leave behind as a mark of their work,' I said. 'A kind of signature. For instance, Feldspar leaves a glass cube –

feldspar is used to make glass; Carnelian always leaves a small carnelian bead at his kills; and his sister, Citrine, leaves a small knife with a citrine stone in its hilt, usually in someone's back, although flaying is her speciality.'

'Charming.'

'I never intended to leave anything,' I said, staring into the distance for a moment, my mind drifting back in time. 'I thought it all rather vulgar and boastful. Mal thought the same and never left anything, either.'

Valerian frowned. 'I don't know any details. Father sent me off after you as soon as Angelica had been found, but maybe they've recovered something you can identify.'

'I hope so. I want to help.'

'Why?'

I looked to the ground for a moment, then back up at Valerian. 'I've hated every moment of being in the Coterie, of protecting my sister – and Mal, for that matter. I've been cut loose, now, and I want it to stay that way. I want to prove to you, to your father, that I'm innocent, earn my freedom, and find a new home somewhere far from my stepmother, where the Coterie won't find me.'

The frown deepened as he chewed his lip for a moment. 'We'd better get some rest,' he said, turning back towards our camp. 'And stop calling me Your Highness or Prince Valerian – Rian's good enough for the others.'

'But-'

'But nothing – unless you want me to start calling you Amethyst,' he said, giving me an artful glance.

'Definitely not.'

'In fact, I think I'm going to shorten your name after this night's adventure,' he said as we walked back to the camp.

'Shorten it? What can you shorten Samphire to?'

'Phire,' he said, grinning at me.

As a High Blood, Rian constantly surprised me.

'She probably only did it to make us trust her,' Sage said to Tarragon from where he rode behind me and Rian.

'Don't be ridiculous,' Tarragon said.

'Why else would she do it?'

I felt Rian tense as he sat behind me, his warm arm still around me to keep me steady on our horse.

'Because those children were in mortal danger?' Tarragon asked.

'She's Lady Merciless, the Coterie's prized assassin. Why would she care about Low Blood children?' Sage asked. 'She's only interested in her own skin and saving them puts her in a good light. You'll be wanting to untie her next.'

'She could've died in Fennel, and that's a damn stupid way to save your skin,' Rian said.

Sage grunted.

For the next two days we rode on through the countryside towards Viridi. Tarragon remained civil to me – kind, really – whilst Rian appeared happy to keep me alive because at the moment it suited him – and because I'd saved his life. But whether that would change once we reached the palace, I didn't know. After all, he was a High Blood, and they could change their minds on a whim. Sage just hated me.

We stopped that night at a small inn situated at the edge of a bustling town of wooden houses. Rian made arrangements with the owner to stay in a little barn at the back of the inn, and a serving girl brought us our evening meal. At the far side of the town, a couple of marble mansions indicated the presence of High Bloods, but Rian and his friends seemed content in the barn. Strange for High Bloods. I'd assumed they'd want to impose on the other High Bloods, but it wasn't something they even considered.

After a reasonable night's sleep, we awoke to sun streaming in the barn door. I sat up, stiff from sleeping in an awkward position with my hands tied and leant against the stone wall as Rian and Tarragon disappeared off to see about some breakfast. Sage sat near the barn door, glowering at me.

'Do you dislike me personally, my profession, or the fact I'm a girl?' I asked, staring back.

'I don't know you, and it certainly isn't because you're a girl,' he said gruffly.

'Then it's my perceived profession.'

'There's nothing perceived about it. I've seen your tattoo. That confirms everything, and as far as I'm concerned, that's all I need to know, assassin.'

There was no point in arguing; it wasn't going to get me anywhere.

Several shadows suddenly fell across Sage and he twisted around, looking towards the door.

'Well, well, what do we have here? A High Blood – a King's Warrior, even,' a dishevelled man said, entering the barn with three others in his wake – four Low Bloods. Two had knives concealed under their coats in sheaths at their waists. I could tell by the tell-tale bulges in the material, but had Sage noticed?

'What do you want?' Sage asked, getting to his feet.

One of the Low Bloods stepped forward, narrowed his eyes, and swiped at him with his fist, knocking Sage down with a brutal blow to the jaw. I winced. He should have seen that coming.

'Your money,' he snarled as Sage sprawled on the straw-strewn ground.

'I don't have any on me,' Sage said, rubbing his jaw, fear in his eyes. His weapons were on the far side of the barn.

'Of course, you've got money, you're a High Blood. Now hand it over,' the Low Blood said. It appeared that they hadn't noticed me in the shadows of the barn.

'I have nothing with me.' Sage wiped blood from the corner of his mouth as he scrambled to his feet.

Hell's teeth.

I could do little to help him with my hands tied; there had to be some way of freeing myself. Just to my left, an old nail protruded from the wall. Keeping to the shadows, I slowly moved towards it and started rubbing my ropes against it. Gradually, the rope began to fray.

'You really expect us to believe that? You have money. Dill, shake out his pockets,' the Low Blood said.

'With pleasure, Mullein,' Dill said, moving towards Sage.

My ropes broke. I took a deep breath through my nose.

'Is there a problem here?' I asked, stepping out of the shadows, and standing in front of a wooden pillar.

The Low Bloods jumped and turned towards me.

Dill leered at me, but I held his gaze. 'Your wench? Maybe we'll take the money from her.'

'She's not my wench,' Sage said. 'She's nothing to me.'

Thanks.

'Now, are you gentlemen leaving?' I asked as pleasantly as I could.

'I don't believe we are,' Mullein said, his lip curling.

'You know, we can do this the easy way, or else we'll do it the hard way. It really doesn't bother me,' I said, stretching my neck.

Mullein hesitated before speaking. 'Dill, take him; Basil, the girl. Kill them both and take anything they've got.'

Dill grabbed Sage by the shoulder and shoved him to the ground. Sage hit his head against a wooden bucket and lay there, dazed.

Basil, a great, hulking man with bad breath even at this distance, tensed, shifted his weight, and flew at me, shoulder dropping before his fist swept towards me. I ducked. His fist smashed into the wooden pillar behind me. He screamed, staggering back to the door, nursing his injured hand. 'Bitch,' he spluttered.

I grabbed my Fan from my waist and flicked it open, taking up a defensive stance, turning my body sideways. I stretched my left hand out in front of me, my right holding my Fan parallel to my body. The familiar, cool metal helped calm me.

Mullein turned to me and laughed, the others joining in. 'You're going to take on all four of us with that pretty little green fan?'

Sage shook his head, trying to clear his vision as he looked at me. 'No, don't, it's too dangerous,' he said, awkwardly scrambling backwards, a little trickle of blood working its way down the side of his head from a cut on his brow.

'For me or them?' I asked, pressing the amethyst at the bottom of the War Fan. The thirteen small knives flicked out.

'What the...' Mullein backed away, but I needed to make sure they fully got the message.

I lunged towards them, slicing at Dill. I then twisted and slashed at Mullein before spinning around, slicing across Basil's front. I swiped at the fourth Low Blood, finishing with a kind of flourish for good measure. Taken by surprise, the men looked on in amazement as their sword and knife belts fell to the ground, including the ones holding the concealed weapons. All severed by the knives in my Fan, which I waved in front of my face as any great lady would and laughed.

They took one look at me, eyes wide, then turned and fled from the barn, not even bothering to collect their weapons. I smiled. I pressed the amethyst, the blades retracting back into the Fan, and closed it, replacing it at my waist before turning to Sage. Crouching beside him, I looked at his wound.

Sage stared back at me, his eyes slightly unfocused. 'Why did you do that?'

'Because you needed help, because I could, and because I hate seeing someone outnumbered,' I said, shifting his hair from his cut. 'It's not bad; you'll be all right.'

Sage pulled back and glowered at me as he gingerly felt his head. His hand was shaking slightly. 'You're still an assassin.'

'And you're a High Blood,' I said, giving him a little smirk. I took a deep breath, trying to relax. My heart still raced after the fight, and my mouth was as dry as the Mere Desert. I'd been lucky, and I knew it. Those men were ruffians. They were slow, inept, unskilled fighters, or else I might have been in trouble.

Sage frowned a moment. 'You could've just left me to die.'

'Ah, but then I'd have no one to argue with.'

'The truth is, she could've left us all to die over the last few days, but she hasn't,' Rian said from the barn door. Both Sage and I turned to see him and Tarragon standing there, watching. 'She could've escaped many times over if she'd wanted, but she hasn't. I don't believe she's guilty – and the fact she's had that weapon with her all along rather proves it,' he said, giving me a long look.

I smiled sweetly at him and stood up.

'She's no killer, and once Father realises that, we can start looking for the real murderer and thief,' Rian continued. 'I won't rest until I see the Fire Opal back in the Cedarwood Throne.'

'None of us will, y'know,' Tarragon said, walking over towards Sage and handing him a small rag. 'We all want to see it returned.'

Sage took the rag in a shaking hand. He dabbed at his lip and brow, mopping up the blood.

'You'll be pleased to hear a full-cooked breakfast is on its way,' Tarragon said, buffing his fingernails on his coat, a smug expression on his face.

'I need it after that,' Sage said, continuing to dab at his wound.

I held my wrists out to Rian. He frowned at me. 'Don't you want to tie me up again?' I asked.

Rian glanced at Tarragon and Sage, then back at me. 'Do I need to?'

I shook my head, surprised. 'No, you don't need to. I'm not going anywhere.'

'Good, then I think we can dispense with the ropes.' A little lopsided grin formed at the corner of his mouth.

Returning to Viridi had caused a knot to form in my stomach. Knowing I had to convince King Finule the Second of my innocence filled me with a kind of anxiety I'd never experienced before, although Rian appeared quite relaxed as we rode through the city and into the palace courtyard. The smell of thyme drifted on the air as I looked around. Seeing the palace in daylight took my breath away. Its white marble glowed in the sun, the walls carved with thyme and other herbs sparkled with inlaid gold leaf, and golden finials on the top of the towers shone like beacons in the blue sky. On the tallest tower fluttered the Aerban flag with its pale green background, dark green border, and at its centre, a sprig of Aerban Thyme, again in dark green – the emblem of Aerba.

Stable boys appeared from the far side of the courtyard as a King's Warrior, with a slight limp, came running down the steps, four Palace Guards close behind him. An angry expression covered his face, and I noted that his features were not dissimilar to Sage's, although he had piercing green eyes rather than brown. He wasn't dressed as neatly as Sage, and his muscles strained the seams of his clothes.

'Your Royal Highness.' The Warrior bowed to Rian, putting his coat under even more stress. 'Is this her? The assassin?'

'No, Sorrel, it's not,' Rian said as we dismounted, handing his horse over to one of the boys. 'But she might be able to help us.'

'We were led to believe you had the murderer with you,' Sorrel said, looking suspiciously at me as his black hair swayed in the breeze. 'The King wants her taken straight to the dungeon, and it'll be a pleasure to do it myself.'

Rian tensed. 'She's coming with me to see my father now. She may be able to identify the real killer.'

Sorrel shook his head. 'I'm sorry, Your Highness, but the King's orders are that she's taken to the dungeon.'

I looked at Rian.

He glanced at me apologetically. 'It won't be for long,' he said, turning back to Sorrel. 'I'll go to Father now,' he said, his tone of voice brooking no argument.

'Yes, Your Highness,' Sorrel said, nodding, as Rian strode up the steps towards the palace door. He watched the prince go, then looked back at me, his eyes looking me up and down. Suddenly, I felt incredibly uncomfortable, naked almost.

Sage paused as he reached Sorrel. 'Brother.' He inclined his head.

'It's good to see you returned safely,' Sorrel said, although the tone of his voice didn't match his words.

'We've all returned safely, thanks,' Tarragon said as he followed Rian up the steps.

Sorrel ignored him, still looking at me. 'You had a good trip, according to the Nightshade.'

Sage gave him a sour expression. 'Do those wretched spies shadow Rian all the time now?'

Sorrel turned to Sage and shrugged. 'Hmm, I don't know, but they do when he's sent on a mission to bring back Crown Princess Angelica's killer,' he said, glancing back at me.

My shoulders drooped.

Sage looked towards me. 'If the Nightshade have been shadowing us, then they know she's been protesting her innocence, not just of the murder but the theft, too.'

'And you're daft enough to believe her?' Sorrel asked.

Sage tensed. 'I'm thinking about it,' he said, a hard edge to his voice.

'What's to think about? You're a fool if you think she's anything but an assassin. Lady Merciless. You really think she can be innocent? She's lying to you.'

Sage narrowed his eyes as he looked at his brother. 'Maybe, but I'm beginning to think maybe not–'

'I've got to go,' Sorrel said.

Sage grabbed his brother's arm. 'Valerian won't want her harmed.'

Sorrel sneered. 'You think I'd want to have my way with *her*?' he asked quietly, but still loudly enough that I would hear. 'Don't be stupid.'

'I know you, remember?'

'And I know you, too, little brother – don't you forget that, either.' He raised his voice. 'Bring her.' He pulled away from Sage, striding off across the courtyard as quickly as his limp would allow.

One of the guards grabbed my arm, pulling me roughly towards the side entrance Sorrel was heading for. My heart lurched. I found myself being dragged along behind Sorrel, and after a long walk through dimly lit passages, down stairs and past less-than-pleasant cells, they cast me into a small, dank room. Mouldy straw covered the floor, and the only light came from a pitch torch outside the cell, which barely illuminated the little room through a rusty grille in the door. This was just as well, considering the foul stench that greeted me.

'You'll stay here until the King summons you, Lady Merciless,' Sorrel said, locking the door. The sound of rusty metal on metal made me flinch.

As their footsteps receded, a constant dripping noise filled the air, setting my teeth on edge – a leaky pipe somewhere, or a torture tactic? I didn't need them to torture me. My sister's betrayal already cut me to the core. It was the first chance I'd truly had to think about it, and what she'd done. How could she? She'd deceived me for who knew how long, and then forsaken me, allowing the Coterie to kill me. That knowledge was torture enough. By nightfall, I sat huddled against a cold wall, wondering if Rian and the others were speaking up for me, or disavowing me instead. Probably the latter. I was sure Mal would've had something positive to say.

Mal.

I'd had little time to dwell upon his fate, either, but now it all came surging back, and grief finally overtook me. Tears fell. A miserable night followed with sleep evading me and my heart aching for my dead brother – and my lost sister.

Sometime early the next afternoon, Sorrel reappeared with Palace Guards in tow. By then my eyes were red and puffy from crying. I just hoped he wouldn't realise and think it a sign of weakness. I stood up. The cold cell had left my muscles stiff, but that didn't matter to the guards who led me back up into the palace at quite a pace along white marble corridors with their green carpets and colourful tapestries of herbs, and into the familiar Throne Room. I glanced towards the throne and shuddered; a gaping hole sat where the Fire Opal had once languished.

On one side of the room, near large, arched windows, stood a long table surrounded by chairs, and close to it were three men. One, an older man in burgundy and gold, wore a golden crown set with diamonds and emeralds, his greying hair caught in the traditional Aerban high ponytail, his belt under pressure. King Finule. Although Finule bent over the table, it was obvious he wasn't as tall as his youngest son. His face was careworn, tired, and not overly handsome. Rian had inherited little of his father's looks or build – leading me to think his strikingly handsome features must have come from his mother's side.

A slightly older man stood beside the King – another High Blood with his burgundy and black coat, his grey eyes watching me intently as I entered the room. Beside him, lounging on a silk-cushioned window seat fiddling with his sleeve, sat a young man, perhaps three years older than Rian. The golden hem of his burgundy coat indicated he wasn't just a High Blood, but Royalty, his features the spitting image of the King's, just thirty years younger – could this be Rian's brother I'd heard them talking about in the barn?

Sorrel took my arm and led me forward.

'So,' King Finule said, 'you're Lady Merciless.' His brown eyes looked me up and down as the guards stopped behind me, Sorrel bringing me to a halt.

I flinched. 'My name is–'

'The King is speaking. Silence!' Sorrel said, squeezing my arm uncomfortably.

King Finule adjusted his crown, staring at me, his eyes hard. 'I hear that you say you're innocent of my daughter's murder?'

I nodded.

'Liar.' I turned to the young man on the window seat. His brown eyes narrowed as he looked at me, his long black hair falling down his back, and his goatee giving him a shifty appearance – the only man I'd seen in Aerba with facial hair. His smooth skin and soft hands spoke of a life of luxury, something I began to suspect Rian hadn't enjoyed in quite the same way.

'Chervil, please,' Finule said, raising his hand. 'Although I happen to agree with my son, Lady Merciless.'

I winced. Why did people have to keep calling me that? 'I didn't kill your daughter, Your Majesty. I admit I was sent to kill Princess Angelica, but I didn't do it.'

'Do you know who did carry out this heinous crime?' Finule asked, his face taut.

I shook my head. 'But if you can tell me exactly what happened, and whether anything was left behind, I might be able to, Your Majesty.'

'She was murdered with Blue Water Hemlock.'

The confirmation of the Hemlock did narrow it down a bit – there were three possible assassins that used that particular poison.

'Was anything left near the princess' body?' I asked.

'What do you mean?' Chervil asked, his forehead creasing as he sat up.

'A glass cube, a small pebble or a red bead?'

Finule shook his head. 'No, nothing, just the Hemlock poison.'

I frowned – this wasn't what I'd expected at all. 'They used the poison I'd been told to use – so it could be any one of three people, Your Majesty.'

'Three murderers, you mean,' Finule said, taking hold of the edge of the table, his knuckles turning white.

I swallowed.

'Their names?' Chervil asked.

'Feldspar, Onyx, and Carnelian, Your Highness.'

'There's only one solution, Father,' Chervil said, shifting his position and leaning forwards.

'Maybe, but first I want to know where the Fire Opal is,' Finule said, his brown eyes boring into me.

'I don't know, I had nothing to do with the theft of the Fire Opal,' I said, trying to maintain my composure.

'Our information is that the Fire Opal has been taken to Iolite,' the man next to Finule said, scratching his nose again.

'Lord Wintergreen is correct. Whether or not it was you, *someone* from Iolite took it, and we want it back,' Finule said.

Lord Wintergreen? Finule's Chamberlain?

'We take robbery very seriously in Aerba, and I take the theft of Aerba's precious Fire Opal personally,' the King continued.

'And I don't take kindly to murder,' Prince Chervil said. 'You may protest your innocence, Lady Merciless, but I still believe you murdered my dear sister. She was a sweet, wonderful person, and would have been a great queen. I loved her dearly, and you snuffed out her light.'

Chervil seemed to be objecting just a little too much. Every now and then, I caught a satisfied glint in his eye, a smile trying to escape from his lips. Because of Angelica's death, he'd now become heir to the Aerban crown, and I had a sneaking suspicion that he was enjoying his newfound position.

'The sentence for murder of a member of the Royal Family in Aerba is execution,' Chervil said, looking at me intently.

Rian should've killed me when he first met me.

'My son speaks the truth,' Finule said, shifting his crown again.

'Give her the choice, Father,' Chervil sneered, getting to his feet. 'It's only fair.' It was only now that I realised how short Chervil was. He certainly didn't have his younger brother's height; indeed, he was shorter than me.

Wintergreen shuffled, his salt and pepper hair swinging from side to side as Finule nodded, making a little shiver run down my spine.

'Your Majesty,' Wintergreen said, his face pale. 'Are you sure this is wise?'

Finule raised his hand, stopping any further protests. 'I will give you a chance to prove yourself, Lady Merciless. The choices are simple: execution, or penance. If you choose the second, then you must swear fealty to me, find out who's behind Princess Angelica's murder, and retrieve the Fire Opal.'

I frowned – he really called that a choice? I only had one option, to do as he asked, somehow, but at least it would earn me what I craved. My freedom.

'Make your choice,' Chervil said, stepping forward, his eyes bright.

What was his problem? 'All right,' I said. 'I promise to serve King Finule, find out who ordered the princess' death, who killed her, and retrieve the Fire Opal.'

'Excellent,' Finule said, rubbing his hands before signalling to Sorrel who had been standing silently beside me all this time.

Sorrel let go of me, the two guards moving up beside me, and headed for the door. My heart skipped a beat. Now what?

'Of course, there are a few conditions,' Finule said.

'Conditions?' My stomach knotted. 'What conditions?'

'Prince Valerian, Head of my King's Warriors, will go with you. Any attempt to escape or deviate from your task, he will kill you, do you understand?'

I nodded. I guess I'd expected that, really. I may not have trusted the High Blood Prince, but I could work with him; we had the same goals.

Sorrel returned with two Palace Guards carrying something between them. Whatever it was sat on a large silver tray and had been covered in a black cloth. They set it down on the table, and Sorrel went to stand beside Chervil, smiling. Chervil grinned back, then looked towards me, his lips curling in a way I didn't like one bit.

'The other condition is that you will carry the weapons of my choice,' Finule said. 'I know you are skilled with a variety of weapons, so this should not be a problem for you. Agreed?'

Weapons? What weapons? The knot in my stomach tightened, and my palms broke out in a cold sweat as I began to see where this was going. Aerba had a set of legendary weapons, fearsome weapons that came with a catch, one I didn't want to entertain. My shoulders rose as my muscles tensed.

'Agreed?' Finule repeated as he moved along the table.

I nodded mutely. I didn't have a choice.

He pulled the black cloth away to reveal a sword with a gold and silver hilt and a clear, three-foot crystal blade. Beside it sat a wedge-shaped shield with slight cut-outs on either side at the top, slightly shorter than the sword in height, but also of clear crystal, with golden enarmes at the back for securing the shield to your arm and hand.

I quietly let out a long breath as my shoulders dropped. These weren't what I'd been expecting. I was expecting to see blood-red crystal weapons, not clear ones. What were these, then, if not Aerba's Cursed Weapons? The Ruby Sword and Shield? The deterrent the Royal Family had used for centuries to rule absolutely.

The sun coming in the chamber windows glistened on the weapons, casting little iridescent rainbows across their surfaces and into the crystal, making them shimmer like living things. They were beautiful, yet a worm of doubt and fear still wiggled in my chest.

'Take them,' Finule said. 'They're diamond. I believe your people think diamond gives courage.'

Chervil watched intently, his eyes glistening with excitement as he struggled to suppress a smile. Sorrel had a similar expression on his face. Lord Wintergreen, however, blanched further and rubbed his nose – he didn't look at all well. Something deep inside me squirmed. Surely, diamond weapons as exquisite as these had to be known throughout the Five Lands, yet I couldn't place them.

'I'm quite happy with ordinary weapons, Your Majesty. You don't have to give me these treasures,' I said.

'Don't worry, you will return them to me when you recover the Fire Opal and bring me the information I want,' Finule said. 'Now, take them.'

My eyes widened at his harsh tone of voice. 'Very well,' I said, walking over to them. They shimmered in the sunlight, the rainbows dancing in a dazzling, mesmerising display. I reached out, placing my arm through the enarmes of the shield and grasping the handle before taking hold of the sword hilt. The crystal weapons were lighter than I'd expected, and so well balanced that they would make formidable tools.

A huge bang echoed around the throne room.

A flash of light brighter than the sun burst from the weapons, making the others turn away, and I closed my eyes, gasping. A sudden jolt of pain spiralled through my body, sending me crashing to my knees, only the sword and shield stopping me from sprawling to the floor as I leant on them for support. The pain intensified, squeezing me like a vice. I gasped for air as my heart threatened to burst from my chest and my muscles screamed from just trying to keep me upright. An unpleasant draining sensation filled my body.

It abruptly ceased.

'Amazing.' Chervil's voice broke through the confusion in my mind. 'I've always wanted to see that.'

I opened my eyes, dazed, and gasped. The sword and shield were no longer clear, but a deep, blood red.

Ruby red.

My heart nearly burst through my ribcage, and my body shook with the enormity of it as I took in what I was looking at. What I'd been tricked into taking up.

Aldorbana. Cwicsusl.

Hell's teeth. I stared at the red crystal weapons in horror.

They were the Cursed Weapons of Aerba, after all – and now my doom.

CHAPTER FOUR

The door to the throne room burst open.

'Father! What have you done?'' Rian stood there, his face as white as the palace marble. He shook his head in disbelief. 'You promised me you wouldn't do it yet,' he said, running over to me.

'Shut up, Valerian,' Chervil said, a spiteful look in his eyes. 'Anyway, it's too late, she's taken them willingly.'

'Did she know what they were?' Rian asked as he reached me, helping me to my feet, his expression full of fear. 'Did you tell her?'

My body trembled as I shook my head, trying to clear it of the dazed feeling.

'Leave it, Valerian, you don't understand,' Finule said, a little smile on his face. 'Lady Merciless, you have willingly taken up the sword Aldorbana and the shield Cwicsusl. You are now bound to them until your death.'

'They'll suck your life energy from you until you're nothing but a dry husk,' Chervil said, grinning from ear to ear.

'Chervil,' Finule said, giving his son a warning look. I felt Rian stiffen as he stood next to me, still holding my arms to steady me as I swayed slightly. 'Although, Chervil is correct – the Weapons will slowly take your life energy. You are now bound to them and they to you, and whilst bound they cannot be taken from you. Neither can you escape them or the Curse. They will be with you constantly as a reminder of your approaching death.'

Chervil grinned at me, a smug expression on his annoying face. I wanted to hit him, but I had no energy to spare.

'As your life force leaves you, they will change back to their original clear-crystal selves. When they do, you will die,' Finule continued. 'Complete your mission and return here before that happens, and I will break the Curse and set you free.'

As Finule spoke, Rian's grip on me increased.

Chervil laughed as he smoothed his coat.

'You bastard,' Rian said.

Chervil smirked. 'Are you going soft on her, little Brother?'

Rian glared at him but remained silent.

'Enough,' Finule said. 'Valerian, you will see that Lady Merciless fulfils her vow. If she doesn't, you are to kill her.'

'Father, I'm sure this isn't necessary,' Rian said, relaxing his grip on me a little.

'She's an assassin,' Chervil said, a vein popping out in his neck.

'She murdered our dear sister and stole the Fire Opal. Of course, it's necessary, Valerian.'

'You obviously don't understand the far-reaching implications of what her actions mean to this country, and to us as a family,' Finule said. 'Not only your age but your lack of understanding show why Chervil is Crown Prince, and you are not.'

Rian tensed once again. I frowned. I could see why two brothers might lock horns, but the callous way Finule spoke to Rian surprised me. He seemed to be treating his youngest son like a complete idiot – and Rian wasn't an idiot.

Finule and Chervil's displays only reinforced my dislike of High Bloods.

Finule moved towards his throne. 'You will set off with her tomorrow morning, Valerian. I want this business sorted out as soon as possible. Wintergreen, Sorrel, take her to the room I've assigned her.'

'As you desire, Your Majesty,' the Chamberlain said with a bow, moving over towards me, Sorrel following him.

'She'd better get on with it; we don't know how long she has,' Chervil said with a smirk.

Rian glowered at his brother. 'It's all right, Lord Wintergreen, I'll take her myself,' he said, waving Sorrel away.

Wintergreen nodded. Sorrel's eyebrows lowered and he glowered, first at Rian, then at me. Rian ignored him and gently steered me out the Throne Room. He took me along a green-carpeted corridor and up a wide staircase.

'I'm sorry it took so long to get you out of the dungeon,' Rian said, glancing at me. 'Father was harder to persuade than I'd thought. It was all I could do to stop him from executing you yesterday afternoon.'

My still slightly-addled brain twisted and turned, trying to work out why he was so keen to help me. 'Thank you for what you've done,' I said, nodding.

A strange look passed behind his eyes. 'I did what I had to to keep you alive,' he said.

'You want me alive to find the Fire Opal?'

'And Angelica's murderer. You're the only one who can help us with that – your knowledge of Iolite will be invaluable.'

I nodded.

'Anyway, I don't think you should die for something you didn't do,' he said, rubbing the back of his neck. 'And...' He hesitated. 'I like you.'

I blinked in surprise. A High Blood liked *me*? That was a first.

'Oh,' I said.

He nodded. 'You've shown great courage, kindness, and determination. Qualities I admire, and you've got them in abundance. Not to mention you're be–' He glanced at me as we stopped outside a highly-varnished wooden door. His lips parted as he hesitated. He took a breath then reached out and opened the door. 'This way,' he said.

The rooms he'd taken me to had luxurious furnishings, pale green silk drapes at the windows, colourful tapestries on the walls, and gold-cushioned seats. From there, he led me into the bed chamber where a half-tester bed sat against one wall with two large, open glass doors leading out onto a balcony. I put Aldorbana and Cwicsusl down by the bed and peered out the windows, seeing the palace gardens where perfumed roses bloomed, and fountains chattered. Under any other circumstances, I would've been in awe of these apartments. As it was, it all rather washed over me.

A young woman, maybe a year older than me, entered the chamber dressed in beige Middle Blood clothing, and bowed. Seeing another Middle Blood came as something of a relief. She wasn't quite as tall as me – mind you, I was tall even for Iolitian women – and her face had a kind quality to it, and an infectious smile.

Rian scowled at her. 'You don't need to bow to me, Willow.'

'I wasn't,' she said, a broad grin on her light sienna face. 'I was bowing to Lady Samphire.'

Rian shook his head and sighed. 'Look after her for me,' he said. 'She needs to rest.'

'I imagine she'll want to bathe first,' Willow said, eyeing Aldorbana and Cwicsusl. 'He did it, then,' she said, a resigned note to her voice.

'Of course, he did. Just as we feared,' Rian said. 'I thought he was going to wait, but he didn't.'

Willow looked at me. 'I'm so sorry,' she said, bowing her head.

'Thank you.' What else could I say?

'Now, about that bath,' she continued, a smile creeping onto her face.

'Sounds nice,' I said, genuinely pleased at the prospect of a good, long soak in a hot bath.

'I'd better be going. I'll see you later at supper,' Rian said, leaving the room.

'Come on,' Willow said, disappearing into a room off the bed chamber, coughing slightly. 'I've already drawn your bath for you.'

I followed her into the antechamber to find a tub of steaming water covered in rose petals and foam. I peeled my clothes off and spent some time relaxing in the hot water before washing my hair. Now smelling of roses and wrapped in a towel, I wandered back into the bedchamber to find clothes laid out on the bed. My own had vanished, replaced by Aerban ones.

'The King had these prepared for you specially,' Willow said, smoothing them out.

'But they're not Middle Blood,' I said, looking at the purple outer coat with a white border that would fall halfway down my thighs. Black suede britches lay with them, boots standing to attention next to Aldorbana.

'Is that what you are? Middle Blood?' Willow asked, stifling a cough. I nodded.

'Same as me,' she said. 'No, they're not Middle Blood. They're not any Blood. They're individual to you.'

'But why?'

'Maybe it's so you stand out. They can keep a better eye on you.'

'Who?'

'The Palace Guards, the Nightshade. Rian.'

I wouldn't put it past any of them, except maybe Rian. I was still deciding about him.

'I'll stick out like a sore thumb, wearing purple,' I said, resenting Finule and Chervil just a little more than I had before.

Willow gave me a pained look, her deep brown eyes almost glowing in the light as her thick, black, slightly frizzy hair swished with her movements. 'You talk about sticking out. I know how it feels. My grandfather came from Mere. He was a successful merchant. King Finule's father gave him special dispensation to marry my grandmother. As you know, Mereans all have dark skin.'

'Hence your colouring?'

She nodded, sitting down on a chair opposite the bed.

'I hadn't thought about it – none of that matters on Iolite. We're so small we always need new blood, so we welcome people from all the Five Lands. They did try to keep things "island only", originally, but they found the children started going a little strange after a while, so the Master put a stop to the practice.'

'I can imagine,' Willow said, grimacing.

'I take from my mother's pale Flosian ancestry rather than my father's golden complexion. Way back, his family were from Trew, but they've been on Iolite for several generations now. But isn't Willow a Trewan name, because of the tree?'

'I'm named after Willowherb. Not the tree. They just call me "Willow" for short. So, it's still Aerban.'

'You know, Mal once said that my eyes were more Aer...' I stopped.

'Mal?'

'My brother.' I bowed my head.

'Rian mentioned him. I'm sorry for your loss.'

I nodded as my heart clenched in my chest. I'd miss my brother until the day I died, which was more than could be said for my sister. I took a deep breath and put the clothes on, struggling with the outer coat. How Rian fought with this going down to his knees, I had no idea – halfway down my thighs made me curse. Iolitian clothes were far more practical, far better for fighting.

'Are you a King's Warrior?' I asked, noting Willow's black headband with red edging.

'Yes and no,' she said. 'Being a Middle Blood means I can't be a true King's Warrior. I'm not allowed. But because of my fighting skills they made me a King's Warrior-Attendant. It basically means I follow them around. Run errands, fight if needed.'

'I'm sorry you're having to look after me,' I said, sitting on the edge of the bed and pulling on the black leather boots.

'Don't be. It's a relief to have a girl to talk to. Most of those King's Warrior boys are tremendously shallow. Not to mention lazy. You can't have a decent conversation with half of them. It's only Tarragon, Anise, Sage, and Rian who are worth talking to.'

I smiled. 'What's Rian told you about me?' I asked, enjoying the soft seat after the cold, hard stone of the dungeon.

'Who you are. What you are. That you're innocent.'

'Do you believe him?'

She looked at me and nodded. 'Rian doesn't lie. He's also a tremendously good judge of character. I have no doubt if he thinks you're telling the truth, then you are.'

Rian, a High Blood that didn't lie? That was a new one.

'Thank you,' I murmured. 'Sage has been a tough nut to crack, though.'

'It just takes a while for him to warm up. To trust people.'

'Particularly when they're assassins.'

Willow smiled. 'How did you get on with Tarragon?'

I frowned. 'Fine. He seems quite easy-going.'

'Tarragon's kind and sensible. Most of the time,' she said, her face flushing slightly.

Now I understood. 'You like him?'

Her face flushed even more. 'He's High Blood. I'm Middle Blood. It's against the Blood Rule Decree.'

She could deny it all she wanted, but she liked Tarragon – a lot. 'The Decree's the same in Iolite, although we have same-sex relationships. Marriages, too.'

'Really? I hadn't realis–' A knock at the door broke her train of thought. 'That's probably Anise. He said he'd come to take you to Rian for supper,' she said, getting up and heading into the sitting room.

I followed her to find the most beautiful-looking young man I'd ever seen entering the room. A King's Warrior, he wore the same clothes as Tarragon and Sage – just as immaculate as Sage's. He looked about the same age as Willow, and his violet-blue eyes darted about the room, taking everything in. He smiled at me, and for a moment I had an irrational hatred of his smooth, glowing, rose-beige skin. Mine always had a dry edge to it. His long, black hair, tied in the high ponytail, fell forward about his face as he moved.

'Lady Samphire, I'm here to take you to Prince Valerian,' he said in a voice as smooth as butter.

'You're being very proper today, Anise,' Willow said, smirking.

'I wish to give the Lady Samphire a good impression, Willow,' he said, standing tall.

'Bobbins.' She laughed a little silvery laugh. 'Well, I guess there's a first time for everything.'

I'd never met anyone like Anise before, and his charming nature immediately appealed to me – even if he was a High Blood.

'Shall we?' he asked, indicating the door. I started to follow him out when a weird sensation struck my back. Willow let out a yelp.

Anise turned, a look of amazement on his face.

A leather strap now sat diagonally across my chest, and another, branching from it at my waist, disappeared around my back where I now sensed Aldorbana and Cwicsusl had taken up residence. Aldorbana sat snugly in its scabbard. Finule had said I was now bound to them, although I hadn't realised he'd meant like this.

Willow swore.

'Interesting,' Anise said, peering at the Cursed Weapons that now sat on my back. 'It appears you can only go a short distance away from them.'

'It would have been nice if someone had mentioned it,' I said, my pulse sounding rapidly in my ears.

'We didn't know,' Willow said, regaining her composure. 'No one has carried them in over a hundred years.'

'I can't think why,' I said, sarcasm filling my voice.

Anise led me the short distance to Rian's chambers, leaving me alone with the prince.

'Shouldn't we be chaperoned?' I asked, raising an eyebrow, well aware of the customs of both our Lands.

Rian smiled. 'No need; there's at least three Nightshade operatives within earshot – they'll be able to report back that nothing inappropriate happened.'

'Three?' I started to wonder if I'd bathed alone or had an audience. 'Your spies take their work seriously if they spy on you, too.'

'I think on this occasion it's more because you're here,' he said. 'How are you feeling?'

'Tired,' I said.

'Come, sit down. You must be hungry.'

I carefully removed Aldorbana and Cwicsusl, resting them up against the wall behind me.

Rian eyed the Weapons. 'You didn't have to bring them with you.'

'I didn't have a choice,' I said.

He raised an eyebrow. 'What do you–'

Two servants came in carrying trays with glasses and bread. Rian showed me to a highly-polished wooden table, where we sat on padded wooden seats. Another servant brought us a wonderful meal of venison and vegetables followed by cakes, all washed down with Pine Wine, an Aerban speciality.

'You get on well with Tarragon and Sage,' I said, lifting my glass to the light and looking at it suspiciously.

Rian laughed. 'It's not drugged, if that's what you're worried about.'

'You're not drinking any,' I said, noticing he'd only had water.

'I hate the stuff,' he said. 'Alcohol in general.'

'I can't say I'm that keen on it, either.'

'Then have water like me,' he said, pouring me a glass from a pitcher on the table.

I still looked at it suspiciously. 'I know what you did last time, and after that I can't be too careful,' I said, taking a cautious sip.

'Sorry about that,' Rian said, a cloud crossing his face. 'I had to make sure you weren't going to run off, although Sage was a little overzealous with it. To answer your question, Tarragon and Sage are my cousins. We've known each other all our lives, grew up together, so yes, we get on well.'

I choked on my water. 'So Sorrel is your cousin too?'

'Unfortunately.' Rian shifted uncomfortably in his chair.

I'd hit a nerve. 'Aldorbana and Cwicsusl,' I said, trying to change the subject as I took another sip of water. 'I assume the names mean something?'

Rian winced. 'Sure, you want to know?'

I nodded.

He sighed. 'They're Old Aerban names – Aldorbana means "Life-destroyer" and Cwicsusl literally means "Living torment".'

'Oh.' I'd had to ask. 'Appropriate, I suppose.'

'I'm sorry. I tried to get Father to give you a chance without the Weapons, but he never takes much notice of me. Neither does Chervil.'

'What's done is done,' I said. 'Besides, if I manage to do everything your father has asked of me before the Curse takes me, he said he'd break it and I'd be free.'

'That's what he said,' Rian said, his brow furrowing as he looked towards the Weapons propped up on his sitting room wall.

I slept little, despite the tiredness I felt. Taking up Aldorbana and Cwicsusl had worn me out more than I cared to admit, but I just couldn't settle. As the sun rose, I ventured out into the misty gardens for a little exercise and some fresh air. I hadn't actually been confined to my rooms, as such, and there was probably someone watching my every move anyway, so I concluded I could probably leave for a short walk. No one stopped me as I left the palace building and wandered amongst the box hedges and jewel-like flowers.

The thought of returning to Iolite filled me with a deep, dark horror I didn't care to examine too closely. I'd hoped to keep the Coterie ignorant of my survival – if Juniper caught me, I'd be dead, although Aldorbana and Cwicsusl might give me an edge in a fight. Returning also raised the prospect of seeing Beryl or Flint, which didn't sit happily with me either, but most of all, the knowledge Mal wouldn't be there became the thing that really tied my stomach in knots. Wave after wave of unsettling sensations rattled through me, which was why I'd decided to go for a walk in the first place: to attempt to settle my nerves.

I walked amongst the herbs and shrubs, their pleasant aromas lingering in the air. The perfume from the rose beds settled around me as I wandered along, well aware that two Palace Guards now followed me. Aldorbana and Cwicsusl clanked quietly on my back. They were going to take some getting used to. I found a hedged garden encompassing a little fountain, and sat on a stone bench, watching the water droplets twist in the air. The dawn sun ricocheted off them, forming sparkles that danced and shimmered in the light, as my tears fell unchecked. My brother had been a huge part of my life; he'd kept me sane. Now he was lost to me forever. He left a huge hole that could never be filled.

The crunch of boots on the shingle path broke through my thoughts, and I hurriedly dried my tears. I looked up to see Rian approaching.

'May I join you?' he asked.

I nodded, although I wanted to be alone right now, and I didn't really welcome his interruption. 'You're up early.'

He shrugged. 'I never sleep well when I know I've got a long journey ahead.' He sat down beside me, and the soft, sweet floral accents of sandalwood engulfed me. 'Are you feeling less tired today?'

'Not really,' I said, trying not to let him see my puffy eyes. 'I didn't sleep well, either.'

He reached out, gently touching my chin, turning my face towards him. 'Your brother?' he asked quietly.

I pulled away. 'Why should a High Blood like you care?' I snapped, annoyed that he'd disturbed me.

'Do you hate all High Bloods, or just me?' Rian asked, a pained expression on his face.

I hesitated. 'I've not had good experiences with High Bloods over the years,' I said, bowing my head.

'So, you don't exactly like or trust any of us?'

'You could say that.'

He chewed his lip for a moment. 'Well, Father and Chervil haven't exactly helped the situation.'

'No, they haven't.'

'We're not all like them,' he said, gazing into the fountain. 'I hope you'll realise that in time.'

I chewed on a nail. I'd already begun to like Tarragon and Anise, despite my prejudice – maybe even Rian wasn't all bad either – but too many things were happening all at once for me to come to terms with anything right now.

'Do you think you'll feel well enough to travel later this morning?' he asked.

'Yes.' I wanted to say no. I never want to leave here; I don't want to go to Iolite. But then Finule would never break the Curse, so I stayed quiet.

'Phire, there's been something I wanted to talk to you about,' Rian said. He fidgeted, faltered. 'I wanted to say, what Father said about the Cu–'

'Prince Valerian, are you there?' A rich, confident voice cut across Rian's words, rising above the sound of the fountain.

Rian jumped to his feet, his face flushed. 'It's Lord Bergamot, Chief of the Military,' Rian said softly, before raising his voice. 'I'm here, Lord Bergamot, by the fountain,' he called, straightening his outer coat and swords.

I got to my feet, taking a few steps back as Lord Bergamot appeared around a hedge. 'Ah, Prince Valerian – oh, Lady Samphire,' he said as he saw me, the portly man's green eyes narrowing as they darted from Rian to me and back again, his left eye twitching. He cocked his head to the left as he continued to look at us, sending a shiver down my back.

'That will be all, Lady Samphire,' Rian said, turning towards me, a warning look in his eyes.

I nodded, giving him a little bow, Aldorbana awkwardly catching on Cwicsusl. 'Of course, Your Highness,' I said matter-of-factly. 'I'll see to it at once.' I turned away, walking back towards the palace.

'Now, what can I do for you, Lord Bergamot?' Rian asked as I walked off. 'If it's one of your sons you're after, I haven't seen Sorrel or Sage this morning.'

Sorrel and Sage were Lord Bergamot's sons? I heard no more of the conversation as I headed back to the building, wondering what Rian would have said if we'd been left alone.

Mid-morning, we rode out of the palace courtyard into a bustling Viridi market and away from the city, cantering along the road towards Borage. The journey would take us around ten days, longer than to get to Tansy, but the harbour was bigger there and the ship Rian had arranged for us to take made its base at Borage. At least the sea voyage would be a little shorter; I could only take so much of the rolling movement of a sailing ship.

That first night, we camped in a little hollow in the hills, the sun sinking below the horizon as the stars came out to litter the sky like scattered diamonds. The Stars held great importance for the Iolitians, and the Temple of the Celestial Bodies took pride of place in the capital, Adamas. I looked up at the stars for a while until my neck stiffened, then returned my gaze to the camp where Sage and Sorrel cooked the evening meal.

'You'll burn it if you do it like that,' Sage said, trying to take the cooking pot away from Sorrel, his earring sparkling in the firelight.

'I know exactly what I'm doing; you're the incompetent one,' Sorrel said.

'I've done far more cooking than you.'

'Hmm, shame you still don't know what you're doing, then.'

Willow looked over towards me and made a face. Quite why Sorrel had joined us, I didn't know, but apparently, he would see us to Borage.

After the evening stew finally made it to our bowls, the others sat chatting while I found myself watching the gentle evening breeze ruffling Rian's hair as he sat feeding the fire with twigs. The glow from the flames set his hair alight with reds and golds as he gazed into the fire. He glanced over at me, a look of confusion – conflict, even – filling his eyes. But something else lingered there, too, something that made the blood rush to my face, and I turned away, feeling a strong urge to study my boots.

'Hey, Rian, we need more wood,' Tarragon said. 'Come with me and we'll get some dead branches from that small copse over there.'

Rian nodded and they disappeared off into the darkness.

'Do you like him, Samphire?' Anise asked from beside me, making me jump. 'It's about time Rian found someone.'

How could I answer that? He was a High Blood.

'What? No,' I said, flustered by Anise's words.

'Don't worry, I'm good at keeping secrets,' Anise said with a grin.

'Don't be daft, we're just working together, that's all. Anyway, he's a prince. We're different Blood Classes.'

Anise snorted. 'The Blood Rule Decree indeed. It ought to be done away with,' he said, gazing across the fire at Sage, his eyes lingering a little too long. 'You can't help who you fall in love with.'

'Does he feel the same?' I asked softly. If he did, they were treading a dangerous path, one leading to possible Demotion of Blood Class, imprisonment, banishment or in rare cases, execution – all at the Aerban King's pleasure, of course.

Anise looked sharply at me. 'Don't know what you're talking about, Samphire,' he said, getting up and wandering over to help Willow, who had started preparing the bedding.

It appeared the Blood Rule Decree was proving a little awkward for several of those sitting around this campfire. I glanced towards the far side of the fire.

'I still don't know what she's doing here,' Sorrel said, nodding at Willow.

'She's the best lock picker we have, and we may need her,' Sage said.

'I'm sure we could knock down any door we needed to.'

'Not everything can be solved with brute strength, Brother,' Sage said wearily.

'Most things can.'

A short while later, Rian and Tarragon returned and quickly had the fire blazing away. It illuminated quite a distance around the camp, and I glanced at the tattoo peeking out from my purple coat sleeve. I angrily pulled the cuff down to cover the brand.

'You don't like that very much, do you?' Rian asked, sitting next to me.

I shook my head. 'It's only ever been a mark of shame,' I said bitterly. 'I'd get rid of it if I could.'

'Here, take this,' he said, removing a leather wrist strap from his arm. 'You can cover it up, then no one will see, not even you.' He passed it over to me. 'Put your wrist in and I'll do it up.'

I pulled up my sleeve and placed my wrist into the strap. He did up the lacing and just as he'd said, it completely covered the Coterie tattoo.

'Thanks,' I said, appreciating his kindness. 'That's much better.'

Rian smiled at me. 'Good. Now, you'd better get to sleep; we'll be up early tomorrow. The sooner we get to Iolite, the sooner we retrieve the Fire Opal.'

I nodded and made my way to my blankets, sliding under them as the others began to do the same. As I lay there, I glanced over to where Rian had made his bed on the other side of the fire. The smell of sandalwood from his wrist strap filled my senses, and my heart skipped a beat. Maybe Rian wasn't as much like his father, or Chervil, as I'd first thought. Both his father and brother appeared to want me dead one way or another. To do "penance", as Finule put it, wasn't going to be easy. Even if I did manage to find out what he wanted, I'd still have to get back and appease the King before Aldorbana and Cwicsusl sucked the life out of me – literally – and that was assuming he kept his word by breaking the Curse. It was all I had to cling to, and cling to it I would. I wanted to survive. As I drifted off to sleep, I found my dreams filled with amber eyes.

CHAPTER FIVE

The next day we set off just after dawn, riding through the hills past sheep grazing happily on the hillsides. Gradually, the land flattened, and fields of herbs encroached on the road with little buildings dotted amongst the fields. In the distance, a copse of oak trees and a few sawmills lay scattered across the countryside.

Anise glanced at me. 'Aerba's very much an agricultural economy, Samphire,' he said.

'You grow lots of herbs, don't you?' I asked.

'It's in the name,' he said, grinning. 'It's Old Aerban for herb. But yes, we have hundreds of varieties, many dried and exported to the other Lands.'

'What are the buildings used for?'

'Mainly drying huts and distilleries. Some of the herb flowers are distilled into medicinal tinctures. I carry a combination of dried herbs and tinctures in my Herb Chest,' he said, patting a pack attached to his saddle.

'He's never without it,' Sage said from in front of us. 'Anise is a real genius with herbs. He can conjure just about any remedy from them.'

Anise's face took on a pinkish hue.

'So, you're a Herbalist?' I asked.

'Not as such,' Anise said. 'At least, I've never had any formal training. I picked things up from my father, and from books, but mainly it's instinct. I just seem to have a natural feel for what herbs to use and combine into remedies.'

'Told you.' Sage grinned. 'He's a genius.'

'And the tree plantations are for wood?' I asked.

'To an extent, although these ones here are oaks grown mainly for medicinal purposes and their galls,' Anise said.

'For both purposes?'

He nodded. 'Oak bark can be made into a tea for coughs, colds and digestive issues, as well as arthritis. The oak galls are growths on the trees formed when certain types of wasp lay their eggs. The galls grow due to the wasp larvae and are harvested for Iron Gall Ink.'

'I know about the ink. So, these are the galls we import into Iolite to make the Iron Gall Ink for the university and the library books, then?'

Anise nodded. 'Iolite is where the bulk of ink is made in the Five Lands because of your iron supplies in the mountains, Samphire.'

'We still have to import Spindle Gum from Spindle City in Trew, from their Acacia Trees, for the ink – so what about things like cereal crops?' I asked.

'We import some, but Aerba grows a lot of crops so we're fairly self-sufficient there, as long as the drought in the east doesn't get worse.'

I looked out over the herb fields and the tree plantations, such different countryside to the more mountainous Iolitian views I was used to. 'Iolite exports our jewellery, although the other Lands aren't as interested in the gemstones' meanings and attributes as we are,' I said. 'They're more interested in the colours and designs of the jewellery we make.'

'Not always.' Anise smiled, reaching under his shirt to pull out a gold chain necklace with a beautiful green Jade Amulet. 'I think this must have come from Iolite – I found it in my mother's things after she died.'

'I'm sorry about your mother,' I said, my heart twisting at his sad words.

'It was a couple of years ago, now. She and Father went to visit relatives in Anisum, in Eastern Aerba. While they were there, there was an outbreak of Morbilli Rash. My parents caught it, too, and died. Since then, I've lived with Sage's family. You see, Lord Bergamot was a close friend of Father's and he took pity on me.'

'You're lucky to have a new home.'

He turned and smiled. 'Since then, I've worn Mother's Amulet for good luck – that's what Iolitians believe jade does, isn't it? Bring good luck?'

I nodded. 'Does it work?'

'I think so. Sometimes, anyway. Do you wear one?'

I pulled out my Amethyst Talisman. 'My namesake. It's supposed to obstruct negative energy, although I'm not sure about that, and it's also for protection, courage, and inner strength,' I said.

'You need inner strength?'

'More than you know.' Blood rushed to my face – had I said too much? 'My Fan is made of malachite for inner strength and protection, too. Mal gave it to me for my sixteenth birthday. I'm not sure if he chose the stone because of how it looked, what it represented, or because of his ego,' I continued, remembering the dazzlingly smug smile he'd given me as I'd opened it. Ego. But I didn't care if it was. I'd give anything to have my brother back. My Fan was even more precious to me now. 'It also has topaz for strength, aquamarine for courage and protection, and an amethyst, along with the sun, moon, and stars embossed on the outside.'

'Do they protect you?' Anise asked.

'I'm still alive. At least, I am for the moment,' I said, giving him a wry grin.

Rian glanced towards me then away as Anise smiled back.

'So, all Iolitians are named after gemstones?' Anise asked.

'Gemstones and semi-precious stones,' I said. 'Things like malachite, beryl, diamond, agate, moonstone, sapphire, ruby, emerald – all the usual things. I guess it was because they thought they shone and sparkled like the Stars we honoured. Beryl was named after Mother. She was called Emerald, and that's a type of beryl, like aquamarine. Aerba follows the Herbs, though?'

Anise nodded. 'We're all herbs or herb-type names. Not flowers, of course, flowers are for Flos.'

I nodded. 'I have a cousin, Jasmine, in Flos. She and her husband, Hyacinth, used to have me and Mal to stay quite a bit when we were younger. Not my sister, Beryl – she didn't like going. We also used to visit my cousin Erica at the palace – she's distantly related to the King somehow.'

'Have you been back recently?'

I shook my head. 'When Father died of sweating sickness, my stepmother reduced our visits, then put a stop to them completely.'

'How long ago did you lose your father?'

'Seven years, now,' I said, my eyes stinging with unshed tears. 'Mal and I were away in Flos when he became ill. He died in a matter of hours, or so they said. That's when *she* forced us into the Coterie – me and Mal, that is. We did it to keep each other safe, and Beryl.'

Rian glanced back at me again, his eyes clouded.

'Juniper didn't train your sister too?' Anise asked.

'I hadn't thought so, but I was wrong. She just trained her in a different way,' I said bitterly.

Later that day we made camp in a little copse of pine trees. The fresh smell filled the air and I soaked it in. Tarragon stood at the edge of the trees, watching some rabbits scampering about in the distance near their sandy burrow. He glanced towards me as I came and stood beside him.

'I was considering whether to supplement our evening meal with rabbit,' he said. 'But by the time I get close enough they'll be long gone.'

'You need a bow,' I said, gazing out at the playful rabbits.

'Never learnt to use one.'

'Why not?'

'Not really an Aerban thing, archery – swords are more our style.'

'But not much use for catching rabbits,' I said, grinning at him.

'Indeed.'

'Where're you going?' Sage came up behind us, his forehead furrowed.

'Nowhere,' I said, suppressing a sigh.

'She just came to talk to me, y'know, she's not going anywhere,' Tarragon said.

'Good,' Sage said, turning back to camp.

'He really doesn't like me, does he?' I asked.

Tarragon watched his cousin walk away. 'It's not really that,' he said in a low voice. 'It's partly because of your profession, but also to do with his loyalties.'

'What do you mean?'

'He's very loyal to the Crown and to Aerba. Anyone he thinks is challenging that, he doesn't trust. I blame his father and Sorrel for that.'

'Why?' I asked, my curiosity piqued.

Tarragon leant against a tree. 'Well, they've always let him down, really. Told him one thing, done another. He eventually found he couldn't really trust either of them, and so he takes a while to warm to people in general, learn he can really trust them.'

'He trusts you and Rian.'

Tarragon nodded. 'Willow, too, but he's known us since we were in our cribs. Other than that, there's only Anise. He trusts him with his life.'

'Every day.'

'What?'

'Well, it's against the Blood Rules, the two of them.'

Tarragon raised an eyebrow. 'You know?'

'I guessed.'

He nodded. 'I suppose you're right. The King could have them executed if he found out. Doubt he would, but yes, he trusts Anise with his life every day. And us, too.'

'It's a big risk.'

'I don't know – when you fall in love with someone, you'd risk everything for them, wouldn't you?'

I couldn't answer that. I'd never been in love. I glanced back at the camp where Anise sat chatting to Rian. As I caught sight of the prince, my heart did a little skip.

I swallowed. 'But how can Sage be so loyal to the Royal Family if he doesn't trust them?'

'He respects them, the institution, just doesn't entirely trust them as individuals. Loyalty to the idea of the Crown and the Land of Aerba are a different thing entirely – a Land can't let you down.' Tarragon turned back to watch the rabbits. 'He'll come around eventually, and when he does, you'll find him a fierce and loyal friend – but in the meantime you'll have to be patient.'

We spent the next week in the saddle, camping or staying at an inn when the opportunity presented itself. When it did, I noticed how Sorrel would often disappear with a lady in tow, despite Sage's disapproving looks.

'It's against the Blood Rules,' Sage murmured to Willow one evening.

'Like Sorrel cares,' she said. 'If your father or the King find out, though, he'll be in trouble.'

I had my own encounter with Sorrel the following night. We'd camped in a barn, a local farmer agreeing to our using it. After our meal, I wandered out of the barn for some fresh air, the smell of horse inside becoming a little overwhelming. I stood at the side of the building enjoying the nip to the night air, watching the stars march across the sky.

'Not tired?' Sorrel asked, limping over to me.

'I'm getting there. In fact, I think I'll turn in now,' I said, moving past him. He grabbed me as I tried to pass, pulling me around so I came to rest against the barn's wall.

'Hmm, why not have a bit of fun with me first, Lady Merciless? Then you'll sleep well, I promise.' The leer on his face did nothing to entice me.

'Let go, I'm not interested,' I said, trying to pull away. The alternative involved causing him considerable pain, and probably breaking something.

'Come on, it'll be fun – I've never had any complaints,' he said, licking his lips suggestively.

'What's going on?' Rian asked, walking around the corner of the barn.

'We were just getting to know one another,' Sorrel said. 'We'll be in shortly.'

'Like hell we will,' I said, satisfying myself by kicking his shin.

He yelled, letting go of me as he bent over and rubbed his leg. I took the opportunity to move over towards Rian.

'You shouldn't have done that, Lady Merciless,' Sorrel said, eyebrows lowering as his hand went to his knife.

Rian took my hand as I got to him, pulling me behind him.

'You want her?' Sorrel asked, his eyes narrowing slyly.

Rian shot him a look like daggers. 'I want her unharmed so she's as effective as possible on our mission for the King. Now leave her alone; that's an order,' he said, moving away, taking me with him back around the front of the barn.

'Thanks, but I can take care of myself,' I said, shaking my hand free of his.

'I know, but Sorrel…' Rian looked at me, hesitated a moment as his pupils dilated ever so slightly, then rubbed the back of his neck. 'I didn't want him bothering you.'

'Why not?' I asked.

'Because you might lose patience with him, break a habit of a lifetime, and kill him. Then I'd have to explain what happened to Lord Bergamot.'

I grinned. 'I might just do that, if pushed.'

'There you are, then,' he smiled back.

'Your cousin's obviously not scared of the Blood Rules, then?'

'Apparently not.'

'We should reach Borage by nightfall,' Tarragon said as we rode through grasslands full of chirping insects that occasionally became a meal for a grassland swallow. The birds dived towards the long grasses, catching their prey like an airborne fisherman.

'Good. I smell of horse and need a bath,' Willow said, glancing meaningfully towards him through her long lashes.

Tarragon's eyes widened as a rosy blush appeared across his face. He cleared his throat. 'I'm sure we'll have time for that before we leave,' he said, looking away over the grasses.

Willow smiled.

'We should be able to sail on the morning tide,' Sage said, ignoring them.

'If you're lucky,' Sorrel said, looking up at the sky.

'You think the weather is going to turn?'

'You can never tell.'

Sage squinted. 'I think you're wrong.'

'We'll see.'

'How long will it take to get to Iolite, Samphire?' Anise asked.

'About three or four days, depending on the conditions,' I said.

'I've never been to sea before,' Willow said, her eyes sparkling with excitement.

'As long as it's calm, it'll be all right,' Tarragon said. 'I hate being out in rough weather. Does nothing for the digestive system.'

'Bobbins. It'll be fine.'

'You don't know what you're saying.'

'Speak for yourself,' Rian said, a smile spreading over his face. 'I love being at sea, whatever the weather.'

Tarragon grunted.

The ground broke up as we approached Borage and the road took us into a series of deep, rocky gullies as the afternoon drew on. We paused at a stream in a gully to water the horses and take a break before our final push to the town. I took Aldorbana and Cwicsusl off my back for a few minutes' respite – they really made my back hot and sticky. I walked down to the stream to splash water in my face, the cold water quickly refreshing me, and I took a sip of the crystal clear liquid.

'I think I'll bathe, too, when we get to the inn,' Anise said, looking at his dusty clothes with distaste. 'Long journeys on horseback can be–'

A yell from behind us made me twist around. A group of men, all dressed in black, appeared from out of the rocks, brandishing curved swords, one carrying a crossbow. A cross bolt whistled towards me. I ducked.

Willow froze, eyes wide with fear.

'This way,' Rian shouted as he leapt across the stream towards a side gully, leading us towards open ground.

I grabbed Willow's shoulder, shaking her into movement. 'Run!'

She looked at me, wild-eyed, then did as I said.

I raced after Rian, the others doing the same.

Rian glanced back at me, his expression changing to concern, and he slowed. 'Your weapons?'

'Don't worry,' I said, running past him. I'd barely taken four steps before Aldorbana and Cwicsusl returned to my back.

'Damn.'

'Your father said we were bound to each other,' I said as we entered an open area where I could draw Aldorbana.

'I didn't realise he meant like that,' Rian said, drawing his own swords.

We held our ground as the black-coated men rushed in. We met their attack, attempting to drive them back. All my companions were skilled fighters, Rian and Tarragon in particular. It was Anise that stepped in first, his swords moving in a flurry of shining steel, immediately taking his opponent off guard. Willow had gotten over her initial shock, and she slashed and dodged with such grace I became quite jealous – the Coterie didn't teach grace, just efficiency. Sage appeared to be more of a refined swordsman than Sorrel, who relied on brute strength, but even then, he seemed lazy in his approach, not taking down his opponent quickly like I thought he should.

A scruffy-looking man sped towards me. I stood, sword foot forward, ready to meet his attack. He lunged at me. I sidestepped, and he plunged past me, swearing. I turned, ready for his next attempt. He twisted around, shoulder dropping, hand pulling back as he prepared to attack. But I didn't give him the opportunity. I struck at him before he knew what was happening. He parried clumsily with the top part of his sword, and Aldorbana cut a nick in it as they met. The man in front of me thought he knew what he was doing. He didn't.

Again, I sliced at him. Again, he brought the top of his sword up to block. I slammed my elbow into his face. He fell, dropped his weapon, and grabbed at his bleeding nose. My heart raced with the adrenaline. I took a deep breath while I could.

Another man came at me from the side. He thrust his sword towards me. I raised Cwicsusl, blocking his blow. As he swiped a second time, I twisted out of the way. He snarled, lips curled, as he swung his sword at me again with such force it made me smile. I sidestepped. His momentum took him on. I spun past him, slamming Aldorbana's hilt into the back of his neck. He fell.

Suddenly, my foot caught on a rock and I fell backwards onto the uneven ground, dropping the Cursed Weapons. My heart thumped uncomfortably in my chest. I was vulnerable. One of the men lunged towards me, sensing blood. He thrust with his sword. Still reeling from the fall, I tried to roll out the way. Not quickly enough. His blade swept towards me.

Another sword parried his blow. It forced him back, saving my life. I looked up to see Rian swinging his sword at my assailant before running him through. I clambered to my feet as he turned and winked at me. I nodded my thanks. His face changed abruptly from smile to horror.

'Phire! Behind you!'

CHAPTER SIX

An arm flew around my neck, trying to choke me.

Just breathe. Don't *panic.*

I stamped hard on my assailant's foot. Smashed my elbow into his liver, ducking under his arm as he released me. He bent over, yelling in pain. Not sufficient pain to stop his fist from flying in my direction, catching my chin. I staggered backwards. Pain radiated along my jaw. No time to think about that now. *Push through the pain.* Push through as I'd been taught.

'Here!' Rian threw me one of his swords.

I caught it as the man stood up.

'You're a feisty one,' he spat.

'You're slow,' I said, my face throbbing.

He roared, swinging at me, his sword stroke wild and uncontrolled. I dodged, which only enraged him more. He swiped wildly at me. I jumped backwards, out of the way, and his sword buried itself in the earth, caught by a rock. It was tempting to kick his arm, but I'd only put myself at risk of being unbalanced. Instead, I brought Rian's sword down into the side of his wedged blade, jarring it from his grip. He looked up at me. Backed away. Ran.

He wasn't alone.

All our attackers were now moving away, grabbing their injured comrades, fleeing back the way they'd come. Sorrel watched them go, rubbing his arm. I bent over, trying to regain some control over my breathing.

'What was that about?' Tarragon asked, anger tingeing his voice as he wiped his weapons, looking around cautiously for any stragglers.

Rian ran over to me. 'I thought he was going to kill you,' he said, resting his hand on my shoulder.

'For a moment there, so did I.' I smiled at him, then wished I hadn't. It sent a whole new jab of pain through my face. 'Ow.'

'Let me see that,' he said, his hand going gently to my jaw. For some reason, his touch made the blood rush to my face. He looked into my eyes. There were questions there, confusion, a look of concern, of worry. 'Anise will have some salve you can put on it. The skin's not broken,' he said, letting go, rubbing the back of his neck.

'Thank you,' I said, passing his sword back to him. Our hands momentarily touched. My fingers tingled at the warmth of his hands. 'You saved me.'

He wiped perspiration from his brow. 'You're a good fighter. And I need you.' He took the sword and turned away.

'Are you all right?' Sage asked, putting his hand on Anise's arm.

'Fine, you?' Anise smiled, resheathing one sword and placing his hand on Sage's.

Sage nodded, then looked at us and cleared his throat, letting go of Anise. 'Good, I just wanted to make sure,' he said, stepping back and walking away from us.

Sorrel screwed his nose up and looked skywards, disgust in his eyes.

'It was the Nightshade,' Anise said, resheathing his other sword.

Rian turned sharply. 'By the Herbs, are you sure?'

Sorrel looked across at Anise, his body suddenly tense.

Anise nodded. 'I recognised their gold rings with the Nightshade flower on.'

'Bugger,' Tarragon said, gazing in the direction the men had gone.

'Tell Lord Wormwood to stay away from us, or I'll send the Coterie after him!' Rian yelled after the retreating swordsmen. 'And that's a Royal Command!'

I raised an eyebrow as I looked at him. He shrugged, his forehead furrowed, and his lips pressed tightly together as he resheathed his swords.

Willow stood beside me, a little smirk on her face at Rian's words.

'He's just like his father,' I whispered to her.

The smirk on her face vanished. 'No, he's not,' she said, shaking her head, the sharpness in her voice taking me by surprise.

'You really think issuing an edict like that'll work?' Tarragon asked.

'It won't hurt,' Rian said.

'Why on earth would the Nightshade attack us?' Sage asked.

'The Nightshade have a thing against Flosians,' Willow said, sliding her swords back into their scabbards.

'What's that got to do with anything?' Tarragon asked.

She cast a sidelong glance at me.

'What, the Nightshade could've been sent to kill me because my grandmother's family came from Flos?' I asked, incredulous at the idea.

'What?' Rian asked as Tarragon frowned.

'My grandmother was Flosian, but she married an Iolitian. You really think that's why they attacked?'

'As Willow said, the Nightshade are rather blinkered when it comes to Flos,' Anise said.

'But why?'

'Something to do with one of our princesses running off with a

Flosian Prince over a hundred years ago,' Tarragon said, rubbing his chin.

'Hell's teeth, you Aerbans hold grudges longer than Juniper,' I said.

'But why would they want to kill Phire when she's on a mission for the King?' Rian asked.

'Who knows, but the Nightshade are a law unto themselves most of the time,' Sage said.

Tarragon looked at Rian, an amused glint in his eye. 'We're calling her "Phire" now, are we?'

'Leave it, Tarragon,' Rian said, sending him a warning look. 'We'd better get back to the horses.'

Aldorbana and Cwicsusl returned to my back as we walked.

Rian raised an eyebrow. 'The Weapons coming to you like that before the fight, and now too – you knew that would happen?' he asked as he walked beside me.

'Yes – they already did it at the palace,' I said. 'I did try to tell you then.'

'There's definitely some sort of Magic at work here.'

'Really? Magic?' Sage scoffed. 'I've never seen any evidence of it in my lifetime. There's no such thing anymore.'

'Bobbins,' Willow said. 'How else is the Curse going to work, then? Surely, it has to be some sort of Magic?'

Sage frowned, looking less sure of himself. 'I don't know – we should get back to the horses,' he said, moving ahead of us.

'You fought well,' I said to Anise.

He smiled. 'Sage says I sometimes jump in too quickly, but I can't help it – there's no point in letting them get the upper hand first.'

'True,' I said, nodding. We returned to the stream, but when we got there, the gully stood empty except for our bags that we'd had the foresight to remove from the horses to give them a break.

'Great,' Sorrel said, cursing for good measure.

'We're only about a couple of hours' walk from Borage,' Sage said. 'We'll be there shortly after dark if we get a move on.'

Sorrel glared at his brother, picked up his bag, and started down the track. We followed Sorrel, walking towards the town, out the gully, beside the stream on its way downhill.

'You really think there's Magic at work?' Tarragon asked Rian.

Rian shrugged. 'Willow's right. The Cursed Weapons must carry some sort of Magic to be cursed in the first place. They are hundreds of years old, so who knows. Maybe it's something to do with the old Elemental Magic.'

'It's possible, I suppose,' Tarragon said, scratching his chin. 'The

Curse itself must go back centuries, well into the times when Elemental Magic ran in the veins of High Bloods.'

'How did it work?' Willow asked.

'The way I understand it is that those who could spin Magic were able to use one of the five Elements,' Rian said. 'Depending on their Magic "Angle", as they called it, they were either Fire Angle Spinners or Water Angle Spinners, and so on. Essentially, they were able to manipulate that Element.'

My father had been interested in the history of the Five Lands and had several books on the subject in his study back in the Crimson Castle that I'd devoured as a child. I knew that not everyone had had Magic in the past. Low Bloods had no Magic at all, but most Middle Bloods were able to enhance the High Bloods' Magic somehow – I'd never understood that part. Even in High Bloods, some were more powerful than others.

'Wait a minute, you got that wrong. There's only four Elements,' Sorrel said. 'Fire, Water, Earth, and Wind.'

'And Quintessence,' Anise said.

'What?'

'Quintessence.'

'You made that up,' Sage said, giving him a long look.

'I did not, Sage,' Anise said, scowling. 'My father told me all about Elemental Angle Spinners when I was small. Quintessence was the rarest; only a couple of Quintessence Angle Spinners were ever alive at the same time.'

'But what was Quintessence?' Willow asked. Her face had an ashen quality to it, and if you looked carefully you could see her hands trembling.

'The highest of the Elements,' I said. 'It was said to permeate the whole of nature and was the most pure and concentrated form of Magic.'

Rian gave me an approving smile. 'You know your Magic.'

'My father had many books on all sorts of subjects,' I said, looking away, tears stinging my eyes at the memories. One of his books, hidden in his study, was solely devoted to Elemental Magic.

'But that's centuries in the past,' Rian continued. 'I think Magic still lingers, like in the Cursed Weapons, but most of it's gone now.'

'Maybe there are those that could still use it,' Willow said, a thoughtful look on her face. 'If only they knew how.'

Sage snorted. 'Elemental Magic died out centuries ago. It doesn't run in anyone's veins anymore.'

Was he right? I didn't know. Anyway, I was a Middle Blood, and it made no difference to me either way.

As night fell, the twinkling lights of Borage came into view, a little constellation sitting next to the sea where the rising moon set light to the waves with silver flames. The wooden town bustled with folk even at dusk, many making their way to the various inns and taverns, others heading for the docks preparing for night-time fishing trips. We stopped at an inn a short distance from the docks. It reeked of stale beer downstairs, and the beds had seen better days, but Willow and I were glad of the chance to bathe and rest in our shared room. During the evening, Rian and Tarragon returned from a trip to the harbour to see the captain of the ship taking us to Iolite the next day.

'We sail on the morning tide,' Rian said. He sat down at our table where we were eating, and yawned. 'Hopefully it won't be long before we get the Fire Opal back.'

'You're quite attached to it, aren't you?' I said as I prodded at the food on my plate. Not only did my jaw hurt when I tried to eat, but I also felt a little nauseous – the aftereffects of the fight still lingering. I'd noticed it was still affecting Willow, too – she was trembling as she looked at her food, rather than tucking into it. The others just looked tired.

Rian nodded. 'It's the emblem of Aerba, our heirloom, and I take the fact someone has stolen it rather personally. I won't rest until it's back in the Cedarwood Throne.'

I'd never seen him look so determined.

'Any of that food for us?' Tarragon asked, snatching a small potato from Willow's plate and popping it in his mouth.

She slapped his hand. 'Order your own. This is mine.'

'But you're not eating it.'

'You can still get your own.'

Tarragon muttered something and wandered off to the busy bar, dodging the noisy, drunken patrons.

'Order for me, too,' Rian called after him. 'Where are Sage and Anise?'

'Bathing,' Sorrel said, a look of distaste on his face.

'What's your problem?' I asked.

He gave me a strange look. 'Nothing,' he said, turning away and rubbing his head. 'I'm going to bed. I've got a headache.' He got up and left the table.

'I might bathe myself, after I've eaten,' Rian said.

'Take Tarragon with you,' Willow said. 'He smells like a horse. I hate horses.'

I stifled a giggle as Tarragon returned to the table with two steaming plates of food and passed one to Rian.

'Might as well eat while I can,' Tarragon said, stabbing a potato.

'What?' I asked, confused by his words.

'Tarragon gets seasick in bad weather,' Rian said, cutting the meat on his plate.

'Some people just can't handle rough weather,' Willow said with a smirk, grabbing one of Tarragon's potatoes and munching on it. She turned a little green. 'Not sure I really wanted that.'

'You've never been to sea; you don't understand,' Tarragon said, a pained expression on his face. 'The weather can be really bad, and then there's the fact you have to keep an eye out for sea monsters.'

'Bobbins.'

'Sea morgens, you mean?' I asked, familiar with the stories of the beautiful Sea-born creatures that took men and women down into the depths with them, never to be seen again. Their song was so beautiful it allegedly drew you into the water – and you didn't care. They'd drown you and feed on you, although some said they took you to their undersea cities of pearl and made you marry them. Neither option appealed to me, and it sent a little tingle down my spine. I'd been on many sea voyages, but never seen a morgen.

'They're real?' Willow asked, a slightly wild look in her deep brown eyes. 'I mean, I know people talk about them – lake morgens too, even at Viridi – but I thought they were stories to frighten children. Stop them from swimming in the lake. They're actually real?'

'I don't know if the lake morgens are real, but the sea ones are,' Tarragon said. 'I've never seen them, but I know they exist. I did see a powler at Fennel Lake once – they're real. Horrible-looking things, y'know. So are Aerban Mynogres, but I think they're just myth, now – they used to live in Cilantro Forest in Southern Aerba.'

'I heard that tree dryads were beautiful,' Willow said. 'I don't know where they're supposed to be.'

'There aren't any dryads in Aerba, as far as I know,' Rian said.

'They're rumoured to be in some of the forests of Flos, but I don't know if that's true or not,' I said.

'There are Merean Blue Death Worms, out in the deserts,' Willow said. 'My grandfather used to tell me stories about them.'

'Of course, you know how all these creatures came into being, don't you?' Tarragon asked around the vegetables in his mouth.

'Whether you do or not doesn't matter,' Willow whispered in my ear, suppressing a giggle. 'He's going to tell you anyway.'

'Five hundred years ago, King Cinquefoil IV, the Aerban King of All the Six Lands, allowed the prolific use of Elemental Magic,' Tarragon said.

'Six Lands?' Willow frowned. 'Have you forgotten how to count, Tarragon? There are only five.'

'No, I haven't forgotten how to count.'

'The Land of Chroma was the sixth, before it was lost under the sea,' I said.

Tarragon gave me a little scowl. 'You know about our history?'

'My father was a student of the subject; I learnt a lot from him.'

Rian gave me a little smile.

'So was I, at the Iolite University,' Tarragon said.

'I didn't know that,' I said.

'There's a lot you don't know about me, Phire. I'm a veritable man of mystery.'

'An open book, you mean,' Willow giggled.

Tarragon gave her a long look then continued, undeterred. 'Anyway, Cinquefoil was King, but Chroma had power as they had greater knowledge of Magic. They'd warned fifty odd years earlier about the dangers of overusing Elemental Magic when a great storm had decimated the Lands, but no one took any notice.'

'Sounds about right,' Willow said as Anise and Sage joined us, hair damp and a healthy pink tinge to their cheeks. 'Tarragon is giving us the full history of Aerba and the Five Lands.'

Sage groaned. 'What, again?'

'I've never heard it all before.'

Tarragon gave her a pointed look, then turned to Sage. 'Do you want to go and order some food?'

'No, thanks, we've already eaten.'

'Then be quiet, I'm talking. So, Chroma tried to get people to stop using Magic for trivial, everyday things, but it didn't work.'

'And Artefacts too,' Anise said. 'At least, that's what Father told me.'

'Artefacts?' Willow asked. 'I haven't heard about them before.'

I had, thanks to Father.

Tarragon beamed at her, buffing his fingernails on his coat. 'Artefacts were special crystals that enhanced Elemental Magic.'

'Sometimes you could use Artefact against Artefact, depending on the crystal, to destroy each other,' Anise said. 'But they're lost, now—'

'The Great Pestilence of 5244 was caused by the overuse of Elemental Magic and Artefacts,' Tarragon cut in, glowering at Anise, who smiled back at him. 'It became known as Cinquefoil's

Folly. Anyway, the Elemental chaos that was unleashed resulted in illness across the Six Lands. Many people lost their lives, and the disruption in nature created the fearsome creatures like morgens and powlers, and several others, too.'

'So, why are there no Artefacts now?' Willow asked.

'Magic was banned after the Pestilence, and Chroma collected all the Artefacts up and destroyed them so they couldn't be used. There are rumours of some being left, y'know, but no one knows what they look like or where they might be now.'

'And what happened to King Cinquefoil? Did he die in the Great Pestilence five hundred years ago?'

'No, he–' Anise stopped short. 'Sorry, Tarragon, you go on.'

'Thank you,' Tarragon said.

I knew exactly what he was going to say next, and I couldn't help but shudder.

Almost as if he had read my mind, Tarragon glanced over at me. 'Chroma decided to punish the King for his folly. They gave him a gift at the End of Year Celebrations, as they usually did. This time it was a crystal sword and shield. But they cursed them, and a short while later Cinquefoil died.'

'And the Kings of Aerba have been using the Cursed Weapons as a threat against anyone who would challenge the Royal Family of Aerba ever since,' Rian finished, his eyes sorrowful and far away.

Willow gasped. 'Bobbins. Aldorbana and Cwicsusl?'

'Aldorbana and Cwicsusl.' As I nodded, a worm of uneasiness wriggled in my heart.

'Chroma was so angry with Cinquefoil and the unbridled use of Magic that they left the Six Lands,' Tarragon said. 'Twenty years later, Chroma was lost beneath the sea in a huge wave. The Five Lands continued with Magic completely banned. They left the Elemental belief system behind. Aerba turned to the Herbs, Flos to the Flowers, Trew to the Trees, Mere to the freshwater Springs and Lakes, and Iolite to the Stars and Celestial Bodies. So, there you have it.'

After that, the conversation died.

We retired a short time later. On the way to our rooms, I caught sight of Sorrel disappearing into his room with a barmaid – Sage had a disapproving look on his face.

'Sage and Sorrel really don't like each other, do they?' I asked Willow as we got ready for bed.

'They don't really approve of each other's romantic choices, amongst other things,' Willow said, getting into her small bed.

'Neither one can call the other one out. If they did, they'd both fall foul of the Blood Rules. End up Demoted. Or worse. It's kind of an unspoken truce. But that doesn't stop the odd minor skirmish.'

'Minor skirmish?'

'Bickering. Like the other night at the camp. Although, I suppose it does go back further. They went out riding together as children. Sage's horse disturbed a pheasant. It made Sorrel's horse shy. Threw him to the ground. He damaged his ankle, hence his limp. I think on some level he's always blamed Sage for that. He told their father it was Sage's fault. Sage hasn't trusted him since.'

'Surely it was an accident? Sage couldn't have known Sorrel's horse would shy away.'

'True. But Sorrel doesn't much care. He needed someone to blame. Still does. Hence the friction.'

That explained a few more things. I climbed into my bed.

'Is it always like this after a fight?' she asked suddenly.

'Like what?' I asked, gently rubbing some salve Anise had given me earlier into my jaw.

'Shaking, nausea, not being hungry.'

'Sometimes.'

'I've practised, but that was the first time I've ever been attacked,' she said, her eyes troubled.

'You fought well.'

'Only after you'd got me moving.'

'We all freeze to begin with. The trick is learning not to.'

'You've fought a lot, haven't you?'

'Mainly it's been training, but I think training on Iolite is different to here. Back home, you really are fighting for your life during each Coterie training session.'

'We just practise moves,' she sniffed.

'I spent almost every day fighting for my life,' I said. 'But don't worry, it'll get easier. And you've got Tarragon. He's a great fighter. He can help you.'

A moan of pleasure came from the room beside us – a woman's voice. Wasn't that Rian's room? Another, longer one made my face flush. Then a louder one. Breaking the Blood Rules didn't really seem his style. At least, he hadn't given me that impression. There was a giggle, followed by a deeper moan – a man this time. Maybe he was a womaniser after all. For a reason I didn't understand, my heart fell.

'They're having fun,' Willow said, a grin on her face.

Is that what she called it? A little tinge of green ice grew in my chest – quite why, I didn't know. Rian was nothing to me, just a

High Blood Prince. A satisfied groan from the next room had me rethinking.

'I didn't think Rian was like Sorrel,' I said, my voice tighter than I'd expected as the moaning continued.

Willow turned towards me and frowned. 'That's not Rian's room,' she said. 'He's down at the end of the passageway on the other side. He's opposite Anise and Sage. Don't worry, he's absolutely nothing like Sorrel.'

'I'm not worried, and anyway, it's none of my business what he gets up to at night,' I said, turning over. *Not worried?* Liar.

She gave a little silvery laugh. 'He's never been with a girl. And I'd know. He and Tarragon tell each other everything. And Tarragon tells me.'

'Hasn't some princess been flung at him?'

'A couple, but he wasn't remotely interested in them.'

'Is he...?'

'Like Anise and Sage? Bobbins, no. It's just that up until now, he's not been interested in romance.'

Up until now? What did that mean? I never found out – she went straight to sleep. Maybe it was just a turn of phrase; maybe she meant up until he met me. A surge of blood raced to my cheeks at the thought. It didn't matter what she'd meant. I could never be interested in a High Blood. Could I?

Despite my tiredness, I couldn't nod off. The realisation that we were going back to Iolite made my stomach churn, and I took to chewing at my nails. The thought of returning there, of finding out what King Finule wanted me to, all under the noses of the Coterie and Juniper, made my blood run cold. Admittedly, carrying Aldorbana and Cwicsusl gave me a little extra confidence, but not enough to stop the gnawing inside my chest. Every time I nodded off to sleep, I woke with a cold sweat covering me like an early autumn dew, with Juniper's shrill voice ringing in my ears – or the ring of swords.

I lay on my back in the early hours, contemplating the ceiling in the light of the one candle we had burning. Willow moved. I glanced in her direction to see her climbing from her bed, tiptoeing towards the door. She quietly opened it and disappeared. Where could she be going at this hour? There was the metallic sound of something moving and twisting in a lock, not the sound of a key, but of a couple of smaller things, then the door opposite our room softly creaked open – the door to Tarragon's room. Well, that answered that, then. She still hadn't returned when I awoke from another nightmare an hour later, but as the moon set, she silently reappeared, getting back into her bed.

I slipped into a deeper sleep, and when I awoke, the fingers of dawn clawed at the window, and Willow and her bags had gone. I sat up. Had they left without me? I scrambled out of bed, dressed, and strapped Aldorbana and Cwicsusl to my back. Quite why I did this, I wasn't sure. After all, they'd do it themselves if I left them. Still, it seemed to be good manners, and I didn't want to offend them. I grabbed my bag and left the room, hurrying down the stairs to find Sorrel sitting in the taproom chatting to the barmaid from last night.

'Where are Rian and the others?' I asked.

'They've left,' he said, looking at me down his nose.

'What, without me?'

'You were asleep,' he said. 'Don't worry, I promised Rian, on pain of death, that I wouldn't lay a finger on you.'

I'd like to see him try. 'I've got to go after them,' I said, turning to leave.

'Hmm, I'm afraid I have my orders and you stay here until Rian's ready to sail. Go back to your room.'

To hell with that. I turned and headed back up the stairs, stopping on the landing to assess my options. Maybe they wouldn't leave for Iolite without me, but in the meantime, whatever Sorrel had promised Rian, I really didn't want to be left alone with him. The evening before, the long night, and my dreams had brought things into sharp relief. I didn't think Rian truly realised how dangerous this mission was likely to be, and that worried me. He might die, or worse, get caught by Juniper. My heart froze at the very idea.

If Sorrel wasn't going to let me leave by the front door, I'd find another way to get to the ship. I opened a grimy window on the landing, salty sea air rushing in, clearing my head. I climbed out the window onto a roof below, scattering a number of pigeons as I went, scrambled along the shingles, then jumped onto a large barrel and down to the ground. I crossed the street, ducking as I went in case Sorrel looked out the downstairs window, and on into an alley towards the docks and Rian.

CHAPTER SEVEN

The early morning sun cast a silvery light over the town. There were few people about as I sped through the alleyways, heading in the direction of the harbour, the increasing sound of seagulls signalling my imminent goal. My heart hammered as I ran, my weapons banging uncomfortably on my back as my breaths tore at my throat, but I didn't care.

I threaded my way through warehouses and storage buildings to the docks, quickly scanning the ships, looking desperately for the thyme pennant that would indicate Rian's ship as salt lingered in the air. There, to the right. I ran towards the ship with its three masts, dodging fishermen unloading their early morning catches, jumping lobster pots, endeavouring to stay upright as I went. I reached the ship and rushed up the gangplank.

'Who are you? What are you doing here?' a large, muscly sailor with one eye asked, pausing in his work as I alighted on the deck, a knife held warily in his hand.

'I'm–'

'It's all right, Captain Feverfew, she's with me,' Rian said, appearing out of the main cabin. The captain nodded and carried on across the deck.

I walked over to Rian.

'He's right, though, what are you doing here?' he asked, raising an eyebrow. 'And how did you escape Sorrel?'

'I climbed out a window,' I said. 'I didn't want you leaving me behind.'

'As much as I'd like to leave you behind where it's safe, I have my orders from the King,' he said, his expression one of unease.

'You're going to need me on Iolite – I don't think you realise how dangerous it's going to be.'

Rian smiled. 'We've done this sort of thing before, you know, and Tarragon knows his way around Iolite.'

'Not as well as I do,' I said. 'This isn't going to be easy, and you don't know how the Coterie work. Or Juniper, for that matter. Iolite is the last place in the Five Lands I want to go, but I made a promise to your father, and I won't break it.'

Rian nodded, his eyes softening. 'I know,' he said, reaching out and resting his hand on my shoulder.

'Good morning, Phire,' Tarragon said with a grin.

The prince hastily pulled back as Tarragon walked over to us.

'Rian, the captain says he's ready to sail when you are,' Tarragon said, nodding across the deck to where the captain talked with another sailor.

'Very wel–'

'Where the devil have you been, girl?' Sorrel asked, limping hurriedly up the gangplank onto the deck. 'You were supposed to stay with me – I thought you'd run off.'

'It's fine, Sorrel. She's a bit impatient to get going, that's all,' Rian said. Why would he cover for me like that?

Sorrel screwed his face up. 'Hmm. Well, she led me in a merry dance. I thought I was going to be executed for losing her. If you ever do that to me again, Lady Merciless, I'll–'

'You'll do nothing, and don't call her by that name,' Rian said, taking a step forward towards Sorrel. 'Her name is Samphire, now. Lady Samphire to you, and don't forget it,' he finished, giving Sorrel a menacing look.

Sorrel looked at him in surprise. 'Whatever you say, Your Highness.'

'As Samphire's here, now, don't you have somewhere else you need to be?'

Sorrel nodded curtly. 'I'll see you all when you get back,' he said, turning towards the gangplank.

'Bye!' Tarragon said, giving him a little wave.

Sorrel turned back and glared at him. 'See you later, Sage,' he called.

Sage looked up from where he studied a map with Anise at the front of the ship and gave his brother a half-hearted wave. Sorrel sent a less-than-friendly glance in his direction, then walked away down the gangplank, soon disappearing into the town.

Sorrel was one High Blood I was glad to see the back of.

Rian let out a long breath. 'Thank the Herbs he's gone. He never fails to raise my hackles.'

'You're not the only one,' Tarragon said.

I smiled as I silently agreed with them both.

The ship set sail, quickly leaving the harbour, and breaking out into open water, slicing through the sunlit wavelets like a knife. The sailors called to each other, and for a while a sea shanty filled the air. The sea remained calm all day, and a good, stiff breeze filled the sails, carrying us along at a decent speed. At this rate, we'd reach Iolite the day after tomorrow. Unfortunately.

I spent the day at the side of the ship holding onto the smooth, varnished rail, watching the white horses that periodically appeared on the water as we glided past. Gulls followed us, flying high above the creaking rigging, the sails flapping like bats above my head, the smell of salt hanging in the air and settling on my tongue, courtesy of the sea spray. The cabin door burst open as Willow ran out, her face an awful green colour, and she proceeded to throw up over the rail on the far side of the ship. Tarragon flew out after her, rubbing her back in a futile attempt to ease her suffering.

Rian walked across the deck towards me.

'What's the matter?' I asked.

'She's seasick,' Rian said. 'But then, she's never been out at sea before. I'll go and find Anise; he can make something up for her from his Herb Chest. That reminds me, how's your bruise?' he asked, peering at my jaw.

'It's…' I'd forgotten about it. I gingerly touched it – nothing. Not even a slight jolt of pain. 'It's fine.'

Rian grinned. 'He's good, isn't he?'

'Amazing,' I said, mystified as to how it could have healed so quickly.

'I imagine he'll break out the ginger and peppermint for Willow. They tend to work a treat. At least, they always have for Tarragon in rough weather,' he said. 'I'd better go and get Anise.'

Later that day, I stood taking in lungfuls of clean, salty air as I watched the cresting waves, their white foam scattering in the breeze. The wind rustled in the sails, then suddenly dropped. I looked up at the sagging canvas, a little chill sweeping down my spine.

Morgens?

My pulse began to sound in my ears as I scanned the water for any sign of the Sea-born.

A gust of wind sped through the rigging, and the sails billowed again. I sighed, relaxing once more. Nothing to worry about after all. The ship carried on cutting through the water, sea spray shooting up into the air as gulls cried above me.

'Enjoying the trip, Phire?' Anise asked, coming to stand beside me. 'May I call you "Phire"?'

'Of course – I'll enjoy it more when we're back on land,' I said. 'I don't dislike a sea voyage like Willow and Tarragon, but I prefer solid ground.'

Anise nodded. 'Me too. I like the green of the countryside, rather than the blue-grey of the sea. I suppose that comes from growing up surrounded by fields.'

'I'd love to hear about your herbal remedies sometime,' I said, smiling at him. This was one High Blood I could spend hours talking to – Tarragon was the same. Had I been wrong, lumping all High Bloods together? Maybe they weren't all bad. Even Rian had his moments.

Anise smiled and nodded, his hand going to his Amulet. 'I'd like that. You know, my father was good with herbs. He could make up a cure for pretty much any ailment. He used to tell me stories of ancient Aerba and how the herbs came into being, too,' Anise said, his eyes distant. 'So many myths and legends.'

'Like what?'

'The Chamber of Earth, for a start.'

I frowned. I knew quite a bit about the history of the Five Lands, but I'd never heard of the Chamber of Earth. 'What's that?'

'The Chamber where the sacred herbs originated,' Anise said as Rian and Sage joined us. 'Kept secret, only known to the High Bloods of the Royal Family.'

'I heard that it was created using Earth Magic,' Rian said.

Anise nodded. 'Father told me that the Chamber of Earth was in the gardens of the Royal Palace in the old Cilantro Citadel in southern Aerba,' he said, a wistful look in his eyes. 'The legend is that Earth Magic was used to create the great variety of Aerban herbs in this special chamber, mainly for healing purposes.'

'Utter rubbish,' Sage said, casting his eyes skyward.

Anise gave him a little glare as he let go of his Amulet. 'They had to come from somewhere.'

Sage shrugged. 'Maybe they just grew?'

I glanced at Rian who had an amused look on his face. He leant towards me. 'They'll argue about this until they're old men,' he whispered.

Sage screwed his nose up at Rian. 'I'm going back inside.'

That evening, we sat in Captain Feverfew's cabin eating a meal of fish and potatoes. The ship's cook had caught the fish himself that morning, and they were delicious. Sage sat opposite me, eating bread and ham.

'I'm allergic to seafood,' he said, looking suspiciously at the fish on my plate. 'Makes me throw up, a bit like this one–' He nodded towards Willow, who sat in a corner looking a little less green than she had earlier, sipping a tea Anise had brewed for her.

'I hope she feels better soon,' I said.

'I'm sure she will, once she's had a few mugs of my tea,' Anise said. 'I've never known it to fail yet, Phire. So, what's this I hear that the King's promised to break the Aldorbana Curse when we get back to Viridi? Can he really do it, Rian?' he asked through a mouthful of fish. Rian gave him a warning glare, and Sage rammed him in the ribs with his elbow. 'Ow!'

'What do you mean?' I looked at the prince, who now wore a slightly anguished expression on his face. 'Rian?'

'You have to tell her, Rian,' Tarragon said, miserably stabbing an unoffending potato with his fork. 'It's only fair.'

A chill colder than the depths of winter's harshest storm swept through me. He didn't have to tell me anything. He didn't need to because I'd already guessed the fateful answer.

Rian looked at me, his eyes full of – what? I couldn't name it, but it sent little sparks scurrying through my body. 'My father lied to you. The Curse is unbreakable.'

'As far as we know,' Tarragon said.

'You think it could be broken?' Willow asked.

'Surely, everything can be broken – you just have to know how.'

'The Curse hasn't been broken since the craftsmen of Chroma gave those weapons to King Cinquefoil IV five hundred years ago,' Anise said. 'What makes you think it can be broken now?'

Tarragon shrugged. 'First time for everything.'

As the others spoke, I hadn't broken my gaze with Rian, and he still stared into my eyes. 'We'll find a way to break it,' he said, his eyes deep, amber pools.

'Hell's teeth, why didn't you tell me?' I asked, my hands making fists. How dare he not tell me? Willow had been wrong – Rian did lie.

'I didn't know how to break it to you,' he said, bowing his head.

I'd trusted him. Stupid. I'd trusted a High Blood, and now look what had happened. My heart pounded in my chest, my blood boiling at the deception. I'd begun to think of him – no, of all these people – as my friends, yet they'd kept this most important piece of information from me. I was going to die, and soon. Nothing known could stop it. I stood up, trying to stop myself from uttering all manner of profanities.

'So, you lied, just like your High Blood father?' Anger and despair took me, and I couldn't stop the words from falling out. He looked sharply at me. 'I'm nothing like my father,' he said, his teeth gritted.

An uncomfortable silence filled the room. Only the sound of the waves and the creaking of the ship drifted into the space. My whole body tingled at Rian's words – said so forcefully and with such indignation and ire. But what shook me most was the tinge of bitter anguish that accompanied them, and I immediately regretted my sharp tongue.

I swallowed. 'I'm sorry, I didn't mean that it's just-'

'I didn't have the courage to tell you,' he said quietly, his eyes full of pain.

A twisting sensation filled my chest. I shouldn't have said that to Rian; I didn't even mean it.

'Y'know, if the knowledge to break the Curse is anywhere, then it'll be in the Iolitian Library,' Tarragon said. 'They hold all sorts of documents within those walls.'

The Library.

If I could find out more about the Weapons, maybe I could find a way to break the Curse. What's more, I had two friends at the library who might be able to help me, and neither of them had much love for Juniper, so hopefully they wouldn't give me away.

Rian looked at his cousin. 'You could be right.'

'The answer has to be in the library,' Willow said, nodding. 'Short of finding Chroma, what else is there?'

Sage laughed as I sat back down. 'Find Chroma? You'll never find Chroma. It's far out under the sea somewhere, assuming it wasn't a myth in the first place.'

'I thought that's where the Cursed Weapons were made.'

'Well...'

'If it didn't exist, where did they come from?' Willow asked, nodding artfully towards Aldorbana and Cwicsusl sitting against the wooden wall, a smug expression on her face.

Sage screwed his nose up at her, tugging gently at his earring.

'We don't need to go to Chroma, just Iolite,' Rian said. 'We'll go to the library as soon as we get to Adamas and look for answers.'

'And your father's mission?' Tarragon asked. 'Are you intending to get into the Crimson Castle to find answers?'

'Father's mission takes second place to this. Besides, we may be able to find some information out at the library. At this moment, Phire's life is more important.'

I looked at Rian, but he wouldn't meet my gaze. He wasn't a typical High Blood after all. If he was, he'd have stared me down.

Tarragon exchanged a glance with Willow.

'Sounds good to me,' Anise nodded.

The library was my only hope.

The next morning, I stood out on deck, the wind whipping my hair into my eyes. I undid the ponytail at the base of my neck and redid it, securing it once more as Anise came and joined me at the rail.

'Are you all right, Phire?' he asked, his hair catching in the wind.

'Not entirely,' I said. 'I didn't mean to upset Rian, I just wish he'd told me.'

'To be fair, he didn't actually lie to you, he just didn't tell you everything – none of us did,' Anise said. 'I confess I thought you already knew.'

I shook my head.

'Rian's right, though,' Anise said, looking out over the water. 'He's nothing like his father. There's not a cruel bone in his body.'

'I'm seeing that now,' I said, meaning every word. Rian wasn't the haughty High Blood Prince I'd thought when I first met him. He was a fair, kind, and decent young man. What I'd said to him last night filled me with shame.

Anise glanced behind us. 'Rian's coming over. I'll leave you,' he said, trying to wander off nonchalantly.

Rian came and stood silently beside me, staring out over the waves.

'I'm sorry,' I said.

He turned to me. 'What?'

'I'm sorry for saying you were like your father. I know you're not, and I shouldn't have said it. I thought I could trust you, and then...'

'You can trust me,' he said, suddenly taking my hand. 'I'd never lie to you.'

I looked into his eyes. 'I know. And you didn't lie.'

'Just didn't tell you everything when I should have.' He looked down at the deck.

'I spoke rashly. I shouldn't have done that. I didn't mean to hurt you, I was just-'

'Upset, and rightly so,' he said, glancing at me. 'It was my own damn fault for not telling you about the Curse sooner. I did try to tell you, at the fountain before we left the palace, but Bergamot interrupted us, and since then, the longer time's gone on, the harder I've found it to broach the subject.'

'I probably should've known already. I obviously missed that part in Father's book – I guess I didn't read about it because I thought it'd never apply to me,' I said with a wry grin.

He hesitated a moment. 'You know, I think my father's wrong.'

'Oh?'

'You have to understand, he's not a bad man, he just wants the best for Aerba and its people. Chervil does, too, for that matter. But they don't always go about it in a way I like. They can be heavy-handed, cruel even, to achieve what they want. You and the Cursed Weapons are one example of that.'

'What would you have done?'

He looked at me, his gorgeous eyes softening. 'Trusted you.'

Surprised, my heart skipped in my chest and I gave him a little smile.

'So, you're not too upset with me, then? For not telling you about the Curse?' he asked.

I hesitantly looped my arm through his, but he didn't back away. 'No. As long as you're not upset with me?'

He rested his head against mine for a moment. 'It's all forgotten. As long as you remember I'm really nothing like Father or Chervil.'

'Don't worry, I'll remember.'

'Captain Feverfew says we'll arrive at Iolite around midday tomorrow,' Sage said, coming over with Tarragon. 'Then we can really start to track down the Fire Opal and Angelica's murderer.'

I let go of Rian and nodded. 'Are we docking at Cinnabar?'

'Yes, that's the plan,' Rian said.

'What's Cinnabar?' Sage asked. 'I thought all the Iolitian towns and people were named after gemstones.'

'I always thought Cinnabar was an odd name,' Tarragon said.

'Cinnabar's a mineral,' I said. 'We use gemstones, semi-precious stones, and a few minerals, for names.'

'Better than being named after a herbaceous border,' Valerian sniffed.

Tarragon nodded ruefully.

Sage shrugged. 'I like my name.'

'My grandmother and her mother were variations on Ara,' I said. 'Some sort of narcissus, I think, because they were from Flos. Of course, I was named after the Iolite tradition because of Father.'

Tarragon raised an eyebrow. 'About your Flosi–'

'Ware!' someone shouted from behind me.

A great snap split the air; I glanced up – the rigging suddenly sagged, and the sound of wind rushing towards me had the hairs on the back on my neck standing to attention. I dived for the deck, pushing Rian out of the way as I went.

A great wooden pulley swung down from the rigging towards our heads, missing us by inches. The pulley smashed into the side of the ship and the wood disintegrated, splintering around us as the others ducked for cover. I took a deep breath and looked up from my prone position on top of Rian to see the shattered remains of the pulley, the ropes hanging impotently from the rigging. Feverfew stared at me, a glint of terror in his eyes. The other sailors made signs to ward off evil as they watched me warily.

I looked down. My face was an inch from Rian's. His eyes were wide, but his cheeks flushed.

'I – sorry,' I said, getting off him and standing up.

Rian scrambled to his feet. 'Damn, are you all right?' he asked, taking my hands.

'I'm fine, really. What about you?' I asked, looking him over for any signs of injury. 'I knocked into you quite hard.'

'I'm okay. That's twice you've saved me, now.'

'Are we counting? You saved me twice outside Borage. I think we're even.'

'Did you see how quick she moved?' one of the sailors said.

'Witchcraft?' another said in a low voice.

No. Just assassin.

'That was too close,' Rian murmured to me before releasing my hands. 'I almost lost you.'

'Then you'd have had to search Iolite without me. Like you said, I'm sure you'd have managed.'

'That wasn't what I meant,' he said, stepping away, rubbing the back of his neck.

Shortly before noon the next day, Iolite came into view. Until now, whenever the island had loomed in the distance across the water, a swirl of excitement had swept through me because I'd see Mal soon; but not today. Today it filled me with sorrow, tears welling in my eyes as I stood at the prow, spray flying up around me. I missed Mal so much my heart ached whenever I thought of him.

Tarragon wandered over to me, looking out over the sea towards Iolite. 'Thinking of your brother?' he asked softly.

I nodded, not trusting myself to speak.

'I only met him the once, but he seemed a decent fellow to me.'

'He was,' I said. 'And he was the only person I could confide in, truly be myself with.'

'We all need a few people like that around us.'

'And I've lost him.'

'You've got us, now,' Tarragon said.

I couldn't hold the tears back any longer. Tarragon reached out and put his arm around me, pulling me towards him, holding me close while I sobbed. He held me until I eventually composed myself again.

'It'll get easier,' he said. 'Being back on Iolite won't help, but we're here with you. You can trust us.'

'Can I? Trust has been a little hard to come by, lately.'

'Not all High Bloods are untrustworthy liars.'

'I know.' It'd taken me a while to realise that, but I now had the upper hand on my prejudice.

'You may even come to like me, y'know,' he said, elbowing me in the ribs, a silly grin on his face.

'I do like you, idiot,' I said, smiling in spite of myself.

'You just need to get through this visit home.'

I stepped back, although he still held my shoulders, and rubbed my eyes. 'This whole trip scares the hell out of me,' I said, glancing over his shoulder to see Rian standing near the ship's wheel, a weird expression on his face. 'What's wrong with Rian?'

Tarragon turned around. 'Probably doesn't like me holding you,' he said, letting go of me.

'Why ever not?' I looked at Tarragon in confusion. Surely Willow would be the one who wouldn't be happy, not Rian?

'Well – don't worry about it, forget I said anything. Will you be all right now?'

I nodded. 'Yes, I'll be fine, thank you.'

'Could everyone come here, please?' Anise called from the cabin door.

'I wonder what he wants,' Tarragon said.

'Might as well find out,' I said, walking over towards the cabin with Tarragon as Rian approached, giving Tarragon a less-than-friendly look.

'She was upset,' Tarragon said as I entered the cabin. 'I'll explain later.'

Anise stood beside the table where six packages sat. 'Our clothes are going to stand out in Iolite, so I took the liberty of arranging some alternatives before we left Aerba.'

'Only you would think of that,' Willow said with a grin. She'd been much better since having Anise's tea and had only thrown up once.

'Well done,' Tarragon said, clapping Anise on the back.

'I'd wondered what you'd been doing before we left Aerba,' Sage said from where he sat looking at a map.

Anise smiled. 'Well, now you know. They're all Middle Blood clothes, so we should be able to move around wherever we need.'

'Thank you,' Rian said as Anise handed around the packages. 'We'll let the ladies change first.'

The young men all left the room while Willow and I moved over to the table and untied our packages. I shuddered as I took in the black tunic and black suede britches that lay before me.

Willow glanced at me. 'Bad memories?'

'That's an understatement,' I said. 'I've got used to wearing purple over the last couple of weeks – I guess I've just got to get on with it.' I started to take off my purple coat.

'It won't be for long,' she said. 'We'll be back here before you know it.'

I hoped so.

The others changed after us, and when they came out of the cabin with their hair in the traditional low ponytails of the Iolitians, I tried to stifle a giggle. They looked so different that Willow stood smirking, too.

'I don't know what you're laughing at,' Tarragon said, an indignant edge to his voice. 'You haven't changed your hair yet, y'know.'

She flinched, and the smile disappeared. She began tugging at her ponytail, a look of annoyance on her face.

'I like it,' Anise said.

'You would,' Sage said sourly.

As soon as we docked, we disembarked and moved into the fishing town of Cinnabar. I already had the hood of my cloak up, which was just as well as grey clouds scudded overhead, threatening rain despite the humid weather. On a flagpole not far from the docks, the flag of Iolite fluttered in the wind. The violet cloth, with its white section in the top right hand corner where the outline of Iolite Island sat, was immediately recognisable.

All the sights and smells were familiar to me. There were no herbs here, only salt in the air, along with the fishy notes of morning catches. Gulls cried overhead, trying to snatch fish from unwary fishermen. We made our way past the docks towards the plain, utilitarian grey stone buildings of the town, some with red streaks on their sides. The townsfolk milled around with their plethora of hair colours, skin tones and eye colours. Iolite was unlike any other Land, a truly cosmopolitan country.

I pulled my hood up a little further over my head; the Coterie had a long arm, with operatives all over the island, and they would be sure to have members lurking throughout the town. The moment they got wind of the fact I was still alive and, more to the point, here, we'd all be in even more danger. We walked up to the horse trader where Rian and Sage purchased six horses for our journey to Adamas. It would be far quicker to ride, we'd get there some time tomorrow on horseback, and money wasn't exactly a problem for the Prince of Aerba.

'Do they have any perfume shops here?' Sage asked, his nose twitching.

'Perfume shops?' I asked, confused. 'No, I don't think so. The town's too small for that sort of thing. Why?'

'Just wondered,' he said, frowning at Anise who was grinning at him.

I showed Willow and Anise where the food shops were, and we went into one to make a few purchases. As Willow paid, I stood out of the way near the door, watching. A man came in, a Low Blood, who started to peruse the bread. Something about the glances he kept casting in Anise's direction had my nerves taught. He moved to pick up a loaf, and his sleeve slipped down to reveal the tattoo on his wrist. Assassin. I backed towards the door, slipping out, walking straight into Tarragon who'd just collected some fresh water.

'What is it?' he asked as I pulled him to one side.

'An assassin's in there,' I said, watching the door nervously. 'Not one I know.'

'Did he see you?'

'No, he's too busy watching Anise.'

Anise and Willow appeared out the shop carrying our food, the Coterie member not far behind.

'You go tell Rian, I'll join the others. We'll try and lose him before we get back to you,' Tarragon said.

I nodded, shrinking back into the shadows of an alleyway as Tarragon sauntered over to Anise and Willow. They quickly exchanged a few words, and Tarragon and Anise walked off in one direction, Willow in another. The assassin followed Anise and Tarragon down the street. I sighed. This was an added complication we didn't need. Willow spotted me and doubled back.

'Tarragon said he and Anise would try and lead the assassin away,' she said.

I nodded. 'Let's get to Rian.'

We took the back alleys on our way to Rian and Sage who were waiting with the horses. I stopped dead at the alley's end, flinging my arm out and stopping Willow from going any further. *Hell's teeth.*

'What is it?' she asked, peering into the street.

'Another assassin,' I said.

Rian and Sage stood across the street, the horses tied to an old wooden rail, and they were being watched, too. This time I recognised the assassin. Feldspar. A particularly nasty piece of work. His dark green eyes were fixed on Rian and Sage, his blond hair catching the wind. Getting to Rian without being recognised would be impossible. We needed a diversion, but what?

The inns along the street bustled with the lunchtime trade as patrons made their way in for a pint and something to eat, becoming rowdier by the minute. Excellent.

'I have an idea,' I said, leading Willow back into the alleys and making our way past the rear of a particularly noisy inn where the smell of stale beer wafted out the window, and on to the next door wine merchant's establishment. I quietly moved up to the door and tested the handle. Locked.

'What are you thinking?' Willow asked.

'A little diversion,' I said. 'But I need to get in there.'

She smiled. 'Allow me,' she said, producing a little bunch of variously-shaped metal tools from her pocket. 'You may have heard I'm quite good at lock picking.'

I grinned. 'I did hear Sage mention it.'

She quickly set to work, wiggling her tools about in the mechanism until there was a small click. She took hold of the handle – it turned silently, and she cautiously opened the door far enough for us to peer in.

'Thank you,' I said quietly. The back storeroom stood packed with barrel after barrel of wine and spirits stacked against the wooden walls, some leaking. A high, dirty window looked out on the alley but didn't provide much light. The powerful smell of alcohol hung in the air, making me screw up my nose. An empty passage led from the room, and a little way down it a flaming torch sat on the wall, illuminating the storeroom with flashes of flickering orange light. I smiled. Perfect. The wine merchant must be in the shop. I stole in, moving quietly across the flagstone floor, and carefully removed the burning torch from its holder on the wall.

'…we may have some out the back.'

I froze as the voice drifted in from the shop.

'Don't worry, I'll have this instead,' came another voice.

My muscles relaxed slightly. I didn't have much time. I carefully selected a leaky-looking barrel, and moved the fiery torch towards it, then hesitated. Hopefully this would work – there'd be a few little bangs and a fire big enough to distract everyone outside, including any Coterie members hanging around, which would give us the chance to escape.

I placed the torch against the damp wood. It immediately burst into flame, blue and orange fire licking voraciously at the side of the barrel. I moved on to another and another – the storeroom flickered with light. I threw the burning torch in amongst some oak spirit casks and ran for the door, closing it behind me.

'That should do it,' I said to Willow, who beamed at me.

'We make a good team,' she said.

I grinned back. 'That we do.'

As we walked away, the fire took on a life of its own. Its voice rose above the sound of the raucous patrons in the adjoining inn, its cry like a ravenous beast as it consumed the contents in the storeroom. I turned around to see flames reaching out the storeroom window and swallowed hard. A chill washed through me.

'Oops,' I said. I hadn't expected something this big. I'd miscalculated badly.

'Oh, dear,' Willow said.

We looked at each other and sprinted down the alley, back to the street, peering out anxiously to see what would happen next.

CHAPTER EIGHT

The blast as the first barrel exploded shook the whole area, shattering glass and sending shards from the wine merchant's windows right across the street. I watched in horror as people scattered and screamed. The wine merchant scrambled out of his shop with two customers in tow just as another explosion rocked the town. This was followed by several smaller pops and bangs as casks exploded and the fire took hold, quickly spreading to the next door inn. Willow winced. Sound ricocheted around the town, echoing through alleys and across streets like a swarm of angry bees, making me flinch. Across the street, Rian and Sage struggled to calm our startled horses. I glanced towards Feldspar.

Inn patrons were fleeing in all directions, all keen to get away from the explosions and the blaze, sweeping Feldspar down the street with them, away from Rian and Sage. I fervently hoped that everyone would get out alive. I hadn't meant for anyone to be hurt, and although I hadn't seen anyone with injuries, I watched the result of my handiwork with dismay. This was supposed to be a distraction, not a full-on catastrophe.

'Let's go,' I said.

We dashed out the alley as Tarragon arrived with Anise.

'Did you lose him?' I asked.

Tarragon nodded. 'As soon as that explosion went off, he vanished. Was that something to do with you two?'

'Maybe, but we need to go,' I said.

'We'll tell you all about it later,' Willow said.

'What's going on?' Rian asked, looking perplexed.

'You were being watched by the Coterie,' I said, leading my horse away from the confusion, the others following. 'We just tried to provide a little diversion so we could get away unseen.'

'By setting light to the whole damn town?' Rian asked, his eyes wide.

I flinched. 'It was meant to be a small diversion,' I said, mounting my horse as we neared the town gates. 'I didn't mean for all those buildings to go up quite like that.'

'They're full of alcohol,' Tarragon said. 'Of course, they're going to go up.'

'I thought it'd just be a small fire.'

'It was never going to be small.'

'I hope everyone got out all right,' Willow said, looking backwards.

'So do I,' I murmured.

Sage glanced at me as we rode out the town, joining the dusty road towards Adamas. The humidity in the air became oppressive as the afternoon wore on, the clouds still scudding above us, and I found myself longing for Aerba's clear skies. I wiped perspiration from my forehead. Willow, who rode beside me, started to cough.

'Are you all right?' I asked.

'I have asthma,' she said, coughing again. 'It always gets worse in this kind of weather. My chest gets tight. I find it harder to breathe. Luckily, Aerba isn't too humid most of the time.'

'I'll make you some of my liquorice and sophora tea as soon as we stop, Willow. That should help,' Anise said from behind us.

'Thanks,' she said. 'What would I do without you?' Tarragon turned and gave Willow a long look. 'Obviously, I couldn't do without you, Tarragon. I need your strong arms to help carry the shopping.' She fluttered her eyelashes at him.

'Was that a compliment?' Tarragon asked. 'I'm not quite sure.'

'I'd take it as one,' Rian said.

A rumble in the distance made me glance around the open grassland, the distant mountains just visible on the horizon. Lightning flashed to the east as thunder rolled over the countryside, a wave of relentless sound. Black clouds moved menacingly towards us. Another flash lit the grasslands, and another, as the thunderclaps echoed around us, faster this time, cracking and booming through the air, making the horses whinny and shy at the sound. The storm swept in, and I watched as forked lightning hit a solitary oak tree about half a league away, sending a shower of sparks and wood splinters in all directions. I desperately scanned the countryside for shelter.

'We're going to need to take cover,' I said. 'Being out here in a thunderstorm isn't wise, and if we're not careful, the horses will spook. There's a barn up ahead.'

Rian nodded. 'Let's head for it.'

We turned the horses towards the building. As we cantered along a curtain of rain approached, obscuring the landscape in the distance, the grasslands disappearing in a dense mist. A brilliant flash of white illuminated everything for an instant before a crash of thunder enveloped us, reverberating around the countryside, shaking the very earth we rode on as the hairs on the back of my neck stood to attention.

'Move!' Rian yelled.

Our horses galloped towards the farm building as the rain hit. It came down in torrents, drenching us to the skin. As we reached the ramshackle barn, we brought our nervous horses to a halt and quickly dismounted, leading them inside as the rain continued to fall. The building couldn't be described as watertight, but it would do. The rain came down heavily, swiftly turning the dry, dusty earth into a muddy quagmire.

There was no point in trying to dodge the water droplets my horse sent flying as he shook himself. Another flash, overhead this time. The crack of thunder that followed shook the building, sending a shiver up my spine at the intensity and ferocity of the storm; I'd never experienced one quite like this before. I looked around at the inside of the old barn – there were stalls for cattle, straw, and a trough of water, just not a complete roof. We tied the horses in the stalls, and I went back to the door to watch the storm as a violent crash overhead made Tarragon take a step backwards, further into the barn.

'Are you okay?' Willow asked, moving over towards him and shifting his wet hair from his cheek.

'I don't like storms. You know that,' he said, his face pale in the dim light.

'Don't worry,' she said, putting a comforting arm around him. 'I'll look after you.'

Tarragon grunted and gave her a peevish look.

'I mean it,' she said.

I smiled, turning away, looking straight at Rian who had a similar smile on his face. He gave me a wink and went back to tending the horses.

'I'll make that tea for you, now, Willow,' Anise said, opening his Herb Chest. 'I can build a small fire by the door if I'm careful. We can use it to dry off, too.'

'Thanks,' she said, sitting beside him with Tarragon.

Sage looked out into the storm. 'This is going to hang around for a while,' he said sourly, drying his hair with a small towel from his pack.

'Then maybe we should eat and rest. We can start out before dawn tomorrow,' Rian suggested as he pulled a dry shirt from his pack. 'We'll go to the library first, see what we can find there, then make plans for the Crimson Castle after that.'

I shuddered. The thought of going back there chilled my bones more than any storm could.

'Sounds good to me,' Tarragon said, nodding.

Rian slipped his damp tunic and shirt off, leaving his top half naked. I couldn't help but watch him as he changed into his dry shirt, his lean, muscular body making my heart flip. I swallowed and looked away. Willow was grinning at me. Blood rushed to my face.

Anise made Willow the tea, sticking his tongue out as he worked. It was something he did whenever he concentrated, and the familiar sight of it made me smile. Having dried off, we ate then rested, Rian settling down to sleep not far from me. I lay looking at his hair peeping out from his blankets, hair that glowed in the last golden light from the embers of Anise's fire. A sudden yearning hit me, but I quickly suppressed it. It was a fanciful thought, one that would never be realised. I'd probably end up in the dungeons as soon as we arrived back at Viridi Palace, and that was if I was lucky.

The sound of dripping water from the roof and broken gutters outside reminded me of my time in the palace dungeon, and it took a while for me to get off to sleep, especially when thoughts of Rian kept assailing me. When we set off the next morning, dawn had started to cast its light over the countryside, and the smell of wet earth and grass surrounded us. Anise sniffed the air.

'Petrichor,' Tarragon said.

'What?' Anise asked.

'That after-rain, earthy, clean smell.'

'It has a name?' I asked, surprised.

'More to the point, how do *you* know what it's called?' Rian asked.

Tarragon buffed his fingernails on his tunic. 'I am a man of many parts.'

'Bobbins,' Willow giggled.

Rian sighed.

Early afternoon, we crested a ridge. The high, grey walls of Adamas City came into view, the great Adamas Mountains looming beyond. The Temple of the Celestial Bodies sparkled to the left. Its white quartz was in complete contrast to the rest of the drab city. It shone in the day, and at night glowed in the moonlight. It was probably the most beautiful building on the island. To the right sat the University of Iolite, surrounded by the only visible gardens. The library nestled within its campus – our goal. At the very centre of the city sat the Crimson Castle, its deep red granite rising out of the grey buildings. The huge, imposing structure was impenetrable, or so they said. A moat surrounded the castle, with only a single drawbridge spanning the deep water. Great towers looked like sentinels on watch, the battlements protecting them, whilst below the castle festered the dungeons from which no one ever escaped. It was my home. I shuddered. No, it *had* been my home. I had no home now. My breakfast rose in my throat and any wisp of confidence I'd had evaporated like mist on a warm day. It was a veritable hornet's nest. I'd only just avoided Feldspar back in Cinnabar. Avoiding the Coterie here would be nigh on impossible, but I had to try.

'Are you all right?' Rian asked, shaking me from my anxious thoughts.

I nodded. 'I guess so.'

'I'm – I mean, we're here for you,' he said, glancing away.

'Thanks,' I said, looking back at the city. 'I think our best bet is to circle around to the north east where the road comes in from Opal Town. It's usually quite busy so we should get in unseen, and it's also the closest gate to the library. There's a copse near the walls where we can leave the horses – we'll be even less suspicious on foot.'

'Very well,' Rian said, nodding. 'Then let's go.'

We rode towards the city, an anxious knot growing in my stomach. We circled the walls at a distance, stopping in the copse I'd suggested, and dismounted. The horses nickered as we tied them up.

'Should I stay with the horses, Rian?' Anise asked, patting his horse's nose.

'It might be an idea,' Rian said. 'We don't want anyone making off with them.'

'Will you be all right on your own, or do you want company?' Sage asked.

'I'd like the company, but I think you may be needed in the city,' Anise said, smiling at Sage who nodded back. 'Just look after yourself.'

Sage grinned and patted Anise on the arm. 'I will.'

'See you soon,' Rian said, pulling the hood of his cloak up over his maroon hair.

We said our goodbyes to Anise and walked towards the Opal Road, joining the many travellers and merchants making their way in and out of the city. I pulled up my cloak's hood, tucking my hair in for good measure. Cartloads of wood rumbled beside us as we entered the city gates.

'What's all the wood for?' Willow asked as we walked up the main street.

'Paper,' I said, looking around for any Coterie members I

recognised. 'They use a lot at the university and the library for the books and academic papers. Most of it comes from Aerba.'

'Then why isn't it coming in from the southern Cinnabar Road?'

'The harbour at Opal is deeper so they can accommodate bigger ships than Cinnabar – the oak galls tend to come in from Opal, too.'

'The what?' Willow asked, frowning.

'Don't you know anything about your country's exports and economy?'

'Not really, no.'

'You need to speak to Anise. Iron Gall Ink is what they use for writing and printing at the university, and for the books at the library. There'd be no library without it, or learning here at all, probably. The galls are mainly harvested from mid-summer to mid-autumn, so they'll be arriving soon. We make ink and paper all year round.'

'You know a lot about it,' Sage said.

'I spent a lot of time in the library when I was younger,' I said, remembering happy days amongst the books with Mal. I swallowed. 'This way,' I said, leading them away from the main street towards the University Campus. It was late afternoon when we reached our goal. A metal railing ran around the university and the library, enclosing the gardens surrounding the buildings. Well-tended flower beds spread out before us, with small fountains, a few trees, and a topiary casting long shadows in the afternoon sun. A few scholars milled around, others sitting on wooden benches discussing all sorts of academic questions.

'I'd begun to think Iolitian towns and cities were all about grey stone and red streaks, but apparently not,' Sage said.

'You're not wrong, really,' I said. 'These are the only gardens in Adamas. Iolitians are too practical for gardens, which I've always thought a great shame. I like flowers.'

'Where's the library?' Rian asked as we paused at the railings.

'It's that carved building with the steps leading up to the double doors.'

'Sage, Willow, wait for us here. I'd rather not draw too much attention to ourselves as a group.'

'If you go down to the building over there, you'll find an inn where you can wait, if you like,' I said, pointing.

'Might be less obvious than hanging around at the gates,' Sage said.

Willow nodded. 'Don't be long,' she said, and they walked off.

I turned back to the library. 'It'll be closing soon, so we'd better hurry.'

Several students wandered down the steps, talking animatedly to each other as they went, books in hand.

'You know, I studied here for a year before my father called me home,' Tarragon said, looking around. 'Nothing's changed much.'

'Your father?' I asked.

'Lord Wintergreen.'

I hadn't realised King Finule's Chamberlain was Tarragon's father. 'Is that when you met Mal?' I asked.

Tarragon nodded. 'Yes, he came to the university for a visit one day.'

'We need to focus,' Rian said, looking around warily as we started to climb the steps.

The doors to the library began to close as we reached the top.

I rushed forward. 'No, wait, please!'

'I'm sorry, Miss, but the library is shutting,' said a man with a port wine birthmark on his left cheek, his belly slightly overflowing the belt at his waist, and his white hair caught in a low ponytail. He started to wave me away.

'Wait, Agate, don't you see who it is? Come in, Amethyst. Quickly, before you're seen. You coming here is most dangerous.' An elderly man, a couple of years older than Agate, ushered us in, firmly closing and locking the doors behind us. He turned to us, his grey hair flowing over his shoulder, his burnt sienna skin glowing in the light from the library lamps.

We were in a marble-floored entrance hall, the walls covered in an elaborate marble mosaic veneer of blues, whites, reds, and beiges. An elaborate lamp hung above us, illuminating the space that smelt of old books and dust.

'Moonstone, it's so good to see you,' I said, giving the man a hug.

'Indubitably, my dear, but we thought you were dead, lost at sea,' Moonstone said, releasing me, his face turning ashen as my cloak slipped slightly from my shoulders and he saw my back. 'Oh, my dear, what has happened to you?' he asked, his sharp nose twitching.

'It's a long story.'

'I say! Master Tarragon, is that you?' Agate asked.

'It is,' Tarragon said, smiling, his golden-brown eyes sparkling as he shook hands with the old man. 'I trust you've been well?'

'As can be expected,' Agate said, giving him a wry grin, his golden skin wrinkling like old paper around his blue eyes.

'We need your help, good Sirs,' Rian said.

'And you are?'

'This is Prince Valerian of Aerba,' I said.

'Indeed,' Moonstone said, giving Rian a little bow. 'We were sorry to hear about your sister.'

'Thank you,' Rian said.

'And how can we help you, Your Royal Highness?' Agate asked.

Rian fidgeted with his cloak. 'We need to know how to break the Curse of Aldorbana and Cwicsusl.'

Moonstone looked at Rian, then at me. 'I'm so sorry, but there isn't a way.'

My heart sank. 'If we can't break the Curse, can we destroy the Weapons themselves?'

'They're made from a single diamond Artefact, Amethyst. Totally indestructible,' Agate said, shaking his head as he waved his hands in front of him.

The Cursed Weapons were made from an Artefact?

Agate and Moonstone's words were a sledgehammer to my chest, and the room tilted ever so slightly, my heart thumping hard against my ribcage even as an icy wave washed through me.

'But...' I couldn't get anything else out. By the Stars, was all hope truly gone? There had to be a way to stop this nightmare I'd found myself in. I felt like a fish twisting and turning in a net, trying desperately to find a way out – any way out. 'How were they cursed?' Perhaps if I understood that...

'Elemental Magic,' Agate said. 'An Artefact contained its own Elemental Magic that could be manipulated by a Magic Spinner of the same Element. For example, a Fire Artefact could be wielded by a Fire Spinner because their Magic Angles were the same – both Fire, in this case.'

Moonstone nodded. 'Unfortunately, no one can wield the old Magic these days. If they could, they'd be able to break the Curse with it and use those weapons to devastating effect. As it is, Aldorbana and Cwicsusl are useless, magically speaking, other than as instruments of the Curse.'

'That's not to say Magic doesn't exist anymore, just that no one knows how to wield it.'

'I'm afraid there's nothing you can do, my dear.'

Was that it, then? Was I doomed after all? Nausea welled in my throat at the prospect.

Agate narrowed his eyes in thought, his right hand scratching his head. 'I'd say that as far as I know, all the books specifically on

Elemental Magic and Artefacts were burnt after the Great Pestilence, when Chroma left the Six Lands, and the knowledge became lost. The King of All ordered the burning, and it was done throughout the Lands.'

No. He was wrong. At least one book had survived. Father's one, hidden in his study. Was it still there?

'King of All?' I asked.

'King of All Five Lands – it had been the Six Lands, until Chroma left.'

'Come upstairs to our office, my dear,' Moonstone said, leading us up the carpeted staircase.

As I followed Moonstone, my legs trembled slightly. I glanced at Rian, but he looked away, unable to meet my gaze. I didn't blame him. I wouldn't be able to look at someone if my father had cursed them, either.

Row upon row of regimented books sat upright on wooden shelves, their spines displaying their titles in gold and silver ink etched into the leather bindings. They stretched off in all directions down dimly-lit passageways, the musty smell of old paper and leather filling the air, bringing back old memories and a warm feeling. How many trees and oak galls had gone into the paper and ink that surrounded us, I couldn't begin to guess, but probably more than I could reasonably imagine. We walked along a corridor, up another small set of curved granite steps, and into their office. A couple of oil lamps lit the room from their sconces, illuminating bookshelves that took up all the available space on the walls, only stopping for the windows, and two large desks covered in yet more books and manuscripts.

'We wondered if you've heard anything about Aerba's Fire Opal?' I asked, knowing more was at stake than just my life. 'It's been stolen, and King Finule thinks it was brought here.'

'I say! It's been stolen?' Agate asked, his face turning grey. 'That stone has protected the King of Aerba from harm and kept peace in the Land for centuries. Whoever has it will be extremely dangerous.'

'But it's not as if the Fire Opal has any powers,' Tarragon said. 'It's just an heirloom.'

'Did you learn nothing when you were here, boy?' Moonstone asked. 'Now the Fire Opal's gone, the King may be in danger – you must know the old saying about Aerba and the King being safe as long as the Fire Opal sits in the Cedarwood Throne?'

Tarragon nodded. 'Yes, b–'

'You must get it back, for everyone's sake,' Moonstone said, his brown eyes worried. 'But as far as we know, it isn't here on Iolite; we'd have heard.'

'Then where is it?' I asked.

Agate shrugged. 'Who else would have cause to steal it?'

'Flos,' Moonstone said.

Rian looked at him. 'You think they'd be that brazen?'

'Well, someone was,' Tarragon said. 'The Flosians don't exactly like us – perhaps it was a coincidence that Angelica's assassination happened at the same time the Fire Opal was taken.'

'Maybe.'

'Finule thought I'd taken it when I was sent to…' I couldn't give the thought voice.

'Juniper should never have sent you to Aerba,' Agate muttered darkly, wringing his hands. 'She has so much to answer for. What she did to you, your father, your brother – it's despicable.'

'What do you mean? What did she do to them?' I asked.

Moonstone looked uncomfortable. 'We've heard rumours,' he said softly. 'Nothing solid.'

'What rumours?' I asked, my heart suddenly thudding uncomfortably in my chest.

'Around the time of your father's death, my dear, there had been talk in the castle about Juniper taking over.'

'Be careful, Moonstone,' Agate said, looking around furtively.

'She deserves to know,' Moonstone said.

'Then be quick – the walls can have ears, even here,' Agate said. 'I'll check no one's about,' he said, moving off.

'I'll go with you,' Tarragon said, nodding to Rian.

'Your father knew nothing of the Coterie Juniper was setting up,' Moonstone said, sitting down at his desk. 'I believe he discovered the truth, told her to dissolve it, and she arranged his death. Had him poisoned, to be exact.'

CHAPTER NINE

The room tilted a little. I forced air into my lungs as Rian's hand slipped into mine.

'He died quickly, mainly due to the huge amount of Blue Water Hemlock he was given. He was dead before he hit the ground.' Moonstone looked at me, his face creasing. 'I'm sorry, my dear,' he said, as if suddenly realising he'd spoken too casually. 'It was around this time your sister decided to ingratiate herself with Juniper and join the Coterie.'

Thoughts tumbled through my mind, and questions screamed out for answers as I took a couple of deep breaths. 'They told us Father died of sweating sickness. No one ever said he'd been poisoned. Why didn't you tell me sooner?'

'Because it wouldn't have helped your plight,' Moonstone said, lowering his voice further. 'And if Juniper had found out you knew, she'd have killed you. Which brings us to your brother.'

'What do you mean?'

'As I think you know, Malachite never returned after you went to Aerba to kill Princess Angelica. He apparently met with thieves on the way back through Flos.'

'Apparently?'

'She arranged it.'

'But why?' Rian asked, still holding my hand.

'There are two possibilities – probably a bit of both, actually. Either, it had to do with the fact she didn't want to honour her promise of him taking over as Master of Iolite on his imminent twenty-first birthday. Or, because she was angry. You see, I think she found out.'

I looked blankly at him. 'Found out about what?'

'That you hadn't ever killed, my dear, despite your orders, and that Malachite was doing your killing for you, to spare you the pain and suffering of doing it yourself.'

I swallowed hard. Mal? He was the one who'd been getting to every mark ahead of me? It suddenly made sense. There'd been no calling card – Mal's way. He'd been the first to congratulate me after each kill, never giving me the chance to tell Juniper someone had got there before me. I'd always wondered why, and this had to be the reason. He'd been the one assassinating my targets, so I didn't have to. All along it'd been him. My big brother protecting me, as he always had. Keeping me safe.

Why hadn't he told me? But even if he had, would I have stopped him? I didn't want to kill, but I hated the thought of him killing for me. My body trembled with the weight of these revelations. The room tilted again and Rian slipped his arm around me, holding me close. Thank the Stars he'd stayed with me.

'So, she killed him, too,' I said, nausea rising in my throat once more.

'No, I don't believe so. I believe she just wants people thinking he's dead,' Moonstone said.

'What – he's alive?' I took a deep breath, hope glimmering. 'But Carnelian found him…'

'Carnelian lies.'

I couldn't argue with that.

'I can't be certain,' Moonstone continued, his voice barely more than a whisper. 'But I believe she felt he could still be of use to her – after all, his skills must be quite superb to have achieved what he has. Those are skills she wouldn't want to do away with. I believe he's alive somewhere and she's keeping him for something important.'

'Then I have to find him,' I said, my heart flaming at the thought of my brother still being alive, anger raging in my soul at the thought of Juniper imprisoning him.

'Take care, my dear,' Moonstone said, resting a cautioning hand on my arm. 'If she knows you know, she may well have him killed.'

I nodded. 'I'll find him before she has the chance.'

'We both will,' Rian said, squeezing my hand.

I glanced at him. A strange flicker sat in his eyes as he looked at me, staring into my soul.

'Even though he killed your sister?' I asked.

'I'd happily save any man who's gone to such extremes to protect you.'

Tears welled in my eyes. 'Thank you,' I murmured, my heart overflowing with relief.

A little lopsided smile played on his lips, a smile that even in my misery made my breath catch.

'I think I'd like your brother,' he said, wiping an errant tear from my cheek.

'We have to go,' Tarragon said, bursting into the room.

'The Coterie know you're here,' Agate said, rushing in with a book in his hands.

'Quickly, out the back way,' Moonstone said, grabbing a candle and opening a door on the far side of the room, leading us out.

'Amethyst, take this,' Agate said, thrusting the old book into my still-shaking hands. 'This contains remedies to all sorts of ailments – you might find something helpful in there for the Curse.'

'Thank you,' I said, taking the book from him.

He shook his head. 'I'm so sorry I can't do more.'

'It's all right,' I said, placing a reassuring hand on his shoulder. 'You've been a great help, both of you.'

I followed Tarragon down the staircase on the other side of the door. The spiral stairs took us to a dark tunnel that ran under the gardens, Moonstone's candle barely giving us enough light to walk by. At the far end, we made our way up a set of stairs to a door that came out in a passageway, not far from the inn where Sage and Willow were waiting.

'Take care of yourselves and don't let her get you, my dear,' Moonstone said, his nose twitching as he looked at me.

'You take care, too,' I said.

'Indubitably.'

'We'll be careful, and thank you,' Rian said, shaking Moonstone's hand.

I gave the two librarians a quick hug as Tarragon said goodbye, and we slipped out into the side street, Moonstone shutting the door behind us as I glanced across the gardens. Four men, with swords drawn, ran up to the doors of the library: Coterie Assassins. I shivered as they started banging on the doors. We hurried over towards the inn.

'You wait here,' Rian said to me. 'You might be recognised inside.'

I nodded reluctantly, sinking into the shadows as the two young men headed to the inn. Things appeared quiet here, except for in the direction of the noisy tavern, as the sun slid towards the horizon. The smell of stale ale drifted on the air as I waited, my heart racing, my hands growing clammy. Time passed. I noticed two men approaching the inn from the far side, and a flood of noise and light cascaded out onto the dusky street as they entered. A chill rushed through me. They were definitely both assassins, and although I couldn't be completely sure at this distance, one might've been Feldspar.

Still Rian and the others didn't come out. What were they doing in there? I wiped my hands on my tunic. Then Tarragon emerged with Willow and Sage, running over to me.

'We have to go,' Tarragon said, grabbing my arm and pulling me along.

'But Rian! Where is he?' I asked, looking back towards the inn.

'We have to go.'

'No, tell me! Where is he?' I refused to take another step until I knew what was going on.

'The Coterie have him,' Sage said, out of breath. 'We weren't sure, but we thought we were being watched. We didn't want to arouse too much suspicion, so we bided our time, then split up in the inn, but they recognised Rian anyway. They must have been specifically looking for him.'

'I have to go and get him,' I said, trying to pull away.

'No, he said to get you away from here, not to come after him,' Willow said.

The two assassins emerged from the inn, pulling Rian with them as three more arrived. I tried to move forward, but Tarragon's grip on me intensified and Sage grabbed my other arm.

'You can't help him,' Willow said, her face desolate. 'It's too late.'

I wanted to throw up. I couldn't leave him. 'Do you have any idea what Juniper will do to him?' I asked as they yanked me away and back to the main street.

'It's nothing compared to what she'd do to you,' Sage said. 'I don't care about me; I care about him.'

I care about him.

I *did* care about him.

By now, the city gates loomed ahead as they bundled me along, dusk wrapping itself around us. I couldn't think straight, despite my training. Whatever else it meant, I knew I had to rescue Rian.

We made our way back to Anise, where Tarragon quickly filled him in as I mulled over my options, but I'd already made the decision to go back. It was just a matter of how to approach things.

'Return to the ship,' I said. 'Leave two horses for me and Rian. Sail the ship to Tourmaline Cove, near Quartz Town on the eastern coast. Captain Feverfew will know where it is. We'll meet you there the day after tomorrow.'

'By the Herbs, what are you talking about, Phire?' Tarragon asked. 'You can't go back; it's tantamount to suicide.'

'Take this,' I said, thrusting the book of remedies into Anise's hands. 'I'm counting on you to have a remedy for the Curse by the time I see you next.'

'But Juniper will kill you, Phire,' Anise said, his eyes gleaming in the moonlight.

'She'll have to get past Aldorbana and Cwicsusl first.'

'Rian will never forgive me if something happens to you,' Tarragon said, his brow furrowed as he rubbed his chin. 'I can't let you go alone.'

'You have to.'

Anise had a doubtful expression on his face. 'Are you sure about this, Phire?'

'You'd do it for Sage, wouldn't you?' I asked.

Tarragon looked at me and raised an eyebrow.

'Of course,' Anise said, his face resigned.

'Then there's your answer.'

He nodded and gave me a hug. 'Be careful,' he said as he released me.

I looked around at them and they all nodded. 'Now go, I'll see you soon.'

They mounted up, the horses restless and snorting, then proceeded to leave the trees.

Tarragon hesitated. 'You're sure I can't change your mind?' he said, turning back to me.

I shook my head.

'Then I'll come with you.'

I rested my hand on his arm. 'No. I've a better chance of getting in on my own. I know the castle and you don't. Besides, Willow would be rather upset if something happened to you.'

Tarragon sighed. 'Very well. Good luck, Phire,' he said, reluctantly following the others out of the copse, glancing back at me before he galloped off. I waited until they were out of sight, then turned back to the Opal Road gate.

Back into the lion's den, after all.

I had a couple of things in my favour: firstly, everyone outside the inner workings of the Coterie thought I was dead; and secondly, under normal circumstances, no one would dare go against Juniper – not even the Coterie – but I intended to be the exception, see if I might throw things off balance. Of course, I also carried the Cursed Weapons, which might give me an advantage of sorts, I concluded as I chewed on a fingernail, if only to scare everyone in the castle. Perhaps I should brazen it out, march right into the Crimson Castle and demand Rian's return. My boldness might just unsettle my stepmother enough to make a mistake.

Rian.

His maroon hair that shifted in the breeze immediately came to mind. His gorgeous amber eyes, his warm voice, that lopsided smile that increasingly made me go weak at the knees. He'd crept into my heart and I'd hardly realised it. Now, he'd taken up a permanent place there, and I couldn't lose him.

Who knew what Juniper would do to him if left to her own

devices? What she would do to the kind young man who had been there for me, held my hand while Moonstone told me things I never could've imagined, things that'd changed my life forever.

And then there was Serpentine.

The thought had me running towards the Opal Gate, pushing my way through the people that still milled around there. I ran on unchallenged and hurried up along the main street, heading straight for the castle entrance. My breaths tore at my throat as I sprinted along, escaped locks of hair catching my eyes, making them sting. This whole trip home to Iolite had been nigh on a disaster. All I'd done was uncover a lot of uncomfortable truths. I hadn't got any closer to recovering the Fire Opal or finding its thief. Nor had I found a way to break the Curse, and to top it all, Rian had been captured.

Home.

Wait a minute.

I paused, catching my breath. I knew more, now. Agate had said all the books about Elemental Magic and Artefacts had been burnt after the Great Pestilence, but Father had such a book, and as far as I knew it still sat hidden in his study. Was that why he'd always kept it concealed? If I was going into the Crimson Castle, then I had to get hold of it. It might have a clue to breaking the Curse.

I ran on, reaching the drawbridge, pleased to see it down, although also slightly concerned. Maybe Juniper expected me to come? I took off my cloak and untied my hair so my copper curls fell about my head – now no one would have any doubt about who I was. Removing Aldorbana and Cwicsusl from my back, I crept over the drawbridge, keeping to the shadows as I made my way into the castle barbican. I had to make this quiet to stand any chance of getting the book and making it to Rian. Pitch torches lined the gatehouse walls, sending grotesque shadows skittering across the passageway and the cobblestone courtyard beyond. I wanted to challenge my stepmother about Father's death, about Beryl's induction into the Coterie, and about Mal. But Moonstone was right. If I did, I'd probably put Mal's life in even more danger. I'd have to find another way to locate my brother.

The guards at the entrance took one look at me and turned white as sheets. So, everyone at the castle really did think me dead? Perfect. Suddenly regaining their senses, they raised their weapons. As the first struck at me, Cwicsusl met his blow, and I sent him careering backwards into the wall. The second lunged at me. Aldorbana parried and Cwicsusl slammed into his face. He fell to the floor, unconscious. Thankfully, they'd gone down fairly quietly, bar the odd clatter.

I strode past their inert bodies, making my way around the edge of the Crimson Courtyard, staying in the shadows, ducking down when a guard walked past, and entered the maze of cold passages within the castle keep. Pitch torches lit the walls, flickering and stuttering as I crept along, dark shapes flitting across the red granite walls, the familiar smell of musty dampness all around me. I turned a corner and clambered up a spiral staircase. At the top, I peered out into a long, dimly-lit corridor. All quiet. Something had to be happening in the Great Hall for the castle to be as empty as this.

I hurried down the corridor, breathing hard, and up another, narrower set of spiral stairs. At the top stood the door to my father's study. I took hold of the iron ring door handle, twisted it, and heart pounding, pushed the door open. The dark room beckoned me in like a gaping mouth, a shaft of moonlight cutting through the blackness and illuminating a section of the small room. My eyes adjusted to the low light and I finally made out Father's wooden desk, still covered with books and papers and a thick layer of dust. Juniper had had no interest in my father's papers or books – she already had everything she needed to run the island and the Coterie before he died.

I ducked under his ornately-carved desk and felt for the hidden button he'd shown me so long ago. There. A little click signalled I'd found the right place, and a small drawer poked out of the woodwork. I moved position and pulled the little drawer open. Inside rested a book, about the size of my hand, bound in red leather and embossed in gold. I slipped it into my tunic and left the room, silently making my way back down the stairs.

As I stepped out into the corridor, a door opened right in front of me. A guard walked out and looked at me, his eyes widening in surprise – then recognition. I rammed my elbow into his face before he could do or say anything, breaking his nose, making his eyes tear up in the process. He yelled in pain. I kneed him in the stomach and pushed him back into the room where he hit the floor, dazed and groaning.

I had no more time. I had to get to Rian now.

I shut the door and locked it before running down the corridor, heading for the Great Hall. I met no further resistance as I raced along the passageways, rushing on, my heart pounding uncomfortably, continuing until I reached the steps that led towards the doors of the Great Hall and, hopefully, Rian.

I took a deep breath.

A little voice inside screamed at me to get out while I still could, demanding to know what I thought I was doing coming back here into the viper's nest for some High Blood Prince from another country. Nevertheless, I had no choice. I had to at least try and get Rian out – not because I owed him anything, necessarily, but because I cared about him. A little ember settled in my heart, warming me even though my hands could've been mistaken for blocks of ice.

Aldorbana and Cwicsusl sat reassuringly on my back as I took hold of the ringed door handles, heaved the heavy wooden doors open, and stepped inside.

People thronged in the Great Hall; Juniper was holding some sort of lavish gathering, like she did occasionally. The general conversation inside the hall began to stutter. The Court members, mainly Coterie assassins and their families, turned and looked at me, their faces quickly taking on looks of shock. The volume gradually reduced like a wave rushing away from the shore, only it was rushing away from me, as people turned and stared.

Juniper sat on her "throne", her fingers toying with her necklace. My fists balled; jaw clenched at the sight of my father's murderess. On her left stood Lord Flint, his beady, brown eyes widening in horror as he saw me, and next to him my stepbrother, Elm, stood fiddling with the hilt of his sword, the jade ring on his index finger glistening. On Juniper's right sat Beryl. My traitorous sister who was happy to see me die. The smile faded from her porcelain face as her hazel eyes locked with mine for a moment. I scowled at her. Did she know that Juniper might have faked Mal's death? That our brother might still be alive somewhere? And just beyond Beryl, chained at the wrists and standing with an anxious look on his face, stood Rian. Thank the Stars Serpentine hadn't got to him yet. The prince's chains ran to a metal ring in the floor, and two guards hovered near him. Rian had no hope of escape as things stood.

As for Juniper, the moment she noticed me, her face drained of all colour and she leapt to her feet, her piercing yellow eyes boring into me. She rarely showed emotion, but now she stood, nostrils flaring, and her mouth set in a hard line as the muscles in her neck tensed. I smiled inwardly; she was very angry. She nodded to someone in the packed hall as Serpentine appeared from behind the throne, his lips twisting in a nasty grin.

Hell's teeth.

I marched towards my stepmother's throne, trying to ignore Rian's sudden look of horror as he pulled on his chains.

'Phire! Look out!' Rian shouted.

Footsteps sounded behind me, then an arm slid around my neck. I grabbed at my assailant's shoulder, twisting my body, bending my knees slightly. Feldspar flew over my shoulder, slamming into the stone floor. He looked up at me, shock in his deep green eyes, his blond hair dishevelled from the fall, and a large bruise appearing on his temple. He really was better at poisoning than hand-to-hand combat.

I glanced up. Rian's face was etched with relief, but concern still filled his eyes as his tense muscles strained at the chains holding him in check.

I continued towards the throne as Feldspar staggered to his feet and disappeared into the spectators, nursing his head.

'Still alive, Amethyst-sweetie,' came a honeyed voice to my right.

I turned to see Carnelian, one of the Coterie's nastier assassins. His dark, lank hair, pale skin, and watery grey eyes did nothing to endear him to me. He had a fearsome reputation – far worse than that of Lady Merciless, if you could credit it – but while I was known for my deftness and skill, he was known for violence and brutality.

'So it would appear,' I said, glowering at him for good measure, desperate to ask him what he really knew about Mal and wondering where his younger sister – Citrine, a master in knife throwing – might be. I didn't want to be blindsided by her in the middle of the hall.

Carnelian smiled, his right eye twitching. A young woman came and stood beside him, slipping her hand into his.

'Amethyst,' she purred. Her brown hair was tied back, and her narrow blue eyes watched me intently. She had four knives that I could see, but probably had another couple secreted about her somewhere. The scar down the left side of her face was a reminder of a disagreement we'd once had.

I nodded curtly. 'Topaz.'

Turning back, I walked on up to the throne, my heart thudding, stopping a good fifteen feet away, trying to stay alert to all around me – after all, I was surrounded by assassins. I half expected to see Sunstone and Hematite, both great brutes of men with necks like tree trunks and muscles of iron, standing behind Juniper somewhere. They acted as her bodyguards when they weren't out on commissions, but today they were, thankfully, absent. A flash took my attention for a split second. The hilt of the Malachite Dagger winked at me from its place on the wall behind the throne. My heart jumped. I glanced at Beryl. What did she know about

Mal? Not that I could ask her, or Carnelian for that matter, and whatever they told me would probably be lies anyway.

'Kill her now!' Juniper pointed towards me, her tall frame shaking with anger as her voice set the air alight.

'No!' Rian yelled, yanking at his chains.

Before I'd had the chance to draw Aldorbana, two guards grabbed me from behind.

Elm sneered, his golden skin shining in the torchlight, highlighting the ugly scar on his right cheek – a gift from Mal during a particularly nasty fight that Elm started and Mal finished.

'On your knees,' he said, rushing forwards and grabbing my shoulder as the guards let go, pushing me roughly to the cold flagstone floor. My knees hit the hard stone with a jolt, sending a sharp pain through my legs, as Elm slid his sword from its scabbard and rested the blade on the back of my neck. I knelt upright, my back straight despite my pounding heart, and glanced at an ashen-faced, helpless-looking Rian, before turning and staring straight into Juniper's dead eyes. Whatever they thought, I wasn't going to make this easy. I took a deep, long breath to steady myself.

Juniper smiled a serpent's smile as it prepares to finish its prey. 'Goodbye, Daughter.'

Beryl sat beside her, grinning again. She truly hated me – but why? What had I done to her?

Elm raised his sword and swung it down towards the back of my unprotected neck. I ducked and twisted out the way as the sword struck the stone floor, jarring free of Elm's hands as his momentum took him down to one knee. I grabbed the sword as it clattered to the floor, turned back to Elm as I stood in one swift, smooth movement, and held it to his throat, my other hand holding his hair, pulling his head back. My stepbrother stiffened as he realised his predicament.

'Mother! Get her to stop,' Elm said, breathing erratically.

Juniper took a step forwards, her eyes narrowing. 'We taught you well.'

I looked up at her. 'Maybe you did.'

'Witch,' Beryl said, pointing at me as her white-blonde hair bounced around her face. I'd always been a little jealous of her hair, seeing as I could never tame mine. As twins, we were both reasonably well-endowed, but when it came to height, I was the taller. I'd been sad when we were young that we hadn't looked more alike, but now I welcomed the fact we weren't identical. 'No one can move that quick.'

'Training,' Rian said, a look of pride on his face. I tried to suppress a smile.

'Why did you come, Amethyst?' my sister asked.

'I came for Prince Valerian,' I said.

'What's he to you?' Juniper asked, her eyes narrowing.

I glanced at Rian. How could I answer that? He was so many things to me now, and none of them would I utter in public. Only ever to him. If he ever wanted me to. His eyes gave me hope that he would. 'He's my friend.'

'Friend? You've never had any *friends*,' Beryl snapped.

And she was right. I'd had family, but just one friend, Onyx, and he was nowhere to be seen tonight. In a way I was glad.

'This isn't your home anymore, Amethyst. We don't want you here,' Beryl said, her voice harsh, her eyes hard as granite.

'What did I ever do to you?' I asked, mystified and unsettled by her hatred.

Beryl stood. Took a step forward. 'You had something I didn't.'

'What?'

'Their approval.'

What was she talking about?

'I don't understand,' I said.

'Father and Malachite. Everything you did, they approved of, applauded you for. You walked first. You talked first. You learnt to ride first. Read first.'

'It was never a competition, Beryl.'

'Not to you, perhaps, but it was to me. They loved you more than me.'

'Don't be daft.' I couldn't believe what I was hearing.

Elm tried to twist away, but I yanked him back.

'But I did do one thing first.' She smiled. 'I killed.'

The blood drained from my face. 'You what?' I knew she was involved in the Coterie, but somehow, I'd never imagined her being sent out on an actual commission.

A slow smile crept across her face. A cruel, harsh smile of victory. 'And neither of them love you now, do they? They're both long gone.'

I swallowed.

Beryl glanced at Rian. 'Perhaps we should kill him now, Mother, rather than ransom him. It could be quite the spectacle – the evening's entertainment.'

I flinched at Beryl's use of "mother". She'd never done it before, not that I'd heard, only ever referring to Juniper as Stepmother. Her betrayal now seemed complete.

My knuckles whitened around the sword hilt. 'Lay one finger on him and I'll–'

'Kill me?' she scoffed, an amused look on her face.

'Yes.'

'Enough.' Juniper stepped forward. 'Prince Valerian will be ransomed back to Aerba. He won't be killed – unless they refuse to pay,' she said, menace in her voice.

'They don't need to pay because you're releasing him now,' I said, tugging on Elm's hair.

'Ow,' he complained.

'Shut up.'

Beryl's hazel eyes narrowed. 'You like him.'

I glowered at her, knowing the warmth rushing to my face was giving me away. My mouth dried out like the desert.

Juniper stared at me, then paused, her lips mottled. 'What's that on your back?' She blanched. 'It can't be,' she said, taking a step back. 'You can't carry those weapons.'

'What is it?' Beryl asked, stepping forward.

'It's those blasted Cursed Weapons of the *Aerbans*,' Flint said, his deep voice trembling. He practically spat out the word "Aerbans".

'The what?' Beryl asked, her forehead creasing as worried mutterings scattered around the hall and people started backing away from me.

'Aldorbana and Cwicsusl, the Cursed Weapons of Aerba,' Juniper said, a strange bitterness to her voice. 'The Aerban *High Bloods* like to keep them as a deterrent to keep their Middle and Low Bloods in check.' Her face darkened as she spoke, and the veins in her forehead and neck looked ready to pop.

I frowned. I'd had a misguided dislike of High Bloods – she hated them.

'King Finule likes to keep his people on a tight leash,' she said.

Rian winced.

'How did you come by them?' Juniper asked.

'You really think I'm going to answer that?' I replied.

'It doesn't matter whether you tell us or not, my girl,' Flint said, regaining his composure. 'The Weapons are bound to you until you die, which, as I understand it, won't be long.'

A nasty smile spread over Beryl's face as she played with her hair.

'What do you mean?' Elm asked, his yellow eyes puzzled.

'They're sucking the life from her even as we speak,' Juniper said, absently caressing her diamond and agate necklace.

'Oh, good,' Elm sneered, once more trying to pull away. I

pressed his sword on the unprotected skin of his neck. He stopped struggling. 'Bitch.'

'Bastard,' I said.

'How dare you–'

I pressed the sword's edge harder against his neck, and a small drop of blood oozed from his skin. The blade obviously had a nick in it somewhere. Elm hadn't been taking care of his weapons properly.

'In the meantime, Stepmother, you'll release Prince Valerian unharmed, or I'll kill Elm and take the castle – and you – apart, one piece at time,' I said. 'You know I can, and I will. Now release him.'

Juniper looked ready to fly apart, which gave me some considerable satisfaction. She preferred to be in control of things. *Well, not today.* 'Unshackle him,' she ordered the guards standing beside Rian, an unpleasant edge to her voice, her serpent eyes never leaving my face. 'Who knows what those Cursed Weapons are capable of.'

Beryl looked at me through her long eyelashes. If looks could kill, Beryl would've had me dead on the floor in less than a second. Her face turned a lovely puce as Rian joined me, rubbing his wrists.

'Thanks,' he murmured.

'Where's Aerba's Fire Opal?' I asked my stepmother, still holding Elm.

Juniper frowned. 'The Aerban Fire Opal?'

'Yes, where is it? You had it stolen when I went to kill Princess Angelica.'

Juniper's yellow eyes slowly narrowed, and she shook her head. 'No, I didn't.'

'But–'

'It may have been stolen, but neither the Coterie nor Iolite had anything to do with it. I don't have it. It's not on Iolite.'

Carnelian was busy smirking at Topaz – I really wanted to wipe the smile off his stupid face.

'She's lying,' Rian whispered in my ear.

I shook my head. 'No. Juniper is a lot of things, but she's not a liar,' I said. 'She twists the truth, but never lies. Very well, we're leaving, and I suggest you let us do it unhindered if you want Elm to remain alive.'

Juniper nodded curtly as I turned towards the doors with Rian, pulling Elm to his feet and along with me.

'I do hope you get home in time, Prince Valerian,' Juniper said.

Rian stopped. He turned back. 'What do you mean?'

I paused, holding my breath, one hand clamped around Elm's shoulder, the other still holding his sword at his throat.

Juniper smiled sweetly. 'The commission for the Coterie to assassinate your sister wasn't the only one. We received three, to be carried out a set time apart. King Finule is next.'

CHAPTER TEN

'You wouldn't dare.' Rian took a step towards Juniper.

Keeping the blade at his throat, I let go of Elm and grabbed the prince's arm, pulling him back.

'I offer a service to those that can pay, Prince Valerian. Of course, I'd dare,' Juniper said.

'Who ordered the assassinations?' I demanded, grabbing Elm's tunic before he could escape me.

Juniper turned her serpent's gaze on me. 'I never betray a confidence. You know that. The contract between customer and Coterie is sacred.' Contract, indeed. I shuddered at her off-hand way of referring to someone's life. 'I'm not going to divulge that information, but I can tell you it's imminent, Prince Valerian. I'd hurry home if I were you, assuming you want to see your father before he dies.'

'You bitch!' Rian said.

'Who's the third?' I asked.

Juniper smiled.

'Who's the third?' I repeated, my voice steely with determination as I brandished Elm's sword against his neck.

'Mother,' Elm choked.

Juniper gave Elm a rather chastising look. 'Crown Prince Chervil. As to when his assassination is scheduled for, that will have to be a surprise. It would appear someone wants you on the Aerban throne, Prince Valerian,' Juniper said. 'At least, for now.'

Rian made a slightly strangled sound.

'Come on,' I said, backing towards the doors, pulling Elm along with us.

'I'm sorry about Malachite,' Elm said.

We were almost at the doors now, but I stopped dead. Elm sneered at me, pleasure written all over his ugly face.

'Now I'll have to take over when the time comes,' Beryl said, a smile creeping across her lips and lighting up her eyes. 'Mal's death came as a great shock.'

I narrowed my eyes. She knew more than she was saying. My knuckles whitened as I held onto the sword hilt.

'So did your betrayal, which rather excludes you from the line of succession now, I'm afraid,' Beryl continued, her voice lilting and triumphant. 'But I think I'll do a better job of leading Iolite than you, anyway. You don't have the stomach for it.'

'If you mean for leading the Coterie and ordering the death of others, no, you're right,' I said. 'But you don't really need a stomach for that, just a lack of conscience.' I glared at Beryl, then glanced at Juniper. She had an air of satisfaction about her, and I tensed, wishing I'd kept silent. I wanted to confront her about Mal, demand to know what she'd done with him, where she held him prisoner, but I'd only sign his death warrant by showing my hand if I did. I said nothing.

'It's such a pity, especially when he'd been about to become Master of Iolite,' Juniper almost purred. 'His death is a great burden to me in particular, but one I will have to shoulder as I continue as Mistress until Beryl is of age.'

I clenched my fist holding the sword. For the first time in my life, I could actually imagine murdering someone.

'We're going,' I said.

'You can't escape the Coterie, Amethyst. You'll always be one of us. We'll always dog your footsteps, no matter where you go,' Juniper said.

A little shiver rolled down my back. I knew no one ever left the Coterie, but maybe I'd be the first – however impossible it may seem.

'Maybe you'll live long enough for us to meet again, Daughter,' Juniper said, toying with the diamonds and agate nestling at her neck. 'But I doubt it.'

'I'm no daughter of yours,' I said, my blood boiling.

'I'll miss you, Sister.' Elm's tongue lingered on the "s" rather longer than I liked.

I snapped. I raised the sword and hit his head with the hilt. He fell to the stone floor, unconscious.

'Move!' I said, grabbing Rian and making it out the doors before anyone could do anything. Together, we heaved the doors shut behind us, and I forced Elm's sword through the handles, barring them shut. Juniper screamed orders from inside the hall as someone tried to open the doors, then slammed against them. 'They won't hold for long,' I said, running down the steps.

We sprinted along a corridor until we reached a fork. Instead of heading back to the courtyard, I turned to the right along a smaller passageway.

'You could've been ki–' Rian started.

'Shh!' I said, putting my fingers to my lips. 'We're going out a different way and I don't want more of the Coterie following us than necessary.'

'We're being followed?' he asked, looking behind us.

'You have the Nightshade, we have the Coterie,' I said, leading him at speed along another passage, down some stairs into a long, narrow tunnel, dimly lit with oil lamps and the odd torch. 'Take one,' I said as we passed two stuttering pitch torches set in sconces on the wall.

We turned into another tunnel before ducking into a side room where I shut the door behind us and locked it, praying there were no secret entrances to this room I didn't know about. I moved over to a wooden packing crate and started to push it to one side towards a wall.

'Let me help,' Rian said, pushing against the crate.

With a grinding noise that set my teeth on edge, we shifted it out of the way to reveal a wooden trapdoor, which I pulled open. In the floor, a black hole that looked like the yawning mouth of hell gaped at us.

'We go down here,' I said. 'There's a tunnel that leads out under the castle and beyond the city walls.'

As I started to climb down the ladder, the door handle moved. Rattled. Then the sound of someone smashing against the door echoed through our little room.

I glanced at Rian. 'We need to hurry,' I said, hastening down the ladder. Rian followed me, bolting the trapdoor behind him, and joining me in the damp tunnel below. Rian's features, visible in the flickering torchlight, contorted as he sniffed the air.

'Sorry about the smell. We're quite close to the sewers down here, in case you wondered,' I said.

We made our way along the tunnel. Water dripped from the roof. The sound of scuttling came from all around us in the dark. Rats. I hated rats. But I hated the thought of staying in the Crimson Castle more. We hurried along, making our way under the castle and on under the city towards freedom.

'Where exactly does this come out?' Rian asked.

'Just beyond the walls, not far from where the horses are,' I said, splashing through a puddle.

'Will it take much longer?'

'Why, don't you like it down here?' I grinned.

'It's not that – I think I can hear someone following us.'

'What?' I stopped, listened, straining to hear any noise back along the tunnel. Sure enough, the distant echo of footsteps reverberated behind us. 'You're right. How did they get through so quickly? We'd better hurry.' Running wasn't ideal in such a cramped space, but we had no choice and broke into a jog.

Ten minutes later, we reached the end of the tunnel and clambered up a ladder. At the top, a bolted trap door blocked my way. I reached up, taking hold of the bolt. No one had been out this way for ages, which wasn't a complete surprise because as far as I knew, only myself, Mal, and Onyx knew about this tunnel. I jiggled the bolt, finally sliding it free, and opened the trapdoor enough to peer out into the darkness.

Night surrounded Adamas. The sweet perfume of Night Jessamine filled the warm air, and clouds covered the stars, which would help camouflage our escape. We climbed out the tunnel into a little group of bushes, shutting the door behind us. We had no way of locking the trapdoor, so we sped from the bushes towards the little group of trees and our waiting horses. We burst through the foliage. The copse stood empty.

'Hell's teeth! Where are they?' I looked around wildly.

'We don't have time,' Rian said, grabbing my hand. He pulled me on through the trees and out onto open ground away from the city. We ran, the Cursed Weapons banging uncomfortably on my back.

'Over there,' came a shout from behind us.

I turned to see four men running towards us from the open trapdoor – guards or assassins?

'Into the trees,' I said, guiding us towards a wood that stood to our right. We sped towards it, diving in amongst the foliage and deep shadows. We plunged on, branches tearing at our clothes, leaves stinging our faces. Behind us, the men had reached the wood and were crashing through the trees, shouting as they hunted us down.

'We'll have to hide,' Rian said, scanning the wood for suitable undergrowth.

'Wait.' Through the trees, the flicker of a campfire caught my eye. 'This way.' Maybe they had horses. I wasn't a common thief, but if they did, I might just bury my scruples for the night. We edged closer to the campsite positioned in the middle of a small clearing. We peered through the undergrowth.

'I'll be damned… our horses,' Rian said, pointing to the beasts tied on the far side of the camp with several other horses, still tacked up. Six men sat around the fire, taking it in turns to drink from three wineskins. They'd already had a skinful, from the way they talked and slurred their speech.

We crept around the camp, well aware of our pursuers close behind, reaching the horses. Silently we untied them and started to lead them away. Our hunters broke into the clearing.

'Wha' the devil?'

'What yer doin'?'

'They're over there – get them!' Carnelian's voice rang out across the clearing.

'Go!' Rian yelled, climbing into his saddle as I mounted my horse.

I urged the beast into the trees, glancing back at the ring of swords. A fight had broken out between the drunken men and our hunters. Carnelian glanced up, sword in hand, and glowered at me, his angry face illuminated by the firelight. I smiled at him and turned away.

Rian followed me as I led the way, twisting through the trees and back out onto open ground, breaking our horses into a gallop as we joined the Opal Road. We stayed on the road for a good league before turning right towards the dark wall of the Adamas Forest, and the eastern coast beyond. We rode through the night, silent as we cantered along. We'd had a close call, and thoughts tumbled through my mind. Our mission wasn't supposed to be like this. I dreaded stopping and having to explain myself to Rian when he'd expressly ordered me to leave and not go after him – how could I say I couldn't leave him behind, that it had nothing to do with his father and the mission, and everything to do with Rian himself?

By dawn, we were well into the forest, surrounded by oak and spruce, the sun reaching through the leaves and sending yellow fingers onto the track we'd found heading east.

'We'd better stop for something to eat soon, and to give the horses a break,' I said.

'I could do with a break, too,' Rian said, stretching an arm. 'What's that up ahead?'

Splashes of white flashed through the trees, and as we got closer a deep thundering sound filled the air.

'A river,' I said as I rode on. Moments later, we came out of the trees at the edge of a fast-flowing river, the water frothing and churning, splashing at its banks as if trying to claw its way out. 'These forest rivers are usually fairly easy to ford. They must have had some rain upstream – it's going to make it difficult to cross.'

'I'll go first. The sooner I'm wet, the sooner I'll be dry,' Rian said, urging his reluctant horse into the swollen river.

'Be careful,' I said, considering his logic. He made slow but steady progress through the swirling water. Halfway across, his horse stumbled in the turbulent torrent, but it quickly found its footing again and Rian soon rode out onto the other riverbank, dripping-wet but grinning.

'No problem,' he called.

I urged my horse into the angry river, the icy cold water grabbing at my legs, trying to pull me off my horse and into the violent swirl. By the time we reached halfway, the freezing water had almost reached my knees. The cold water chilled my legs to the bone, and my horse snorted. Suddenly he stumbled, and the river took the opportunity to sweep his legs out from under him. I was launched into the angry water and immediately went under.

Water rushed past my ears as I struggled to reach the surface. I felt my head break through, and I took an urgent gasp of air.

'Phire!' Rian yelled before the river pulled me under again.

The water stormed past, deafening me as it dragged me with it. I tried to swim for the surface, but the river repeatedly pulled me back under, twisting me around until I didn't know which way was up. My ankle banged painfully on a rock, and I had to stop myself from screaming. My lungs burned, desperate for oxygen, my throat seared, and my fast pulse thudded uncomfortably in my ears.

I fought back, determined that the insatiable rush of the river wouldn't take me. As I struggled, my strength gradually drained from me, sapped by the cold, churning water. Now dizzy, my vision began to darken from lack of oxygen. I had no energy left. If I breathed in, it would be over.

I dimly remembered Elm saying something once about drowning being quite pleasant, once you'd stopped struggling.

I stopped struggling.

My head broke the surface; I coughed and choked, gasping for delicious, sweet air. The water pushed me over towards the riverbank, and I found myself in an area of slack water. For a moment I floated, attempting to get my breath back. My whole body protested as I slowly dragged myself out of the river, onto the rocky shore where for several minutes I lay on my side, relishing the air going in and out of my lungs. When I finally sat up, shivering and numb with cold, the world spun alarmingly.

Somehow Aldorbana and Cwicsusl had stayed attached to my back, and I couldn't help but swear silently.

'Phire,' Rian called, and I looked up to see him riding along the riverbank towards me. Quickly dismounting, he ran over and pulled me up. 'Are you okay?'

'Yes, just a little dizzy,' I said.

He swept me into a hug. 'I thought I'd lost you,' he said, holding me close as the smell of sandalwood surrounded me.

'I'm fine, really,' I said. 'What happened to my horse?'

'He's gone,' Rian said, pulling back a little and looking down the river after the lost animal.

'Bother.'

'We still have my horse. It'll be fine. Look, let's find somewhere to camp where we can eat and rest for a while.'

I nodded. My ankle, although bruised, held my weight, and I followed Rian as he took hold of his horse's reins. We made our way into the forest, finding a little thicket to camp in far enough off the track to light a small fire and not be spotted. I huddled close to the fire, shivering in my damp clothing. After a hot meal, cobbled together from the provisions in Rian's pack, he got his blankets out while I continued to sit close to the fire, the shivering intensifying. I just couldn't get warm. With my bags now gone, I had no blankets or any other dry clothing.

'Take your leggings and tunic off, hang them up to dry on that bush near the fire, then get under these blankets with me,' Rian said, arranging his bedding. 'I'll warm you up.'

'I beg your pardon?' I looked at him in horror.

'I'm not going to see you get hypothermia for the sake of propriety,' he said, indicating the blankets now covering him. 'The Blood Rules don't say we can't share bedding, and I assume you still want to break the Curse and rescue your brother, if at all possible?'

'Of course, I do.' I knew he was right. The Blood Rules certainly didn't preclude us from sharing blankets, just other more intimate things.

'Then do as I say before you damn well catch your death of cold.'

This trip wasn't going according to plan. I reluctantly got up, took off Aldorbana and Cwicsusl, and removed Father's book from my tunic. Its outer cover looked rather bedraggled, so I placed it near the fire to dry as well.

'What's that?' Rian asked.

'Something I picked up in the castle that I'm hoping will help us,' I said, peeling off my damp outer clothes, glad I was still relatively decent in my shirt and undergarments. Even so, blood rushed to my face. I placed the wet clothes on the bush to dry and moved over to where Rian lay on his side, watching me, and slipped under the blankets next to him. He looked at me, a little furrow on his brow, his face flushed as he swallowed. Hesitated. Then he moved so his body rested beside mine.

'May I?' he asked, his voice catching.

I nodded and didn't resist as he slid his arm around me until it lay gently across my still-damp undershirt and stomach. He tensed, awaiting my response, so I rested my hand on his, smiling as I sensed his muscles relaxing. I'd never felt so safe, so secure. So content. I snuggled into him as I gratefully accepted the warmth from his body. I could feel his heartbeat, and I slowly became aware of the familiar, sweet, woody smell of sandalwood. I relished his arms holding me, relaxing even more as a tingling sensation corkscrewed through my body at his touch.

'Better?' he whispered into my ear, his voice a warm summer breeze.

'That's one way of putting it,' I said, a longing I'd never experienced before growing inside my chest.

Rian's words back at the Iolite University had profoundly affected me. I'd already concluded my dislike of all High Bloods to be irrational. My affection for Rian had been growing for some time, but when I'd found out about Father's murder, Beryl's further betrayal, Mal's imprisonment, and his decision to do my killing for me, Rian's reaction had only further endeared him to me. Instead of being judgemental, of taking against Mal for Angelica's death, he'd supported me, looked after me. There was a kindness there I hadn't expected, a gentleness that I'd not foreseen in a High Blood son of King Finule. And I cherished him for it. We lay there for a while, my shivering gradually diminishing until it ceased altogether.

I glanced down at his wrists. They were both red, sore from the shackles Juniper had placed on him. My heart skipped.

'I'm sorry,' I said.

'Whatever for?' he asked.

'I should've protected you, stopped you from being caught. I wanted to come and get you at the inn, but the others wouldn't let me.'

'I told them not to. I didn't want you getting captured, too.'

'But if I'd freed you then, you'd never have been hurt like this,' I said, gingerly touching one injured wrist.

'I'm fine, really,' he said, raising himself up onto one shoulder. 'Anise has salves for this sort of thing. But it's kind of you to worry about me.'

Kind? That didn't come close. Kindness wasn't what drove me now.

'I just wish I could've spared you the pain,' I said.

'You spared me much more than that by coming to get me,' he said, smiling at me. 'I'll always be grateful to you.'

'I had to. I could never have left you with them,' I said, shuddering at the thought.

We lay silent for a few minutes, listening to the sounds of the forest and our breathing.

'You smell of roses,' he murmured, moving a damp curl from the side of my face, which proceeded to flush annoyingly.

'You have something of sandalwood about you,' I replied, glancing into his eyes then quickly away. Inside, a swirl of emotions twisted and turned. Yearning bubbled to the surface.

'We should sleep for a while before continuing on,' he said. 'Is that all right with you?'

I turned back to him and nodded. 'We probably should get some rest. I arranged to meet with the others near Quartz Town tomorrow, so we'll have no problem getting there in time.'

He lay looking up at the blue sky. 'You still shouldn't have come after me, you know,' he said.

'Whyever not?'

'Because you could've been killed.'

'And if I'd left you, and your father hadn't paid the ransom, *you* would have been killed. Probably in the most excruciating way Juniper and Serpentine could've thought of. I couldn't allow that; you're too important.' My face warmed and I turned away, embarrassed.

'It's because *you're* important I didn't want you risking your life for *me*.'

'Would you have come to get me?' I asked, looking back at him.

He moved another strand of damp hair from my face. 'There's no question I'd have come for you – whatever the cost. I'd have ridden into hell to get you back.' I glanced at him. His face was pink, stripped bare, his eyes full of longing. He swallowed. 'Now get some rest,' he said, his voice husky.

As I lay in his arms, I couldn't think of a time when I'd been happier.

The sound of horses' hooves clattering on the track through the forest woke me, and I opened my eyes to find Rian lying partially over me, his hand over my mouth. I lay still as he looked out through the trees, his muscles tense, until the noises receded.

'Damn, that's the second time in the last hour,' he said softly, removing his hand from my mouth, looking down at me as my heart jumped around like a jack rabbit. His hair fell around his face as his eyes studied me.

'The Coterie,' I said, not breaking his gaze, my mouth suddenly dry.

Our faces were inches from each other, so close I could feel his warm breath on my face. His lips looked velvety and soft. Intoxicating. I wanted to…

'I–' He hesitated as his amber irises dilated. His breath hitched and he cleared his throat. 'Sorry, I didn't want you making any sudden noise or movements,' he said, moving off me.

'It's fine,' I said, trying to control my breathing. 'Maybe we should get going. I think there's another track a little south of here. We just need to follow the river.'

He nodded.

I quickly dressed, tucking Father's book back in my tunic as we gathered our things, then quietly led the horse back towards the river. Once there, we followed the water south until we came across another track. From the grasses covering it, this one appeared less well used than the one we'd been on. Rian mounted his horse, pulling me up behind him, and we rode on towards Quartz. Glancing up at the sky, I noted that the sun had not long slipped past noon. We'd reach the town by late afternoon, in time to set up camp and wait for the others.

We rode on through the forest at a canter, only slowing periodically to rest our horse. Finally, the trees thinned and ahead of us stood the small fishing town of Quartz, its little grey houses huddled by the coast where the sun scattered its rays like diamonds over the water. Tourmaline Cove was visible in the distance, but I couldn't see a ship, not that I expected to until tomorrow morning.

'We could get a few supplies in Quartz, if we're careful,' I said.

'Good idea,' Rian said.

We rode towards the town, dismounting before we reached the buildings. I kept an eye out for assassins as we made our way into the bustling market, but I didn't see anyone I recognised. The smell of bread led us to the bakery where we purchased some loaves and pastries for our evening meal. As we came out, a figure across the street caught my attention. A face I recognised. A friendly one, who waved me over. I sighed with relief.

'Come with me,' I said to Rian as he finished stowing the food in the saddlebags. I crossed the street, venturing into the alleyway where I'd seen the figure.

'Ama, in here,' a voice called from a half-open storeroom door.

Rian tied the horse up outside. 'Are you sure about this?'

I nodded, walking into the storeroom full of wooden barrels and sacks of grain, only to be picked up in a bear hug and swung around, much to Rian's annoyance – at least from the look on his face.

'Onyx, put me down, you idiot,' I said, giving him a friendly punch.

Onyx laughed, his sienna skin crinkling around his hazel brown eyes as he looked at me. 'By the Stars, Ama, I'm so glad you're not dead.' He was wearing his Low Blood moss green tunic over a light mail shirt, his black suede britches tucked into his boots. His familiar rose quartz ring sat on his little finger.

'So am I,' I said, my hand unconsciously going to where Flint had hit me with the oar.

'I assume this is Prince Valerian,' Onyx said, giving Rian an appraising look.

Rian stood straight, his face taut.

'News travels fast,' I said.

'And you are?' Rian asked, his voice curt and princely. In fact, he sounded a little like Chervil as he spoke.

'I'm Onyx, one of the Coterie's finest assassins. I would say at your service, but you'd have to go back to Adamas and pay Juniper if you did want me to kill someone, and I guess you won't want to be doing that,' Onyx said with a flourishing bow before linking his arm with mine.

I pushed him away, Cwicsusl catching on Aldorbana.

Onyx looked at the Cursed Weapons and took a step back. 'Are they what I think they are?'

'Unfortunately, yes,' I said.

He glanced at Rian, who stood stony-faced, then back to me.

'Can you break the Curse?' Onyx asked, his eyes full of concern.

'Maybe, although Agate and Moonstone aren't sure,' I said.

He nodded. 'Did they say anything else?'

'That Mal's alive. Is it true?'

'I believe so,' he said, his eyes far away for a moment. 'The whispers I've heard indicate your dear stepmother has him imprisoned somewhere, although the bitch would deny it if you asked her.'

I winced. He hadn't lost his flair for words since I'd last seen him. I'd forgotten how he liked to refer to my stepmother when he was away from the Crimson Castle. He had no love for her or the Coterie. He did what he did because, like me, he had no choice.

He'd been forced into joining the Coterie, too, only he'd learnt to kill. I hadn't.

'I think Flos may know where,' he continued.

'The Land of Flos?' I asked.

'Yes... she's been working with the nastier elements in the Flosian and Merean Royalty for a while, but I think Flos might be more likely to have answers. Probably someone high up in the Royal Family knows where he is, or at least something that may help.'

'It would have to be Flos, wouldn't it,' Rian muttered.

Onyx sniffed and gave Rian a long look before answering. 'Aerba and Flos don't exactly get along, do they?'

'That's putting it mildly.'

'If you ask me, I think the bitch's ultimate goal is to destabilise all of the Five Lands,' Onyx said. 'She has an insatiable desire to control. I think she'd have all the Lands under her thumb if she could.'

'You'd think she was holding some sort of major grudge against the Five Lands, the way she carries on,' I said.

Onyx made a face. 'Maybe. She could have one we don't know about. After all, no one knows much about her past before she came to Iolite. She just arrived from Trew one day with Elm in tow. Who knows what chaos she left behind her?'

'Yes, but even she'd have trouble taking over all the Lands. It wouldn't be possible,' I said. 'Do you know anything about the Fire Opal?'

'I know it's been stolen.'

'Juniper says it's nothing to do with her.'

'Then I believe her. If you end up in Flos looking for Mal, it's probably not a bad place to start looking for the Fire Opal.'

'Why?' Rian asked. 'You think they have it?'

'As we know, Flos isn't Aerba's best friend. Taking the Fire Opal seems a little extreme, but it would be a place to start looking. The Royal Family there might be able to help with that, too.'

'You think they'd help us?' Rian scoffed.

I frowned. 'My cousins might be able to.'

'Jasmine and Erica?' Onyx asked.

I nodded.

Onyx sniffed. 'Not a bad idea. They hear things – especially Erica.'

'Exactly,' I said.

Onyx shrugged. 'Worth a try, then. Look, you better be going, I'm not the only member of the Coterie in Quartz.'

'Fine, we'll leave now,' I said.

Rian started towards the door.

Onyx stepped in front of him, raising his hand to stop the prince. 'Look after Ama.'

'She's Samphire, now, not Amethyst,' Rian said, straightening so he stood taller than the assassin.

Onyx shrugged. 'Well, whatever you call her, look after her, because if you don't, I'll find you and kill you for free,' he said without a trace of a smile.

'Stop it,' I said, hitting his arm.

Rian glanced at the tattoo on the assassin's wrist and back at Onyx. 'I have no intention of doing anything else,' he said, turning to me. 'I'll see if the way's clear,' he said, slipping out of the room.

I took a step, intending to follow him, but Onyx grabbed my arm. 'Wait,' he said.

'You could've been nicer to him,' I said. 'He's done nothing to you.'

'He has, though,' Onyx said, holding my hand. 'He's stolen my Amethyst.'

'Don't be daft.'

He shrugged. 'You were my best friend.'

'I still am. That's not going to change.'

Onyx grunted.

I frowned at him. 'It isn't. And as far as everyone else is concerned, well, he's helped me to escape.'

Onyx sniffed, let go of my hand, and sighed. 'Not yet, you haven't – the bitch will hunt you down. I'm just worried about my dear friend.'

I squinted at him. 'I'm fine. Anyway, I thought Ruby was making a play for your friendship too, not to mention other things – you're not exactly going to be lonely without me around.'

'The new kitchen maid? Hardly. I'm not the slightest bit interested in her.'

'Have you met someone, then?'

Onyx glanced towards the floor.

I smiled. 'You have, haven't you? Who are they?'

'It's early days and he's currently away, so I don't know if it's going anywhere yet,' he said, taking hold of my Amethyst Talisman that had slipped out of my tunic. 'I've always liked this, how it catches the light and the way the silver wire swirls around the crystal.'

I glanced at it. 'I love the purple colour of it.'

'It's really old. Back then, there were lots of crystals about. Now, only Iolite produces them, makes jewellery. Did you know some types of crystal don't mix?' he asked, letting go of my Talisman.

'What?' I asked, slipping it back under my tunic and out of sight.

'Never mind,' Onyx sniffed. 'Look, there's something you need to know – Beryl hasn't taken kindly to you coming back, or so brazenly rescuing your prince. She'll have the Coterie kill him if you stay with him.'

'Then I'll have to protect him,' I said.

Onyx looked at me. 'You know how difficult it'll be.'

'Phire, we need to go,' Rian called from outside.

'You know what you should do.'

I looked towards the door. 'You think I should leave him?'

Onyx looked at the ground, exhaling a long breath. 'If you love him and want him to live, yes. You have to leave him.'

'What?' I turned sharply towards Onyx, my face doing an excellent impression of a beetroot. 'Love him? Don't be ridiculous.'

He looked up at me. 'You do, don't you?'

'I...'

'I've known you long enough, Ama. I can see from the look in your eyes you love him, and the way he looks at you isn't dissimilar.'

Onyx had always been good at getting straight to the truth of something, and today appeared no different.

'You think so?' I asked quietly.

Onyx nodded. 'I do. And I wish it were simple for you both to be together, but what matters to me most is that you're safe.'

'How can I be safe with this Curse hanging over me?'

He smiled. 'You'll work out how to break it, I know you will. And if you do, and you insist on staying with your High Blood Prince despite the Blood Rules and Beryl, there's an archipelago due east of Trew where they don't follow the Decree and the Coterie don't go. You'd both be safe there. I might even join you one day.'

'I've never heard of it.'

'That's kind of the point – the Pax Archipelago is secret. Few know the islands are even inhabited, let alone that they don't follow the Decree.'

I hesitated a moment before resting my hand on his arm. 'Come with us. You'll be safe.'

'You know I can't. My mother still works in the kitchens and refuses to leave, and if I flee the Coterie, the bitch's made it quite clear she'll kill her. You of all people should know that no one ever leaves the Coterie.'

'I've heard it mentioned,' I said ruefully.

'Now go. Get yourself and Prince Valerian out of Quartz before you're spotted. If I hear anything about Mal, I'll try and send you word somehow.'

'Thank you,' I said, giving him a quick peck on the cheek. 'Stay safe, Onyx.'

He nodded and smiled, though his hazel eyes flickered with worry. 'Go on, get out of here.'

CHAPTER ELEVEN

I slipped out the door, joining Rian, who had a questioning expression on his face. 'I'll explain later,' I said, pausing to wave at Onyx.

We mounted our horse, leaving Quartz through a back alley before heading up the coast towards Tourmaline Cove as the sun set. We continued on to a rocky area near the sea, finding a secluded dip where we'd be hidden from any prying eyes, although we judged it best not to light a fire. As the last light left the sky, I climbed up the rocks and looked out over the darkening countryside. A distant glow marked the position of the town, but other than that there were no lights, no sign of any life out in the countryside. I clambered back down to our natural little amphitheatre looking out towards the sea and sat down beside Rian.

'So, who is Onyx, and what was so important he had to say it to you alone?' Rian asked, looking out across the now moonlit water, his body tense.

'Onyx grew up in the castle with us,' I said, suddenly consumed by a sense of awkwardness. 'His mother is from Mere, his father from Iolite, but they settled here in Iolite. His father died when he was a baby, and his mother works in the castle kitchens. Anyway, when Mal and I were pushed to the fringes, he became more than a friend.'

'More than a friend,' Rian repeated, the muscles in his face taut in the moonlight. 'I always wondered if someone in Iolite had your heart.'

'I only meant that he became like family, nothing more,' I said, glancing at Rian. 'He was telling me to look after you, that's all.' My heart hammered with the intensity of a blacksmith at his anvil.

Rian raised an eyebrow as he turned to look at me. 'Why should he care about me? He doesn't even know me.'

My face grew hot, and I looked away. I couldn't tell him his life could be in danger and it was all my fault. 'Does it matter?'

'It might do,' Rian said.

'He's worried that if your father and brother are in danger, you might be, too, so he was telling me to take care of you.' I felt unable to tell him the full truth, and the thought of voicing what Onyx had suggested I do broke my heart. Despite the risk to both of us, I couldn't bear the thought of now leaving Rian.

'And that's it, nothing more?' he asked. I shook my head. 'And you're sure you're just friends?'

'I'm sure,' I said. This really couldn't be any more embarrassing if he tried. 'Anyway, Onyx has a boyfriend.'

'Oh, I didn't realise.' Rian hesitated a moment. 'Does crossing Blood Classes bother you?' he asked, looking out towards the sea again.

'Other than the fact that to do so would mean Demotion or death, you mean?'

He gave me a wry smile.

'Someone said to me recently, you can't help who you fall in love with,' I said.

'Who said that to you?' Rian asked, frowning.

'Anise.'

Rian nodded and sighed. 'Yes, he would say that – Willow and Tarragon have the same problem.'

'I can't say I've noticed it stopping them,' I said.

'I'll have to tell them to be more careful,' he said with a smile. 'I intend to get the Blood Rule Decree changed, do away with it entirely.'

'Why was it introduced in the first place?'

Rian chewed his lip. 'I was told that eighteen hundred-odd years ago, King Yarrow introduced the law. It was supposed to keep the Blood Lines pure, so the blood of royalty and the nobility wasn't muddied by the middle classes, and the middle classes stayed clear of the lower ones. It also dictated your path in life, whether prince, merchant or farmer. You could only ever stay in your allotted place. Everyone was forced into a Blood Class and there they've stayed ever since, generation after generation. Asinine, really.'

'You think you can change it?'

'I hope so. However it was intended, it's become oppressive. If you love someone, you should be able to be with them. Even if they come from a different Land.' He glanced towards me.

'I think you're right about that,' I said, glad he couldn't see my red face in the darkness. 'But didn't an Aerban Prince try to overturn the law once before and end up being executed for it?'

'Yes, but I don't intend to make the same mistakes as Prince Mace. Let's get some rest.' He organised his blankets and I joined him under them. We hadn't had the opportunity to buy more, and a part of me was secretly glad.

I looked up at the sparkling night sky. 'No Iolitian has ever had my heart,' I said quietly.

My feelings for this young Aerban Prince were growing exponentially every day, and I couldn't stop them even if I wanted to.

Rian slipped his arm around me, pulling me to him. 'Good,' he murmured.

My pulse was loud in my ears as I felt his breath on my neck. 'Is there someone in Aerba that has yours?'

'No, never,' he said, sleepily. 'And they never will, now.'

My heart pounded at his words. It was as I'd hoped. As Willow had said. He had no one special back in Aerba.

I now had the distinct impression he felt the same for me as I did for him. But it wasn't that simple. The Blood Rules saw to that. Rian may want to change them, but at present, that was how things stood. Even if he wanted to be completely open with me, make the first move, he couldn't, and I understood why. And for the same reasons, neither could I. It was an invisible line that neither of us could cross, however dearly we might want to. His breathing altered and slowed as he went straight to sleep. I lay in his arms under the stars, a steady yearning coursing through me. Sandalwood gently caressed me, calming my mind and my body, and eventually, I slipped off to sleep.

The sun woke me as it rose in the sky, gulls crying over the water as puffy white clouds drifted overhead. I sat up. Rian still slept peacefully beside me, and I took the opportunity to move a wisp of maroon hair from his cheek.

I pulled Father's book out from my tunic and opened the pages. Some had stuck together after getting wet, but most were still fine. A large section of the book talked of Elemental Angle Spinners, of the five Elements, and a little about Quintessence Angle Spinners. There were never more than two alive at any one time, and they could be identified by a birthmark on one wrist – not that the book had an image to show what it looked like. There was also a large section on Artefacts, and how Spinners could focus Magic through them and enhance their powers. Finally, I turned a page and found a section on curses.

'What are you doing?' Rian asked, opening a sleepy eye.

'Looking at my father's book,' I said.

'Is that what you took from the castle?'

I nodded. 'It's a book about Elemental Angle Spinners and Artefacts.'

Rian sat up. 'But I thought all those books had been burnt.'

'Not this one. Father was interested in history and he showed this to me. He had it hidden in a special drawer in his desk, but until our visit to the library I hadn't realised why.'

'Does it have anything that will help us break the Curse?' he asked, peering at the pages.

'I'm not sure yet,' I said. 'I've just come across this bit which says *"Curses can only be placed on Artefacts by Quintessence Angle Spinners. They, too, are the only ones that can break those curses, regardless of the Elemental Magic contained in the Artefact."*

'That's a start.'

'Don't suppose you know any Quintessence Angle Spinners that might be able to break a curse?'

'There aren't any anymore,' he said. 'Anyway, how would you identify one?'

'The book says something about a birthmark, but it's extremely vague.'

'So, we're no further ahead.'

I flicked through the pages. I came to a couple stuck together and gently prised them apart. ' *"Some Elemental Curses can be broken using particular natural remedies. The 'Remedy For All Ills' is one such elixir."* A little butterfly of hope danced in my chest. Maybe all wasn't lost.

Rian moved my hand to look at the page himself. 'Could that be in the book Agate gave you?'

'Let's hope so,' I said, desperate to get back to the ship and find out.

'So, how did a Magic Spinner use their Magic?'

'From what I've read, they simply had to focus on what they wanted their Element to do.'

'I wish I'd been taught properly about this,' Rian said.

'Why weren't you?'

He shrugged. 'Probably because Magic was in the past, not something used these days, so it wasn't seen as being relevant. Tarragon only learnt about it because he came to the University here.'

'Why didn't you come?' I asked.

'I wanted to, even managed to get myself a place, but in the end, Father wouldn't allow it. Said I'd learn more being in Aerba.'

'But Tarragon went anyway?'

Rian nodded. 'Lord Wintergreen is more open to learning than my father.'

'Just think, if you'd come, we might have met earlier.'

'We might,' he said, gazing at me.

The distant sound of horses' hooves made me roll out from the blankets and jump to my feet.

'What is it?' Rian asked.

'I'm not sure, maybe nothing,' I said, putting the book back into my tunic and scrambling out the amphitheatre, looking out towards Quartz. Not far away, a group of horsemen galloped in our direction, led by Feldspar. I glanced over towards Tourmaline Cove where a sailing ship cut its way towards the bay. Time to go.

'It's the Coterie,' I said to Rian as I climbed back down.

He swiftly got to his feet, grabbing his bags.

'Leave them,' I said, launching myself onto our horse as Aldorbana and Cwicsusl appeared on my back.

Rian joined me and we rode towards Tourmaline Cove as the sailing ship made its way into the calm waters, its sails billowing in the wind. I looked at the terrain ahead then glanced at the chasing Coterie Assassins.

'We're going to have to jump and swim for it,' I said, the wind catching my breath as we galloped along.

'What?' Rian asked from behind me.

'We'll never get down to the beach quickly enough; the path is too treacherous,' I said, steering our horse towards the cliff top and away from the little scree path. With the Coterie almost upon us, we dismounted and ran towards the cliff edge.

I peered over, looking down at the water. It wouldn't be too bad – only about thirty feet high, nothing we couldn't manage.

'Ready?' I glanced at Rian – why did he suddenly look so pale?

'Let's do it,' he said, taking hold of my hand.

We took a few steps back, then ran for the cliff edge, launching ourselves off into emptiness. Air rushed past my ears in a blast before I hit the water, bubbles hurtling around me as I sank down. I came to a gradual halt and struck out for the surface, pushing up, kicking hard, breaking through the waves, Aldorbana and Cwicsusl not hindering me as much as I thought they might. I twisted around in the water, trying to find Rian, but I couldn't see him. An icy hand clutched at my heart.

'Rian!' I spun around, desperately looking for him, but the churning water refused to give up her treasure.

'Phire, he can't swim,' Tarragon yelled from the prow of the approaching ship.

'Hell's teeth.' My heart froze as I scanned the surface of the water, but I couldn't see Rian anywhere – why hadn't he said something before we jumped? 'Where is he?' I shouted back.

'He went in over there.' Anise pointed to a patch of sea not far from me.

I swam over towards it, fighting my way through the swirling waves as they rushed towards the cliffs, and then took a deep breath before diving down into the water. Fish and seaweed swept past me, but no Rian. Running out of air, I swam back to the surface, my pulse beating away in my ears. Again, I dived back down, fear and desperation circling me like vultures as I searched for him underwater, fighting the currents. Where was he?

I couldn't find him, couldn't see him in the water. I surfaced again. I'd almost lost him once to Juniper; I wouldn't lose him to the sea. I dived again, further down into the darker depths of the churning water – over there.

I saw him, struggling against the current, but each stroke he took was a little weaker than the last. I swam towards him, desperation spurring me on. I grabbed the neck of his shirt and pulled him skyward. He kicked feebly, trying to help me and, after what felt like an eternity, we broke the surface. I gasped as I grabbed Rian under his arms, keeping him afloat as he choked and coughed.

'Are you all right?' I asked, my heart hammering away, worry filling me as I held him tighter than necessary.

'Thanks to you,' he said, his voice weak. 'I thought that was it for a moment.'

'Don't try and swim. I'll pull you; you just lie still,' I said, moving us towards the waiting ship. 'You should've told me you couldn't swim.'

'We didn't have much of a choice at the time,' he said.

'You still should've told me,' I said as he coughed again. If only he'd said, I'd have found another way to get to the ship – one that didn't involve him drowning. As we reached the ship, Captain Feverfew dropped a rope ladder over the side, and Rian slowly climbed aboard. I followed, clambering up onto the deck as Rian sank to his knees, coughing again. I put my arms around him. I could feel him shaking, but whether from the cold water or shock or both, I couldn't be sure.

'I'm all right,' he said, still catching his breath.

I rested my head on his shoulder, shaking a little myself. I'd so nearly lost him. Tears welled in my eyes, but I blinked them away.

'You had us worried,' Sage said.

'We thought you were going to drown,' Tarragon said as I let go of Rian.

Anise ran over, brandishing a small, red glass vial of liquid. 'Drink this, Rian. It'll help,' he said, handing it over.

Rian looked up. 'Thanks,' he said, shakily taking the tincture bottle and swallowing the contents of the vial. 'That whole experience is one I want to forget.' He passed the empty vial back to Anise.

'Bugger me, Phire, you saved his life,' Tarragon said, pulling me to my feet and giving me a hug. He and the others were back in their Aerban clothes, their hair up in high ponytails.

'Again,' Rian said, a rueful expression on his face.

'Let's get underway,' Willow said, moving off towards Captain Feverfew.

'Tarragon, we need to get back to Viridi as quickly as possible,' I said, wiping water from my eyes. 'The Coterie have a commission to kill King Finule and Prince Chervil.'

'What?' Tarragon asked, all colour draining from his face.

'It's true,' Rian said, standing up with Anise's help. 'Apparently someone wants me on the throne.'

'But who?' Sage asked, his earring sending a flash of light across the deck as his face paled.

'Juniper wouldn't say, but they're both in danger,' I said, the cold from the seawater and my damp clothes making me shiver.

Tarragon nodded and ran off towards Willow and Feverfew.

'Would she really do that?' Sage asked, looking at me with a horrified expression on his face.

'She would,' I said. 'She has no compunction about killing – as long as she gets paid.'

'Did you find out anything about the Fire Opal?' Anise asked.

'Only that Flos may be a place to start looking,' Rian said, wringing water out of his hair.

'Flos? This just keeps getting worse,' Sage said, a sour expression spreading across his face.

'We will get it back,' Rian said, a grim note to his voice.

'Are we any closer to finding the princess' murderer?' Willow asked as she and Tarragon returned. 'Or who commissioned it?'

'We know who killed her, just not who arranged it, or who's arranged the other assassinations.'

'So, who killed the princess?' Sage asked, holding the hilt of his knife.

'One of the Coterie, as expected,' Rian said.

'And where is this Coterie member now?'

I waited for Rian to tell them about Mal, but he simply said,

'He's either dead or imprisoned somewhere, but wherever he is, he's beyond our reach.'

'Shame,' Sage said, letting go of his knife hilt. If Sage ever did find out it'd been Mal that'd killed the princess, some very fast talking would be required.

'You two better get out of your wet things,' Willow said.

We headed into the ship, Rian pulling his tunic and shirt off as we went, leaving him naked down to the waist. As the outside door shut, he suddenly stopped in the passageway and turned towards me. I hadn't realised what he was doing and walked into him, my hands bracing on his lean, muscular chest as I came to a halt. I could feel his heart beating under my hand, his skin warm despite the cold water. My hands lingered for a moment before I realised what I was doing. I swallowed and took a step back.

'Sorry,' I said, flustered. I quickly drew my hands behind me, knowing full well my face was going red.

He looked at me, his eyes soft, as a small smile spread over his face, lighting his pupils with fire. 'That's all right. I just wanted to say thank you. You saved my life, and I won't forget it.'

'I wasn't going to let you drown.'

'I don't think you'd have worried about it when we first met.'

I cringed as I thought back. 'Mind you, I seem to remember you had a knife at my throat in that creek.'

He winced. Rubbed the back of his neck. 'I did, didn't I?'

'But things have changed a lot since then, haven't they?' I said.

'They have?'

'Of course. You're my friend now.'

Was that a flicker of disappointment in his eyes?

He looked down. 'I thought that maybe–'

'And I care about you,' I said, my heart skipping.

The flicker vanished. A little lopsided grin appeared.

'I care about you too,' he said, reaching out and running a finger down the side of my face. His warm hand did nothing for my heartrate as sandalwood swirled in the air around me, but it did help my shivering. He wasn't a High Blood Prince to me anymore. He was something far more. He stepped back.

'You know, if the Coterie succeed, you'll be king,' I said, looking at him. 'You'd be able to rip up the Blood Rule Decree, change things in Aerba.'

His smile faded.

'Sorry, I shouldn't have said that,' I said, mentally kicking myself for my unguarded words. What would he think of me, suggesting he was better off without his father and brother?

'The same thing's crossed my mind since Juniper spoke of the assassinations,' Rian said, a conflicted look in his eyes. 'But not only can I not let my father and brother die, I'm not sure I'd want to be king.'

'Even if you could make those changes?'

'My dearest wish is to make things better in Aerba, for the people, the Land. But I'm not sure I'm cut out for something like that.'

I didn't think that was true. He'd shown me so many of those qualities already – leadership, diplomacy, mercy, and above all, kindness.

'I think you could do it if you had to,' I said. The ship hit a wave, making me lurch forward. I came to rest, my hands once more lying on Rian's bare chest. I glanced up at him, my heart pounding. He covered my hands with his, leaving mine resting where they were on his warm skin, his wrists still red and raw from the shackles.

'I'm touched you have such faith in me,' he said.

'I trust you, that's all.' I could feel his heart racing under my fingertips.

'I'm glad because I trust you too.'

I looked up into his eyes, struggling to breathe, his touch scorching, his eyes flickering embers as his pupils dilated. His lips parted slightly as he leant towards me a little. Then all at once, he stepped back, letting go of me.

'We'd better get changed,' he said, moving away.

As I watched him go, my heart pounded and my breath caught in my throat.

Putting my purple coat on again couldn't have made me happier, and as we sailed away from Iolite, I took one last look at my home. So many varied emotions had bubbled to the surface during this visit, most of them unpleasant, but in some ways the experience had been cathartic. As Iolite slipped into the distance, Rian came out of the cabin in his burgundy coat, his hair back to normal.

'How are your wrists?' I asked.

'Fine,' he said, glancing at them. The angry red had been replaced by pink. 'Anise gave me something for them.'

I nodded, holding Father's book that I'd retrieved from my wet tunic. It was even more bedraggled now, and I feared I'd lost its contents for good.

'Do you know if Anise has been through the whole remedy book?' I asked.

'He's just finishing up now,' Rian said. 'In fact, he sent me to get you.'

'*He* sent *you*?' I asked. 'I thought you were the prince.'

Rian made a face. 'I make an exception for Anise. Let's go.' Rian took my hand and led me to the cabin where everyone waited.

The aged remedy book looked as if it would crumble to pieces at any moment, creaking and rustling like dry leaves as Anise flipped through it. The writing had dimmed with age, and in some places, you couldn't make it out at all.

'Have you found anything?' Rian asked, peering at the page Anise studied with interest.

'There's a possible remedy I've come across,' Anise said. 'But I'm not sure about it.'

'Is there a "Remedy For All Ills"?' I asked.

Anise looked at me sharply and frowned. 'That's the one I was looking at. You've heard of it?'

'I collected a book of my fathers from the castle, and it said that some Elemental Curses could be broken by the "Remedy For All Ills".'

'If you've come across it, too, then maybe it is the right one,' he said, running his finger down the page, his face now alight with excitement. He was totally in his element. 'Hang on, yes, this bit, *"An elixir of Wormwood, Mint, Saliivia, and Cilantro Moonflower petals"*.'

Rian groaned from where he stood beside me.

'The only problem is the Cilantro Moonflower,' Anise said.

'Why?' Sage asked, turning to him.

'They're almost impossible to come by.'

'Almost?' Sage asked.

'They grow in southern Aerba, in the Cilantro Rainforest, in areas that are sometimes flooded by acidic rivers,' Anise said. 'They're extremely rare, only blooming between sunset and sunrise for one night, hence their name. I believe they're most likely to be found in the gardens of the ancient palace in the Old Cilantro Citadel ruins.'

'Aren't there monsters in the Cilantro Rainforest?' Willow asked.

'That's just a myth,' Tarragon said, looking unconcerned. 'I think there are some still in Burnet Forest, but not Cilantro. They've all been killed down there.'

'And what time of year do these Cilantro Moonflowers bloom?' Rian asked.

'Late spring or early summer, so anytime now,' Anise said. 'Although, they're toxic, too.'

'There's always something,' I said, rolling my eyes.

'The other herbs aren't too hard to come by, though.'

'I need to try and get these things together; it may be my one chance,' I said, looking at Rian. His face had so many different emotions etched into it I couldn't begin to unravel them all.

'I'll help you, Phire,' Anise said. 'You'll need me to prepare the Moonflower Elixir.'

'Thank you,' I said, smiling at him.

'But if the Moonflower is toxic...' Sage paused, looking at his boyfriend.

'Many herbs are toxic, Sage, but if used correctly they can be safe remedies,' Anise said.

'It's not as if I'm not going to die anyway,' I said, glancing over my back at the Cursed Weapons. 'I have to take any chance I can.'

Rian nodded. 'Let's get to Borage first,' he said. 'We can make further plans from there.'

We spent two days with good winds and calm seas. Despite this, Willow had to make use of Anise's remedies.

I sat below deck on a barrel, on my own, having found a quiet corner to think. Onyx's words kept swirling in my mind – and I knew he was right. It'd been growing for a while, and now my love for Rian was undeniable. I really did love him, and if I loved him, how could I leave him? But how could I, in all good conscience, stay with him and possibly be the cause of his death? I couldn't. I bit my lip. I'd have to leave, let him go. I swallowed. A dull ache formed in my chest at the prospect. I had to keep him alive, and I knew that would be the only way. Beryl would leave him alone once she knew I was nowhere near him. She'd have no reason to kill him then if she thought I wasn't interested in him, because it would make no difference to me. Killing him wouldn't hurt me. It was Rian's only chance.

I still needed to find the Elixir, though, and for that I'd need Anise. Once we got back to Aerba, Rian would probably feel duty-bound to return to his father and report what had happened before we went in search of the ingredients – assuming King Finule would even consider letting us go to find them. I couldn't risk that; I didn't have the luxury of time. I'd have to give Rian the slip before we got back to Viridi. In fact, I needed to head south the moment we reached land to get to the Cilantro Citadel – and I needed Anise with me.

I left my barrel and went out on deck. The others were sitting near the bow, chatting happily as the last of the sun dipped below the flaming horizon, but not Anise – maybe he was in the main cabin. I walked over and peered into the room. I'd found him.

'How many of those have you made for Willow, now?' I asked Anise as I stepped into the cabin and sat down, watching him make up one of his remedies for seasickness.

Anise grinned. 'More than I can count,' he said in his butter-smooth voice. 'I'll need to stock up on herbs before we go on any more voyages.'

'Is Willow's seasickness the worst you've had to deal with?'

'No.' Anise shook his head. 'Chervil's is worse.'

'Chervil.' I screwed up my nose at the mention of his name. 'I've only spent a few minutes in a room with him, but I wouldn't want to spend a whole sea voyage stuck on a small ship with him. I'd probably end up throwing him overboard.'

Anise smiled. 'Rian almost did once.'

'Really?'

'Chervil started an argument about something trivial and turned it into a fight – this was about seven or eight years ago, so they were a lot younger. Anyway, Rian almost had Chervil over the rail when Finule stopped them. He gave Rian a real dressing down.'

'But not Chervil?' I frowned.

Anise paused, his eyes far away for a moment. 'Queen Myrtle, Rian's mother, died when he was very young. She was a beautiful woman, or so they say – I was only small when she died. Anyway, Rian takes after her, not just in personality, but in looks, too. It seems Finule found that hard to deal with when she died. In fact, I don't believe he's ever accepted it.'

'That's why Finule treats Rian so badly, because he reminds him of his mother?'

Anise nodded.

'That's horrible,' I said, my heart breaking for Rian.

Anise shrugged. 'After his mother's death, Rian was pushed to the side. He's never been considered important in the line of succession, until now, and Angelica and Chervil always treated him quite badly. They inherited the ruthless streak from their father, whereas Rian's always had the kindness of their mother. The thing is, Rian isn't soft like they think; he has a steel inside him, a strength they don't understand because it doesn't come with cruelty.'

I nodded. The more time I spent with Rian and his friends, the more I understood the prince. And the more I cared about him.

'Chervil certainly doesn't endear himself to anyone,' I said, 'he truly hates me, but then, he's convinced I murdered his beloved sister.'

Anise laughed.

I looked sharply at him. 'What?'

'Chervil had no great love for Angelica, quite the opposite.'

'But he said to me–'

'Whoever killed Angelica did him a favour,' Anise said, adding another herb to his concoction. 'Chervil always wanted to be king but would never have moved against Angelica himself. When Angelica died, he couldn't let anyone know how pleased he was, least of all Finule, who doted on Angelica as much as he did Chervil. No, Chervil's had to put on a front, make out he's devastated at the loss of his "dearest sister", and make sure all the blame's with you. Things couldn't be better for him.'

I sat there, taking in Anise's words. Everything he said made sense. That was why Chervil had reacted the way he had that day. He really had been protesting his love for his sister too much.

'Rian only found a purpose, and a place, when Lord Wintergreen suggested he lead the King's Warriors,' Anise continued. 'After that, I think Rian was happier, and he got to spend time away from Court with Tarragon, Sage, and me.' He turned and smiled at me, the loveliest smile I'd ever seen.

Anise had succeeded in charming his way into my heart these past few weeks, and I cherished him for it. And not just him. I suddenly found myself surrounded by friends – true friends. People I could actually trust. It felt strange, but wonderful, too. But it couldn't last. I knew deep down what I had to do. By staying together, I was endangering Rian's life – something I couldn't do for much longer. I didn't want to leave him, but Onyx was right – I had to leave him to keep him safe.

'Anise?'

'Yes?'

I bowed my head. 'I've been told the Coterie are after Rian – at least as long as I stay with him.' I looked up – Anise had stopped what he was doing. 'Would you consider coming with me, alone, to make the Moonflower Elixir?'

Anise took a long breath. 'Without any of the others?'

'I don't know how else to keep them all safe.'

'Does Rian know about the Coterie?'

'He knows he might be in danger, but only because the Coterie already have commissions for his father and brother – not the real reason.'

'You staying with him? Being together?'

I nodded. 'I'm worried that if I tell him, he'll insist on staying with me anyway.'

'If you leave without him, Rian *will* come after you.'

'Because of his father's orders?'

He shook his head. 'No, not because of that.'

My heart did a little flip. 'If I stay, I'm putting everyone in danger because they could get caught up in any assassination attempt. Rian's the one in their sights, and the whole idea of the Coterie killing him makes me...' I hesitated. 'I don't want him to die because of me, Anise. And I don't want to go back to Viridi before we head south, which Rian may feel obliged to do – I don't have the time. I have to go now.'

Anise nodded slowly. 'I understand all that. But you do realise that he really stands the best chance of survival with you by his side, don't you?'

'You think so?'

'I do. You have the skills and the determination to protect him.'

I chewed on a nail. 'And if I can't protect him? If he dies, it'll be all my fault.'

Anise sighed. 'Even if I come with you, he'll never agree to letting you go after the Moonflower Elixir without him.'

'Does he have to know we're going ahead of time? We might be able to slip away without him knowing exactly where we've gone, before dawn, the day after we get to Borage.'

The King's Warrior rubbed his chin. 'Maybe. Let's see how things turn out once we get to Borage. Whatever happens, though, I will come with you to get the ingredients – one way or another.'

I smiled. 'Thank you,' I said, encouraged by his words. I would keep Rian safe. 'Please don't tell him he's in danger because of me – I don't want him thinking ill of me.'

Anise looked at me. 'I won't, but you should tell him. I don't think he'll mind. I mean, he'll want to know, and he won't think any less of you because of what the Coterie are doing. After all, he does lo–' Anise hesitated. 'It doesn't matter. But he won't mind.'

'I will tell him – when the time's right.'

On the third day, I took up residence at the prow, welcoming the salty air and the rushing of the waves. Footsteps came up behind me, then hesitated. I turned to see Rian, his face pale, strained.

'Phire, the shield,' Rian said, his voice taut.

'What about it?' I asked, taking the shield off. I froze, goose pimples covering my body.

Tarragon, who stood behind Rian, had a face that said it all.

'Oh, bobbins,' Willow said, peering over Tarragon's shoulder. 'The colour's beginning to drain.'

Although most of Cwicsusl still shone blood red in the sun, the very top of the shield now stood crystal clear. I grabbed Aldorbana from its scabbard. The top of the sword by the hilt stood clear too. A cold rush swept through me and I struggled to swallow, my throat and mouth suddenly as dry as the southeast Aerban deserts.

I didn't feel any different in myself – a little tired, perhaps, but that was only to be expected under the circumstances. Still, the Weapons told a different truth.

I slipped Aldorbana back into place between my shoulder blades, bile rising in my throat. 'It's not as if we didn't know this was going to happen,' I said, gritting my teeth, returning Cwicsusl to my back.

'But not so soon,' Rian whispered.

I tried to smile at him. 'I'm not beaten yet. We have a remedy for the Curse now.'

At least, I hoped we did.

CHAPTER TWELVE

I couldn't sleep that night as I swung in my hammock below decks. So many things spiralled and spun about in my mind. Mal's fate. Father's death. Beryl's betrayal. Moonflower Elixirs and Cursed Weapons. Rian.

Rian.

Amber eyes filled my mind. The memory of his warm body next to mine filled me with a calmness and contentment I'd never felt before. And all because I loved him. I knew that without a doubt now.

It could never work, though, and I think we both knew it. The longer things went on, the more I knew it was true. He was High Blood, and I was Middle Blood, not to mention an ex-member of the Iolitian Coterie of Assassins. Hardly prime material for a Prince of Aerba at the best of times. As it was, the Blood Rules were clear, and neither of us were in a position to do anything about them. Not without significant risk to both our lives, at any rate. I sighed. My cause there was lost before it had even begun. I should just concentrate on breaking the Curse and finding Mal.

It just wasn't that easy. I couldn't turn my feelings on and off. And it was because of that I'd have to go. Parting from him would keep him alive, although it would kill a piece of me. In some ways, Beryl would succeed, whatever happened.

I shifted and almost fell out of the hammock. *Hell's teeth.* I climbed out and quietly made my way up the steps and out onto the deck. I stood at the rail, looking out at the splash of red and purple on the horizon, heralding the dawn. My hand clasped my Amethyst Talisman, and I ran my fingers over its facets and wires as I thought. According to what Feverfew had said at our evening meal last night, we should reach Borage late this afternoon. I'd abscond with Anise, before dawn, to find the herbs for the Elixir. I just had to persuade Anise that it was the best thing to do. I'd no idea how long I had left, now; neither did I have any idea how long Mal had. The sooner I broke the Curse, the sooner I could find him.

'Mind if I join you?' Rian had appeared from the sleeping quarters.

I shook my head. 'Sorry, did I wake you?'

'No, I haven't been able to sleep that well since we got on board, not without–' He hesitated, a touch of red appearing high on his cheeks, his hand going to the back of his neck. 'It's the movement.'

I took a deep breath of sea air to calm the rising sensation of warmth filling my chest. 'At least getting up at this time means it's quieter on deck,' I said.

'You prefer the silence?'

'Not necessarily silence, just fewer people. I don't have to look over my shoulder quite so much if the place is deserted.'

'That sounds rather lonely,' Rian said, his expression grave.

'Yes,' I said. 'It can be. But it feels safer.'

He frowned. 'I get the impression you've lived your life in constant fear.'

'Only since Father died. Up until then, things were fine. More than fine. The last few years have been hard, though. And lonely.'

'You know, I've always had people around me,' Rian said, leaning on the rail as he watched the foaming waves. 'But, despite that, sometimes I've felt so lonely. Mother doted on me, but died when I was young. She was the only one who I really think cared about me. She's been gone for so long; I just have impressions of her now. Her love, her warmth. Until you, those feelings were just wonderful memories. Now, with you by my side, for the first time since then, I feel whole again.'

My breathing grew shallow as I gazed out at the water so he couldn't see my red face. It was funny, but I rather felt that way as well, although it just made things harder.

'You really mean that?' I asked.

'I do.'

I hesitated a moment. 'My mother died when I was young, too, but I still had Father, Mal, and Beryl. Or, so I thought, anyway. We all got on well, until Juniper wormed her way into the castle. Once she'd ensnared Father, Mal and I were on the fringes of everything. Beryl and Elm were the favoured ones. She managed to distance me from any friends I'd had, except for Onyx.'

Rian stiffened slightly. 'Maybe I should thank him – for sticking beside you.' His voice was strange, not quite in tune with his words.

'He was just too obstinate to listen to her threats. Stayed by me and Mal when everyone else was scared off.'

'A real friend.'

I nodded. 'We needed his friendship more than ever when Father died, or should I say, was murdered,' I said, watching the flaming sunrise. Rian's tense muscles relaxed as he slipped an arm around my shoulders. 'After he'd died, Mal and I found ourselves being trained as assassins. We had no choice in the matter, and we were too young to escape. I hated every moment of it, so did Mal, but however reluctant we were, we had to comply. Ever since Father died, Juniper has had this hold on us.'

'You mean Beryl?' Rian asked, a softness to his voice.

I nodded. 'If we'd known Beryl was working with her all along, perhaps Mal and I could've escaped, but we didn't,' I said, a bitter tinge to my voice. 'Juniper did her best to split Mal and I up, sending one of us on a mission while keeping the other at the Castle, or sending us in opposite directions. All part of her elaborate scheme to keep us in check. So, you see, I've known loss and loneliness, too, in my own way. Until I met you,' I said, turning towards him, glad the angry sunrise would mask the blush on my face.

Rian turned to me, pausing a moment to gaze into my eyes before pulling me to him. He held me in his arms, his warm breath on my neck, the smell of sandalwood swirling around us. I could have remained that way forever, safe in his embrace. He moved back ever so slightly, lifting his fingers to gently stroke the side of my face. 'In some ways, you seem quite an old soul.'

I shrugged. 'No more than you. We both had to grow up quickly, that's all.'

'Well, neither of us will ever be lonely again. We have each other, now,' he said, his gorgeous amber eyes dilating. 'I swear it.'

I wished it were true, but I knew I'd be leaving him in a few hours. I gazed into his eyes for what seemed like an eternity, drowning in pools of amber liquid, imprinting this memory into my mind for when I didn't have him with me. If only he'd kiss me, give me something to cling to in the hard days and cold nights ahead...

But I knew he wouldn't, however much his body language said he wanted to.

There was a shout from the Crow's Nest high above us, and the captain came running out onto the deck.

'Everyone outside!' Captain Feverfew yelled, ringing the ship's bell. 'We've got a storm coming in.'

'What?' I turned to where the captain looked. On the horizon, dark, menacing clouds gathered as if waiting to pounce on us.

'That's not only a pretty sunrise,' Feverfew said, coming over to us as Rian let go of me. ''Tis a warning.'

'What is it?' Tarragon asked, running out on deck.

'There's a storm coming,' Rian said.

Tarragon turned green. 'Anise! Where are you? I'm going to need your Herb Chest.'

I looked back out at the roiling clouds moving towards us as he dashed off to the main cabin. Sailors appeared on deck, rushing to adjust the sails, climbing the rigging, and tying down any loose cargo. The wind suddenly picked up, catching the waves which rose to form large monsters that crashed over the side of the ship's rail.

'Get into the cabin,' Feverfew ordered. 'This is going to be a rough ride.'

Rian nodded and grasped my hand as we headed into the main cabin.

'You're sure?' Willow asked.

'That's what the captain said,' Tarragon replied as he watched Anise hastily preparing a tincture.

'I don't like being at sea.'

'Neither do I. If we make it back to land, I'm never going on board a ship again.'

'If?' Sage raised an eyebrow.

The ship lurched as a wave crashed over the deck, sending water into the cabin. Rian and Sage quickly pulled the doors shut. The pitching and rolling had me grabbing for a post to keep me upright. The howling shriek of the wind, as waves broke across the ship, rose in a thunderous bellow. The wood around me groaned, chains clanked, the rigging creaked, and above it all, the ship's bell rang out a mournful, irregular rhythm.

I stood there clinging to the post, desperate for the sea to calm. Tarragon and Willow's faces were green, even though Anise had given them his tincture. The others clutched whatever happened to be nailed down as the storm began throwing the ship around like a child gleefully tossing about a rag doll. We lurched violently, vibrations rattling through the floor and tearing through the hull. The sails wailing on the masts high above the deck wept for those below. I shuddered.

For more than an hour, we endured the horrific weather as rain joined the onslaught. Then, suddenly, an enormous grinding sound jolted through the timbers of the ship, followed by the crack of splitting wood. The cabin doors were yanked open, rain and seawater gushing in with a blast of wind. Above the ship, the foremast stood broken, sails flapping impotently.

'We've hit rocks!' Captain Feverfew yelled. 'Get above deck. We're going down.'

Easier said than done.

The ship listed, sending me away from the doors as I clutched at the post, holding on until the ship lurched the other way. The others started to scramble and climb towards the doors. Rian grabbed my hand, pulling me along. We reached the doors and hauled ourselves out onto the deck as a huge wave crashed into the side of the ship, and I lost hold of Rian's hand. The force of the water threw me backwards into the cabin, slamming me against the far wall, shutting one of the doors.

'Samphire!' Rian's alarmed yell rang above the storm as he clung onto the doorframe.

A huge creak made the hairs on the back of my neck stand on end. The ship lunged to the starboard. Rian was launched across the deck, disappearing from view as the broken foremast fell. The other door slammed shut as an almighty crash echoed outside, the sound of splintering timbers rising above the storm. I scrambled to the doors. Pushed on them. Another jerk knocked the cabin lamp free. It hit the floor, smashed, and suddenly the cabin lit with the orange glow of flames. I threw myself against the doors.

They wouldn't budge.

The mast must have come to rest against them, wedging them shut. I turned. The flames licked at the tarry wood, desperate for food. I'd wondered if I might drown – burning to death at sea hadn't even occurred to me. I heaved on the door again, but to no avail. Fear stalked me. There was no way out through the door, and the cabin window rested against rocks. I had no escape.

My heart hammered in my chest as the ship rocked again, and a moment later the main mast came screaming through the ceiling of the cabin. I ducked as planks and splinters of wood cascaded around me, stabbing into the floor and walls. A sudden chink of light broke through the cabin roof. The hole the main mast had gouged out provided me with a sliver of hope, although my escape route happened to be on the other side of the fire.

I slipped the Cursed Weapons from my back – they'd return to me soon enough. I took a couple of steps, then launched myself across the cabin, jumping the fire. I clambered up the broken wood, doing my best to avoid getting splinters, reached the mast, and started to climb. As I clawed my way up, I found my route blocked by fallen rigging. I grabbed my Fan, flicked it open, and pressed the amethyst button. The blades leapt out. With my heart thudding, I started to saw through the rigging. The ropes were old and tough, and although my War Fan was sharp, it took time to slice through them; time I didn't have, with the flames moving towards me. My muscles strained as I worked, the fire moving ever closer. I used all my strength to cut the ropes, and finally the rigging gave way – just as the flames licked the wood at my feet. I dragged myself up and out onto what remained of the quarter deck, resting on my hands and knees as I took a moment to get my breath back, the rain pummelling my back and head. That had been close. I pressed the button to retract the blades, then flipped the Fan shut, and looked around to the people clinging to the deck as my heart continued to pound in my ears. Immediately, an icy wave splashed over the deck, washing me to the rail. I shivered, gasping for air.

Suddenly, Rian appeared beside me, grabbing hold of me. 'Are you all right? I thought you were trapped.'

'I got lucky,' I said, bracing as another wave washed over us. 'We've got to get off this ship.'

'I know,' Rian said, a look of fear in his eyes I'd never seen before. That was when I remembered he couldn't swim.

'We'll do it together, trust me,' I said, squeezing his hand.

He turned and looked at me. 'I do trust you, with my life.'

A little chill ran through me at his words. I looked down over the broken deck. Sharp shards of splintered wood protruded at strange angles, making walking across it hazardous at best, suicidal at worst. The third mast wavered precariously above us as the rigging creaked and moaned in pain. The sea roared mercilessly as it crashed over the ship, and persistent rain lashed at those hanging onto the deck. Willow clung to Tarragon, who hung on to the remains of the main mast.

The wind tore at my face, whipping my wet hair around and sending it stinging into my eyes. The salt air burnt my lungs, and a chill grasped for my bones. A huge wave crashed over the deck, taking two sailors with it into the maelstrom. They broke the surface of the angry sea and were swept away. I shivered. Anise and Sage held on to a rail, both looking quite ill in the fiery glow from the cabin. Anise had his Herb Chest strapped to his back.

A wrenching sound, followed by a crunch, echoed above us. Rian ploughed into me, and the two of us fell onto the deck just as a great pulley swung inches over our heads. Rian landed on top of me, coming to rest with his face a whisker away from mine. For a moment, we lay staring into each other's eyes as the storm raged around us.

'Are you okay?' he asked, composing himself and pulling me up.

'Yes, thanks to you,' I said.

The fire had taken hold, and the heat from the flames fought the cold from the sea, sending a golden glow out over the water. The protesting timbers of the ship creaked and groaned, slowly pulling apart with a prolonged, ear-splitting crack.

'She's going to break apart,' Feverfew yelled from the main deck. 'Abandon ship!'

'We'll have to swim for it,' Tarragon said, his voice almost lost in the storm.

'How far away are we from land?' Sage shouted.

'Far enough,' I said, looking out towards the coast, which had to be a good half mile away across the boiling sea.

Another wave broke over the deck and a sailor went hurtling into the sea, vanishing beneath the large waves rising and falling around the hamstrung ship before reappearing – only to be dashed against the rocks on that side of the ship. The shocking sound of the ship's back breaking shuddered through the timbers. As the ship started to splinter apart, Willow and Tarragon made it to the side. The last I saw of them, they were making a grab for the rail, just as a huge wave came crashing over the deck, sweeping them into the sea along with several others.

I peered over the rail to the sea below us; a piece of broken deck from the front of the ship floated not far from the side. 'Get ready, we're going to jump,' I said, pulling Rian along with me.

'W-what?' His eyes widened in the dim light.

'Trust me and don't let go of my hand – we're aiming to reach that piece of decking. Ready? One, tw–'

A huge wave cascaded over the ship's side from behind us with all the fury of Juniper on a bad day, hurling us into the sea. Our clasped hands were wrenched from each other's grasp as the cruel waves yanked us apart.

CHAPTER THIRTEEN

The cold sea immediately had me in its clutches, tugging me remorselessly under the waves. I struggled against the raging water, swimming for the surface, only to be pulled down again, spiralling around as if caught in a whirlpool. I sank, despite my increasingly desperate attempts to escape the depths. It wouldn't beat me. I fought against it again. Kicked. Clawed at the water. Then my head burst through the surface of the sea. I coughed, gulping in the sweet air whilst trying to stay afloat in the huge waves. Rian surfaced only a few feet from me, and I swam over to him, grabbing his collar, pulling him towards the wooden decking as he choked and tried his own futile attempts to remain above the water.

'Hold on,' I said, grabbing hold of the slippery wood as best I could while the sea threatened to drag us back under. Rian grasped the decking, his knuckles white. 'Get on,' I urged, pushing him onto the wood.

'What about you?' he asked, trying to pull me up beside him.

'No, it won't bear both our weights. I'll hang on. I'm fine,' I said, looking around.

'But–'

The flaming ship cried out in a final lament, drowning out his words as it sank beneath the waves, a few sailors still on board, their cries chilling my soul.

The bell rang no more.

The Cursed Weapons suddenly appeared on my back. With their additional weight, I stood no chance of joining Rian on his raft, now. The wind continued to shriek, the waves crashing around us, and in the distance, the cries of the drowning sailors sent shivers down my spine. I tried to locate the others in the dim, grey light of the storm as the waves pummelled us, and I held onto the wood with increasingly numb fingers. Sage and Anise floated about twenty feet from us, hanging onto a broken piece of mast. Willow clung to a barrel, Tarragon swimming beside her. Several sailors thrashed about in the water, trying to reach their own makeshift floats. Relieved our friends were relatively safe, I started kicking, propelling us slowly but surely towards shore.

The closer we got to dry land, the bigger the waves grew, foaming with fury, before finally spitting us onto the beach. Rian and I clung to each other as we staggered from the water, stumbling as the surf washed around our legs, maliciously attempting to pull us back. We collapsed onto the wet sand, gasping for air. I shivered with cold and relief.

'I never want to go to sea again,' Rian muttered from where he lay beside me, attempting to catch his breath.

'Neither do I,' I said.

The survivors gathered on the beach as the storm blew itself out, and a hazy afternoon sun appeared in the clearing sky. Our party had all survived, along with a number of the crew, but Captain Feverfew and several of his men had been lost with the ship. I looked up and down the beach, searching for something that might help us. We had no packs, no supplies; nothing other than our weapons. I sat shivering, watching the surf running up the beach, shock riddling my mind as I tried to take in all that had happened.

'Get up and move,' Rian said, grabbing my arm and pulling me up. 'You need to warm up – I can't have you dying of cold.'

He rubbed his warm hands up and down my arms in an attempt to get my blood flowing.

'Don't you ever feel cold?' I asked him, surprised at how warm his hands were.

He shrugged. 'No, not really.'

I sighed.

'Well, that was fun,' Sage said from his place on the sand, a sour note to his voice.

'You're all right?' Anise asked, his hands on Sage's shoulders as he crouched in front of him, checking him over.

'I'm fine. Really. What about you?' Sage asked, looking into Anise's eyes.

'As long as all my herbs have survived, I'm fine too,' Anise said, moving to sit beside him now that he was certain he was okay. Opening his Herb Chest, Anise began inspecting the contents, his tongue poking between his lips.

'Put that away.'

'What?'

'Your tongue.'

'Leave me alone, I'm concentrating,' Anise said, studying the vials and bottles.

On our other side, Willow and Tarragon were lying on the sand, holding onto each other, breathing hard.

'I thought I'd lost you,' Willow said to Tarragon. 'One moment you were there, the next you went under and I couldn't see you. Then the water just seemed to spew you out.'

Tarragon tried to shrug within Willow's embrace. 'I rather hoped it would. Do you know where we are?' he asked a bedraggled sailor sitting on the sand near to them.

'We've washed up just east of Borage,' the sailor replied. 'It shouldn't be more than a couple of hours' walk. We were so close to making port when we went down.'

'I'm sorry about Captain Feverfew and your men,' Rian said.

'Comes with the territory, I'm afraid,' the sailor said. 'It's not my first wreck. It's just one of those things.'

Although I tried to keep moving in an attempt to warm up, a wave of exhaustion filled me. I removed Cwicsusl for a moment, to adjust its straps. I gasped as a shard of ice stabbed repeatedly in my gut, my heart suddenly racing. The scarlet had drained further, leaving a bit more of the shield crystal clear – was this why exhaustion plagued me? Or could it be that the more I struggled the quicker the Cursed Weapons drained my life energy? I sighed and replaced the shield, catching Rian's eye as I did so. From the look on his face, he'd noticed the change in the shield, too.

'Let's get going,' he said, taking my hand and leading the way. 'The sooner we get to Borage the better.'

We finally reached Borage at dusk, taking rooms in the same inn as last time. My clothes had pretty much dried on the walk, but a chill still sat in my core, although that may have been more from knowing I would be leaving Rian shortly. We talked as we all sat together eating a hot, herby stew with dumplings, Rian on one side of me, Anise on the other.

'Before dawn, tomorrow,' I whispered to Anise.

He glanced at Rian, then nodded. 'Sage won't be happy,' he murmured, his eyes flicking towards his boyfriend on the other side of the table. 'But it can't be helped.'

'First thing tomorrow, we'll get new provisions, horses, and the herbs for Anise's Elixir that we can here,' Rian was saying.

I prodded miserably at a dumpling. This was my last meal with Rian and the others. My heart wrenched in my chest as I thought of what Anise and I were about to do.

'Tarragon and Willow will ride to Viridi to warn my father and brother that the Coterie are coming,' Rian said. 'Anise, make a note of the other Elixir ingredients you'll need, then you, Sage, and Phire will ride south with me to the Old Cilantro Citadel.'

I stopped poking my dumpling and looked up. 'You don't want to take me back to your father first and warn him about the Coterie yourself?' I asked. I hadn't expected him to want to go straight to Cilantro Citadel.

He turned to me, determination in his eyes. 'From the look of Aldorbana and Cwicsusl, we don't have any time to waste. Going to Father first would only delay us, and he may not even let us go on to Cilantro since we haven't found the answers he wanted. We'd be wasting time you don't have, and I'm not prepared to risk your life while Father locks you in the dungeon deciding what to do until...' He hesitated a moment, his forehead furrowing before continuing. 'Until you run out of time, which he's quite likely to do. Tarragon and Willow are perfectly capable of warning him and Chervil without me.'

'But–'

'Don't you want me to come with you?' he asked, a sudden glint of fear crossing his face, a vulnerability in his eyes I hadn't seen before.

'Of course, I do.' But I didn't. I wanted him away from me. Safe. 'I just thought you'd want to go back to Viridi first, and maybe leave me and Anise to find the herbs for the Elixir.'

'You're still in my charge,' Rian said. 'Father made it quite clear to me you weren't to leave my sight, and I intend to honour that.'

'Oh,' I said, bowing my head – if he wanted to stay with me, I'd hoped it might have been for another reason. 'I understand.'

He looked at me, his eyes softening, his hand moving to cover mine where it rested on my thigh under the table. 'Besides, I couldn't let you go without me – not now,' he said in a low voice as the others started talking about the next day's plans.

Blood surged to my cheeks.

'Told you,' Anise whispered into my ear on my other side.

'Then it's settled,' Tarragon said, giving his chin a scratch. 'Make that Elixir, break Phire's Curse, and get back to Viridi as quickly as you can.'

'We'll try, Tarragon, but these things are never easy,' Anise said. 'I suggest you speak to anyone who might have any other suggestions about curse breaking when you get to Viridi, just in case it doesn't work.'

Willow nodded. 'We will. Good luck on your journey. Don't get eaten by monsters.'

'Thanks for your concern,' Sage said as Willow giggled.

'At least we're heading south,' Anise said. 'Far eastern Aerba is being gripped by drought and it's heading west, just like in Trew.'

I glanced up to see Rian looking at me. The tenderness in his eyes set off a tingling sensation in my chest, and any final trace of cold melted away.

Later that evening, I went to the room I was sharing with Willow – the same one we'd stayed in before. This time, however, there were no strange noises from the room next to us as we got ready for bed.

'So, if you were a Magic Spinner, what would your Angle be?' she asked.

'Could you choose?' I asked. 'I didn't know that.' Father's book hadn't mentioned anything about choosing Magic Angles.

She shrugged. 'Don't know. But if you could, what would it be?'

'It's not something I've ever thought about. I'm not a High Blood.'

She sighed. 'Just pretend! What would you choose?'

'I don't know – Water maybe. I'd never be without a drink, then. What about you?'

'Earth. I could grow all sorts of things.'

'Isn't that more Anise's Angle?'

'Probably. Air, then. I could blow any ship I was on to the next harbour really quickly. I reckon Sage would be Fire.'

I laughed. 'If Tarragon was Water, that would be rather ironic.'

She grinned at me. 'He'd hate it. What about Rian?'

I squinted as I thought. 'Quintessence. He'd be the most powerful.'

'Why? Because he's a prince? Or because you *like* him,' she said, grinning impishly at me.

'So, will you be picking the lock to Tarragon's door again tonight, or is he going to let you in this time?' I asked, raising an eyebrow.

She looked at me, eyes wide with horror, face flushing. 'You know about that?'

I nodded.

'And you've kept quiet all this time? Thank you.'

'It's none of my business what the two of you do, I just wish you didn't have to creep around to do it,' I said.

'So do I. It gets very tedious. But it is quite exciting, too,' she grinned. 'You should try it sometime.'

'I've got enough to worry about.'

'I'd recommend it.'

'Go to sleep – you'll be awake later.'

Early the following morning, we made our purchases and said our goodbyes to Tarragon and Willow, watching them ride off down the road to Viridi as we buckled up our saddlebags. We mounted our new horses and set off south towards Cilantro, churning up the muddy road as we went.

'Did you manage to get all the herbs you needed in Borage?' I asked Anise, as we rode out into the countryside.

He shook his head. 'I wasn't able to get any Saliivia,' he said.

Rian made a strangled sound, turning away.

'What's wrong with you?' Sage asked, his earring jingling as he moved his head.

'Saliivia. It's the damn devil's work,' Rian said, turning back with a scowl.

'But your father and Chervil approve of it – promote its use, even,' Sage protested, shaking his head.

'Only so it makes the people more tractable because it addles their brains.'

'That's a slight exaggeration, Rian,' Anise said, adjusting his reins.

'Are you saying long term use doesn't affect your brain and memory?' Rian asked, scratching his head.

'Well, it does depend on the dose, but…'

'We have Saliivia in Iolite, but I've never tried it. I don't like the thought of not being in control.' I shuddered.

'That's the assassin coming out in you – you have to be in control to feel safe,' Rian said, flashing me a smile. 'I took it once. It almost killed me.'

'You don't strike me as someone who'd try that sort of thing,' I said, surprised by his revelation.

'I didn't take it on purpose – it was all Chervil's doing. He tricked me into it.'

'Really? You've never told us about this,' Sage said.

'When did this happen?' Anise asked.

'It was about five years ago, now,' Rian said. 'I should've known something was wrong because Chervil had invited himself to my rooms for breakfast. He'd brought a tray with him. I thought he was trying to be friendly at the time, to make up for all his years of antagonism. Anyway, he gave me a cup of pine tea and put some sugar in it, at least that's what he told me it was. I hadn't had much when Father called for him, sending him to Hops for a few days on some diplomatic mission or other. The hallucinations started shortly after I'd had the tea. Then came the dizziness and nausea, and for a brief while, a high fever.'

'How much did he put in?' Anise asked.

'A couple of heaped teaspoons.'

Anise stared at him as the colour drained from his face. 'No wonder you had such a bad reaction to it, Rian, that's about five times the normal dose. You're lucky to still be here. I've heard of people dying after a double dose, let alone five times.'

'All I can say is when the hallucinations finally stopped after three days, I spent a fun week filled with anxiety and dizziness. At one point I couldn't get out of bed. The room was spinning so fast, I really thought I was going to die.'

'Was that when you missed Angelica's birthday party?' Sage asked.

Rian nodded.

'I remember her being quite put out about it,' Anise said. 'She wanted to be the centre of attention and, instead, everyone was talking about your absence.'

'Sounds like she should've taken it up with Chervil,' I said, swatting a fly from my horse's ear.

'I don't think Chervil ever realised what he'd done,' Rian said. 'That's why I've always been so against Saliivia. I've experienced it first-hand, maybe in a much higher dose than you're supposed to have, but the anxiety was crippling and the dizziness – I never want to go there again – and as for the hallucinations...' He screwed his face up. 'I think it should be banned completely.'

'I always wondered why you were so against it, but it makes sense now,' Anise said. 'It's fine in small doses, but you're right, it *can* do things to some people's minds, particularly over a long period.'

'Will Phire be all right if you're going to use it for her Elixir? How much will you be using?'

'Only a sprinkling, not a normal dose, and nothing like the huge amount you took.'

Well, that was a relief.

Rian nodded, looking a little happier.

After that we spoke little, still feeling the effects of yesterday's awful storm. Although I'd slept, it had been somewhat fitful, and when I'd managed to drift off, my dreams had been less than pleasant.

We rode hard all day through fragrant fields of mint, thyme and rosemary carpeting the countryside around us. I glanced at Rian as we rode, his hair streaming out behind him. The fact that he'd insisted on coming with me warmed my heart, although my head still counselled against his being anywhere near me. At least, being out in open countryside, we were relatively safe. The Coterie tended to operate in built-up areas – easier to hide, easier to escape. Out here, there was none of that, and although I didn't relax, the risk to Rian was a lot less – and, of course, they had to find us first.

No one would be able to follow us out here undetected. I was making extra sure of that by looking over my shoulder every few minutes, which Anise noticed.

That night we camped in a rocky valley close to a little stream, eating a simple stew that Anise had concocted for our evening meal. Between them, Sage, and Anise were excellent cooks. The two young men wandered off as the sun set, to stretch their legs. I sat on a large, flat rock next to the fire, warming my hands, as Rian came over to join me.

'I know the circumstances haven't been ideal, but I'm so glad I met you, you know,' Rian said with a smile, throwing a twig into the fire.

'And I'm glad I met you, Prince Valerian,' I said, slipping my arm through his, grinning.

His beautiful amber irises dilated slightly, then his smile faded. Suddenly he looked quite serious, and my heart did a little flip. Surely, he wasn't going to break the Blood Rules – was he?

'Phire, you make me feel things I've never felt before. You make my heart sing – it races at your touch. You make me want to hold you close. Protect you.'

Blood rushed to my face at his words. 'I thought *I'd* been protecting *you* recently,' I said. He looked sheepishly at me and I poked him in the ribs. 'You need to learn to swim – but I know what you mean. I feel exactly the same way.'

He smiled a warm, lopsided smile that made my breath catch.

'You're my light,' I said. 'I think that without you now, I'd be lost, forever in the dark.'

He took hold of my hand, squeezing it.

'I'll always be here,' he said, gently resting a hand over my heart, which started to pound. 'Don't ever forget that.'

I smiled until I caught the flickering fire reflecting off Aldorbana. The top stood completely clear now, the firelight dancing in its crystal blade. 'I'm not sure I have long left, though,' I said, the warmth I'd felt earlier seeping away to be replaced by winter's chill.

He reached towards me, gently turning my face towards him. His hand lingered longer than necessary as he looked deep into my eyes. 'We'll make the Moonflower Elixir and free you from the Curse. Don't worry.'

'But we don't have much time,' I said. 'I have a few weeks at best. The trip to Iolite and the storm tired me out, and things are only going to get worse.'

'We will find a way,' he said, suddenly pulling me to him,

holding me in such a way his touch seared my heart, scorching my mind. He wasn't going to cross that invisible line after all. And I didn't blame him.

Damn the Blood Decree and damn its stupid Rules.

We stayed like that until the crunching of boots on stone made him let go.

'Probably time to get some rest,' Sage said as he and Anise returned. We unpacked our new blankets and settled down to sleep.

Every time I drifted off, fire and water filled my dreams. I woke, my hair plastered to my sweaty face as my heart raced and my body trembled. I turned over, trying to calm my breathing, only to find Rian looking at me from his blankets on the other side of the fire. He glanced over to where Sage and Anise slept peacefully before getting to his feet, quietly making his way over to me and crouching down.

'Nightmares?' he asked softly. I nodded. 'Would you like me to join you?'

'That would be nice,' I said, and he slipped under my covers, placing his blankets over us both and pulling me close. He radiated warmth, and I smiled as his body rested against mine.

'I'm here, now, so try and get some sleep,' he said, burying his face in my hair. His presence calmed my racing thoughts, his touch filling me with a warm glow, and I relished his closeness. Just having him next to me like this made a world of difference, and I was finally able to fall asleep.

When I awoke, Anise had already started preparing breakfast, sporting a big grin on his face as he looked towards me, Rian still holding me. I gave him a little glare, but that just made him grin all the more.

'Problem, Anise?' Rian asked from behind me.

The grin evaporated. 'Not at all, Rian, no, of course not.'

'I already told you, Phire must have got cold in the night. Rian was only being gentlemanly,' Sage said, walking over with some newly-caught fish from a trip down to the nearby stream.

'Of course. What else did you think?' Rian asked, stretching. 'Don't answer that, Anise, it's a rhetorical question.'

After a breakfast of fried fish, we set off, the sun beating down on us. I dabbed my forehead, wiping away the perspiration as the horses snorted in the warm weather. We rode hard once more through plantations of spruce and pine, past sawmills, desperate to get to the ruined Citadel as quickly as possible. The next day, we reached forest cover, the canopy providing some much-appreciated shelter from the unyielding sun. The fresh, earthy scents and the chatter of the forest birds made a welcome change from the insects of the grasslands. We camped that night at the edge of the forest, knowing the next night we'd have proper beds in Cotula Town.

Miserable was the only way to describe the next morning. I woke to rain dripping through the canopy and a damp blanket covering my shivering body. Although Rian hadn't shared my blankets last night, he had taken up position right next to me, much to Anise's amusement. I wasn't sure that Sage approved, though. We rode out of the trees into a curtain of rain, cloaks on and hoods up. It didn't take long for the steady, incessant rain to soak us to the skin.

The horses' hooves dug into the muddy road, sending up clods of earth, making the going difficult. The herb fields we passed looked bedraggled as rain dripped from their bowed leaves, suppressing their fragrance. We didn't bother stopping for a midday meal, determined to reach Cotula and shelter as soon as possible. By late afternoon, the town was in sight, and we rode through the wooden buildings where water dripped from shingle roofs, down drainpipes, and into collecting barrels. The inn appeared well-kept, fairly clean, and free of the smell of stale beer – and patrons, for that matter. We took rooms, drying out our clothes as best we could, Anise and Sage slipping back out to find some Saliivia before our evening meal. When they returned, I noticed the scent of roses, lemon, and violet – had Sage found a perfume shop here? He looked pleased with himself, whatever he'd discovered in town. Our meal of steak and vegetables quickly warmed me up, and the pine tea helped to thaw my bones. I peered out the taproom window to see that the rain had stopped, and the dusky sky had cleared.

'I might go and see if the farrier's still open,' Rian said. 'I think my horse's shoe is getting loose, and I'm hoping he can sort it out first thing tomorrow.'

'I'll come with you,' I offered, and we left the table to Anise and Sage, making our way out into the twilight. We walked along, nodding to the few folk still out on their business, before reaching the corner of the main street and an alley where the farrier's shop stood.

I stopped dead as the hairs on the back of my neck stood up.

Something was wrong.

I glanced along the street. A heap of rough wooden crates sat outside the front of the farrier's, sending deep shadows along the wall behind them. Cool air brushed my face as the smell of horse drifted into the air around us. The clink of the farrier still at work in his forge echoed around the buildings.

Rian stopped beside me, muscles suddenly taut. 'What is it?' he asked, his voice strained.

I twisted around towards the alley just in time to see the glint of lamplight on a knife. In one swift, fluid movement, I pulled my Fan free from my belt. Flipped it open. Flicked it across Rian's unprotected back as the knife hurtled towards him.

CHAPTER FOURTEEN

The knife collided with my War Fan, careering off the malachite into the shadows, skittering across the cobblestones. Instinctively, I ran into the alley – by the Stars, I recognised that style of throw. We'd been taught it at the beginning of our assassin training. This had to be one of Beryl's Coterie at work, just as Onyx had said, and when it came to knife throwing? Citrine was the obvious candidate. Topaz was a possibility, but Citrine and Beryl were close friends, so it was more likely Citrine. She had great skill in the use of knives, rather like her brother, Carnelian, in his use of poisons, and her reputation for brutality rivalled his – flaying was her speciality.

When I reached the point from which the knife had been thrown, the dim alleyway stood empty. I couldn't see her. I swore. I'd never find her, now. She could've gone anywhere – ducked into a house, hidden behind a barrel, escaped off over a roof top, the possibilities were endless…

The one consolation was she wouldn't return tonight – that much I did know. It was an unwritten Coterie rule.

I sighed, walking back to Rian who had picked up the knife.

'One of yours or one of mine?' he asked, inspecting the weapon.

'Why would the Nightshade want to kill the Prince of Aerba?' I asked.

'They attacked us before. Although hopefully, my message got to Wormwood and he's backed off.'

'To be fair, they attacked you very half-heartedly last time; they were far more aggressive towards me. I think they were after me, then, but this has all the marks of the Coterie about it, and more particularly an assassin called Citrine,' I said, taking the knife from him, noting the faceted citrine stone set in the handle of the knife – her signature.

'By the Herbs, so Juniper really *is* trying to kill me, now, as well as the rest of my family? *Nice.*'

'It's not Juniper,' I said, immediately wishing I hadn't.

'What? Who, then?'

I'd dug myself a hole, now, but I still couldn't tell him everything. 'Beryl.'

'Why would Lady Beryl want me dead?' Rian asked, shaking his head in disbelief.

'She's no lady,' I said through gritted teeth.

'I noticed that.'

I had never asked him what had happened when the Coterie captured him, but I couldn't help but wonder what had gone on. I spotted a stable to our left, a lamp flicking outside. 'Let's go in here,' I said, slipping the knife in my boot and unhooking the lamp, leading the way in. I climbed up into the hayloft and sat down on a bale of hay, Rian joining me. 'What happened?'

'I'm sorry?' Rian looked confused in the lamplight.

'Back at the castle. What happened to make you say Beryl's not a lady?'

'Oh, well, after they caught me, they took me straight to the castle, to the Great Hall and Juniper,' Rian said. 'She already seemed to know me and didn't appear particularly keen on harming me – probably due to relations with Aerba and the suggestion she was going to ransom me. After a while, Beryl came in.' Rian's face took on a pained expression. 'It was the way she looked at me. I've never had anyone look at me like that before, as though I was a piece of meat. She started asking Juniper about me, wanted to know about you and me.'

'What did Juniper say?'

'Nothing. Lord Flint and Elm came in, Beryl went quiet, and that was the end of the conversation.'

I laughed. 'I imagine it was.'

'I don't understand.' Rian looked questioningly at me.

'Beryl's been after Elm for ages. With both Mal and me out the way, I dare say she wants to make sure of her position as the next Mistress of Iolite, and with Elm as her husband, no one will question it.'

'Her own brother?' Rian asked, looking sick.

'Stepbrother, not brother, remember? Beryl's not that perverse. Juniper already had Elm before she married Father.'

'Of course, I forgot. Anyway, you arrived not long after and rescued me.' He grinned.

'You're welcome.' I smiled back.

'So, why is Beryl trying to kill me? Just because I escaped?'

How could I tell him it was really because Beryl wanted to hurt *me* by killing him? 'Maybe, but I've discovered recently you can never tell with Beryl.'

Rian frowned. 'You said Onyx knew I was in danger, but I'd assumed you meant from Juniper. Not Beryl.'

'I'm not really sure it matters who's behind it,' I said.

'How did you know? That Citrine was there?'

I shrugged. 'Just a feeling. I guess all that Coterie training is paying off.' I grinned ruefully before standing up. 'She won't bother us again tonight. We'd better get back to the inn, deal with your horse's shoe tomorrow.'

Rian stood up and took my hand. 'I owe you my life again,' he said, a wry grin on his face. 'This is becoming a habit.'

'It's the line of work,' I said, my heart clamouring against my ribcage as he pulled me into a hug. I felt his warmth and his strong muscles as his arms enveloped me. He kissed me on the head, my veins now running with fire as the familiar scent of sandalwood held me in its grasp.

'Thank you, all the same,' he said, taking a step back. He let go of me. 'It's a good thing you're with me.' He grinned. 'I'm glad I've got you to keep me alive.' He turned and climbed back down into the stable below.

I flinched as I watched him go. I wasn't keeping him alive, though. I was doing the exact opposite – putting his life in danger. Maybe I *should* leave. It would be best for him. And yet, I didn't want to.

What I wanted, more than ever, now, was for him to kiss me. I *needed* him to kiss me. I longed for his velvet lips to be pressed against mine. I yearned for his touch on my face, his arms around me, pulling me so close I could feel his heartbeat through his chest. I took a couple of deep breaths, trying to calm the frantic sensations raging inside me, before following him, replacing the lamp on its hook outside the stable and returning to the inn.

We told the others about our encounter with Citrine and spent the rest of the evening chatting before turning in for the night. I went to my room, placed Aldorbana and Cwicsusl against the wall, and climbed into bed.

I lay staring at the ceiling, trying once again to decide if I should leave, especially as the Coterie now knew where we were. The encounter with Citrine had shaken me. Rian wouldn't be safe until I left. But how could I leave when I felt the way I did? Or was that even more reason to go? Was it as Onyx had said: if I loved him, I should leave him? The thought set off a gnawing ache in my chest. I couldn't leave him. I loved him. I'd stay and protect him, like Anise said – but if I failed? I couldn't bear to think about it.

If I left now, I'd be long gone by dawn. He'd never find me. Probably. Then again, if I did go, I'd never get the Elixir, unless I could persuade Anise to come with me covertly. Perhaps staying and protecting Rian until I had the Elixir would be the thing to do, then leave him. Maybe we both had a shot at surviving that way, even if it meant we were eventually apart.

What sort of existence it would be without him, now, I didn't know. I'd got so used to being with him over the last weeks. I relied on him and couldn't bear the thought of being without him.

Our friendship – what had become more than friendship – had been forged quite literally in blood and fire, and now we were right at the top of Beryl's kill list. Maybe even Juniper's, too. I wiped an errant tear from my eye with the back of my hand, ignoring the soreness from one of my chewed nails. The Moonflower Elixir – that's what I had to focus on. We'd get the Elixir and then I'd go, leave Rian, however much it cost me, and find Mal.

The next day, we left before dawn in an attempt to shake off Citrine, heading out on the east road towards Tulsi before doubling back and hiding in a thicket of gorse. As the sun rose, a lone rider sped eastwards. Citrine. Once she was well out of sight, we headed back, taking a track along the side of Lake Cotula, fields full of sheep and cows lining our other side. I kept glancing over my shoulder, half expecting to see the assassin following us, but it appeared we'd successfully given her the slip.

Rian spent some of the morning extolling the virtues of my War Fan. I rode along, a tiredness aching in my bones. Some of my fatigue may have been due to a restless night, but a lot was down to the Curse and its continuing effect on me.

'Maybe we should get some War Fans; they're small, but really versatile,' Rian said.

'Men with Fans? I don't think so,' Sage said, screwing his nose up. His sour expression made me want to laugh out loud, but I didn't think he'd appreciate that much, so I remained quiet and looked away. Rian caught my glance and grinned, which didn't help.

'I wouldn't care about that,' Anise said with a smile. 'It would be practical in hot weather as well as a fight. Think of the different styles and colours you could have. I think it's a great idea.'

Sage groaned and pursed his lips.

The sun bounced off the lake's surface, blinding me. I wiped perspiration off my brow as we rode, the sun high overhead, such a complete change in weather to the day before. By late morning, we paused for something to eat and for the horses to take a drink from the lake.

'Should we stop here?' I asked, scanning the water. 'I mean, how deep is this lake?'

'It's quite safe; you don't need to worry,' Sage said, a patronising edge to his voice as he rode his horse over to the water to drink. I glared at him, but he ignored me and turned to Anise. 'Are you sure you know how to make this Elixir?'

'I've made elixirs before, Sage, it shouldn't be a problem,' Anise said, dismounting.

I slipped off my horse, Rian following me, and I wiped my forehead again.

'As long as you're su–' Sage never finished his sentence.

I glanced over towards the sound of splashing water and gasped.

Sage yelled as he fell from his horse. The horse bolted. Rising out of the lake was a grotesque creature – a green-skinned beast with the face of an old hag, all creased and wrinkled like ancient parchment. It had long, dark-green hair, and teeth as sharp as knives. Metal, armour-like plates covered its body, and it wore an expression of insatiable hunger. The smell of rotting flesh accompanied it as it moved, its hair dripping with water and weeds. It had to be at least twelve feet tall, with long sinewy arms and huge hands tipped with dagger-like claws which wrapped around Sage, dragging him towards the water.

'A powler!' Anise yelled, running towards his struggling partner, drawing his swords as the creature hissed menacingly from between its cracked lips.

For a second, I froze.

It was the first time I'd ever seen a powler. The rancid smell of decay that lodged in my throat made me gag as I grabbed Aldorbana and Cwicsusl.

Rian lunged forward, slicing at the green flesh. The powler held Sage in one hand and tried to swat Anise and Rian away with the other, but they both ducked, sidestepping out of the way.

I bided my time as the creature moved, jerking from side to side, waving poor Sage in the air like a rag doll. Anise twisted, slamming one of his swords into the powler's side. It screamed. Yellow blood, or what I assumed to be blood, oozed from the wound. It swiped at Anise, sending him tumbling over the grass, leaving him stunned. Dragging itself from the water, the powler staggered towards Rian, who slashed at it, drawing more blood, before dodging backwards to avoid its flailing arm.

As the powler punched at Rian, I sprang forward, pushing the prince aside as I put myself between us and the creature, raising Cwicsusl to protect us. The creature's fist slammed into Cwicsusl. The sound of bone breaking set my teeth on edge. The force of the powler's punch shot up my arm, causing me to grit my teeth against the pain. The beast shrieked in agony. As it recoiled, I lunged forward, slashing at the creature's other arm, slicing through its armour with Aldorbana. The powler's far shoulder fell as it pulled back its arm, preparing to strike at me again. As it did, I dived out the way, slashing at the limb. It howled in pain, moving back into the lake.

Sage finally fell free of the creature's grasp and into the water, sending splashes in all directions.

The powler screamed as it waved its maimed arms around before sinking below the water, leaving behind an oily, yellow tinge on the surface. I took a deep breath, trying to calm myself. I'd never faced anything like that before and I never wanted to again.

Sage quickly swam for the lakeside, scrambling up the muddy grass bank, breathing hard. Anise clambered to his feet and ran to Sage, immediately taking him into a hug, kissing him and holding him in an embrace that looked as if they'd never let go of each other ever again.

'Are you all right?' I asked Rian as I pulled him to his feet.

'I'm fine, thanks to you,' he said, slipping a shaky arm around me as I flexed the fingers on my aching shield arm. 'You're an amazing fighter, you know? I really love that about you.'

'What?' I looked up. Did I just hear him right?

'Thank the Herbs Sage is all right,' he continued as if he hadn't realised what he'd said.

I glanced over at Sage and Anise – the two were standing, foreheads resting against each other, both a little weepy. 'They really do love each other, don't they?' I murmured.

Rian nodded, then looked at me, his pupils dilating. 'And I–' He hesitated, then rubbed the back of his neck. 'I'm going to rip up that damned Blood Rule Decree if it's the last thing I do.'

'I thought you wanted the Fire Opal back most of all.' I smiled.

'That, too.'

'Maybe we should ride on a bit and try to stay away from the lake. There must be a stream around here somewhere for the horses to drink.'

Rian nodded. 'Hey! You two, put each other down and let's ride on before that thing's friends come visiting.'

Anise looked up, his face red and eyes glistening as he nodded back.

Sage's face had a pale tinge to it as he walked over to me, dripping wet. 'You saved my life,' he said. 'I know I wasn't exactly friendly to you when we first met, and I apologise for that. I know you didn't kill the princess, and, without you just now – I'd probably be dead.'

Anise stood behind him, his eyes swimming in tears.

'I misjudged you, Samphire,' Sage said, using the name for the first time. He gave me a quick, wet hug. 'Thank you, truly, thank you. And – you've known about us for a while and not judged us. I thank you for that, too.'

A warm sensation spread through me at his words. At last, we'd finally reached an understanding.

Anise rushed at me, catching me in a huge hug, squeezing me so hard I could barely breathe.

'Put her down,' Rian said good-naturedly, although a hint of warning tinged his voice.

Anise let me go. 'Thank you, Phire.'

'You're both very welcome. You know, someone said to me once that you can't help who you fall in love with, and they were right.' I glanced sideways through my eyelashes at Rian as Anise turned tomato red. 'Perhaps you two should move to Iolite. Your relationship wouldn't be a problem there – although Juniper is there, of course, so maybe not.'

Sage smiled at me, although I could see he was shaking after his ordeal.

Rian chewed his lip and looked at me. 'I– Let's get going,' he said.

We caught and mounted our horses, riding hastily along the track and staying as far from the lake as we could. We paused at a stream to water the horses and have a quick bite to eat. Not that I felt particularly hungry after the fight. Once we'd eaten, Anise rummaged around in his Herb Chest, eventually fishing out a small, blue glass vial. He held it up to the light, his spare hand going unconsciously to his Amulet.

'Take this tincture,' he said, passing the vial to Sage.

Sage looked up at him from his position perched on a dead log, his face still pale, eyes glassy. 'What is it?'

'It's to help with the shock.'

'I don't need it. I'm fine.'

'So, you've stopped shaking, then, have you?' Anise asked, gazing intently at his boyfriend.

Sage looked at his still-trembling hands. 'Well…'

'Take it.' Anise thrust it into Sage's hands.

Sage nodded and uncorked the bottle, gulping it down in one swig. He pulled a face and re-corked the vial. 'Thanks,' he said, a sour note to his voice as he passed it back.

Looking satisfied, Anise returned the vial to his Herb Chest, then sat down next to Sage, draping an arm around his shoulder. His boyfriend didn't object.

I glanced at Rian. He was no longer shaking, but there was a wildness in his eyes.

'You've never fought one of those things before, either?' I asked.

Rian shook his head. 'Never.'

I nodded and glanced over at Sage and Anise. 'I think we were lucky.'

'Very lucky,' he murmured.

I glanced at the stream and the flowers around us. Beside me grew a plant with tall flower stems reaching up from a clump of leaves. A sweet scent drifted from the many small, white flowers that made up the flowerheads. The flowers were a little larger than the Rock Samphire in the marsh where Rian had found me. I leant towards them and sniffed.

'Valerian,' Rian said, glancing in my direction.

'What?' I turned towards him.

'That plant, those flowers, it's Aerban Valerian, my namesake.'

'It's beautiful,' I said, taking another sniff. 'And smells quite intoxicating.' I could have been talking about him. I swallowed. I looked back at him. My heart skipped. There was something in his eyes that made blood rush to my face. He held my gaze, a little smile working its way slowly along his lips and into his eyes.

'Perhaps being named after a herbaceous border isn't all bad,' he said.

I cleared my throat. 'No, not bad at all.'

As we rode on later that afternoon, colour returned to Sage's face and he visibly relaxed. We continued until late evening when we'd cleared the lake's end and could camp well away from the water. I cast the occasional, suspicious glance in the direction of the lake, but when sleep found me, I slept like a baby, and in the morning, I managed to eat a good breakfast.

As I picked up Aldorbana, a weight settled on my chest. The blood-red crystal had drained a little more, probably due to yesterday's exertions. No wonder I'd been so tired. I sighed, resheathing the sword and placing Cwicsusl on my back. I looked up to see Rian gazing at me, worry etched into his face, concern flickering in his amber irises.

'I'm fine,' I said, moving over to my horse.

'But for how long?' he asked.

That, I didn't know.

Our journey took us along the Cotula River, through perfumed fields of basil, sage, and lemon balm, small buildings dotted around for the drying and mixing of herbs. When we joined the main road, we met several travellers and merchants going about their business before finally taking the southern road to Cilantro. We rode through the foothills of the Cilantro Mountains, the up-and-down nature of the road slowing our progress. We passed merchants with logs from the mountain tree plantations, sawmills visible in the distance. A cool wind wafted down from the mountains where, high above, forests covered them like cloaks, the breeze drifting on to the increasingly humid foothills and fertile coastal plain below. After five days of riding, the Cilantro Rainforest appeared in front of us.

'We should make it to the forest boundaries by nightfall,' Rian said. 'We can camp there.'

I nodded. 'Sounds good. We'll be rather exposed if we stay out here.'

Anise looked a little unsure but didn't protest.

We kept going as fast as we could as the sun gradually faded from the sky, the shadows growing longer, until we reached the forest. I found the humidity here particularly unpleasant, and I'd long since removed my coat in the heat. The trees and plants here were alien to me, their leaves far bigger than anything I'd seen before, and the sounds of the chirping insects quickly put me on edge.

'There's a good-sized thicket up ahead, off the road to the left,' Sage said. 'We can stop there for the night.'

We dismounted, leading our horses to it, and pushed our way inside. The dense thicket had an open centre, and we had room to picket the horses at one end and sleep at the other. We unloaded our bags and ate a cold supper as the light completely vanished, the forest filling with darkness.

The silhouettes of the trees beyond our hiding place threw inky-black shadows into the gloom as the moon cast an eerie, pale light the colour of milk through the trees. I lay on my blanket next to Rian, sweating in the heat and humidity, and listening to the night-time sounds of the forest: animals scurrying around, a bird hooting, something stirring in the bushes to our right. A distant howl echoed through the trees and the insects, intent on keeping me awake, scuttled around, making increasingly more irritating sounds.

As I lay awake, I had the inexplicable sensation that these strange trees were watching me, many eyes scrutinising my every move.

I shuddered and looked up – something wasn't right. Silence crowded in on me. The animals were suddenly conspicuous by the absence of their night calls, and the sinister quiet frightened me.

'What's going on?' Anise asked, a nervous edge to his voice.

A shrill scream pierced the night air, cutting through the stillness with the sharp edge of a knife.

CHAPTER FIFTEEN

I sat up as Rian placed a warning hand on my arm.

'Don't make a sound,' he whispered in my ear, his lips grazing my cheek.

My breaths came in ragged gasps and my rapid pulse beat loudly in my ears, making it difficult to hear anything else. A yell broke through the silence, making me jump; the ring of a sword being drawn followed, then another cry, and a deep, throaty growl. The hairs on the back of my neck rose, my hands turned to ice, and a shiver coursed down my spine. I didn't like this one bit. I took hold of Aldorbana's hilt, although I didn't draw it; wielding it in the small thicket would prove difficult, but I felt safer, more in control, knowing it was in my hand.

The sound of horses cantering thundered past our hiding place. I glanced towards Sage and Anise as they peered out of the thicket, Sage holding his earring to stop it from jingling. Rian stared into the darkness as a cloud drifted away from the moon, illuminating small sections of the forest with shafts of pale, milky light.

The sound of scurrying feet drifted through the night, moving along the road we'd been following, and the outlines of two men flashed past, heading towards the edge of the forest. Judging by the jingling sound of the coins in their pockets, I assumed them to be merchants. They careered past our thicket at a full pelt, gasping for air as they went, with the sound of something vast following in their wake, grunting as it went. *No.* It was more than one thing, but I couldn't make out what the black, ominous-looking shapes were as they sped past our hiding place. Rian stifled a gasp from beside me and I glanced at him, but he'd already regained his composure. Piercing cries rang through the trees, suddenly cut short, followed by growls, snarls, and other horrible squelching, tearing sounds. I threw my hands over my ears in a futile attempt to stop the noises. Horror and nausea filled me.

My heartbeat hammered against my ribs as my mind did cartwheels, imagining what had happened to the men. They had to be dead, but what had killed them? And why? I desperately hoped we wouldn't find out. I glanced at Sage who looked out through the undergrowth, trying to see what I probably didn't want to, as the sound of dragging swept towards us from the roadway. The moonlight vanished and we had no chance of identifying what was happening on the road. After the dragging sounds had passed, everything went quiet again for a few minutes before the tranquil, nocturnal sounds of the forest returned.

'What just happened?' I whispered in Rian's ear.

'I'm not sure, but we want to get to the ruins and out the other side of the forest tomorrow,' he said.

'You'll be lucky – the Moonflower only blooms at night,' Anise said. 'We may have to spend another night here.'

I shuddered at the thought.

My dreams raged with strange beasts and screams, which made for a change from the shipwreck of recent nights. I slept fitfully, waking as the silver light of dawn penetrated the forest, turning over to see Rian still sound asleep. I lay for a while, listening, but I couldn't hear anything out of the ordinary, just the usual forest sounds, so I sat up. Sage and Anise snored happily. My mind raced, full of questions about what had happened the previous night, like where were the men, now? How long would it take to get to the ruins? Would I be able to take the Moonflower Elixir today? And, finally, when would I have to leave Rian?

'Penny for them?' Rian asked.

I twisted around to see him looking curiously at me. 'My thoughts? Just thinking about the Elixir.'

Sage yawned and prodded Anise, waking him up. 'We can eat then move on,' he said, moving to the bags and handing out some bread.

I was glad to get moving again. My stiff muscles protested after the long night, and I groaned as I moved. We stowed our blankets away, tacked up our horses, and started off with Rian leading the way back to the road. He stopped abruptly in front of me, and I walked straight into him.

'Damn,' he said.

'What's the matter?' I asked, peering over his shoulder. A trail of crimson covered the stone road in both directions in front of us. The evidence of someone being dragged whilst bleeding so heavily made me shudder, a profound reminder of the incident the night before. 'Hell's teeth.'

'I think we should move on quickly,' Sage said, resolutely looking up and away from the awful sight, his face haggard.

I nodded. Although blood didn't affect me much, it obviously bothered Sage. The pungent smell of blood and earth surrounded us absolutely.

'What happened?' Anise asked, his face pale.

'I'm not sure we want to know,' I said. 'Sage's right, let's keep moving.'

We mounted our horses and followed the road south through the forest. I attempted to steer mine around the bulk of the congealed blood, alarmed and horrified as the quantity increased, until we arrived at the scene of the men's obliteration. That was the only word to describe what had happened to them, given the quantity of scarlet blood and gelatinised guts splattered over the bushes and leaves. One tree trunk sported a particularly dark stain.

'What could have done this?' I asked, trying to suppress the wave of anxiety breaking through me.

'I don't know. Some sort of creature? Definitely no ordinary animal,' Rian said, his face pale.

'The monsters Willow mentioned?' Anise asked as he looked nervously into the trees.

'They're myth here, now, remember?' Sage said, although I caught him glancing into the undergrowth beside the road.

'Care to hazard another guess at what did this, then?'

Sage hesitated. 'We need to keep going, and quickly. We don't stop until we've got the Moonflower and we're out the other side of this hellhole,' he said, urging his horse on through the dappled sunlight streaming through the trees.

I didn't argue.

'Do you know where the Citadel is, Anise?' Rian asked as we rode on.

'Roughly,' Anise said. 'We should reach it this afternoon, if we're lucky.'

'And we're just going to ride into it?' Sage asked. 'It's on the road?'

Anise wiggled his nose. 'Sort of. I don't think we're going to ride straight through it, but it's close to the road, so we should be on the lookout for ruins.'

'Ruins? Here amongst the vegetation of the rainforest? We'll never see anything in this.'

'Just keep your eyes open,' Rian said.

We moved swiftly along the road through the trees, across clearings, past thickets, the reasonably flat terrain and the stone paving making the going good, despite the heat and humidity. None of us bothered with outer coats, only wearing our shirts, which clung to us with sweat. I wiped my forehead with my damp sleeve and took a drink from my waterskin as I looked at the trees.

We ate on the go, not daring to stop for more than a moment at a time. We passed no other travellers; the only sounds were those of birds and forest animals amongst the trees.

As the day wore on, I gazed into the surrounding undergrowth. Something caught my eye. A large doorway emerged from the forest's grasp. I stopped my horse, for a moment doubting my own vision.

'What's the matter?' Rian asked, bringing his horse to a halt.

'Over there.' I pointed to the doorway in amongst the trees and twisting vines.

He looked at where I indicated.

'What is it?' Sage asked, coming back as Anise reached us.

'There's a doorway in the forest,' I said.

'Exactly what we're looking for,' Anise said, slipping from his horse's back and hacking his way through the undergrowth towards the doorway.

'What do you mean, "exactly what we're looking for"?' Sage asked.

'It's the entrance to the Old Cilantro Citadel, of course.'

'Here?'

I scanned the surrounding trees for anything suspicious, listening for animals – or, rather, for a lack of animals – but insects chattered, birds chirped, and a forest squirrel jumped from tree to tree, totally unconcerned.

'Then we'd better get in there,' Rian said, dismounting.

I followed Rian as he made his way through the undergrowth, through the bracken and ferns, towards the doorway. I studied the arched doorway as I approached it. It was made of blackish-grey stone, covered in green, slimy-looking lichens, and strangling vines. Intricate carvings rose around the sides, harking back to ancient times and happier days. The aged door frame had a beauty about it, although the great wooden door that had once hung there had long since rotted away. The trees surrounding the doorway had grown up on either side, forming a wooden arch of branches and vines across the top and, as I drew closer, walls emerged from the undergrowth so obscured by forest plants that the casual observer would never notice them.

'Come on, this is where it gets interesting,' Anise said, a hint of excitement in his voice as he used his sword to slice through the vines and undergrowth and ventured through the doorway.

'I don't like this,' I murmured, a chill of uneasiness and foreboding vibrating down my spine despite the fact that my shirt stuck to my back with sweat, but I followed all the same.

We entered a short tunnel, coming out onto a covered colonnade supported by immense grey stone columns intricately carved with herbs. I looked out between the columns, awestruck – the afternoon sun shone on a vast complex of buildings below us, stretching out for some distance. I gazed down on the ancient, ruined city, overgrown and tangled in vines and ferns. Its stone towers reached out of the encroaching vegetation towards the sky like fingers, ornate with carvings, green and black with age, some shrouded in cascades of small white and blue flowers as they surrounded huge, vine-choked squares. A long slope led from the colonnade down into the first of these squares. Beyond that loomed another square, and in the centre of the city, surrounded by a lake, stood a palace. The building climbed majestically out of the lily-strewn water with columns and arches, towers, and overgrown gardens. I'd never seen anything like this in my life, and my breath caught at its beauty.

'The ancient Cilantro Citadel,' Anise breathed.

I tore my eyes from the buildings to look at him. His eyes were wide and he had a big grin on his face.

'It used to be the capital, but they moved it after most of it was destroyed in the Great Storm around seven-hundred-and-fifty years ago,' Rian said.

'You know your history of Aerba,' I said, gazing back over the old city of Cilantro.

Rian shrugged. 'That was one thing they did teach me. But as you know, Tarragon's the real history buff – he could write you a book on the subject,' he said.

Looking to the right, out over the trees, the rainforest's edge was just about visible, forming a dark splash against the lighter colour of grassland. An hour on horseback and we'd be clear of the trees. A kind of relief settled on my shoulders at the thought of being so close to the forest's edge.

'Let's head for what looks like the palace. Hopefully we'll find what we want in the old gardens,' Rian said.

We led the horses down the wide, stone-paved slope that took us towards the first square below. The lichen-covered slope made the going slippy in places, and we had to pick our way across the stone; a horse crashing to the ground here wouldn't be ideal. We reached the first square where the remnants of buildings reached through the overgrown forest as if searching for freedom.

'I wonder what it was like when it was new,' Anise said, his eyes sparkling as he took in the vast scale of the place.

'It was known as the Jewel of Aerba,' Rian said, his face awed by the vista. 'At least that's what the other Five Lands called it at the time.'

'It's such a shame it was abandoned,' I said.

Rian nodded. 'People came from distant lands just to visit and walk around its squares and gardens.'

'I don't blame them,' Sage said, gazing around as we walked.

We made our way under a crumbling archway and along a street, stumbling on malicious vines that did their best to bring us down. Insects buzzed in the undergrowth, and birds in bright, jewel-like colours chirruped as they swooped around us in the ruins, catching the insects. We made our way around the remnants of a fallen archway, down another slope into a larger square where a small tower rose from its centre. At the top of the tower, a polished stone shone white in the sun like a pearl.

On the far side of the square, a bridge led across a lily-strewn moat to the palace complex. We made our way across, avoiding the areas where the stones had begun to crumble into the water, and tethered our horses in what remained of the palace courtyard.

'We need to find the gardens then wait,' Anise said. 'Hopefully, we'll find at least one Moonflower about to bloom.'

'We'd better,' Rian said, glancing at my back and setting off shivers inside me. Had more of Cwicsusl turned to clear crystal? From the look on his face, I could only glean one answer.

We took our packs off our horses to give them a break, and took the bags with us, walking around the edge of the palace to the gardens behind. They must have been magnificent eight hundred years ago, but were now only a tangled mass of vines, roots, and undergrowth. I took hold of Aldorbana and started slicing through the vegetation, ignoring the blade's colour change. Old stone pathways made their way through the gardens; in some places, they were almost pristine, in others, crumbled and broken, sticking up like broken teeth intent on tripping us up. Around us, flowers of blue, purple, and pale yellow bloomed, their sweet, almost fruity scents drifting on the early evening air.

'What exactly are we looking for?' Sage asked. 'I assume a Moonflower is white?'

Anise nodded. 'Yes, they have delicate petals and are about eight inches wide when fully open. It's actually a special kind of cactus, the Aerban Moonlight Cactus, and they grow on the outside of trees, about six to fifteen feet up. These gardens are the perfect sort of place because it looks like they flood, which the plants like.'

I started looking around at the trees for any sign of flowers. 'And they open only at night?'

'Yes, about now. And they bloom for twelve hours, then die.'

'Let's split up,' Rian said. 'We can cover more ground that way. Anise go left with Sage. Phire and I will take the right side of the gardens. Yell if you find anything.'

We set off searching the gardens, moving through the undergrowth looking for the elusive flower.

'We will find it, you know,' Rian said, taking my hand. 'We *will* save you. I won't rest until we do.'

I looked at him, his eyes glistening in the dusky light, almost glowing. 'I know. Thank you.'

He reached out with his other hand, tenderly touching the side of my face, his fingers lingering as he ran them gently down my cheek, setting off sparks and starting wildfires that twisted inside me. 'In the weeks I've known you – I really can't imagine being without you now,' he said, suddenly stepping back and letting go of my hand. He turned away slightly, rubbing the back of his neck. Was his face flushing? 'I–'

'Over here!' Sage's voice cut through the moonlit gardens. 'I've found one!'

Rian grabbed my hand, immediately pulling me towards Sage. We forced our way through the plants and flowers to where Sage and Anise stood looking at a large bud on a tree about seven feet off the ground.

'Is that it?' I asked, a little twist of excitement funnelling its way through me.

Anise nodded. 'Now all we have to do is wait for it to open.'

We sat on a fallen tree and ate a cold supper while we waited for nature to take its course. The moon rose and, ever so slowly, the Moonflower opened its petals until it reached its full size, glowing in the moonlight.

'It's beautiful,' I said, getting up to inspect it. A fragrant honeysuckle scent lingered around the flower, and I reached out towards it.

'Stop!' Anise jumped up, grabbing my hand before I could touch it. 'It's poisonous.'

'To the touch? And you're going to give it to me to drink?'

'Only very little, and by the time I'm finished with it, it won't be anywhere near as potent as direct contact with the skin.'

'That's good,' I said, not attempting to hide the sarcasm in my voice.

'So, how are you going to touch it?' Sage asked.

Anise turned, grinning at Sage, and pulled a pair of leather gloves out from his britches pocket. 'With these,' he said, putting them on and gently tugging two petals off the Moonflower. He carefully wrapped them in a cloth and stowed them in his bag.

'If we're done here, we might as well get back to the horses,' Rian said. 'I noticed we're not far from the southern edge of the forest – we could be out of the trees before midnight.'

'Sounds good,' Sage said, nodding.

I led the way back through the gardens, around the side of the palace to where we'd left the horses. Standing next to the horses, a curved knife in each hand, stood Citrine, a nasty smile on her pale face and her watery grey eyes sparkling with excitement.

'Amethyst,' she said, nodding to me, moonlight glistening off the stones in the hilts of her knives.

'Why are you here, Citrine?' I asked.

''Cause I'm going to kill your prince,' she said, throwing a knife into the air and catching it.

I stepped in front of Rian, pushing him behind me. 'That's *not* going to happen.'

'I missed him last time 'cause of you, but this time I won't let you get in my way. And, if you do, I'll kill you as well.'

The hairs on the back of my neck suddenly rose. Sage started to take a step forward, but I threw my hand out to stop him and the others from going any further, putting my finger to my lips, urging them to be silent.

Quiet and stillness surrounded us.

Even the horses stood quietly, the whites of their eyes showing.

Something was definitely wrong.

'What's the matter with you?' Citrine asked, her eyes narrowing as she glanced warily out into the city, her black hair dancing in the night breeze.

Sage looked at me, shrugging his shoulders, confusion etched into his face, but Rian nodded, looking out into the vine-choked city beyond the courtyard as if he immediately understood my thoughts. With all my senses heightened, I strained to hear the forest sounds. Nothing. No insects, no birds, no animals; nothing. I glanced at Rian, my heart beginning to race.

No sounds.

Just like last night. I couldn't bring myself to think about what had come next. Rian took my hand, pulling me back towards the side of the palace, indicating to the others to do the same.

Vegetation rustled in the Citadel beyond the bridge, and I strained to see what could be causing the sounds in the pale light.

A crash of timber. A guttural growl.

Crouching in the adjoining square not far from the bridge, illuminated by the moonlight, was a creature. It stared right at us.

A creature from the very worst of nightmares.

About the size of a horse, it crouched on its bulky, muscular back legs, forearms thrust out in front of it. Four large, lethal-looking claws issued from each paw, and black, dried blood clung to the talons. Long, matted black hair ran down its back, the rest of the creature's body covered in short, dark hair.

I shuddered as my gaze reached higher. Two large horns rose from the top of its head, curling around the sides of its ears. It had a squashed nose, and the vicious fangs protruding from the mouth sat covered in dried blood, with old, rotten flesh caught between the teeth. But the thing that froze my heart was the eyes, the glowing red eyes. They looked directly at me. Into me. My heart skipped in terror as Citrine swore and backed away from the creature, her knives raised.

CHAPTER SIXTEEN

'What the devil is that?' Citrine asked, her voice strained.

'An Aerban Mynogre,' Rian said.

'I thought they were myth now in Cilantro Forest,' Anise said, his face ashen. 'Tarragon said they were a myth.'

'Apparently not,' I muttered, moving slowly backwards towards the gardens with the others.

'I'm going to have a word with him when we get back.'

'*If* we get back,' Sage said, drawing his swords.

The mynogre roared. Close up, the sound was so excruciating that I wanted to hold my hands to my ears. Immediately, the creature's bellow was answered by a roar from the left and another two from the right, followed by a low, guttural growl.

'Why don't we carry bows?' Sage asked. 'Forget the War Fans, we ought to carry bows.'

I'd used one, but never carried one – perhaps I should? The sound of more creatures crashing through the undergrowth set my teeth on edge and my heart pounding.

We fled, leaving Citrine gawping at the creatures as they sprang forward across the bridge. We sprinted back into the gardens, the horses snorting and screaming behind us as the mynogres gave chase. Citrine hesitated before following us – I could do nothing for her, even if I wanted to. She was too far away.

'Now where?' Sage asked, slicing undergrowth out the way.

'Down here,' Rian said, leading us along a vine-strewn pavement, through trees and shrubs as ferns and vines grabbed at our legs.

Behind us, a shriek of abject horror and pain cut through the night air. Citrine screamed again as the sound of mynogres feasting drifted towards us. Nausea welled in my throat as I ran on. Her screams stopped abruptly.

The sound of the pursuing mynogres got louder as we sprinted along. We'd never out-run them at this rate. Hiding may be our only hope, but where could we hide here? The moon reflected off a half-overgrown pond, illuminating the trees as we ran past and – *a door*? It loomed out of the darkness to my left in a kind of grotto.

'Over here,' I said, cutting away from the path, forging my way through the vines and weeds with Aldorbana before reaching the grotto and making my way to the door. Made of stone, it sat near the pond, carved with all manner of herbs. I heaved on it, but it stood unyielding before me. 'Help me!'

Rian arrived and began pushing with me, hands flat on the cool stone. The door gave a little with a grinding stone-on-stone sound that made me wince. The mynogres were right behind us, crashing through the gardens. They were searching for us, drooling, and making hideous sounds. In the distance, a horse shrieked. A shiver swept down my spine at the sound of the poor animal's terror, my heart pounding.

'Open!' I yelled, losing patience, and hitting the door with the palm of my hand – it sprang open.

Rian glanced at me, then pulled me after him through the doorway and down damp, slippery steps.

'How do we shut it?' Anise asked, but as we descended the steps it closed behind us with an echoing boom. The sound of snarls stopped abruptly as the door shut, blocking out the horrifying sounds of the primal beasts close behind us.

We paused at the bottom of the steps surrounded by total darkness, the sort you find in caves where it has a life of its own, touching you and caressing your face with its blackness, a living entity of its own. As my eyes adjusted, I made out a green, ethereal glow coming from up ahead.

'Let's keep going,' I said, leading Rian on.

As we ventured along the tunnel, the light gradually got brighter. We reached a great hall illuminated by the soft green glow of several leafy plants, interspersed with shrubs and bushes that covered the floor. At the far end, a little waterfall chattered merrily as it entered the chamber from a crack high up in the wall and descended into a glowing pool before exiting via a gurgling stream that slipped underneath the left hand wall. Some of the plants had flowers of yellow and white that glimmered in the darkness, helping to illuminate the chamber.

'Is this what I think it is?' Rian asked, his voice trembling slightly with awe.

I frowned at him. 'What do you think it is?'

'I think so,' Anise said, his voice similarly hushed in reverence. 'The Chamber of Earth.'

'This isn't just legend after all,' Sage murmured, looking around. 'I didn't think it was real.'

'I'd always hoped,' Anise said as he began to study the plants around us, tongue out as he crouched down to look at a leaf.

'It's beautiful,' I said. No other word would ever come close to describing this chamber. The feeling of calm surrounding me lay at odds with my pounding heart and the fear lodged in my chest, but gradually the chamber overtook my body's anxiety and calm settled on me like a familiar blanket.

'Do you think the mynogres can get in?' Sage asked, glancing warily back towards the entrance.

'They'd be in here with us by now if they could; they weren't far behind us,' Rian said, putting his bag down.

'So, what now?'

'I think we can safely say the mynogres are nocturnal,' I said. 'We saw nothing of them in the daylight hours – only their handiwork.'

'Then we'll wait until dawn and move on to Cilantro Town, down on the coast,' Rian said. 'We can get passage on a ship there and head back to northern Aerba.'

'Whenever dawn is,' Sage muttered. 'How are we going to tell?'

I gazed up at the ceiling of the chamber to see a little shaft of moonlight seeping through the roof from a chink. 'We'll know when it's light,' I said, pointing towards it.

'Can you make the Elixir?' Rian asked suddenly, turning to Anise.

Anise shook his head as he stood up. 'I need a fire and everything in here is too damp, Rian. Besides, I don't feel it would be appropriate to light a fire in this chamber.'

Rian nodded. 'You're probably right. We might as well rest until dawn, make ourselves as comfortable as possible while we can,' he said, sitting on the moss-covered ground.

Sage gave him a sour look.

Anise grinned, moving off into the plants, inspecting each one as he went along, studying the leaves and flowers alike with one hand, his other resting on his Jade Amulet. 'Maybe I'll find something new that I can cultivate,' he said, looking at a reddish-green leaf.

Sage looked to the ceiling; Anise was in his element and it made me smile.

The chamber had an earthy smell and such a warm feel to it that we didn't need blankets as we lay on the soft ground to rest. I gazed at a glowing green plant growing not far from me.

'How could this place have been forgotten?' Rian asked, gazing around, his eyes like that of a child's in a toy shop.

'The mynogres may have seen to that,' Sage said. 'No one is going to do much exploring around here. And if they did, they'd be lucky to see the night out. I think the only reason we survived last night was because they already had prey.'

'Maybe.'

Sage turned over, trying to make himself comfortable.

'I'm sorry about your friend,' Rian said, looking at me.

'She wasn't my friend,' I said, shuddering at the thought of her demise.

'Even so, that was a bad way to go.'

'Yes, it was, and I wouldn't wish it on anyone. Not even Citrine.'

I lay there trying to calm my racing mind, enjoying the scents and the calm of the Chamber of Earth as the night progressed. Sage nodded off, snoring softly. I looked over at Rian and grinned.

'I have to put up with this almost every night,' Anise said from where he now lay resting.

'I'm sure he's worth it,' I said.

Anise turned to look at Sage, a smile breaking out over his serene features as he shifted his hair. 'Oh yes, Phire, he is.'

Eventually the pale yellow light of dawn slipped through the crack in the ceiling as daylight broke over the rainforest.

'Let's eat something, give the sun time to get up properly, then move on,' I said.

Rian nodded as Sage elbowed a sleeping Anise awake. By the time we'd finished eating, strong sunlight streamed through into the chamber.

'I'm loath to leave here, really,' Anise said, looking around as he collected his bags.

'Did you find any interesting plants?' I asked, sitting Aldorbana and Cwicsusl on my back.

'A couple,' Anise said. 'I'm going to see if I can cultivate them when we get back home and test them to find what medicinal uses they might have.'

'Let's go,' Rian said, shouldering his pack and leading the way towards the steps.

'How are we going to open the door?' Sage asked.

'We'll just ask it to open,' Rian said. 'It worked last night.'

Sage muttered something under his breath that I didn't hear, and Anise chuckled. We climbed – or tripped, in my case – up the dark steps to the door.

'Open, please,' Rian said as we got there.

'Please?' Sage asked him.

'There's no need for poor manners,' Rian said, placing his hand flat on the door.

I reached out, too, the stone cool on my palm. 'Have your weapons ready, just in case.'

The door made a grating sound and gradually opened. Bright sunlight streamed in, making me shy away for a moment. As my eyes adjusted to the light I turned back to the gardens, bathed in yellow as they sat proudly in all their overgrown glory, the plants closest to the chamber door trampled and flattened by the mynogres. The sun hung in the bluest sky I'd ever seen, as the sounds of insects and birds greeted us. Even this early in the morning, the air was thick with heat and humidity. Flowers of blue and yellow flourished near the pond, while on the water itself, white and pink water lilies lay strewn across the mirrored surface, fully open in the morning light. The perfume from the flowers drifted around the gardens, sweet and light, as we stepped out of the doorway, making our way back through the gardens and around the side of the palace. In the daylight I could see into some of the palace rooms, riddled with vines and other plants.

'This would have been an amazing place hundreds of years ago,' I said, glancing over the lily-covered moat to the crumpled buildings beyond.

'Imagine having lived here,' Anise said.

'Imagine having to leave it,' Sage said, screwing his nose up.

'That would have been tough,' Rian said, 'but after the Great Storm, they had no choice.'

I rounded the corner to the courtyard where we'd left the horses. 'Hell's teeth,' I said, turning away in an effort not to gag. The remains of Citrine's body lay beside the palace wall, just her bones and the odd bit of flesh left behind, the citrines in the hilts of her discarded knives sparkling in the sunlight.

It appeared that the mynogres had eaten our horses, too. Horse flesh and bone lay scattered around the courtyard, blood and guts splattered across the stone.

'We'll be walking the rest of the way, then,' Sage said.

'Try not to look,' Rian said, and we made our way out of the courtyard and over the bridge. 'We need to go southwest – let's see if there's an old road heading that way.'

We crossed the stone-paved square, turning south, jumping blocks of fallen masonry and vegetation where necessary. I climbed over a rotten log and followed Rian through a half-fallen archway into the next square.

'Over there, Rian – that road looks to be heading in the right direction,' Anise said, pointing across the square.

We walked towards it, under an archway, and exited the city, finding ourselves walking along a wide, partially-overgrown, ancient road with broken paving stones sticking up in places and trees attempting to encroach on the stone roadway. We followed the road through to the edge of the forest where we left the trees behind in the early afternoon. I paused and took a long breath. Thank the Stars we were out of there. I glanced back into the trees for a moment, then turned to the open ground and followed the others. The old roadway took us towards Cilantro Town, across gently sloping grasslands. After another couple of hours walking, and Sage complaining, we finally reached the town.

Nestled against the coast, Cilantro Town had a bustling feel to it. Wooden buildings rubbed against each other, some at odd angles, while others had become worn by the salty sea air. People filled the streets as they haggled for goods at market stalls that left the air filled with aromas from their wares. The strong smell of fish also filled our nostrils, and the salty tang of the sea drifted in from the water, clinging to everything it touched. We took rooms at an inn Sage had stayed at before, next to a little beach, not far from the natural harbour.

Sage spoke to the innkeeper before heading off with Anise and his Herb Chest into the kitchens.

I sat outside on the sand with glistening eyes, looking out over the sea, the sun dancing on the waves. Although I knew we were safe from the Coterie for a while after Citrine's demise, her persistence had forced my hand. As soon as I took the Elixir and I knew it had worked, I'd find a ship and get as far away from Rian as I could. It broke my heart to even contemplate it, but I had to keep him safe. Beryl would then call off the Coterie and he'd be left in peace, and I…

I would concentrate on tracking down Mal, because if I didn't, then I'd just sit in a heap, pining for Rian, and then I might as well have let Aldorbana and Cwicsusl kill me with their Curse after all. The sun kissed the horizon by the time Rian came to find me.

'It's ready,' Rian said, offering me his hand.

I inhaled deeply and took his hand. We went up to Sage and Anise's room and opened the door. Anise stood by a little table stirring a foul-smelling concoction, his tongue sticking out slightly as he concentrated.

'…and this is going to work?' Sage asked, looking at it suspiciously. 'You're not going to kill her?'

'A few weeks ago, that wouldn't have bothered you, Sage,' Anise said.

'Well, it does now.'

'It bothers us all, now,' Rian said, shutting the door behind us.

'And me most of all,' I said, eyeing the bright green liquid.

'You won't die, Phire,' Anise said, handing me the Elixir. 'Drink it – all of it.'

'How long will it take to work?' Rian asked, concern in his eyes.

Anise shrugged. 'No way of knowing. Although, if the Weapons haven't changed in twenty-four hours, I'd say it's failed. But that's not going to happen,' he said, winking at me. 'It'll work, don't worry.'

'All right,' I said. 'And I shouldn't have any ill effects from the Moonflower or Saliivia?'

'No.' Anise smiled.

I nodded, downing the whole Elixir in one go. I feared if I tasted it, I'd back out. I coughed. The foul-sweet liquid cloyed and burnt my throat, and I had to force it down, swallowing hard.

'You okay?' Rian asked, resting a hand on my shoulder.

I nodded. 'But I never want to drink it again,' I said emphatically.

'Then don't pick up any more Cursed Weapons,' Rian said with a grin.

'Very funny. Any change?' I asked, peering over my shoulder.

Sage shook his head. 'No, nothing yet.'

'It's a bit early, really. You've got to give it a chance to work,' Anise said.

We took our evening meal in the inn dining room. The whole time we sat there, I kept expecting something to happen – a flash, a bang, a sudden shockwave slamming through my body. But nothing happened. All I sensed was the bone-numbing tiredness that had been getting progressively worse over the last few days. After we ate, we sat and chatted for a while as the inn filled with noisy, regular patrons.

'I'm going up to bed,' I said, yawning.

'I'll take you,' Rian said, standing up.

'No, I'm fine, really,' I said, making my way to the stairs and starting to climb them. The stairs tilted. Cramping pains shot through my stomach and the stairs lurched again. A black wall rushed towards me. I tripped, falling onto the stairs as the stomach cramps intensified. I tried, unsuccessfully, to stifle a yelp of pain. As I lay writhing on the stairs, footsteps ran towards me, then someone held me tenderly in their arms.

'Phire? Anise, get over here, dammit!'

I looked up at Rian, trying to focus on his blurry face before he vanished as the black wall engulfed me like a wave.

CHAPTER SEVENTEEN

'I'm going to kill him.'

Beryl looked at me, her face red and her full lips white as she pressed them together. A glowing blue dress surrounded her like a cloud, shifting and undulating. We were in a prison cell, grey walls around us and a shaft of sunlight cutting into the gloom of the cell from a grate high above.

'Lay one finger on him and I'll kill you, bitch,' I said as colours swirled around me.

Beryl snarled. 'He will die. One way or another. He will die.'

She disappeared as a white mist drifted and spiralled every way I turned.

Warm arms slipped around me from behind and I turned to see Rian gazing at me, his eyes molten pools that I wanted to drown in and never leave. We were in a cave that glowed with all the colours of the rainbow, crystals lining the walls and shimmering like living things.

'You're safe, I'm here,' he said.

'But Beryl, she wants you dead, she—'

'There's no Beryl, only the two of us,' he said, pulling me closer and looking into my eyes. 'I love you, Phire.'

'I love you, too,' I said.

'Kiss me, then,' he murmured, leaning into me. His intoxicating, velvet lips caressed mine as a shock went through my system, a silken thread knotted in my stomach, and my veins erupted in fire. I'd never felt such desire, such love.

'Don't ever leave me. I want you. I need you,' I said.

'I won't leave you, Phire. I'll never leave you; just don't you leave me. I couldn't bear it, now,' he said brokenly, his voice cracking. 'Don't leave me.'

'But I have to leave you. I have no choice.'

'Why?'

'You're not safe.'

A deep red shadow loomed out of the glowing walls.

The ethereal light glinted off a blade as the shadow lunged.

Colours swirled around me.

Mal sat hunched up, shackled to a tall pine tree in the middle of a great stone hall. The walls were of green marble, the beige floor polished to a mirror finish. Above, the ceiling opened into a dark sky and rain fell, cascading into the hall, drenching my brother.

'Mal! Mal, where are you? I have to find you.'

He raised his head, his wet strawberry-blond hair plastered to his head. His blue-green eyes were blank and his face was devoid of all thought.

I shuddered, pulled back, and once again the mist swirled around me. The green hall fell away.

'Mal!' I screamed, reaching for him, but he had vanished, just like Beryl and just like Rian.

I didn't understand. Where had they all gone?

I was falling. Water rushed past my ears. A pain burned in my stomach like a cold flame.

Bright greens and reds clouded my vision before turning to yellows and greys. Again, the colours changed until I was in an open, grassy field, the sun beating down on my head. Rian lay on a bed of soft, purple silk cushions. His face was pale and he groaned in pain, clutching at his stomach, bending double.

'What is it? What is it?' I ran forwards.

Flames erupted around him, beating me back. The heat seared my face, the bright fire insisting that I stay away.

He screamed and my heart stuttered.

'Rian? Rian!*'*

'Samphire, wake up,' Rian said from beside me. 'Can you hear me? Are you all right?'

I opened my eyes. Sweat beaded on my brow. My shirt stuck to me like a limpet to a rock. My heart thundered in my chest and I gasped for air to soothe my sore lungs. I groaned. Everything hurt – my head, my arms, my chest. I turned towards Rian, his tired face etched with fear and relief in equal measure.

'I hurt all over,' I said, my voice croaky and my throat like sandpaper.

'You gave me – us – quite a scare,' he said, moving a curl from my face. He lay on the bed beside me, raised up on one shoulder. Other than a couple of candles flickering on the other side of the room, the place was in darkness.

'What happened?' I asked, still trying to clear my aching head.

'You had a bad reaction to the Elixir.'

'Did it work?' I asked, a sudden flash of hope escalating inside me.

'No, I'm afraid not,' he said, bowing his head. 'I'm so sorry. Anise is beside himself.'

Wretchedness washed over me. We'd failed. All that time, the mynogres, the Moonflower – everything had been for nothing. I could've been looking for Mal, but now it was too late. A surge of tears filled my eyes and a sob threatened to escape my lips as despair rolled through me. I choked it all back and tried to swallow.

'Tell Anise not to worry, and thank him for trying,' I said.

'You've had a bad fever and some violent hallucinations.'

'Oh.' Hallucinations? They'd seemed so real.

'Do you remember any of them?'

'No, not really,' I lied, remembering everything in minute detail. 'Can I have some water please?'

'You probably need it after all that,' he said, reaching for a glass of water beside the bed.

'What? Did I say something?' I asked, horrified at the thought.

'Nothing particularly intelligible,' he said, giving me the glass. He helped me sit up and I sipped on the water.

'Thank you,' I said, lying back down. 'How long have I been out?'

'A couple of days,' he said, putting the glass back.

'That long?'

'You were really quite ill. Look, I'll let Anise and Sage know you're okay,' he said, slipping from the bed and leaving the room.

A couple of days? *Hell's teeth*. My stomach ached as though someone had been using it to bounce on, and every time I moved, I couldn't help but groan. The door flew open and Anise rushed in.

'You're all right, Phire? Truly?' he asked, his buttery voice quivering as he knelt beside my bed. 'I was so worried about you. When you reacted like that – the fever, the hallucinations – I felt awful because it was all my fault. I'm so sorry, I had no idea that would happen. We've all looked after you, but Rian insisted on staying with you the whole time. He hasn't left your side for a minute.'

'It's all right, I'm okay. A little achy, but I'm fine. Really,' I said, taking his hand. 'Thank you for trying.' I paused. 'Rian's been with me the whole time?'

Anise nodded. 'He said you were saying some weird things, but I'm glad you're okay. I'm sorry it didn't break the Curse.'

'Don't worry,' I said as Rian and Sage entered the room. I'd said not to worry, but a heavy, dark cloak settled around my shoulders, pushing down on me. The Curse still prevailed, and I was doomed.

'I've been through the remedy book three times while you were ill, but there's nothing else that will help. I'm so sorry there aren't any other remedies to try.'

I squeezed his hand. 'Thank you anyway.'

'Thank the Herbs you're awake,' Sage said, giving me a relieved look. 'You had us all worried – some of us more than others, of course,' he said, giving Rian a knowing look.

Rian ignored him.

'It's time you rested now, though,' Anise said, standing up as I let go of his hand, his impossibly smooth skin glowing in the candlelight.

'All right, but just for a while. Then I think I'll want something to eat,' I said.

'In the morning, Phire, I don't think your stomach could take it at the moment,' Anise said as he and Sage left the room, closing the door behind them.

Rian moved over to the window and sat in a chair.

'What are you doing over there?' I asked, sitting up.

'I'm going to get some sleep, now you're back with us. Why? Did you want something?' he asked, frowning.

'Get over here. I need you with me.'

He smiled, leaving the chair ,and climbing under the covers with me. He turned towards me, gently stroking my hair. 'I thought I was going to lose you earlier.'

'I'm tough as old boots, me.' I grinned.

'You're not as tough as you think,' he said, kissing my forehead as his words sank in.

'You stayed with me the whole time. Anise told me.'

'It was nothing. I'd move the stars for you,' he said, holding my hand and gazing into my eyes.

My eyes swam with tears at his heartfelt words. He would move the stars for me. But why bother? The Elixir hadn't worked and I would soon be dead. The heavy, black cloak pressed against me.

'What is it?' he asked, frowning.

'It didn't work. I've put you through all this for nothing…' The sob I'd been holding back finally escaped and the tears began to fall. Finding the ingredients and taking the Elixir had filled me with such hope, but now…

'We had to try. We had to see if the Elixir would work,' he said, taking me into his arms as I sobbed. 'Hope isn't gone yet, Samphire. Tarragon may have found something. We can still do this – I damn well won't let you die.'

I couldn't get any words out as my body shook, wracked with disappointment and despair. He leant his forehead against mine and his hot tears mingled with my own warm ones. He held me close, murmuring into my ear, slowly lifting the black cloak away from me until I lay exhausted in his arms, cried-out yet comforted by his words and embrace.

'Get some sleep,' he said gently, pulling me even closer.

The following afternoon, I sat on the edge of the bed, glowering menacingly at Aldorbana and Cwicsusl who stared back at me, scarlet now only filling half of the Weapons. Rian and Anise had insisted I stay in bed all morning, and had brought food and drink to my room, but now I rebelled. I wanted to stretch my legs.

'You can go for a short walk, but only if you agree to holding my arm,' Rian said. 'You're bound to be a bit wobbly after the last couple of days, and the last thing I want is for you to stumble down the stairs or go careering off a cliff edge into the sea, never to be seen again.'

'Fine,' I said taking his arm, actually glad of his support as the room lurched.

'Are you all right?' he asked.

'I feel a little as if I'm on board a ship in a storm.'

'Then don't let go of me.'

'I won't.'

We left the inn, slowly making our way down to the beach. I sat next to him on the sand, watching the fishing boats out at sea, as a beautiful breeze wafted around me, keeping me cool.

'When do you plan to sail?' I asked.

'Not tomorrow. You need at least another day's rest before we go,' he said. 'The day after, we'll head for Hops and then Viridi.'

I nodded. He was right, I needed the rest and I definitely had something of a balance issue at the moment, too. I knew I wasn't well enough to leave him now, as I'd planned, and with the failure of the Moonflower Elixir I'd also lost any chance of finding Mal before the Curse took me. A worm of fear and despair wriggled uncomfortably in my chest.

I spent the next day resting as instructed by all three young men but, the morning after, we boarded *The Sea Urchin* bound for Hops. The First Mate, a man in his mid-thirties, welcomed us on board. As I walked past him, I noticed a strange look of recognition flicker in his sea-green eyes upon seeing the Weapons on my back. Did he know what they were? If he did, he didn't say anything and carried on welcoming Anise and Sage onto the ship.

As I stood on the deck, a little shiver slid down my spine as I remembered how the last sea journey had ended, but I put those thoughts out of my mind. The two-and-a-half day journey to Hops gave me a further chance to rest and recover from my ordeal. The combination of the Curse and the Elixir had taken their toll, although I didn't like to admit as much. That evening, Rian and I stood at the ship's rail in companionable silence, gazing out over the water.

'Would you really kill for me?' he asked suddenly.

'What?' I looked sharply at him.

'When you were hallucinating, you said something about killing to keep me safe.'

What else had I said out loud? 'I thought you said I didn't say anything when I was hallucinating?'

He rubbed the back of his neck. 'There were fragments. Bits and pieces, here and there.'

'I'd rather not kill – you know my feelings about that. But, I suppose, if push came to shove and it was the only way to save you, then – yes, I would kill to keep you safe.'

He turned, giving me a little smile.

'What else did I say?' I asked, searching his face for answers.

'Nothing I could make out,' he said, turning back to the sea.

By the next morning, my balance was much improved, but the fatigue remained. I rested as much as possible, but I'd never been the best patient and preferred to be out on the deck, as opposed to being in the cabin or stuck below in a swinging hammock. I stood at the prow watching a curtain of rain approaching – as long as it didn't turn into a full-blown storm, I didn't mind the rain. The wind got up, flapping the sails above my head, whipping a loose strand of hair into my eyes. I re-tied my hair as the first few raindrops started to fall. In moments, the few had become a deluge, and I made a dash for the cabin as the deck became slippery.

'Quick,' Rian said, coming up from the sleeping quarters, heading for the cabin. As I moved, my balance and the treacherous deck decided to play a joke on me and I slipped, grabbed for the rail, and missed. Rian grasped my hand, saving me from falling and making a complete idiot of myself. His fingers intertwined with mine as he held me upright, and my heart skipped about like a jackrabbit. 'Come on.'

We made our way into the cabin, turning back to watch the raindrops bouncing on the deck and splashing off ropes. The wind continued to whistle high above in the rigging as the sailors went about their work.

'At least it's not like last time,' I said, gazing out into the veil of rain.

'I don't want to experience that again,' Rian said, screwing up one side of his nose.

'I'm amazed you got Anise out to sea once more after the shipwreck,' Sage said from where he sat at a table with Anise.

'The ship was the lesser of two evils – I'm not going back through the Cilantro Rainforest ever again,' Anise said, looking through the remedy book.

'Is there anything else of use in there?' Rian asked.

Anise shook his head. 'I don't think so. I've been through it several times, now, but unless you want a cure for a bunion or an ingrown toenail, I don't think it'll be of much use to you.'

'I never asked you if your father's book had survived,' Rian said to me.

I pulled it out of my coat where I'd kept it since leaving Iolite. 'Take a look,' I said, passing it to him.

He picked up the bedraggled book and tried to open it. Most of the pages were stuck together. 'Oh.'

'It's more of a keepsake than anything, now,' I said as he passed it back to me. A solitary page fell open.

'Does that say anything helpful?' Rian asked.

I glanced at the open page. Nothing made much sense. 'Something about Quintessence Angle Spinners sometimes using Artefacts against each other and sometimes with each other. That doesn't help much.'

'My father used to say something about Artefacts being used against Artefacts,' Anise said, looking up from his book. 'I never entirely understood what he meant, but he never said anything about Spinners doing it, but maybe I wasn't listening properly.'

'The Weapons are both Artefacts – could they be used against each other in some way?' Rian asked, a hopeful look in his eye.

I shrugged. 'We can try,' I said, removing Cwicsusl and Aldorbana from my back. 'What do you think I should do with them?'

'Hit them together?' Anise suggested.

I took a deep breath and hit the shield with the sword. Nothing happened.

'It was worth a try,' Rian said, his shoulders sagging.

'Perhaps it didn't work because they're made from the same Artefact?' I said, returning the Weapons to my back and the book to my coat.

'Maybe.'

The rain continued to fall and the wind whistled as the morning wore on, drawing into afternoon. We ate a decent fish lunch, except for Sage, and I went back to watching the rain out the cabin door.

Until it stopped. Abruptly. The wind fell to nothing, the ship slowing to a stop.

A little shiver ran down my spine.

'What's the matter?' Rian asked, coming to join me.

I stepped out on the deck. Every last one of the sailors had stopped their work and were looking around, out over the rail, worried expressions on their faces. Some grabbed hooks and knives, readying themselves for something.

'What is it?' Rian asked the nearest sailor to us, but I didn't need a sailor to tell me.

The sailor looked at Rian, fear in his eyes. 'Morgens.'

I sped over the wet deck to the rail, looking out at the water like everyone else, my pulse racing as I feared what may come next.

'Morgens? But–' Rian stopped.

An ethereal, melancholy song soared over the still water – one voice first, then another and another until a whole choir sang in unison. Their chorus rose and fell, then harmonies intertwined with single voices, the lilting tones turning into a mesmerising melody. I turned back to the sailor. His face had changed from fear to a terrifying blankness, and he moved slowly towards the ship's rail. I turned to see the other sailors doing the same, shuffling towards the railings. One man down by the prow jumped over the side.

I peered over the rail. The sea glowed with an unworldly green and, right below the surface, the sylph-like figures of women floated in the water, their long, dark hair flowing around faces of such exquisite beauty that any man, or woman, would be forgiven for finding them attractive. But their seductive song held no appeal for me.

'What's going on?' Sage asked, running out of the cabin with Anise.

I turned towards them and froze. Rian had that same blank expression on his face. He took a step towards the rail.

'They've been enchanted,' I said, running back to Rian. I took hold of his arm, but he pulled me along with him. 'Stop,' I yelled at him.

He took another step towards the rail – and his impending death – as a sailor close to us threw himself over the side.

'We have to stop them,' I said, a sense of panic rising within me.

'How?' Anise asked, horrified by the desperate scene playing itself out around us.

'Grab them, tie them down,' Sage said. 'Or knock them out. It's the only way.'

I desperately tried to slow Rian's progress towards his watery doom but failed miserably. *Hell's teeth.*

There was only one thing I could do – exactly what Sage had suggested.

So, I hit the Prince of Aerba.

Hard.

CHAPTER EIGHTEEN

The right hook I'd planted on his jaw sent Rian tumbling across the deck, and I immediately regretted the force I'd used, but I'd be damned if I was going to let those creatures take him from me into the watery depths of their realm. The morgens' song continued to swell around the ship, the sails sagging in the lifeless air, the sky overhead taking on an unhealthy, greenish tinge. I shook my throbbing hand as I looked around.

'We have to stop as many as we can from jumpin' in,' a sailor yelled, climbing down from the rigging, his weathered skin sparkling with raindrops. I recognised him as the First Mate.

Sage and Anise had already started grabbing sailors, rendering them unconscious as I raced to find a coil of rope. The First Mate helped me tie Rian's hands and feet so that when he came to, he couldn't go anywhere. Between the four of us, we managed to restrain over half the crew, either by knocking them out or by tying them up, but the rest threw themselves overboard in a hypnotic stupor, disappearing below the still water, taken to the depths by the morgens.

I now found the song irritating, rather than seductive, and it rang in my ears as we slumped on the deck, exhausted by our efforts. I wiped sweat from my forehead and took a sip of water from a waterskin, taking in the sight of the unconscious and tied-up men. The conscious ones writhed, fighting against their bonds, but we'd tied them so tight they had no chance of escape. Some of them cried out as they tried to get into the water with the morgens.

'I'm Hyssop, by the way, and thanks for your help,' the First Mate said, sitting beside me on the deck.

'Nice name,' I said.

He smiled, his deep green eyes sparkling. 'Actually, my parents just didn't have much imagination. I was born in Hyssop, on the north coast, so they named me after it.'

'Could've been worse,' Sage sniffed. 'You could've been called Sorrel.'

Anise looked at him and smirked.

Hyssop frowned.

'Long story,' I said. 'So why aren't we affected by the song?'

Hyssop looked a little uncomfortable for a moment, glancing at Anise and Sage. 'I take it the two of you...'

'We're together,' Sage said emphatically, with no hint of embarrassment.

'You're like us, Hyssop?' Anise asked.

The sailor nodded. 'Not that I'd normally admit it, thanks to the Blood Decree.' He glanced nervously at me. 'I assume my secret is safe with you?'

'I won't betray you. I come from Iolite, so you don't need to worry about that,' I said, looking over towards Rian. I reached over, moving his hair to see a red mark where I'd hit him. I winced. That was going to be sore. 'But what about me?'

'I guess that saved you,' he said, pointing at my Amethyst Talisman that had slipped out from my tunic during the excitement.

'What?'

'It has the power of protection, doesn't it?'

I wore my amethyst for inner strength, but there were those on Iolite who believed that amethyst could be worn for protection. Was that what had happened here? I slipped the amethyst back under my tunic, intrigued.

'You're with the Coterie?' Hyssop asked, looking at my naked wrist.

I glanced at my arm and moved Rian's leather strap back across the tattoo.

'Not anymore, she's not,' Anise said.

'I didn't think anyone ever escaped the Coterie,' Hyssop said.

'There's always a first,' I said.

'I heard the Coterie sent Lady Merciless to kill Crown Princess Angelica. Is that true?'

Anise glanced at Sage. 'Well…'

'They sent her, but she didn't kill the princess,' I said, fidgeting with Rian's wrist strap.

'I know Princess Angelica didn't have the best reputation, but it's an awful way to go, and now people are sayin' someone at the Court ordered her assassination.'

'What?' Sage asked, looking quickly towards Hyssop and making his earring jingle. 'Someone at Court commissioned the assassination?'

'You didn't know?' Hyssop asked, a surprised look in his green eyes. 'That's the rumour goin' around – it might even have been someone in the Royal Family, so the whispers say.'

'Don't be ridiculous. No one in the Royal Family would do such a thing.'

Hyssop shrugged. 'It's just a rumour.'

Sage grunted, looking out over the water. 'If only the wind would get up,' he muttered, clenching a fist.

The singing reached a crescendo, the soaring melody so loud that it drowned out my thoughts. I'd just started contemplating going to the side of the ship to shout profanities at the morgens in an attempt to get them to shut up when the song ceased abruptly. Wind returned to the sails, the green tint to the water and sky vanished, and rain fell once more.

'Oh, great,' I said, looking sourly up at the sky.

'At least we're moving again,' Sage said, tugging at his earring.

The men around the deck began to come to once the ship started moving, their blank expressions replaced by looks of horror and fear. We cut them free and, although they got on with their work in the pouring rain, they all looked like haunted men.

'Don't tell them about me,' Hyssop said quietly.

We nodded as we cut Rian free, carrying him back into the cabin. I got a cloth, cooled it in some water, and held it to his jaw. As I watched him, memories of my hallucinations returned and I saw him once more, lying in pain, surrounded by fire. I tried to shake the image from my mind, but it was impossible, and it left an uneasy sensation in the pit of my stomach.

Eventually he came around, the same haunted look in his eyes as in the other men's. He started shaking, sweat beading on his brow, his face pale.

'Hey, it's all right, you're okay,' I said, gently touching his head, still holding the cloth to his jaw with my other hand.

'W-what happened?' he asked. A jolt of pain flashed across his face as he reached gingerly for his jaw, his hand resting gently over mine.

'I'm so sorry. I had to hit you,' I said, wincing and looking down. 'It was the only way to stop you from jumping overboard.'

'You saved my life. I don't think a bruised jaw really matters,' he said, the haunted look beginning to fade, although the shaking continued. 'I didn't know what I was doing. I felt this yearning, this pull from the sea.'

'They were morgens, the beautiful Sea-born creatures who call people into the water.'

The haunted look returned. 'I had no control. I couldn't stop it. I tried, but I couldn't.'

'You can't fight that sort of Magic, Rian,' I said, trying to reassure him.

Sage, who sat in the corner of the room, looked to the ceiling and made a face.

'I'm so sorry,' Rian said, bowing his head. 'I let you down.'

'No, you didn't,' I said. 'It's not your fault they tried to lure you to them.'

He rubbed the back of his neck. 'I know, but I still don't want you thinking any less of me because of it,' he said, his cheeks flushing slightly. Sage tried, unsuccessfully, to suppress a chuckle. Rian apparently hadn't realised Sage and Anise were in the room until then, because his eyes widened, and his face flushed all the more.

'Don't be daft,' I said. 'Of course I don't think any less of you, it wasn't your fault. The only reason these two weren't affected was because they're too wrapped up in each other,' I said, casting Sage a long look. Sage's face turned a delightful red and he looked away. Anise smiled broadly, then looked through his Herb Chest.

'And you?' Rian asked.

'I was too busy trying to stop you,' I said with a grin. 'I didn't have time to think about jumping overboard.'

Something flickered in Rian's eyes that set my pulse racing.

'Here, take this,' Anise said, moving over to Rian and giving him a little red glass vial as his other hand went to his Amulet. 'The tincture will help you to calm down.'

Rian took it and held it up to the light. 'No Saliivia?'

'No, Rian, no Saliivia,' Anise said with a grin.

The rest of the journey passed uneventfully. I noticed Hyssop now gave the orders, the captain having jumped overboard to his death. I stood on deck as we approached land, one hand fiddling with my Amethyst Talisman as I leant on the rail with the other hand. I watched a thunderstorm far out to sea, the lightning striking at the water like a fisherman with his spear, thunder barrelling across the water. A warm hand covered mine on the rail – Rian's fingers interlacing with mine as he stood beside me, his maroon hair catching the wind. He didn't say anything, just stood there holding my hand until we docked. He let go as we turned to leave the ship, collecting our bags before heading for the gangplank.

I paused as I reached Hyssop. 'Thanks for your help, Captain Hyssop,' I said with a grin.

'It's been my pleasure – and thanks for yours,' he said with a smile. Then a frown crossed his face as he glanced towards my back. 'You know what you're carryin'?'

I nodded. 'I'm afraid so.'

'You don't have long.'

'I know. But how do you–'

'Come on, Samphire,' Sage interrupted from the dock below.

'Good luck,' Hyssop said, walking back across the deck.

'And to you, too,' I said. How had he known about the Weapons? I wanted to talk to him more, to find out what he knew, but Anise grabbed my arm and tugged me towards the gangplank and the dockside.

Hops wasn't dissimilar to Cilantro Town, bustling with folk. Like all fishing towns, the smell of salt and fish lingered in the air as we made our way further up into the buildings, taking rooms at a wooden inn at the edge of town. Rian had decided not to begin travelling so late in the afternoon, so we set about stocking up on supplies ready for the journey to Viridi. If we started early tomorrow, we'd arrive the afternoon of the following day. Sage arranged horses for the journey, and we met in the taproom for a meal as the sun began to set, casting its golden threads between the buildings.

The barmaid brought us our food, a hearty meal of stew and dumplings, and four mugs of mead. I didn't particularly enjoy mead with its cloying honey flavour which rather stuck in my throat, but the fresh water here had been tainted by the sea following a recent unseasonal storm, so it would have to suffice. Rian took one look at the mugs of mead and went to the bar.

'Doesn't he like mead?' I asked, stirring my stew with a spoon as I waited for the near-boiling liquid to cool enough to eat.

Sage shook his head. 'Hates it. He'll be after a mug of Pine Tea, I expect.'

A man after my own heart. 'Rian – can you get me a mug of tea, too, please?' I called. He turned, smiled, and nodded.

We had far more in common than I'd have guessed when we first met.

A few minutes later he came back with two steaming mugs.

'Thanks,' I said, taking one from him.

'Not keen on mead, either?' he asked.

'No, I'm with you on that one,' I said, glancing up towards the door.

A hooded figure near the entrance reached out to open the door. Its sleeve slipped back, and a cold hand grabbed my heart at the sight of a tattoo. The figure turned slightly. Dark, lank hair slipped out of the hood.

My head whipped back to our table – on the tray that'd brought our drinks and food sat a small red bead. A signature.

Rian picked up his bowl of now-cooled stew, about to take a spoonful. I smashed it from his hand before it met his lips, and it clattered to the floor, sending the beige liquid and dumplings splattering across the wooden boards.

'Don't eat or drink anything, any of you,' I said, dashing from the table and out the door before any of them could speak. I scanned both ends of the twilight street – where was he? There, ducking into an alley. I sprinted after the figure – this could be one person and one person only. Carnelian. He liked the poison route, particularly in large quantities. It killed quickly but spectacularly, causing his victim to convulse, foam at the mouth, and quite often to scream uncontrollably until they died, left in a contorted shape, face cast in a hideous grin.

I reached the alley just in time to see him heading towards a horse. He wasn't getting away, not if I had anything to do with it. I ran down the alley, climbed up onto a low-roofed stable, and sprinted across the top of it, taking me parallel to Carnelian's escape. He mounted his horse and looked behind him with a smile, completely unaware I was shadowing him above. He urged his horse into a trot. I jumped from the roof and slammed into him, knocking him from his horse, rolling to my feet before he'd even realised what had happened. I immediately pounced on him, my War Fan in hand, the amethyst button triggering the blades which now rested against his throat.

He looked up at me in shock. 'Amethyst-sweetie,' he said, trying to compose himself, his honeyed voice not quite as confident as usual. 'As sprightly as ever, I see.'

'Who sent you, Carnelian?' I demanded, my Fan pressed hard against his neck. I needed to know for sure if Onyx was right.

He smiled. 'The Coterie, of course. Your princeling isn't their favourite person right now.'

'*Who* sent you?' I pressed on my War Fan so that the tiniest of rivulets of blood trickled down the side of his throat.

He gave me a particularly nasty smile. 'Your sister doesn't like you very much, does she? She wants Prince Valerian dead. As long as you stay with him, that is. So, I volunteered.'

Hell's teeth.

'The bitch,' I cursed.

'Language, Amethyst-sweetie, language,' Carnelian admonished me, his right eye twitching.

'Shut up, Carnelian.' For a moment, I wondered if he knew about his sister's demise, but his demeanour made me think otherwise. When he found out, there would be hell to pay, and I wasn't going to be the one to tell him.

A rat shot out from a stable, spooking Carnelian's horse. The beast reared and stepped backwards, knocking into us. I rolled clear as the horse stumbled and fell over a water trough. Carnelian scrambled out of the way. Or at least he tried to. The horse's downward trajectory caught him in its path, and the beast landed on top of the assassin. I looked up to see the horse unable to get back on its feet, most likely due to a broken leg, and Carnelian lying on the paved ground, blood running from his ear. The horse shifted and snorted in pain.

'Are you all right?' Rian asked, running over with Anise and Sage.

I nodded as he helped me up. This had sealed it. I had to leave Rian. I'd do it tomorrow night, once we'd camped and he'd gone to sleep. 'His name's Carnelian,' I said. 'He'd been sent to kill you. You didn't eat or drink anything, did you?'

'No, none of us did,' Rian said, shaking his head.

'Why don't we eat at a different inn?' Sage suggested. 'He can't have got to all of them, and I'm not eating in that one, now. Who knows what else he might have poisoned?'

Rian nodded. 'Let's do it.'

'Are you just going to leave them here, Rian?' Anise asked, looking at the bodies of the young man and the still-writhing horse.

'We'll have a word with the stable lad on the way back,' Rian said. 'I saw him in another stable back there. He can get the owner to sort out the accident.'

I glanced at Rian. 'I didn't kill him.'

'I know, we saw what happened,' he said, patting my shoulder.

I retracted the blades on my War Fan, flicking it shut and returning it to my belt. Sage led the way back to the main street after pausing to speak to the stable lad. We ate in a clean enough-looking inn, although my appetite had gone. A combination of the attempt on Rian's life, and what I had to do, had suppressed my hunger entirely.

When we got back to our inn, I lay in bed for several hours, staring at the ceiling. I was so tired that sleep would never come, now, and I was aware of the tears streaming down my face. I couldn't leave it any longer. I couldn't wait until tomorrow night. The longer I waited, the longer Rian's life would be in danger, and all because of me. It was possible that Carnelian wasn't the only Coterie assassin in town.

I climbed out of bed, wiped my eyes, and dressed. With dawn

still a couple of hours off, I left my room with my bag, creeping down the stairs, my senses heightened for any sign of discovery, only putting my boots on once downstairs. I left the inn, opening the door with shaking hands, and slipped out into the lamp-lit street.

Walking along the street I paused to look back at the building that held my love, my eyes once again glistening with tears. Leaving him and doing it now tore my heart to pieces. Onyx had been right all along, though. I had no choice in this if I was to keep Rian alive. My shattered heart didn't matter; the only thing that mattered was his life.

I had no choice.

My heart wrenched in my chest, but I had to keep him safe, even if it meant losing him forever. A little voice at the back of my mind said I wouldn't make it out of town before I turned back. It was probably right, but I had to try. For his sake. I knew the ache that now lodged in my chest would never leave me.

Rian had captivated me with his lopsided smile, his kindness and intelligence. He'd seduced me with his rich voice, his understanding and strength. And now I was his. Leaving him would change none of that.

I turned away and collided with a hard body.

I gasped.

'Where do you think you're going?' Rian stood in front of me, frowning. He glanced at the pack on my shoulder. Was that fear in his eyes? 'You're leaving me?'

CHAPTER NINETEEN

His words cut me to the core.

'Y-you don't understand,' I said.

'It seems fairly clear to me,' Rian said, his face downcast as he reached out and gripped my shoulders. 'You've got your pack – you're going without me. You can't do this.'

'I have to,' I said miserably. 'If I don't, you'll die. Don't you see?'

He shook his head, his eyes glassy. 'No, I don't. You can't go. I need you!'

My heart stuttered. 'Every day I stay with you, you're in danger.'

'But–'

'Onyx said Beryl wants you dead because you're with me. Citrine made two attempts, Carnelian tried again last night, but there *will* be others. They're just two of many. But the attempts will only continue while I stay with you. If I leave, Beryl will call the Coterie off. She only wants to kill you to hurt me, and I can't let that happen. I won't. I have to leave you to keep you safe. I have to–'

'Slow down,' he said, loosening his grip, but still holding me. 'It won't stop just because you leave.'

I frowned. 'But...'

'She'll have me dead anyway if it's to hurt you. And even if your sister does let it go, I don't think Juniper will. She wasn't happy that I escaped. I wouldn't be surprised if she plans to kill all of the Aerban Royal Family.'

My eyes widened. 'But why would she want to do that?'

'To step in? To take control by herself? It was something Onyx said about her insatiable desire to control everything, to rule the Five Lands, which got me thinking, and I believe he's right.'

'The control part certainly sounds like her,' I said, looking at him. 'But I don't want you to die because of me.'

He glanced away into a side alley, then pulled me along with him into a stable lit by one small lamp where two horses stood in their stalls, nickering softly. Having checked we were safe from prying eyes, he turned to me, his eyes burning with an intensity I'd never seen from him before. 'I don't want you to go because I can't live without you.'

My heart skipped.

'If you leave me now, I might as well be dead,' he continued. 'I need you with me. I *want* you with me, whatever the risk, whatever the cost. If you go, Beryl and Juniper might as well kill me because

I honestly don't think I could go on without you. I don't *want* to go on without you by my side.'

I swallowed.

'My heart was breaking as I left,' I said miserably. 'I didn't want you in any more danger. I didn't want to be responsible for the death of the person dearest to me.'

'Then stay with me, Phire. You're one of – if not *the* – most skilled fighter I've ever known. You've proved that over and over, saving our lives more than once. With you next to me I stand the best chance of staying alive.'

'That's what Anise said.'

'You told Anise, but not me?' Hurt swelled in his eyes.

'I didn't know how to tell you. This happening – you being in danger – it's all my fault. I told Anise because I asked him to come after the Elixir with me, alone, to keep you safe, but then you insisted on coming anyway and we never got the chance. I just wanted to keep you alive, and I still do.' I paused. 'I didn't want you thinking badly of me because of what Beryl was trying to do to you – all because of *me*.'

Rian's eyes clouded. 'You shouldn't have worried about that. I could never think badly of you.'

'I-I don't know what to do,' I said helplessly as a tear finally escaped my eye, rolling down my cheek.

Rian tenderly brushed it away. 'It's quite simple; we stay together, whatever the risk,' he said, pausing for a moment. 'But you should have told me everything sooner – told me and not Anise.'

'I know. I'm sorry. I didn't want you to worry, and I suppose I didn't want you to know you were in danger because of me, because I lacked the courage to leave you.'

He smiled. 'The last thing you lack is courage. Just promise you'll speak to me in future. No more secrets.'

'I promise,' I said, nodding. 'No more secrets.'

'I'd probably have been in danger from the Coterie sooner or later, anyway. The one thing I'm not letting you do is leave me, because of me. I'd do anything for you – I'd walk unarmed into a room of assassins if it meant I got to be with you. As far as I'm concerned, staying with you far outweighs any risk from the Coterie. Together, we're stronger than they are.'

One moment my heart was shattering into a million pieces, the next it swelled with love again. 'But the Curse – I don't know how long I've got.'

'I don't care how long you've got. We'll find a way to break it. I need you. I *want* you. Stay with me, Phire, please.'

I nodded, not trusting myself to speak.

'Is that a yes?' he asked, the lopsided smile appearing again in the lamplight.

'Yes. Yes, I'll stay with you. I'm not sure I'd have made it very far, if I'm honest. I was having second thoughts even before now – I'd probably have been back by breakfast time,' I said ruefully, feeling a little ashamed of my lack of resolve.

He smiled. 'I'd have come after you once I'd realised you'd gone,' he said. 'I'll never let you go now, Samphire Amethyst.' He pulled me towards him into a bear hug.

'I don't want you to,' I said, suddenly desperate for him to kiss me. The yearning that I'd felt before, now went deeper; the longing I'd had for his touch increased, and my desire for him now outshone everything else. I loved him so much I ached.

'You still smell of roses,' he said, pulling back a little and reaching towards my chin, gently turning my flaming face, and forcing me to look into those eyes I so desperately wanted to drown in. He leant towards me, tilting his head.

He was going to do it. He was going to cross that invisible line. And I would let him because I would cross it with him. We'd cross it together, hand in hand. My breath caught in my throat.

My heart pounded as his lips brushed mine so tenderly that they set off all manner of sparks within my body, but then he pulled back. 'Is-is it all right if I kiss you?' he asked, hesitantly. 'I'll only do it if you're sure, *absolutely* sure.'

I nodded, my heart skipping in my chest, and a tingling sensation working its way through me. 'Yes, I'm absolutely sure,' I said.

'The only thing is, if I do kiss you, I may never stop,' he murmured, his breath hitching as he gazed at me.

'I don't want you to ever stop,' I said, staring into his eyes, drowning. 'Don't stop–'

This time he leant towards me with purpose. He gathered me into his arms, pulling me close as he kissed me, gentle and a little hesitant at first, his hot, velvet lips triggering raging wildfires in my veins. Any shyness vanished as the kiss deepened. His breathing changed, became heavier as wonderful new sensations swept through me that I couldn't even begin to put names to. I ran my fingers through his hair, sandalwood enveloping me as I pressed my body into his. By the time he finally pulled back, I was lightheaded and breathless. He gazed into my eyes and smiled, his pupils dilating, his eyes burning with the same desire I felt.

One kiss wasn't enough. I pulled him back to me, my mouth

meeting his sweet, intoxicating lips. I'd never tire of this. I sensed his heartbeat, his warm body, his scorching touch. We lingered in each other's arms; our true feelings finally laid bare. Eventually we parted.

'I want to tell you something that I should have told you a while ago,' he said, his voice hoarse.

'Go on.'

He hesitated a moment, taking hold of both my hands then looking into my eyes before speaking.

'I love you. I've loved you for some time, now, but I've been too afraid to tell you because of the Blood Rules. I love you with all my heart. In truth, I've felt something for you from the moment I fished you out of that damned samphire creek, it just took me a while to work out what it was. I've wanted to kiss you before, more than once, but in the end I didn't dare. But when you were ill, I realised how deep my feelings went. In fact, there was a time we thought we might lose you, and I found that I couldn't bear it. I knew then that I had to tell you how I really felt, Blood Rules or no Blood Rules. Whatever the cost, I had to kiss you at least once. I had to tell you I loved you. I love you more than I ever thought possible.'

Blood rushed to my face and my heart leapt for joy, doing its best impression of a blacksmith with his anvil. 'I love you too, Rian,' I said, my voice croaky. 'Since the creek, I've found I can't get you out of my head – or my heart – and I don't want to.'

He reached out, shifting my hair from my eyes. The look he gave me would've melted the hardest of hearts. My soul sang at his words, and I knew I'd never be happier than I was at that moment. He leant towards me, his mouth meeting mine once more, triggering a heat that spread from my fingers to my toes as I tasted the sweetness of his warm tongue. He held me close, his hands on my back, mine around his neck.

'We'd better get back,' he said finally, drawing away. 'It's almost dawn.'

I took a deep breath. 'The honest truth is – I couldn't leave you because of my love for you. And loving you has put your life in danger, and that's all my fault.'

He gazed into my eyes. 'None of this is your fault, so stop thinking like that. It's the Coterie's. Even if it was, I wouldn't change a thing. I'd still want you, still need you – still love you – despite any danger or risk.'

'But–'

'No,' he said firmly, resting his finger over my lips. 'We *both* fell in love. *Both* want to be together. And from now on, we will do everything together. Yes?'

'Together.' I nodded, my heart thundering away. He loved me for me. With all the baggage I brought, with all my scars. None of it mattered to him. 'I love you.'

Rian smiled, bent forward, and kissed my nose. 'And I love you, more than anything in this world.' He took my hand, gently intertwining his fingers with mine, and kissed it, sending sparks up my arm. 'But we'd better not hold hands on the way back, just in case we're being watched.'

'At this hour?'

'With the Nightshade you can never be too sure. Just know, in my head, I'm walking back with my arms around you, and in my heart, I'm holding you.'

My breath caught at his words. It turned out that Prince Valerian could be quite romantic. He started to move towards the door.

'Why were you out here?' I asked, reaching out to stop him.

He paused, my hand on his arm. 'Oh. That,' he said, glancing away. 'I couldn't sleep. You see, I've been – I've been having nightmares since you were ill. I keep losing you in my dreams, and I didn't want it to happen again tonight, so I went for a walk to clear my head.'

'You didn't lose me, I'm right here,' I said, still holding on to his arm, stepping closer to him and resting my head on his shoulder.

'Maybe I should've just come to your room and climbed into bed with you,' he said.

'As long as we didn't get caught, Prince Valerian. There'd be hell to pay if we did.'

'You have no idea. It'd probably be death for the both of us,' he said with a grin.

'You've never tried it before?' I asked slyly.

'There's never been anyone like you before,' he said. 'It's never even been a thought that's entered my head. Besides, isn't it the same in Iolite?'

I nodded. 'Only, if you get caught there, you get tortured before they execute you. And for the record, no, it's not something I've ever entertained, either.'

'It's a good thing that no one knows we shared blankets when we were camping.'

'That was perfectly innocent,' I said indignantly.

'It was, then. I don't know about now. I guess we've already crossed the line by admitting our feelings for each other – but I'm seriously beginning to think about breaking all the Blood Rules.'

'Oh, really?' I arched an eyebrow. 'What are you suggesting, Your Highness?'

'I intend to show you one day, one way or another,' he said, his eyes full of love. We left the stables, heading back to the inn – but we didn't hold hands, just in case.

The day dawned clear, and we set off early, Rian keen to get back to Viridi as soon as we could. As we rode along, I hummed happily, removing Cwicsusl from my back to find a more comfortable position for it. I stopped humming. Well over half of Cwicsusl shone clear with little rainbows dancing inside the crystal. How long did I have left with Rian? The more I exerted myself, and the longer time went on, the quicker the red crystal depleted. Even if I rested, the probability of the Weapons retaining any colour for much more than another week had to be slim. Nausea rose in my throat. I silently returned Cwicsusl to my back.

'Are you all right, Phire? You look a little peaky,' Anise said, riding up beside me.

'I'm fine, still rather tired, that's all,' I said. I looked ahead to where Rian was riding quietly – he'd hardly said anything since we'd left Hops. 'Anise, I don't have long left. Will you make sure Rian's looked after when I'm...'

Anise's eyes glistened. 'We'll look after him, but there's still a chance we can break the Curse.'

'I can't see how. Not now. We've run out of options.'

'There's still Tarragon.'

We rode hard during the day, stopping for the night at an old barn a short distance off the road. The next day we'd reach Viridi, and the thought terrified me. As far as King Finule was concerned, I'd failed in my mission. I hadn't found out who was behind his daughter's death. I did know who'd killed her but telling him about Mal wouldn't help. And as for the Fire Opal? Well, an excursion to Flos seemed to be the only way to find answers. My chances weren't good. Even if Finule did have some way to break the Curse that we didn't know about, I doubted he'd use it, given the circumstances. We sat while Sage prepared a lovely stew, and after we'd eaten, we chatted for a while.

'It looks like a nice evening, so I'm going to make the most of it and stretch my legs for a while,' Sage said, then looked at Anise. 'Coming?'

Anise nodded. 'Don't wait up for us, we might be a while.'

Sage flushed. 'I like long evening walks sometimes,' he said, but I didn't believe a word of it.

'Take your time,' Rian said, not noticing their sudden discomfort, his mind elsewhere. The two young men walked out of the barn and around the corner, disappearing out of sight.

'I think I'm going to get some sleep,' I said, searching for my blankets.

'Before you do, I wanted to talk to you,' Rian said, moving to sit beside me on a hay bale.

'Oh, what about?'

'While we were riding today, I did some thinking. I've thought about it a lot and I've made up my mind.'

A chill shot through me. 'We can't be together because of the Blood Rule Decree because our Blood Classes are different?'

'What? No, not that, you know I don't care about that.'

'But–'

'I really couldn't care less.'

'But your father won't let you muddy the High Blood Class with my Middle Blood.'

'Forget my Father and Blood Classes for a moment, will you?' he asked, a pained expression on his face. He took hold of my hand and kissed it. I reached out with my free hand, touching the side of his face as his cheeks tinged a lovely rosy colour. Letting go of my hand, he glanced away momentarily, rubbing the base of his neck before turning back to me, his irises alight.

'I wanted to ask you…' He looked at me, seeming to change his mind and instead, slipped his arms around me, pulling me into a scorching kiss. My veins were set alight, my heart pounding in my ears at the touch of his velvety lips. Love spread through me as I held him close, running my fingers through his hair, delighting in his touch, but as we paused for breath, I couldn't stop the Curse from forcing its way back into my mind, putting out the fire in my veins.

Tears sprang to my eyes. 'The Weapons are draining faster than ever. The Curse is killing me, and we won't have the chance to be together for much longer. Indulging ourselves is only going to make it harder, when the time comes.'

He looked at me, his amber eyes full of love. 'I'll take every minute I can with you. That's what I wanted to say – I want you for as long as you're here, and that's all there is to it. Stay with me as long as you can. Marry me.'

I looked sharply at him. 'Marry you? But the Blood Rules–'

'Forget about the damn Blood Rules,' he said, laughing now. 'And the Curse, for that matter. I don't care about either of them. All I care about is you and the time we have left together. I love you. Marry me, please? Be my wife.'

If I'd been standing, I'm sure my knees would have given way. My whole body started to tremble, and I nodded, unable to form the words I wanted to say.

'Was that a yes?' he asked, the firelight illuminating his lopsided smile.

'Yes.' I nodded again. 'Yes, I'll marry you.'

'My Samphire Amethyst,' he said, gathering me in his arms and kissing me once again, his mouth warm, his tongue sweet. His love for me was unquestionable, and there was no doubt in my mind as the scent of sandalwood swept around us. The desire and want in that kiss sent a thrill throughout my entire body, and as I kissed him back and wrapped one arm around his neck, I felt his body responding to me. No, I had no doubts at all.

'We may still find a way to break the Curse,' he said. 'Tarragon may have found out something. We'll break the Curse, and then we'll change the law so that we can be together. And if that doesn't work, we'll leave the Five Lands.'

I stared at him in amazement. 'You'd leave Aerba for me?'

'I'd move the stars for you. I'd even find Chroma, if it'd help,' he said, a dopey grin appearing on his face. 'I love you so much I'd drain the ocean to be with you.' He gently brought me towards him. Although I found his lips intoxicating, I pulled back.

'If we don't find a way to break the Curse, will you promise me something?' I asked.

'Anything,' he said, looking into my eyes.

'Promise me you'll still try and change the Blood Rules so our friends can finally be together? So they can show how they really feel in public, and, if they want to, marry? I hate the way they have to skulk around, hiding their true feelings, in constant fear of being found out and punished.'

Rian nodded, still holding me firmly around the waist. 'I promise.'

'Thank you.'

'Don't give up hope yet, though,' he said. 'I'm still counting on Tarragon.'

'Me, too,' I said, glancing down. 'I don't want to leave you now.'

'And I don't want you leaving me.' He hesitated. 'I told you I loved you when you were ill,' he said, resting his forehead on mine.

'I heard you, but I didn't realise it was real.'

'I told you not to leave me then, too.'

'I thought you did,' I said. 'What did I really say when I was hallucinating? I must've said something at least vaguely intelligible.'

Rian hesitated a moment. 'There was a point where I think you were swearing at your sister.'

I laughed. 'No change there, then,' I said, pausing for a moment. 'Did you really ask me to kiss you, or did I hallucinate that, too?'

He glanced away. 'I didn't realise you'd heard.'

'And did I?'

'You were out of it at the time. You weren't in any fit state to do anything, and I wasn't about to take advantage. Not that I didn't want to. It was just wishful thinking on my part, thinking out loud.'

'But I remember kissing you,' I said, frowning. I remembered the silken knot in my stomach so vividly, the gentle caress of his lips, the desire.

'Well, you didn't. The first time we kissed was last night – well, this morning, although that's not to say I wouldn't have liked to do it before then, if only I'd plucked up the courage. I think your imagination was running riot.' He paused. 'You called my name a couple of times, though. Why?'

I swallowed, wanting to forget the flames and heat of the nightmare. 'In my dreams, you were ill and surrounded by fire. I couldn't get to you. I couldn't save you.'

He raised an eyebrow.

'It was just a hallucination, but it's left its mark,' I said, unease filling me once more.

'Forget it, you were very ill,' he said, brushing my hair from my face. 'For a while, though, I did think I was never getting you back. I thought I'd lost you during those hallucinations.' He watched me for a moment, his eyes glassy. 'You're so precious to me. Will you kiss me again?'

'I'd love to,' I said, leaning towards him. As our lips met, the tenderness of his kiss formed that same knot in my stomach. My breathing changed as I held him, his arms sliding up my back. As he moved in closer, he lost his balance and we fell off the bale, rolling onto the soft hay that lay scattered across the barn floor.

His eyes widened as he came to rest on his back. 'Sorry.'

'Don't be,' I said as I took advantage of the situation and straddled him, one hand resting on either side of his head.

A little frown slipped across his forehead. 'I can see I've got my hands full with you, Lady Samphire,' he said, taking hold of me once again.

'Oh, I do hope so, Prince Valerian. I do hope so.'

CHAPTER TWENTY

By the time Sage and Anise returned, we were asleep. We set off early the next morning, the grey clouds scudding across the sky as a nervous fluttering started in my stomach. The thought of seeing King Finule again made me feel sick.

'I think you should probably know this before we get back, Rian,' Sage said as we rode along. 'One of the sailors on the ship said there was a rumour going around that one of the Royal Family ordered the assassination of Princess Angelica.'

'What?' Rian stared in horror. 'Who would do that? It wasn't me, Father doted on her, and Chervil wouldn't have done it.'

'I'm just repeating what he said. I just thought I should warn you.'

Rian nodded, chewing his lip for a moment. 'Unfortunately, I'm the prime candidate because everyone knows we didn't get along.'

'There'll be no proof against you, though, because you didn't do it,' I said. 'They can't accuse you without real proof, even in Aerba.'

'Phire's right, Rian,' Anise said. 'Anyway, it's just a rumour. But if it wasn't Chervil or the King, who else would have had a vested interest in Angelica's death?'

'I don't know. I mean, it could've been anyone, really,' Rian said. 'She wasn't exactly popular in a lot of quarters, but arranging her death is a step I can't see anyone at Court taking.'

'Then who?'

I glanced at Rian, his brow deeply furrowed in thought. As the morning wore on, my stomach started to churn, and by the time Viridi City and its accompanying lake of sunlit diamonds came into view, nausea nestled in my chest. I took a deep breath. What could King Finule do to me that he hadn't done already? He'd already given me a death sentence when he tricked me into taking up the Cursed Weapons.

We crossed the drawbridge over the poisoned moat, the sun reflecting off the water. Palace Guards stood at the gate, questioning the business of everyone who dared enter the city. As we rode to the gate, one of the guards looked up, quickly saluting Rian.

'Your Royal Highness,' he said, bowing. 'The King has asked that you and your party go directly to him on your arrival.'

'Thank you,' Rian said, nodding, before leading us through the busy city. On our way to the palace, I noted a number of guards milling amongst the people, standing at main thoroughfares, watching intently.

'They've upped the security,' Sage said, taking note. 'Tarragon obviously got the message through.'

Rian nodded. 'I assume Father's fine, seeing as how he's left instructions for us to go straight to him.'

'I'd take that as a positive sign.'

'Depends on what he wants to see us about,' Anise murmured.

I looked at Anise, who shrugged. The guard at the palace gate bowed to us, and we rode into the courtyard, dismounting as the stable boys arrived to take the horses.

'Prince Valerian, how good to see you,' Lord Wintergreen said, coming down the palace steps. 'We'd become concerned for your welfare,' he said, glancing at me.

'We were a little delayed, but we're here now, Lord Wintergreen,' Rian said.

'Did you break it? The Curse, I mean?'

I shook my head.

'I'm sorry. Truly, I am,' Wintergreen said, scratching his nose. 'I'd rather hoped you'd found a way to break it. I trust you know the King has no remedy for it?'

'It has been mentioned to me,' I said.

'She knows Father lied,' Rian said pointedly.

Wintergreen's grey eyes darted towards Rian and a wisp of a frown appeared on his face. 'His Majesty desires to see you immediately. We mustn't keep him waiting any longer,' he said, leading the way into the palace.

My heart thudded as we walked along the corridors to the Throne Room. Even here, extra Palace Guards lined the halls at strategic points.

'Where have all these extra guards come from, Lord Wintergreen?' Anise asked, voicing my thoughts.

'Conscripted from Middle Bloods in the main,' Wintergreen said. 'When Tarragon returned with your message, the King immediately increased the security, not only in the palace but in the wider city.'

'We noticed,' Sage said.

'Have there been any attempts on Father's life while we've been away?' Rian asked.

'No, Your Highness, so far things have been quiet,' Wintergreen said, 'but we're prepared to foil any attempt on his Majesty's life, if and when necessary.'

'Good,' Rian said as we reached the Throne Room.

The two guards standing at the doors nodded to Lord Wintergreen and opened them. We followed Wintergreen into the chamber. At the far end of the Throne Room, sitting on his Opal-less throne, was King Finule, resplendent in his burgundy and gold coat, studying some papers. Chervil sat nonchalantly lolling in his favourite window seat. The Crown Prince sat up as we entered, glowering at me, although a hint of surprise played in his brown eyes.

'Are you still alive, Lady Merciless?' he asked, fiddling with his burgundy sleeve.

I winced and nodded. 'As you can see, Your Highness.'

He glanced at Cwicsusl as I passed and grinned. 'But not for long, I think. I wonder if you'll see the week out?'

Rian turned, his muscles tensing, but I put a steadying hand on his arm.

'It's not worth it,' I whispered.

He reluctantly turned away, still tense, and we approached the throne.

'Prince Valerian and Lady Samphire, Your Majesty,' Wintergreen said, bowing to Finule.

'Father, we're back,' Rian said. 'I'm glad to see you're well.'

'No thanks to your Lady Merciless,' King Finule said, looking up from his papers and nodding to Wintergreen.

'On the contrary, Father, it's because of Samphire we discovered the plot against you and Chervil.'

'You would have discovered that without her, Valerian.'

'Father, I–'

'So, Lady Merciless, what news do you bring me that I may remove the Curse?' Finule asked, handing his papers to Wintergreen.

I flinched.

'She knows, Your Majesty,' Lord Wintergreen said quietly from the position he'd taken up beside Finule's throne.

The King pursed his lips. 'What news?' he repeated, his eyes boring into me.

'I'm afraid we were unable to discover who ordered the assassinations, Your Majesty,' I said, feeling about as big as an ant.

'So, you failed in the first task. What about the assassin that murdered my dear daughter, assuming you still claim to be innocent?'

'I don't claim to be innocent, Your Majesty. I *am* innocent. I didn't kill her.'

'You will not speak to the King of Aerba like that,' Chervil said, jumping up from his seat and marching towards us.

'Leave her alone,' Rian said, stepping towards his older brother.

'Shut up, Valerian,' Chervil said, glowering at him. 'You can't still believe her lies. Surely you're not that stupid? Has she enchanted you in some way? Beguiled you?'

'I do believe her, but only because she's telling the truth,' Rian said, turning to his father. 'We did discover the identity of the Coterie assassin that killed Angelica, but he was killed on his journey back to Iolite. He's beyond our reach now.'

'His name?' Finule rumbled, his face darkening.

'The Coterie assassin, Carnelian,' Rian said.

I noticed a cloud pass over Wintergreen's face, and he rubbed his nose as I silently thanked Rian for protecting Mal. I hoped the confused glances exchanged by Sage and Anise would go unnoticed by the King and his Court.

'And the Fire Opal? Where is it?' Finule asked.

'We don't know,' I said. 'But the information we got indicated that we should look to Flos for answers.'

Finule's face turned purple, anger radiating from his very being. 'Wintergreen, did you know about this?'

'No, Your Majesty, I did not,' Wintergreen said, frowning.

'Guard, get Lord Wormwood in here now; I want to know what the Nightshade have to say about this. If it's in Flos, they would have already known. Why haven't they told me?'

'Hmm. The head of the Nightshade should know something about this,' Chervil said, stroking his goatee thoughtfully.

'Sage. Anise. You may go,' Finule said, waving them away.

'Your Majesty,' Sage said as he and Anise bowed, casting us anxious glances before leaving.

I looked at Rian, who appeared unconcerned – or was doing a good impression of a High Blood who appeared unconcerned. A few minutes later, the doors opened and a tall man with long salt and pepper hair, and a goatee not unlike Chervil's, entered the room. His angular face spoke of vigilance and suspicion, and he watched me intently as he walked across the Throne Room and bowed to Finule.

'Your Majesty,' he said, his voice like gravel. 'How may I be of assistance to you?'

'Lady Merciless has brought news that the Fire Opal may be in Flos, Wormwood,' Finule said. 'What do you know of this?'

I wanted to scream at them to stop calling me that, but I held my tongue.

'We don't actually know it's in Flos, Father,' Rian said. 'Just that we should start by making enquiries there.'

Wormwood scratched his arm. 'We received a report this very morning intimating such a thing. We're in the process of making the inquiries Prince Valerian has alluded to, Your Majesty.'

'Well, look into it faster, Wormwood. Bring me news as soon as you have it, understand?' Finule said, getting up.

'Maybe Samphire and I can—' But Rian never got to finish.

'You don't understand, Valerian,' Finule said, not even looking at his youngest son. 'Leave this to me and your brother. Chamberlain Wintergreen, Chervil, come with me.'

'As you desire, Your Majesty,' Wintergreen said.

'Why are you still here, Wormwood? Go and investigate.'

'Of course, Your Majesty.' Wormwood bowed again.

Wintergreen followed Finule out of the Throne Room, Chervil sauntering along in their wake, pausing only to give Rian one last glare before he left.

The side door shut tight behind them.

Wormwood turned sharply to face Rian. 'I understand from my operatives that you shared a room with Lady Merciless in Cilantro Town, Prince Valerian.'

Hell's teeth. A cold winter's blast swept through me. How did he know that? And what else did the Nightshade know?

'If you know that, Lord Wormwood, you'll also know Lady *Samphire* was very ill, and we all helped to look after her,' Rian said, unfazed by the revelation.

'But you were alone with her, Your Highness,' Wormwood said, his eyes narrowing as he looked at Rian. 'For some time.'

'Because she would have died without care,' Rian said, his voice hardening. 'The King wouldn't have thanked us for leaving her there to die.'

'I suggest you watch yourself, Your Highness,' Wormwood said. He drew himself up to his full height. 'She can still make a world of trouble for you before the Curse takes her.' Wormwood bowed and strode out of the chamber, the main doors closing behind him.

Rian's fist clenched.

'The Nightshade are everywhere,' I said, looking around the room. I half expected to see feet poking out from underneath one of the tapestries on the far wall.

'The palace is riddled with them,' Rian said, his jaw tight. 'Come on, let's find Tarragon and the others.'

We left the Throne Room, heading towards Rian's rooms, passing several guards along the way.

'Thank you for not mentioning Mal,' I said softly.

'It wouldn't have helped you or Father,' Rian said.

'Welcome back, Prince Valerian,' Sorrel said, appearing around a corner. He glanced at me then back at Rian. 'I understand your little side excursion was, how shall I say, fruitless?'

'News travels fast,' Rian said, moving past Sorrel without hesitation.

'Hmm, I'm so sorry for your loss,' he said.

'What did you say?' Rian asked, turning back to his cousin.

'Nothing, Your Highness,' Sorrel said, bowing and moving away, a smile playing on his lips.

'Bastard,' Rian cursed.

'Leave him,' I said. 'Let's find Tarragon.'

Rian nodded, and we turned a corner, entering his chambers. Tarragon, Willow, Sage and Anise were already there.

'It's so good to see you,' Willow said, hugging me. 'I really missed you.'

'I'm sorry the Elixir didn't work,' Tarragon said, offering his own hug.

'Have you found any other answers, Tarragon?' Rian asked.

I held my breath, awaiting his response.

Tarragon shook his head. 'I'm afraid not,' he said. 'We spoke to the best minds in Aerba – when your father and Chervil weren't about, that is – but no one has any ideas.'

My last chance had slipped through my fingers. I glanced at Rian, who chewed on his lip.

'So, you two have been getting along well,' Willow said, fluttering her eyelids, a big grin on her face. Her attempt at distraction.

Rian glared at Anise and Sage.

'It wasn't me,' Sage said, holding up his hands.

'I might have let something slip,' Anise said, his cheeks flushing as he looked away.

'I suggest if we're going to talk about this, we go somewhere else,' Tarragon said, nodding towards the walls. 'Why don't we go into the gardens? I'd like some fresh air.'

'Do we really need to discuss this as a group?' Rian asked, looking annoyed by everyone's interest in our relationship.

'Wait,' Willow said, resting her hand on his arm, an earnest note to her voice. 'You must hear him out.'

'Very well,' Rian said, 'let's go.'

We made our way out into the gardens, past the herbaceous borders, the hedges, and the fountains, out into an area of open, grassy parkland I hadn't seen before. Tarragon only stopped when we'd reached a spot a good hundred yards from a tree or bush in any direction. We sat on the grass, the sun beating down on us.

'Now, what's so important?' Rian asked.

'We know you and Phire are getting...' Tarragon coughed delicately. 'Close.'

Rian glanced at me as if seeking approval. They were all going to find out sooner or later. I gave him a little nod.

'You could say that – we're in love and I've asked her to marry me,' Rian said. 'And she's said yes.'

Silence surrounded us. I looked around at the others – did they disapprove? Willow and Anise had broad grins suggesting otherwise.

'We're pleased for you, really,' Sage said, a worried look crossing his face. 'But they'll never let the two of you marry, any more than they would us,' he said, glancing at Anise.

'We're both of marriageable Aerban age,' Rian said. 'I'm nineteen and Phire's seventeen.'

'What's the date?' I asked, a little shiver running down my spine. I'd lost track of time and dates, thanks to the chaos of the last few weeks, and only now did I realise that I might have missed something important.

'It's the tenth,' Willow said.

Oh.

I had missed something.

'I turned eighteen yesterday,' I said. Eighteenth birthdays were celebrated with grand parties and balls back on Iolite, signifying you formally becoming an adult, even though you could marry younger than that. Not that I regretted missing a ball in the Crimson Castle, but I did regret the fact I hadn't realised yesterday had been my birthday.

'You were eighteen yesterday?' Rian asked, his eyes softening. 'You should've said.'

'I didn't realise – can't imagine why,' I said with a half-smile. 'If I had, I would've mentioned it. Although, yesterday was pretty special anyway,' I said, glancing at him as my face warmed.

He smiled back and took my hand. 'It was, wasn't it?'

I grinned at him.

'Anything you two would care to divulge?' Willow asked, raising an eyebrow.

'No,' Rian and I said in unison.

She grunted and looked away, disappointed.

'Anyway, I don't see what the issue is with us getting married,' Rian said.

'Have you forgotten the Blood Decree?' Anise asked, his face pale and sad.

'I'll change the rules,' Rian said, his body tensing. 'It's about time they were changed; they're unfair, outdated, and positively asinine.'

'We don't disagree with you,' Tarragon said, bowing his head.

'But Prince Mace tried that once and was executed for his trouble,' Sage murmured.

'Bobbins,' Willow said. 'That was six hundred years ago. Times have changed.'

'Not that much,' Anise said, a wistful look in his eyes as he glanced at Sage.

'Changing things for you and Phire may not be necessary, y'know,' Tarragon said.

'What?' Rian frowned at his cousin. 'We can still find a way to break the Curse in time.'

'I'm not talking about the Curse, I'm afraid. I've been doing a little historical research since we've been back,' Tarragon said, rubbing his chin.

'He's very good at that, you know,' Willow said, chuckling. Her silvery laugh caught at the back of her throat, making her cough.

Tarragon glanced at her as she got her coughing fit under control. 'It's about Phire's family,' he said. 'It was something Phire said about her grandmother and great-grandmother having Ara-type names, so I looked into it. Your grandmother was Arabis and great-grandmother Ara, yes?'

I nodded. 'But how did you—'

'And your great-great-grandmother?'

'I'm not sure, but I think she was an Ara-something, too.'

'What about Aralia?'

'Yes, that's it, but why?' I asked, completely confused as to where Tarragon was going with this.

'Aralia is a herb, not a flower,' Sage said, his eyes narrowing.

'Interesting,' Anise said.

'It is?' I asked.

'Your great-great-grandmother was Aerban?' Rian asked, his eyebrows raised, eyes widening.

'I-I don't know,' I said, my heart suddenly skipping.

Was she?

'Not only was Phire's great-great-grandmother an Aerban, but she was also King Finule the First's daughter,' Tarragon said, a smug expression on his face.

CHAPTER TWENTY-ONE

'What?' I couldn't believe this.

'The same Princess Aralia who eloped with Prince Gaillardia of Flos and caused the rift between Aerba and Flos over a hundred-and-twenty-odd years ago?' Anise asked, sitting up straight in surprise.

'Yes, the very same,' Tarragon said, nodding.

Rian had a strange expression on his face as he chewed his lip – one I couldn't read.

'King Finule the First would've had her executed if she'd stayed in Aerba with Prince Gaillardia, so they eloped to his Kingdom and lived happily ever after,' Tarragon continued.

'I have family in Flos,' I said. 'Distant cousins. Jasmine and Erica.'

'Didn't King Finule Demote Aralia?' Anise asked.

Tarragon nodded. 'As he couldn't execute her, he decreed she and her offspring be made Middle Bloods for her perceived crimes against the Blood Decree, since she didn't have permission to marry a man from another Land.'

'Harsh,' Willow said, suppressing a little cough.

'Better than execution, though – stupid law,' Sage said, scowling.

'The King of Flos was livid about the whole thing, y'know, and the relationship between our two countries hasn't been the same since,' Tarragon said. 'Actually, the Flosians still hate us for not allowing the marriage, let alone the Demotion.'

What were they saying? A little shiver crept slowly down my spine as Rian turned to look at me, his eyes seeming to flicker.

'So, Phire has Aerban ancestry,' Rian said, his voice with a thoughtful edge.

Anise grabbed me in a sudden hug. 'You're an Aerban like me, Phire,' he said, grinning.

'Put her down,' Rian said.

Anise let me go. 'I always knew I liked you.'

I looked skyward but couldn't help smiling.

'But it's more than that, though,' Tarragon said, putting a hand on Rian's shoulder. 'Don't you see? Technically, Phire's a High Blood, she's a cousin to me, Sage, *and* you, albeit a very distant one. But, most importantly, she's a High Blood.'

'Distant cousins,' I murmured, trying to take it all in.

An impish grin spread over Anise's face. 'So, as she's technically High Blood, you can marry her whenever you want to, Rian,' he said.

My eyes widened.

Rian's face glowed scarlet. 'Whether or not Phire is High Blood makes no difference to me. If I want to marry her, I will – and I do.' My eyes widened a little more, and my heart did its impression of folk drums, beating away at the inside of my ribs. 'And anyway, as I've said before, I intend to put a stop to the whole Blood System,' Rian said.

'Really? And just how are you going to do that?' Sage asked, raising his eyebrows questioningly. 'Neither your father nor Chervil will ever let that happen. They'll never let you marry Phire. They'll say she's a Middle Blood, and that'll be the end of it. Unless you want to flee the country, of course.'

Rian looked at me. 'I'll do whatever's necessary,' he said, his eyes full of love in a way that made me tremble and quiver inside.

'You know I can't ask you to do that,' I said.

He took my hand. 'You're not asking. I'm telling you what I'm prepared to do to be with you.'

I wanted to melt into a puddle right there.

'But where would you go? All the Lands follow the Blood Decree,' Anise said.

'There's an archipelago east of Trew. I understand things are different there – they don't follow the Decree,' I said softly, looking at Rian. 'Onyx told me – they're hidden, for the most part, and they're left alone to follow their own rules.'

'I thought it was just a rumour,' Willow said. 'I'd never dared to hope it was real.'

'As far as I understand, it's true. They have a free society where you can have a relationship with whoever you want without fear of repercussions.'

Rian's eyes widened at the news, a small smile creeping across his face. 'Sounds perfect.'

'Well, if you do go, Willow and I are coming with you, y'know,' Tarragon said, a determined note to his voice.

'Do I get a say in this?' Willow asked, looking at him in surprise.

'I thought you loved me,' Tarragon said, a hurt expression creeping over his face as he pouted at her.

'I do.'

'Then, if that's how we get to be together, wouldn't you do it?'

Willow hesitated for a moment, looking a little embarrassed. 'Of course, I would. I just never realised it was an option. Yes, I'd go with you,' she said, looking at him through her long lashes as her face flushed. 'Bobbins, I'd go to the ends of the earth with you.'

'Well then.' Tarragon grinned smugly.

Willow sighed.

Anise looked at Sage, who nodded. 'We'd come too,' Anise said. 'Not only would we get to be free, but you'd get into far too much trouble without us.'

'I knew you were scholarly, Tarragon, but I didn't realise quite how much,' Sage said, turning to his cousin.

Tarragon buffed his fingernails on his tunic. 'As I've said before, I'm a man of many parts, and history happens to be a hobby of mine.'

'And thank the Stars it is,' I said, giving him a quick peck on the cheek.

Tarragon's face changed to a beautiful red.

I'd been given the same chambers I'd stayed in previously and I went to bed early, but despite my fatigue, I couldn't sleep. My mind raced. My family's history, the fact I was really a High Blood, swirled in my mind.

A High Blood. How ironic.

I turned over, looking out at the stars twinkling through the windows, and sighed. The moon glinted off Cwicsusl, the scarlet crystal section reduced to a mere three inches. Why was it draining so quickly? Perhaps, now that I knew the end was near, my emotions and mental exhaustion were also affecting it in some way, making it drain all the faster?

I sat up as a quiet knock sounded at my chamber door. I grabbed my dressing gown and made my way out to the sitting room, cautiously unlocking the door and opening it, peering out. Illuminated in the light from the corridor lamps stood Rian.

Before I could say anything, he put his finger to my lips and leant towards me, whispering into my ear, his lips brushing my skin with sparks. 'I just wanted to say goodnight,' he said. 'But I can't stay; the Nightshade will be watching,' he said, kissing the side of my cheek before withdrawing down the corridor.

I shut my door and moved over to the window in my bedchamber, my skin still burning where he'd kissed me. The moonlight glistened on the fountains, sending flashes into the air, rather like the wonderful sparks I felt swirling around inside my chest. I brought my hand to my cheek as I moved out of the moon's light and sat on my bed, cold desperation replacing the warmth – I didn't have long and, at this rate, I'd never get the chance to marry Rian.

'How did you sleep?' Willow asked as she fussed around me the next morning. She'd had my clothes cleaned overnight, and currently had a comb in my hair trying to pull it through my tangled mop.

'I've slept better,' I said, wincing as she pulled the comb through a knot.

'I slept really well,' she said as she attacked my hair.

'Uninterrupted?'

'You know how these things are,' she giggled.

'I wonder how many sleeps I've got left,' I said, flinching as she tugged at the comb.

She stopped her assault on my scalp. 'I'm sure–'

A knock at the door interrupted our conversation.

'Come in,' I called.

Rian walked in. 'I wanted to let you know I'm going to see my father and tell him we're getting married,' he said, immediately turning back to the corridor.

'What? Now?' What was he doing?

'No time like the present, and under the circumstances, I don't want to wait,' Rian said, pausing. 'He needs to know how I feel, and I'm going to tell him before he hears something twisted from the Nightshade.'

'But–'

'I just wanted to let you know,' he said, leaving the room.

A dark horror coursed through my veins and my pulse rapidly accelerated at Rian's words.

Willow's face had an ashen look to it as she put the comb down. 'This won't go well. But we'll never stop him. You know what he's like once his mind is made up.'

'Then what can we do?'

'Nothing,' she said. 'Come on.' She opened the door and hurried down the corridor.

I quickly tied my hair back and ran after her, the Cursed Weapons joining me. 'Where're we going?' I asked, catching up with her.

'There's a gallery overlooking the Throne Room. We can hide there and hear what happens.'

'I'm not sure I *want* to hear what happens,' I said, but followed anyway. We ran up a set of stairs and along a narrow corridor before reaching a small wooden door.

Willow produced her lock-picking tools from her pocket and carefully set about unlocking the door. She wiggled and twisted the metal picks until the lock clicked.

'When we go in, you make no noise,' she said. 'No talking at all, or they'll hear us below.'

'All right.' I nodded, my palms sweating.

She opened the door and we quietly entered the gallery area, closing the door behind us and ducking down behind the wooden balustrade. I peered through the balusters to see King Finule standing at his long table, shuffling through a pile of papers and documents. We heard the doors below us open.

I swallowed.

'Father, I need to speak to you,' Rian's voice sounded clear and strong from the Throne Room floor.

'And I want to speak to you,' Finule said. 'The Nightshade have informed me you shared a room with Lady Merciless in Cilantro Town. Care to explain?'

'There's nothing to explain. She was ill.'

'You were alone. You know the Blood Rule Decree and you broke it.'

'Nothing happened. I was looking after her, that's all, and we didn't break the Decree. Father, she almost died because we were trying to find a cure for the Curse – the Curse *you* told her you'd break, whilst knowing that you couldn't.'

I winced. Not a good start. Willow screwed her face up.

'You don't understand, Valerian. I agreed to give her the Cursed Weapons because that is exactly the outcome I wanted. Even if she didn't kill your sister, she is complicit in the actions of the Coterie and therefore guilty of other heinous crimes.'

'But she's never killed anyone. She only did what she did to survive, just like any of us would've done,' Rian said, stepping forward so I could see the top of his head.

'So she says,' Finule said, adjusting his crown. 'But you can't believe the word of an assassin and a liar.'

'What she said is true. It was confirmed on Iolite – she's completely innocent in this.'

Finule snorted. 'The last thing she is is innocent. But no matter, she will be dead soon – Aldorbana and Cwicsusl will see to that. I must say, she's proved stronger than I thought; I expected her dead days, maybe even weeks, ago.'

Rian shuffled where he stood. 'She's a good person, Father, if only you'd see that and give her a chance.'

'She's a member of the Coterie, and from now on, I want you to stay away from her until she dies. It shouldn't take too long.'

'No.'

Finule looked up at Rian. 'I beg your pardon?'

'No,' Rian repeated, his voice level. 'I've come to tell you that we love each other and I'm going to marry her.'

'You what?'

'I'm going to marry Lady Samphire.'

'Even if you put aside the fact that she's an assassin and an Iolitian, she is Middle Blood – it's not possible. You'd be breaking more than one of the Blood Rules. You're being ridiculous, Rian. She's used some sort of enchantment on you. You've been beguiled by the first woman who's bothered to look at you twice.'

'She hasn't beguiled me, and I'm not being ridiculous. Tarragon has been doing some research, and actually, Samphire is High Blood, so, if you gave your permission for me to marry an Iolitian, we wouldn't be breaking any of the Blood Rules.'

Finule frowned. 'High Blood? And how have you come up with this theory, then?'

'Princess Aralia was her great-great-grandmother,' Rian said. 'Samphire's not only a High Blood, but she has *Royal* Blood.'

'Her family is from Flos?' Finule asked, his eyebrows knitting together.

'Her great-great-grandmother was Aerban.'

'An Aerban traitor,' Finule said, his voice rising. 'You wouldn't understand, but Aralia is the very reason our relations with Flos are so bad, maybe even the reason they stole the Fire Opal – our Opal stolen, all because Lady Merciless' great-great-grandmother ran off with a Flosian princeling. And this is the young woman you want to marry?' He shook his head.

'We don't know Flos stole the Fire Opal, Father. And I do understand, but what happened over a hundred-and-twenty years ago isn't Samphire's fault. You can't punish her for that.'

'King Finule the First Demoted Princess Aralia, and that Demotion still applies to her lineage. I was against your relationship before, but after learning of her ancestry? I expressly forbid it. You will have nothing further to do with her, do you understand me?'

'You can't stop us being together,' Rian said, a steely note to his voice which made me shiver.

'Oh, but I can,' Finule said. 'Guard! Take Lady Merciless to the dungeon.'

A shard of ice slammed into my chest and my clammy hands froze.

'Father, no,' Rian said, his voice outraged and pleading at the same time. 'Please don't do this.'

'This discussion is over, Valerian. You've forced my hand. *I* will find you a suitable Royal High Blood wife from another Land in order to consolidate our power. You will have no say in it. You will do as you are told and produce an heir. Now get out.'

Terse footsteps echoed across the marble floor, then a door closed, and I turned to Willow. She gestured to me and we silently left the gallery, moving back into the corridor and closing the door behind us.

'Well, that went to hell in a handcart,' I said.

'I think we only have one option,' Willow said, her eyes darting up and down the corridor. 'Bobbins. Why did he have to go and do that? Come on, this way.'

'Where are you taking me?'

'Away from your apartments,' she said, leading me down narrow passageways and staircases. 'It's the first place the Palace Guard will look. I need to get you to sanctuary.' Twice we had to duck into doorways as guards passed down the corridors. The few servants we saw ignored us or nodded as they walked past. We moved out towards the back of the palace, pausing at the kitchen storerooms where a row of cloaks hung on wooden pegs. 'Here,' she said, passing me a cloak and taking one for herself. We moved out towards the back door to find a Palace Guard on sentry duty. 'Bobbins. Wait here. Get out when you can.'

I grabbed her arm. 'What are you going to do?'

'Distraction,' she said with a broad grin lighting up her eyes. 'I'll get him away, and you make your way across the courtyard. Get out into the street. I'll meet you in a few minutes.' She squeezed my hand and moved off towards the door.

I ducked down into the shadows, my heart thudding uncomfortably and my mind cartwheeling as Willow discussed something with the guard and they disappeared back into the building. I cautiously slipped into the corridor, hurried to the doorway, and peered out into the rain. The back courtyard stood empty. I had assumed the Palace Guard were concentrating security on the main areas where Finule and Chervil frequented, however, I felt, as a former assassin, this wasn't the best use of the extra men. I pulled the cloak's hood up over my head and made my way around the side of the courtyard, out the back gate into a busy street. A Palace Guard who'd been keeping watch chatted animatedly to a passer-by. I ducked away from the gate and into an alleyway on the opposite side of the street and waited. The rain fell, dropping off my hood, dampening my clothes. Gutters dripped with water, and puddles formed in the street, making it a muddy quagmire. A few minutes later, Willow reached the back gate and came out into the street. She looked around, saw me, and joined me in the alley.

'We only just got out in time,' she said, warily looking around the street. 'They're searching the whole palace for you.'

'But where can I go?' I asked. 'I'll never get out the city gates; the guards will already have been told to stop me if I go that way.'

'We'll go to the Temple of Herbs,' she said, moving down the alley. 'They won't touch you there. You can claim sanctuary.'

'Are you sure about that?' I asked doubtfully, knowing full well the Coterie would take no notice of the boundaries of a temple when on a mission. Whether the Nightshade or Palace Guard would, remained to be seen, but I didn't have high hopes.

She nodded, leading me down a multitude of alleys. Eventually she stopped, peering out into the main street.

'Let's go,' she said. We threaded our way through the crowd and into the deep green marble temple with its grand carvings of thyme. Inside, people huddled in small groups in the large, open space where oil lamps flickered on the walls, herb incense filling the air and producing a cloying, choking effect.

'That better not be Saliivia,' I said, shuddering at the smell. The memory of the Moonflower Elixir and its side effects were all too fresh.

'Come this way,' Willow said, passing a small pool in the centre of the hall, taking a side staircase up to a small, empty room. 'They use this for quiet reflection,' she said, ushering me into the room where a little waterfall trickled from a crack in the wall into a tiny pool which overflowed into a grate in the floor. It reminded me of The Chamber of Earth. Stone benches lined the walls for those wanting to partake of that "quiet reflection".

'I've never seen anyone in here,' she said. 'It's always empty.'

'Let's hope it stays that way,' I said.

'Just keep your cloak up. Don't talk to anyone. Just look as if you're... contemplating.'

'Contemplating? Great.'

'I'll go and get Rian. I won't be long.'

'Won't they be watching him, as well?'

'They're looking for you, not him,' Willow said with a grin. 'Besides, he knows a few secret ways out of the palace. Don't worry. We'll be back soon.'

CHAPTER TWENTY-TWO

Willow left the room, closing the door behind her and leaving me alone, my mind in turmoil as I chewed on a nail. I couldn't see what use staying here would be; surely the best thing would be to leave the city? But word had probably already reached the city gates. Finule had me totally trapped.

I sat, my senses strained, listening for footsteps on the stairs, for any hint of someone coming, but all remained silent. I wasn't sure if that boded well or not, but finally, soft steps echoed on the staircase. I got up, my hand resting on Aldorbana's hilt as the door opened. Rian stepped in. I'd never been so glad to see him, and I rushed over to him, kissing him, and hugging him.

'Were you followed?' I asked, glancing towards the door.

'No, I don't think so,' he said, shaking his head.

'You should never have gone to your father,' I said, pulling away and giving him a little scowl.

'I'm sorry. I had to get things out in the open so he knew how I felt. And I needed him to hear it from me, not the Nightshade. I wanted to give him the chance to accept my choice before we made the decision to leave for the archipelago instead.'

'But now he just wants me to die in the dungeon,' I said as he shut the door. 'And he wants you to marry some foreign princess.'

'You heard all that?' Rian's eyes widened.

'Willow and I were listening from above. Look, as soon as he finds me, he'll stick me in a cell until I di-'

'Not if we marry. Once you're my wife, he won't be able to do that,' Rian cut in, a determined note to his voice.

'Your wife? But it's against the Blood Rules.'

'If we're married by a priest, even Father won't go against that.'

'Are you sure?'

He smiled and nodded. 'Look, I have a friend – a priest here in the temple – who's sympathetic to our cause. He'll marry us.'

'What, right now?'

'Do you have somewhere else you need to be? This may be our only chance, but only if you're happy about it.'

'It's not entirely how I saw my wedding taking place.'

'You've imagined your wedding day before?' he asked with a smile.

'No more than any other girl, but I certainly didn't imagine it under these circumstances.' I frowned as I thought. I loved him. I wanted to marry him, spend my life with him, however long I had left, whether it be five minutes, five days, or five decades. I nodded. 'Let's do it.'

Rian went back to the door. 'Tarragon, get Cardamon,' he said before turning back to me. 'You're absolutely sure about this?'

'However long I have left, I want to spend it with you,' I said, nodding.

Rian smiled the most engaging smile I'd ever seen, and I very nearly melted into a puddle right in front of him.

Tarragon returned with an old man, his white hair caught in a high ponytail, his white robes rustling as he walked.

'Prince Valerian.' The priest bowed low.

'Priest Cardamon, will you marry us?' Rian asked.

Cardamon glanced at me with a smile. 'I will, Your Highness.'

'Thank you.'

'Hold hands, please,' Cardamon said. 'For this to be an official marriage, I must ask if either of you–'

The sound of heavy footsteps from the stairs made Tarragon turn towards the door. It burst open; four Palace Guards forced their way past Tarragon, Sorrel right behind them. My heart fell.

'How dare you enter this place in such a manner,' Cardamon berated them. 'I must ask you to leave, immediately.'

'We've come for her,' Sorrel said, sneering at me.

'How did you find us?' Rian asked, his face taut.

Sorrel smirked. 'I followed you, of course.'

Rian glanced at me and bowed his head. 'I'm sorry, Phire.'

'Don't be,' I whispered back, squeezing his hand.

'Take her to the dungeons, but remove her weapons first,' Sorrel said.

'No, dammit,' Rian said, his voice strained with a myriad of emotions.

'She is under the Temple Priests' protection whilst within these walls,' Cardamon said.

I didn't feel particularly protected. I had no room to draw Aldorbana, let alone wield it – although I still had Citrine's knife and my War Fan. I was running out of options, and much quicker than I liked.

'That's not how the King sees it, Cardamon,' Sorrel said. 'Resist, and you'll be joining her. Guards, seize her.'

'No one's going to the dungeons,' Rian said, stepping in front of me, only to be grabbed by a guard as another took hold of me.

Cardamon's face turned red. 'The King has no control her–'

Sorrel grabbed Cardamon, whipping out his knife and resting it against the old man's throat, a bead of red welling where it pierced the skin.

Tarragon took a menacing step towards his cousin.

Rian strained against the guard holding him. 'Sorrel, stop this!' The guard holding the prince suddenly held a knife to his neck.

Tarragon hesitated, wide-eyed.

'I told you not to interfere, old man,' Sorrel said to Cardamon. 'Take him to the dungeons too,' he said, releasing the priest and shoving him towards the remaining guards hard enough that he fell to the ground. One of the guards pulled him to his feet again and dragged him from the room. 'The King wants to see you at once, Prince Valerian. Tarragon, if you get in our way, you'll be joining Lady Merciless and the priest in the dungeons.'

'Don't call me that,' I said from between gritted teeth as I found myself being pulled away from Rian's side. Aldorbana and Cwicsusl were stripped from my back, Citrine's knife taken from my boot, and my War Fan unclipped.

'Leave her alone,' Rian protested, struggling against the guard holding him.

'Take them,' Sorrel said, no emotion evident in his voice.

My heart pounded as they dragged me past a miserable-looking Tarragon, down the stairs, and through the great chamber where more guards waited to escort us. The people in their huddled groups looked at us in surprise as we were marched through the temple and out into the rainy street, back to the palace. When we got to the palace courtyard, they dragged a still-struggling Rian up the steps. He glanced back at me, anguish in his eyes. As he was manhandled into the building, I found myself hauled towards the familiar side entrance. Poor Tarragon, who'd followed us through the city, stood in the middle of the courtyard in the pouring rain, his eyes darting one way then the other, not knowing which way to go or what to do.

They yanked me along the dim, stone corridors, down a granite staircase, and into the dungeon, although this time they took me to a different cell. At the end of a wide corridor, where small cells with wooden doors and tiny grates sat on either side, two empty cells waited with floor-to-ceiling bars. One side of each cell looked out into the corridor, but the other three were grey walls of granite with tiny grates near the ceiling where the grey daylight crept in and a trickle of rain gently ran down the wall. They threw me in the right-hand cell, onto the mouldy straw.

'Put the Weapons there,' Sorrel said, pointing close to the cell bars, out of reach but not far enough away for the Cursed Weapons to come to me of their own accord. 'Make sure they're near one of those wall torches; the King wants her to see her precious weapons and her life draining away.'

'Bastard!' I yelled as they closed the door. I grabbed at the bars, rattling them in frustration.

Sorrel laughed. 'I'm sorry your wedding was interrupted, but Aerba takes a dim view of different Blood Classes intermarrying.'

'I'm High Blood. I'm the same as Rian, the same as you,' I said. 'I'm your cousin, great-great-granddaughter of Princess Aralia.'

'The traitor princess?' Sorrel asked, his eyes narrowing. 'Then it's a good thing we saved Valerian from such a fate as marrying you.' He turned on his heel and left with the guards, leaving me alone to contemplate my fate – and Rian's.

My blood boiled. I held the bars of my cell, my knuckles white. What could I do?

The day wore on into night, yet no ideas came to me. I did my best to ignore the musty, dank smell surrounding me, but at times it was hard. The sky above cleared, and a small chink of moonlight fought its way through into my cell, illuminating a small patch of straw where I sat resting against the cold wall. I shivered. What had been going on up above in the palace? I didn't want to think about what had happened to Rian. Tears welled in my eyes – how could I really have expected a different outcome? I was going to die. The moment I'd picked up Aldorbana and Cwicsusl I was doomed.

I'd fallen in love with a wonderful young man, but our love had turned out to be rather like the Moonflower – blooming fast at dusk, and over before dawn.

I looked at his wristband still firmly attached to my arm, covering the Coterie tattoo, bringing it to my face and inhaling deeply. The smell of sandalwood still lingered, but only just, and suddenly my eyes swam with tears as I sat shivering, desperate for Rian's touch, the warmth of his body, his calming influence.

If only we'd been able to find a way to break the Curse. The closest we'd come was finding that Quintessence Angle Spinners could break it, and that they could use an Artefact against an Artefact, but we had no Angle Spinners of any sort, and only one Artefact, even if it was in two pieces.

Sometime after midnight, a bell rang mournfully somewhere high up in the palace towers. It was a clanging sound that continued on and on, until I thought I'd go mad. Had they replaced my last visit's dripping with this ringing torture instead? I stuck my fingers in my ears, but I could still hear the melancholy sound echoing in my head. I wanted to climb up that tower and run the bell-ringer through so the incessant noise would stop.

Soft footsteps roused me from my dark thoughts and I looked up to see someone moving in my direction, keeping to the shadows as they headed down towards my cell. My heart leapt – was it Rian? But, as the figure moved into the torchlight, I recognised Anise.

'Samphire, are you there?' his voice drifted towards me.

'Yes, I'm here,' I said, moving over to the barred wall. 'Is Willow coming?' I asked, hope welling in my soul at the prospect of her lock picking skills.

'I'm sorry, it's just me. She's looking for Rian.'

'What's going on?'

His face looked pale in the torchlight, but it was the agonised look in his eyes that sent fear smashing through me. 'King Finule is dead. He was assassinated.'

My heart froze. So, the Coterie had succeeded. With how poorly the back entrance of the palace was defended, I wasn't surprised. One of the newest recruits to the Coterie could've got in without being caught. 'How?'

'Poisoned dart. It was quick, but the convulsions were awful, or so I heard.'

'Was anything left with his body?'

'Yes – a small red bead. How did you know?'

Carnelian? But I'd seen him die, hadn't I? There was no doubt that the red bead was his signature, though, and I shuddered at the thought he was still alive and roaming around Aerba. 'Lucky guess. Is Rian all right?'

'That's the thing, he had an argument with the King when you were brought back to the palace and King Finule banished him to his rooms. They both said things that, well, couldn't be unsaid. Chervil was there at the time and heard everything. The moment Finule died, Chervil had Rian put under arrest.'

'He thinks Rian killed Finule?' I asked, aghast.

'I don't know what he really thinks, but he's putting the word out that Rian killed him because of his argument with his father over you.'

I bowed my head. 'Where is he?' I asked quietly.

'I don't know, he's vanished,' Anise said. 'Tarragon, Sage, and Willow are trying to find him. We thought it best for Willow to help them find Rian before coming to you.'

I nodded. 'It was the right thing to do.'

'The thing is…'

'Rian may already be dead,' I said, finishing Anise's sentence.

Anise bowed his head, nodding. 'It's quite possible. Chervil sees him as a threat now.'

'Enough to murder his own brother?'

'I'm not sure that even fratricide would be a step too far for him these days. Look, I'm going to try and find the keys to get you out of here.'

'No, it's too dangerous.'

'But–' The sound of marching boots drifted along the dungeon tunnels, cutting Anise short.

'You'd better go,' I said. 'Thank you for telling me. Now get out of here, and don't get caught.'

Anise looked back along the passageway, then passed a golden glass vial through the bars. 'Here. It won't break the Curse, but this tincture will give you a little extra strength in case you need it.'

'Thank you,' I said, taking it from him.

He nodded, the flickering torches revealing a conflicted look on his face as his eyes glistened in the light. 'Take care, Phire.'

'Go!'

Anise slipped into the shadows and out of sight as I slid hopelessly to the floor, clutching the vial. Rian had disappeared. He was missing, possibly dead. Tears filled my eyes.

Had he died because of me after all?

The footsteps got closer and turned the corner towards me. Six guards, with a limping figure in the lead, dragged a tall, bound man towards my cell.

Sorrel led the way. 'Put him in that one,' he said, gesturing to the cell next to mine. 'They can spend their last night together – well, almost together.'

I strained to see who it was in the torchlight.

Rian.

Thank the Stars he was still alive.

I scrambled to my feet.

His face looked haggard – drawn, even – with a bruise sitting proudly on the left side of his face. His hair was dishevelled, and his Warrior's headband gone. He glanced at me as the guards cut his bonds then threw him into the next door cell, a look full of pain and hopelessness etched on his face.

'We'll see you in the morning for your execution, cousin,' Sorrel said.

The door clanged shut, and Sorrel and the guards walked away while far above us, the bell continued to clang mournfully.

'Rian, Rian!' I slipped Anise's vial in my pocket and pressed up against the bars at the edge of my cell. I couldn't see him, though I knew he was there, and it drove me insane.

'I'm all right,' he said, his voice strained.

'What did they do to you?'

'Beat me about a bit, but I'm okay. Not that it matters much; Chervil is having me executed tomorrow as payback for Father's assassination.'

'But you're innocent.'

'Are you sure about that? You didn't hear our last conversation. I said things I shouldn't have. I might as well have killed him,' he said miserably.

'The Coterie killed him, not you.'

'How do you know?'

'Because Anise told me what happened. It's their style – Carnelian's actually. I thought he was dead, but maybe he isn't. He left a red bead.'

'I never should've spoken to Father like that,' Rian said, as though he hadn't heard me. The tone of his voice stabbed at my heart; even though he hadn't got on with his father, he'd obviously loved him, and his death had affected Rian deeply.

'It's not your fault,' I said.

'It doesn't matter much, now. I'll be dead at dawn.'

I clenched my fists. My blood flared in my veins. Had Chervil been waiting for an excuse to get Rian out of the way? 'Chervil can't do that.' I slipped my hand through the bars towards his cell. His warm hands grasped mine.

'Chervil's king now; he can do whatever he wants. And what he wants is me dead.'

'But will Lord Wintergreen and Lord Bergamot allow it?'

'They know better than to stand in his way – if they do, they'll be executed, too.'

'I'm so sorry,' I said, tears welling in my eyes. I could do nothing.

There was a pause. 'You know, it was my idea that Father give you the Cursed Weapons.'

'What?' My blood froze in my veins. Suddenly every breath was a struggle. Had I heard him right? 'Why? Why would you do that?' I asked, pulling my hands away from his. How could he have done this to me?

'I did it to try and keep you alive,' he said, the sorrow in his voice cutting my soul.

'I don't understand,' I said, shaking my head as a hundred questions forced their way into my mind as my body trembled.

'Father intended to have you executed the day you first arrived here all those weeks ago. I tried to persuade him not to. I told him you were innocent, that you could help us, but he wouldn't listen. It was only when I suggested he give you the task of finding the assassin and the thief while carrying the Cursed Weapons that he agreed to delay your execution. I wanted you to have the chance, and the time, to maybe prove your innocence before Father even gave them to you, but he made you take the Weapons quicker than I was expecting. Despite that, I still thought we could find a way to break the Curse. I was wrong.'

He'd done this to give me more time? Saved me by cursing me? I couldn't form any words as I tried to take in what he'd said. I wanted to shout, to swear, to cry – anything to vent my fury at the path I'd found myself on and my rage at its inevitable conclusion.

'I was trying to keep you alive for as long as I could,' he said, his voice strained. 'But back then, I didn't know I was going to fall in love with you, because if I had, I'd never have put you through any of this.' He sniffed.

It wasn't Rian's fault. He'd done what he thought best at the time. He'd tried to save me the only way he could. I sat, resting my head on my knees, and took a long, deep breath.

'I suppose you don't love me anymore? I can't say I blame you. I've caused all of this.' His voice echoed around the cells, bitter and wretched.

I pulled myself up and reached back through the bars, feeling his hand take mine in an urgent grasp.

'Of course, I still love you,' I said. 'You did what you did to try and save me. You *did* save me. If you hadn't persuaded your father to give me the Cursed Weapons, I'd have been dead weeks ago.' I glanced at Aldorbana and Cwicsusl winking at me in the flickering light. 'You gave me – you gave *us* – time. Time we'd never have had. Time to find each other, to fall in love and be together, and that time has been so precious to me.'

A strangled sob came from the cell next to me, and I could feel him shaking. 'I thought you'd hate me for it, but I had to tell you. I said to you we'd have no secrets – I had to be honest with you.'

'I don't blame you for what you did. And I could never hate you. I love you all the more for the time you've given us. I understand, and I'd like to think I'd have done the same.'

'Samphire, I love you,' he said, his voice still tight and full of emotion. 'I just wish I'd been able to marry you.'

'Me too,' I said, wiping my eyes, trying to keep my voice level.

'But I don't think there's a single priest in the Five Lands that would marry us now.'

'Then let's make our own vows,' he said. 'Pledge ourselves to each other here, now.' His warm grasp was so tender it broke my heart.

'All right – you go first,' I said. I needed time to think.

'I'm forever yours, my Samphire Amethyst, and no one else's,' he said, his voice catching. 'I was missing something in my life and it was you. You've made me complete. You've become my best friend. You're courageous, kind, and beautiful. With you in my life, I'll never want for anything. You're the soulmate I never knew I needed; never thought I'd have. I can give you nothing but my body and soul, and they are yours for all eternity. I'll love you and protect you until my last breath, Samphire. I love you and take you as my wife.'

I wiped a tear from my cheek. 'I'm yours, too, for always and forever,' I said as he gently squeezed my hand. 'There's never been anyone but you. You're my first and only love, Prince Valerian. You were there when I needed you. You're handsome, kind-hearted, and strong. You fill my heart and my soul. I'm the person I am today because of your love. I'd never have made it this far without you. You're my best friend and my soulmate. I have nothing to give you but my love, and you'll have that as long as I live. I'll care for you, defend you, and be your shield until my last breath.' My trembling voice was beginning to fail me. 'I love you so much, Rian, and I take you as my husband.'

He held my hand tighter and for a moment we just shared the silence, the distant ringing now a wedding bell.

'Hang on,' Rian said, letting go of my hand. A shuffling sound came from his cell then his hand reappeared, his gold and diamond ring held in his fingers. 'I want you to have this – I know it's not a proper wedding ring because if it was, I'd want it to have an amethyst in it, but it's all I have on me.'

I took it from him. It was the ring from his little finger. I slipped it on and gazed at it. The torchlight illuminated the gold ring and its intricate vine of thyme engraved into it that circumnavigated the ring, weaving in and out of tiny diamonds that lay around its surface; it was beautiful. 'This is perfect. I wouldn't want any other ring. I don't have a ring for you, but– I know, have this instead,' I said, taking my Amethyst Talisman off. I slipped my hand through the bars and pushed it into his.

'I can't take this,' he said, holding it so the amethyst dangled and caught the torchlight, scattering the light into brilliant purple beams.

'Of course, you can. I want you to have it. The amethyst is for inner strength. Wear it and I'll always be with you,' I said, trying not to let my voice crack.

'Very well. Then you'll always be close to my heart, as well as in it.' He put it on, then took hold of my hand again. 'I *so* want to hold you,' he said in a voice that nearly broke me. 'I want to kiss you.'

'And I want all those things too, and more,' I said, a wave of fatigue washing over me. I steadied myself against the wall.

'You need to rest,' he said.

'But if this is my last night with you, I don't want to rest.' Silent tears ran down my face; my love was so close, yet so far from me. Despair filled me. We sat in our cells clasping hands, dreading the dawn, and talking quietly.

The bell finally stopped ringing.

'What does it mean?' I asked.

'Chervil has officially taken the throne,' Rian said quietly. We sat in silence, still holding hands as the night wore on, until the slightest of silver flecks began to seep through the grating. Gradually, the silver turned to gold as dawn broke. Footsteps echoed around the dungeon corridors, getting louder by the second.

'Hell's teeth,' I said, clinging to Rian's hand.

'I only wish I'd known you longer, Phire,' Rian said.

'I love you.' I had no other words.

'You'll be in my heart until the end,' he said as the Palace Guards walked into the corridor, Sorrel once again leading the way. 'Look, when they get me out, I'll try to-'

'Time to go, Valerian,' Sorrel said in a triumphant voice, drowning out Rian's words. 'Hmm, I'm sorry you won't get to witness his death, Lady Merciless, but King Chervil wants you to stay here.'

I clenched my fist. 'You son of a—'

'Come now, Lady Merciless. You won't be without him for long,' Sorrel said, glancing at the Cursed Weapons.

Rian let go of me as the guards opened his cell, pulling him out. He twisted out of their grasp, lunging towards my cell, and reaching through the bars. Our lips collided in an urgent, desperate kiss as his fingers closed around my shoulders.

The guards grabbed him and yanked him away from me. I

reached out towards him, but they dragged him along the passage, my Amethyst Talisman swaying around his neck. He struggled against them, causing a scuffle to break out. One of the guards' fists connected with Rian's jaw with a sickening thud, and he tumbled into Aldorbana and Cwicsusl.

'That's enough, Valerian. I expected you to be more stoic about this. You can't escape, you know. Get him out of here,' Sorrel said, leading the way as the guards yanked Rian to his feet.

'I love you,' I said, tears escaping my eyes as I pressed up against the bars.

'I love you, too,' Rian replied, his eyes full of unshed tears, but the glance he gave me as they forced him down the corridor had a flicker of hope in it that I didn't understand.

I shook my head in despair. My heart shattered as a dull ache began in the centre of my chest, my breath coming in ragged gasps, my mind somersaulting.

I screamed with all the frustration and rage I could muster.

CHAPTER TWENTY-THREE

I twisted my wedding ring around my finger as the first rays of sun broke through the grate high in my cell, reaching into the dungeons. It lit the semi-precious stones on Citrine's knife and my War Fan and made Aldorbana and Cwicsusl sparkle and dance with rainbows in the golden light. As I watched the weapons illuminate the room, it occurred to me the Cursed Weapons were further away now. When Rian had struggled with the guards, he'd deliberately tumbled into them and knocked them further down the corridor, unnoticed.

If I could get far enough away from them, they'd come to me. Maybe I *could* get out of this hellhole and rescue Rian after all. I moved to the far side of my cell, pressing myself up the corner, flattening myself into the wall as much as I could, screaming at them to come to me.

But the Weapons didn't move.

They were still too close.

I sank to the floor, shaking. The glass vial Anise had given me poked into my hip. I pulled it out of my pocket and looked at it. Was there really any point in taking it? What could I hope to achieve? Then again, if this was my last chance to save Rian, I had to know that I'd tried everything. I unstopped the golden bottle and tipped the contents into my mouth.

It tasted of rosemary, fresh mint, and summer. Whatever Anise had put in this tincture, it immediately hit me, a warmth spreading through my body as a surge of energy filled my muscles. I became more alert and revitalised. I had the strength to fight. Hopefully, I'd get a chance to thank Anise.

I looked at Aldorbana, half expecting to see the ruby red colour returning to the crystal, but it remained static. I let out a long breath, disappointment welling in me.

A single set of footsteps echoed through the corridors and passageways, and Sorrel turned the corner. By the Stars, what did he want now? I slid back to the floor and looked up at him through my dishevelled hair, my face hopefully conveying defeat and pain, rather than the renewed energy I now felt.

He paused in front of my cell and sneered. 'Well, Valerian's on his way to the scaffold,' he said, his voice full of satisfaction. 'Chervil's going to make me Head of the King's Warriors. Tarragon, Anise, and Sage will be Demoted to menial work –

maybe I can get them to clear out the moat. They won't survive long, of course, but it does need a good clean. Willow might make a good personal maid. I'll have to think about that.'

I bowed my head so he couldn't see the anger and disgust in my eyes as my hands formed fists at his words – fists I wanted to smash straight into his smug face.

'We never did get to finish what we started outside that barn, did we?' he said, causing a shudder of revulsion to shoot down my spine. 'Maybe now's the time to rectify that.'

I heard the jingle of keys, the turn of the rusty lock that set my teeth on edge nearly as much as Sorrel's foul words. The rusty hinges protested as he forced the door open. A hand touched my shoulder.

I exploded like a coiled spring, lunging straight into him.

Taken by surprise, he didn't even yell as he fell backwards, keys flying to the ground. I scrambled to my feet, heading for freedom, but he grabbed my foot and I fell. I tried to kick him off as he grabbed me with his other hand.

I launched my elbow into his face, the tell-tale sound of bone breaking filling the cell as he screamed, rolled sideways, and clutched at his bleeding nose. I got to my feet and unleashed a hefty kick to his stomach before grabbing the keys and dashing from the cell, locking it behind me. I stood there a moment, getting my breath back as my heartbeat like an Iolitian drum in my chest.

'Bitch.' He spat, blood splattering on the stone floor.

'Lady *Merciless*, you mean,' I said, before turning away.

A shocked guard appeared at the end of the cells. I sighed; this wasn't going to be easy, was it? He lunged towards me. I sidestepped, tripped him up, and sent him careering into a stone wall. He dropped to the ground, motionless. I grabbed my Fan and Citrine's knife, glancing at Aldorbana and Cwicsusl. It would be quicker to let them attach themselves to me than for me to struggle with the straps. I glanced at the crystal blade and shuddered – only the tip remained red. I prayed I had enough time and strength left to save Rian.

I gave Sorrel a wave and left him groaning in my cell, then hurried down the corridor, turned a corner, and ran straight into two more guards. Aldorbana and Cwicsusl appeared on my back. I took the first by surprise, shoving him out the way with Cwicsusl, slamming his head into the wall. The second recovered quick enough to draw his sword and take a swipe at me. I parried his blow with Aldorbana then kicked him in the shins. Never kick high – it's too easy to be knocked off balance. I slammed Cwicsusl into his face, launching him backwards into an empty cell. He lay there, groaning. I banged the cell door shut, locking him in, and made my way out of the dungeons.

I reached the palace courtyard and took the opportunity for a breather. My heart was racing, my mouth dry as I peered into the empty space. Everyone had to be at the execution, but where would they hold it? I didn't know Viridi that well and didn't know where to begin looking for Rian. I made my way up the steps towards the palace door, wishing I'd forced the location out of one of the guards before I'd rendered them unconscious. I'd have to find someone else to get the information from. Voices inside the palace entrance made me pause and I hid near the door, listening.

'…lica, Finule and Chervil were supposed to die, not Valerian, too,' Wintergreen said.

'I have no control over what Chervil does.' That honeyed voice made me shudder. Carnelian. He was still alive, after all.

'The whole point was to get Valerian on the throne. Now the commission is pointless. He would have made a good, fair king. Ushered in reform. Chervil's desire is to just crack down on everything and everyone. My plan will never work with him as king.'

'You don't want Chervil killed now?' Carnelian asked. 'I'm happy to still do it. It would be easy enough – the last one was.'

I gasped and crouched down, clamping a hand over my mouth. That bastard.

'If Chervil's killed, Bergamot will become king, followed by Sorrel, and they will be worse than Angelica, Chervil, and Finule combined.'

'I can kill *them* for you too, for the right price.'

'No. This has gone far enough.'

'Then you'd better let Mistress Juniper know, but you do realise you won't get any of your money back?'

'I don't care about the money. I'll write a letter to her – can you deliver it?' Wintergreen asked.

'Of course,' Carnelian said. 'Hadn't you better go? They'll be expecting you at the execution, won't they? I hear it's to be quite the spectacle.'

I shuddered.

'I'm leaving now; Retribution Square isn't far. I'll meet you this evening with the letter at our normal time and place.'

Lord Wintergreen commissioned the assassinations? *Hell's teeth.* Hyssop had been right, someone in the Royal Family really had arranged Angelica's murder; people were just looking a little too high up the family. Wintergreen had never occurred to me. I ducked into an archway, then followed Wintergreen as the tall man made his way on horseback to Retribution Square. I kept to the shadows, far enough behind him not to be noticed. I'd no idea where the square was, and the fact that he went straight there came as a relief. As we got closer, the crowds flocking towards the square grew, so I ducked into a back alley, climbed up a drainpipe, and took to the rooftops.

I scrambled over the tiled roofs until I reached the bottom left hand corner of the square where I looked down. I swallowed. Below me, the large square stood packed with people, the sound of their chatter reaching such a crescendo that I could barely think. Halfway along the left hand side of the square stood a wooden scaffold set in front of the buildings and, on the top, stood a block with a large axe sitting in it, waiting. A chill drove its way down my spine. There were so many people between me and the scaffold that getting there would be near impossible. I had so little time to plan this. A little niggling voice in the back of my mind said that I'd fail, that Rian and I would die together on the scaffold, which strangely gave me a sense of calm.

I focused on the platform, considering my options; if I could get there, I could fight my way past the two guards at the bottom and take out the executioner without a problem, but getting away would be harder. Maybe for once in my life I'd wing it completely, rather than plan all the details. A drum sounded to my right, silencing the crowd, and from the far corner of the square, a procession of Palace Guards appeared. Two rode on horseback, holding ropes, leading Rian, one of his wrists tied securely to each rope. The sight tore at my heart. Behind them, also on horseback, rode Lord Wintergreen, Lord Bergamot and Lord Wormwood, but leading them all, a triumphant look on his face, was Chervil – hardly appropriate for the morning after his father's murder.

Nausea threatened to overwhelm me. Fear wedged in my chest. I couldn't lose Rian now. *Concentrate.* Just concentrate on getting him free, not on the look of resignation and hopelessness etched into his dear face. I gave myself over to my assassin training and its calm focus. Determination to save my love lit a fire in me and it raged, filling me with stubborn purpose.

I searched for a way down off the roof as the procession made its way through the crowd, the now-silent people moving reluctantly aside for them. The scene before me gave me the distinct impression that the people of Aerba weren't happy that their youngest prince faced execution. I climbed down to the ground, hiding in the shadows of a greengrocer's store where the sweet, peppery smell of parsnips, and the taste of dried herbs in the air did nothing for my queasy stomach. A guard cut Rian's bonds and steered him up onto the scaffold at sword point. Chervil remained on his horse, a flicker of a smile on his face as he turned to address the city folk.

'People of Aerba, I address you today as your new King,' Chervil said. 'As you know, my father was murdered last night, but I'm here to tell you that it was my brother, Prince Valerian–' He pointed to where Rian now stood on the top of the scaffold– 'who killed him.' A shocked gasp rippled around the square, and many shook their heads in disbelief. At this moment I wanted to get my hands on Chervil's neck and squeeze the life out of him. Rian had wanted to know if I'd kill for him, and the answer was yes, unequivocally. 'He argued with my father because he had been beguiled into believing himself in love with Lady Merciless of the Iolite Coterie of Assassins who murdered your beloved Princess Angelica.' Another murmur moved through the crowd.

I clenched my fists, blood surging around my body. Perspiration sprang from my brow.

'I intended to show him mercy,' Chervil continued. *Liar.* 'But Prince Valerian would not repent or see the error of his ways, so I have no choice but to punish him for patricide and regicide, and to invoke the Blood Rule Decree for his relationship with a Middle Blood of another country. It is therefore with a heavy heart that I pass the sentence of execution on my only brother. I deeply regret this necessity, but the Royal Family is not above the law, and I am determined, as your new King, to demonstrate to you from my first day on the throne that I will not shy away from my responsibilities.'

I couldn't believe what I was hearing, and Chervil was clearly enjoying every moment of it as he fiddled with his sleeve.

'To this end, I wish to announce that the Fire Opal of Aerba has been tracked down to the Land of Flos. Our old enemies saw fit to steal our national emblem from us, but we will not stand for this. I have ordered the Nightshade to take steps, and I have also, reluctantly, taken the decision to order Lord Bergamot to prepare our army for war.'

Chervil didn't waste any time, I'd give him that, but full-on war with Flos? Had the Fire Opal really been tracked there in the last few hours? It wasn't possible. I shook my head in disbelief at the lies Chervil was spinning.

Worried voices echoed around the square. I looked towards the scaffold where Rian stood, his hands now bound behind his back. He stood tall, proud, and defiant, with a guard on either side, his muscles tense, anger emanating from his core. He looked every inch a Prince of Aerba. A High Blood Prince that, despite my initial reservations, I now loved with everything I had. If I could save him, I would, even if I died doing it.

I had to move now or it would be too late. I drew Aldorbana and Cwicsusl, took a deep breath and moved forward, blessing Anise's tincture. I walked into the crowd. Tarragon and Willow appeared to my right, as Anise and Sage emerged from the crowd to my left matching my movement towards the scaffold.

'Where did you come from?' I asked Tarragon.

'I could ask the same of you, y'know?' He grinned, his swords drawn. 'I thought you were supposed to be indisposed.'

'Is that what you call languishing in the palace dungeons? I'm afraid I got bored, so I decided to look for something to do.'

Despite our dire situation, Tarragon chuckled. 'Spoken like a true King's Warrior.'

'Not sure Chervil would see it like that.'

'We will not lose the Fire Opal to our enemy. We will recover it and return it to its rightful place in the Cedarwood Throne,' Chervil's voice rose above the crowd. 'Aerba will not tolerate thieves and traitors. They will be brought to justice. But first, execute the murderer and renegade, Prince Valerian!' He pointed at Rian. The crowd broke into a frenzy, impeding our progress towards the scaffold.

The guards grabbed Rian by the shoulders, forcing him to his knees in front of the block. The black-hooded executioner picked up his axe and took a few practice strokes on the far side of the scaffold. I pushed forwards, desperate to get to Rian in time.

'I want to say something,' Rian yelled above the commotion. The guards suddenly looked unsure and hesitantly allowed him to stand up. He drew himself up to his full height, proud and magnificent.

The crowd quieted and looked up at him expectantly, even as we continued to weave our way through the people.

'Shut up, Valerian. Guards, proceed with the execution,' Chervil said, his voice raised. 'Traitors to the crown have no right to last words.'

'You're the traitor here.' Rian struggled against the Palace Guards holding him. 'You're the threat to Aerba, not me, or Samphire. You'd really go to war with Flos without diplomacy first? Without proper evidence? Our people's lives thrown away in a war without justification?'

Spoken like a true king.

And he was right. Chervil had no evidence.

People jostled, getting in my way as they tried for a better view of the spectacle.

'Move!' Tarragon shouted, his deep, husky voice imposing.

'Clear the way!' Sage said with such a loud, commanding voice that people immediately scurried out of our path.

I forced my way through the remaining crowd, Cwicsusl giving me the opportunity to shove stragglers away as I hurried to the scaffold. Four guards now stood at its base. I smashed the first out the way with Cwicsusl, Tarragon took the second, while Anise and Sage made short work of the other two.

I scrambled up the steps to the two guards and the executioner. Rian turned, a flicker of hope flashing in his eyes. One of the guards grabbed Rian's shoulder, forcing him to his knees again, his neck thrust onto the bloodied block. The other swiped at me with his mace, a weapon I'd never faced in combat before. My palms broke out in a cold sweat. I parried. The mighty stroke jarred Aldorbana from my damp hand, sending my sword tumbling off the scaffold and into the crowd, turning my fingers numb. I looked up in horror as the mace swept towards me again. I raised Cwicsusl, ducking behind it as the mace impacted on the crystal. The shield stopped the blow, but I fell backwards under the force of the stroke. Cwicsusl slipped from my sweaty grasp. The guard struck at me again. I rolled in the opposite direction, out the way. The mace hit the wooden scaffold, splinters shooting in all directions. He tried to pull the mace free of the wood, but it was well and truly stuck.

I leapt to my feet.

Neither Aldorbana nor Cwicsusl were far enough away to come back to me on their own, and I swore. I grabbed my War Fan and flicked it open, sweeping the sharp metal points towards the soldier's unprotected side. He let go of the mace, pulled a dagger from his waist, and countered my attack, parrying my slice. He swung his dagger towards me. I caught the blade in the spokes of my Fan, twisted the weapon, and wrenched the dagger from his grasp.

Willow reached the top of the scaffold, grabbed the guard from behind, unbalancing him, and hurled him off the wooden structure into the crowd, stunning the people gathered below into silence. She turned and grinned at me, dusting her hands off. There was no sign of her freezing this time.

I smiled back, then turned around. The second guard let go of Rian and lunged at me with his sword. I ducked beneath his swinging arm, twisting around his back, closing my Fan as I went, and slammed the handle into his head. He fell.

The executioner paused, his axe over Rian's unprotected neck.

Rian looked at me, his eyes pleading for help.

'Get away from him,' I said, my voice full of menace and steel. I was about seven feet from them, but I didn't dare step closer in case the executioner began hacking at Rian's neck. I put my Fan away and pulled Citrine's knife from my boot. I'd learnt to throw knives as part of my training, and I'd been quite good, too. But could I do it now, when it really mattered? My heart stuttered in my chest.

The executioner hesitated.

Pandemonium erupted in the square.

'Kill him!' Chervil screamed over the noise.

The executioner raised the axe over his head. I didn't wait. I threw the knife in a smooth, underhand cast. The jewelled blade sparkled and dazzled as it spun one revolution in the air. It buried itself in the executioner's left shoulder. He staggered backwards, dropping the axe behind him, reaching for the dagger protruding from his bleeding body. I swept forward, my War Fan open once more, but he took one look at me and jumped from the scaffold.

The sound of the crowd had changed – were they daring to cheer our rescue attempt?

My tense shoulders dropped, a sense of relief filling me as I turned. Rian was on his feet, his eyes containing so many emotions that I couldn't name half of them. I cut his bonds, the jewels on the War Fan glittering in the light. I closed it and, before he had a chance to protest, pulled him to me, kissing him.

For a moment the square fell away. The noise of the crowd vanished. We held each other, revelling in each other's warmth, and taking comfort in our love. Then the noise of the crowd returned.

'This really isn't the time, y'know,' Tarragon said from behind me.

Rian released me and winked, making blood rush to my face. He grinned, love shining in his eyes. Screams and cheers filled the square, filling my ears and drowning out whatever obscenities Chervil was shouting at us. Rian grabbed my hand and we followed Tarragon, jumping off the back of the scaffold, moving away from the square.

Guards quickly appeared around us as Aldorbana and Cwicsusl returned to my back. Anise gave Rian one of his swords and, between us, we cut our way through the men. A guard wielding a sword appeared in front of me, aiming his weapon at my head, but I blocked it with Cwicsusl. I twisted, parrying another. Sidestepping, I smashed the hilt of Aldorbana into bone. A mace swept towards Rian's unprotected back, and I put myself and Cwicsusl in the way, deflecting the blow. Rian turned, eyes wide, and nodded. I swung Aldorbana around, driving another soldier away from Anise. With every step, we were closer to escape. Willow fought like three men, holding her own, overwhelming them with her speed, agility, and whirling blades. Sage and Tarragon sliced and chopped with powerful blows. Gradually, we forced our way through the guards, forging a direct path away from the square, scattering the crowd in front of us like wolves scattering sheep.

'Down here,' Sage said, indicating an alley. At the end stood five horses with packs, waiting patiently.

'You weren't expecting me, were you?' I asked, trembling slightly from the exertion as I wiped sweat from my face and dried my palms on my britches.

'We knew you'd get out if you could, but you were at least safe in the palace. Rian was another thing, though,' Anise said. 'We'd planned to come and get you later, Phire, so you've saved us a trip.' He grinned at me.

Rian mounted his horse, pulling me up behind him. I clung on to his waist, his warmth filling me. The others mounted their own horses, and we rode out of the alley.

'We'll take the south gate, head in the direction of Hops,' Rian said.

We urged our horses down the street at a gallop. There were few people here, most still being in the square, and they scattered as we rode until we reached the Hops Gate where six guards stood, barring our way.

'Damnation,' Rian muttered, reining in our horse a short distance from the gatehouse.

'We're buggered now,' Tarragon said, looking at the guards.

Willow drew a sword. 'We'll just ride through them.'

'They're Gate Guards and some of them have spears. It's unlikely we'll make it through without them bringing down at least one of the horses,' Sage said. 'And at least one of us, too.'

'Then we fight,' Rian said, still holding one of Anise's swords. I drew Aldorbana again and held on to Rian with one hand. Rian yelled, kicking our horse on, the others following behind.

A wave of dizziness passed over me – whether from the Cursed Weapons or the fight, I didn't know, but I clung on to Rian's waist.

The guards in their red suede uniforms ran forward, brandishing their spears. I took a deep breath. Rian swiped one spear out the way as we reached the gate, trying to force our way through. Our horse reared. I slid backwards, unable to maintain my hold with one hand, landing in a heap on the cobblestones, the wind knocked out of me.

A guard grabbed me and swung his hand back. As he punched towards me, I shifted my head. His hand connected with the stone road. He recoiled in pain.

Anise blocked a spear lunge aimed at my head and I scrambled to my feet, gasping for air. I grabbed Aldorbana, parrying a blow meant to kill Sage's horse. A guard pulled Tarragon from his beast, but Willow acted immediately, and, with a yell, she jumped from her horse's back, knocking the man out as she landed on him.

'Thanks,' Tarragon said, pride in his eyes as he got to his feet.

'You're welcome, my lover.' She grinned.

'Move!' Rian urged us, holding his hand out to me, but a guard thrust his sword at us. I blocked the blow with Cwicsusl, forcing him into the gatehouse wall, rendering him unconscious just as another guard pulled Rian from our horse. The beast cantered off onto the drawbridge that crossed the poisoned moat. The others were making their way over the bridge; Sage and Anise were in the lead as Willow and Tarragon remounted and followed them.

The sound of horses' hooves made me turn. A lone horseman, sword drawn, charged down the street towards us. Sorrel.

How had he escaped?

His swollen, bloodied face had a look of grim determination, almost indomitability. I edged backwards, wondering if Rian and I could ride away before Sorrel reached us, but it quickly became apparent that Rian hadn't noticed Sorrel and was too busy fighting with the guard, making their way out onto the bridge in a macabre dance.

I backed away from Sorrel, moving through the gate. It was the first time I'd been this close to the poisoned moat for any length of time, and its acrid smell made my eyes sting. My heart skipped a beat as Sorrel plunged towards me, his face red, a vein pulsing in his neck. He wanted revenge.

'You're mine, Lady Merciless,' he said, flinging himself from his horse. I tried to move out of the way, but there was limited room and he crashed into me. We fell backwards onto the bridge; the cold hilt of Aldorbana jarred from my hand, clattering across the wood. The force of the landing knocked what little air I'd got into my lungs back out again. Dazed, my lungs screamed at me once more for air. I tried to get up. Pain spiralled through my chest, threatening to overwhelm me. *Push through it.* I tried to clear my head, but my usual speed eluded me. I shook as I gasped for air, the pain from my lungs searing my mind as the Curse took its toll on my body.

Sorrel rolled to his feet and jumped on me, knocking me back to the ground. His sword rested at my throat, his nose still glistening with wet blood. Cwicsusl was useless, pinned to my back.

'And now you die, Lady Merciless,' he said with a grin, eyes narrowing. 'Hmm, I'm going to enjoy this.'

I looked him in the eye, daring him to kill me.

CHAPTER TWENTY-FOUR

I lashed out, kicking Sorrel in the knee.

Rian grabbed him from behind with both hands, jerking him off me and sending him hurtling back towards the gate. Sorrel landed heavily but quickly scrambled to his feet. His injured knee gave way. He stumbled and tripped on the raised edge of the drawbridge, falling backwards. He screamed as he hit the water. The poison immediately got to work, biting into his skin like acid. I was still gasping for air as Rian pulled me up. I watched in horror as a guard tried to pull Sorrel out of the toxic water, only to have his own hand burnt in the liquid.

My vision was like looking down a long tunnel. Only my central vision was in sharp focus – and I could taste blood.

A voice spoke, but I didn't catch what they said.

'Phire!' Rian said again, his voice clearer this time. 'Come on.'

I turned towards him.

'Let's get out of here,' he continued, mounting our horse. He reached out to me and I took his hand, allowing him to yank me up behind him, Aldorbana returning to my back as we rode off the drawbridge. Sorrel's screams of anguish rang out around us. Sage gazed across at his struggling brother.

'You can't help him; it's too late,' Anise said softly.

'Who said I wanted to help him?' Sage asked. He turned, riding after Tarragon and Willow.

I didn't look back.

We rode to the top of a small hill where Rian paused. The distant palace shone in the sunlight. The glistening water of the great lake only added to the breath-taking, heart-breaking view as he looked back at the home he would never return to. I slipped my hand into his in silent comfort.

'Are you all right?' he asked. 'You're shaking.'

'Just the fight,' I assured him.

He nodded, but something in his eyes told me he wasn't convinced. In truth, I wasn't sure what it was. Was it a reaction to the fight, the Cursed Weapons draining me, Sorrel's demise or relief at our escape? It could have been any or all of them.

'I'll be all right, and so will you.' I said. 'We're together, and with our friends.'

'With you by my side I can survive anything – you've already proved that,' he said.

I shivered slightly at his words.

'Come on you two, we need to keep going!' Tarragon called.

'Coming.' Rian took one more look at the palace before kicking our horse on, riding after the others.

We galloped in silence for some time, trying to put as much distance between us and Viridi as we could. We rode to the east of the main road, keeping away from any travellers and hopefully away from the Nightshade's spies. I held on to Rian, but I could sense my strength failing, Anise's tincture having almost run its course. When I'd last seen Aldorbana lying on the bridge, only a drop of red remained in its tip, but in the confusion of the fight no one had noticed, not even Rian. I clung on to him, relishing every moment I had with him, for they were likely to be my last. Rian would be all right with the others to look after him, but I feared for Mal's safety, though I could do nothing for him, now.

'Thank you all for coming to save me,' Rian said as we finally slowed.

'Of course we'd come to rescue you. You didn't think we'd leave you to die on that scaffold, did you?' Tarragon asked, grinning broadly. 'Not when there was a good fight to be had.'

Rian raised an eyebrow. 'I guess not. I should've known you'd be mad enough to try and get me out.'

'Of course,' Tarragon said, buffing his nails comically.

'Where do you want to go, Rian?' Sage asked.

'We can't stay in Aerba,' Willow said. She blinked several times, her fatigue obvious. The fights had taken their toll on her. 'Chervil and the Nightshade won't rest until they've hunted us down.'

'Maybe we should take the opportunity to head for the archipelago,' Rian said.

'Sounds good to me,' Tarragon said, nodding.

'Then we should continue to Hops and take the first ship out of here,' Anise said.

'To where, though?' Willow asked. 'There won't be any going direct to the archipelago.'

'It doesn't matter where to at the moment, so long as we're away from Aerba,' Rian said. 'We can worry about chartering a ship to the archipelago later.'

'Lord Wintergreen arranged the assassinations,' I interrupted, the information suddenly feeling very necessary.

Tarragon brought his horse to an abrupt halt and looked sharply at me. 'What did you say?'

Rian stopped our horse.

'Lord Wintergreen arranged for the Coterie to kill Angelica, Finule, and Chervil in order to put Rian on the throne,' I said.

'But why?' Rian asked, twisting around in the saddle, his forehead furrowed.

'Because he thought you'd make a fair king, one that would usher in reform.'

'Well, he got that right, but to commission the Coterie – I can't believe it,' Tarragon said, scratching his chin. 'How do you know that's what happened?'

'I overheard him on my way out of the palace. He was talking to Carnelian.'

'Carnelian – I thought he was dead?' Anise said.

'He looked pretty dead to me last time we saw him,' Sage said.

'I'm afraid he survived,' I said. 'He was the one who killed Finule. Because Chervil was going to have Rian executed, Lord Wintergreen said he didn't want the rest of the commission carried out. He wants Chervil left alive.'

'I can see why Wintergreen would stop the commission if Rian was dead, but surely he'll carry it through, now – if Chervil was dead, then Rian would be the King,' Anise said.

Rian shook his head. 'Chervil has already had my name removed from the line of succession – it was the first thing he ordered when he had me arrested, so it would go to Lord Bergamot.'

Sage shuddered. 'Father as king? No, thank you. That would be a disaster for the whole of Aerba.'

'That's rather what Lord Wintergreen said, actually. And then, when that failed, it would've been Sorrel,' I said.

Sage blanched. 'And that would've been even worse,' he said in a sour tone.

Tarragon shook his head. 'I'd no idea Father had ordered the assassinations,' he said looking over at Rian. 'I'm so sorry.'

'Don't be, it wasn't your fault,' Rian said.

'But even so…'

Willow rode up beside Tarragon, placing a reassuring hand on his arm. He turned to her and gave her a wan smile.

Rian twisted around. 'Can I tell them?' he asked quietly, his hand resting on mine, his fingers brushing my wedding ring.

I smiled. 'If you like.'

'I want you all to know that Phire and I pledged ourselves to each other in the dungeons,' Rian said. 'We're married.'

Sage narrowed his eyes. 'You do know that it's not really official?'

'It is to us,' Rian said, his voice firm.

'Then that's all that matters,' Anise said with a smile.

'Does that make you a princess, then?' Willow asked.

Tarragon gave her a nudge.

'What?' she asked, all innocence. The thought of being a princess hadn't even occurred to me but seeing as Chervil had removed Rian from the line of succession, and my demise wasn't far away, I didn't think it mattered too much. 'Princess Samphire. That sounds good. Not a herb, of course. But good all the same.'

'Samphire can be used as a herb,' Anise said. 'Didn't you know?'

'Oh, that's fine then,' Willow said, grinning broadly. 'Princess Samphire it is.'

Rian ignored her.

'I'm very pleased for you both,' she said.

'So are we,' Anise said as Sage and Tarragon grinned.

'Shame you couldn't have had a proper ceremony,' Tarragon said.

'We were a little pushed for time,' I said.

'The executioner was calling,' Rian said, grinning. 'But that's all behind us, now.' Had he forgotten the Curse? 'Let's keep going, maybe we can get to Hops by the early hours if we keep riding.'

'We'll have to stop at some point, give the horses a rest,' Sage said.

'Then we'll stop at dusk for a short while.'

We rode on, continuing through until twilight before stopping for a brief rest in a small copse of trees. Rian dismounted first, and I slid from our horse straight into his arms.

'You came for me,' he murmured, stroking my hair away from my face. 'Were you able to get the Weapons to you?'

'No, they weren't far enough away, even after your little subterfuge,' I said. 'But thank you for trying.'

'Then how?'

'Anise brought me a tincture to boost my strength for a while, and then Sorrel came and let me out.'

'I wondered where your renewed energy had come from. But did Sorrel really let you out? Willingly?'

'No, I had to give him a little encouragement,' I said, flashing him a grin.

'And you still haven't killed,' he said.

'Not quite,' I said, rather rueing the fact I'd lost Citrine's rather nice knife.

He looked into my eyes and moved closer, holding me in his arms, his warm, velvet lips caressing mine as he kissed me. This was no ordinary kiss – if there is such a thing. It was a scorching kiss, full of want and desire, setting light to the blood in my veins, my heart exploding with love as a molten pool settled in my core. I kissed him back with such passion I felt him hesitate a moment before replying with equal ferocity. If he'd asked me, I'd have given myself to him there and then. I wanted him and I knew he wanted me. This just wasn't the time, and I didn't think there would be one for us now.

He pulled back, his lopsided grin doing nothing for the weak feeling I already had in my legs. 'I can't believe how lucky I am to have you,' he said, before moving over to help Tarragon and Willow with the horses, while the others got food from their packs.

The world tilted for a moment, and I grabbed a tree to keep myself upright. The Curse appeared to be rapidly reaching its conclusion, and the benefit I'd felt from Anise's tincture was all but gone. Rian hadn't seen Aldorbana and Cwicsusl, hadn't realised how close my end was. I had. I slid to the ground, dizzy. I tried to breathe deeply, calm the rising sensation of panic twisting and knotting inside me. It wouldn't be long, now. I forced the panic down deep inside and pulled myself up, going over to join the others.

We set off again once darkness cloaked the land, starting the last leagues to Hops bathed in moonlight that lit the countryside, painting it silver. After a few hours, the lights of Hops came into view, a warm orange glow illuminating the horizon.

'Almost there,' Anise said.

'Thank the Herbs,' Tarragon said. 'I can't feel my backside. It's gone completely numb, y'know.'

'Baby,' Willow said.

'I won't be sorry to leave the horses; their smell tends to linger,' Anise said, sniffing his sleeve and screwing his nose up. 'I need a bath.'

'The only problem is Willow and Tarragon don't really like sea voyages,' Sage said. 'I hope you thought to bring your Herb Chest with you, Anise.'

'I don't go anywhere without it, Sage. You should know that by now – even executions,' Anise said, patting a bag attached to his saddle.

Rian laughed. 'We can always count on you, can't we?'

'I like to think so. Are you all right, Phire? You're very quiet,' Anise said.

I blessed the darkness for hiding the state of the Cursed Weapons from them. 'I'm fine, just tired,' I said, the biggest lie I'd ever told. I wasn't fine. The last vestiges of life were ebbing from me as Cwicsusl and Aldorbana sucked out what little life remained in me, draining me of my last remnants of energy. 'I'll be better once I've had a rest.' Only I feared the rest to come would be somewhat permanent.

We rode towards Hops, entering the quiet fishing town. Two guards stood at the entrance.

'What's your business here?' the taller one asked.

'We're on the King's business,' Tarragon said, making sure the guards could see his headband in their lamplight.

'King's Warriors? I'm sorry, sir, I didn't realise,' the guard said. 'We're not used to travellers at this time of night.'

'That's perfectly all right,' Tarragon said. 'We wouldn't be travelling at this time if our mission wasn't urgent. I usually prefer a nice, soft feather bed at this hour.'

'Don't we all,' the second guard chuckled. 'Safe journey.'

'Thank you,' Sage said, and we rode into the town making our way through the streets, down towards the docks.

Other than the two guards, the streets were quiet at this hour – only a cat on its nightly hunt crossed our path. We rode down the steep street to where the ships sat moored, the salty sea air tonight more vibrant than ever; I could even taste it.

'There are several ships down there, and I think one of them may even be Hyssop's,' Sage said, squinting in the moonlight.

I strained to see, but my vision suddenly blurred.

'Yes, I think it is. Maybe he can grant us passage,' Rian said.

'Not sure I want to go back to Cilantro,' Anise muttered.

'Why not?' Tarragon asked.

'Too hot, does nothing for your personal hygiene.'

'By the Herbs, is that all you're interested in?'

'No, but as I've said before, being well turned-out is important, particularly if you want to be taken seriously,' he said, giving Tarragon a long look.

Tarragon frowned and straightened his coat.

'Come on,' Rian said. 'Less chat – we don't want to wake the whole town.'

As we rode the last few yards to the ship, the blurriness got worse until my eyes could barely register a thing. The sound of the horses' hooves and the waves lapping on the docks took on an echoey, ethereal quality, and although my arms and hands firmly clasped Rian's waist, a numb sensation started at my fingers and slowly spread up my arms.

The horses came to a halt on the quay.

'Find Hyssop,' Rian said.

Anise and Sage dismounted and walked up the gangplank, striking up a conversation with the sailor on night watch.

Complete exhaustion hit me like a wave. I had no strength left, not even to hold onto Rian and stay on our horse. The numb sensation grew and I lost hold of him, slipping from the saddle, the ground rushing up to meet me. Cwicsusl rolled free. I gasped more in surprise than pain. In the lamplight from the ships, I could see that the shield had just a single fleck of red remaining at its tip.

'Phire!' Rian jumped from our horse, falling to his knees beside me, gathering me up in his arms, tears in his eyes. 'Hold on, don't leave me,' he murmured brokenly in my ear.

'Not sure I have a choice,' I said, my voice barely more than a whisper as I tried to focus on his face.

Anise and Sage ran back down the gangplank towards us, Captain Hyssop following behind.

'Get her on board,' Hyssop said, his brow creased.

Rian scooped me up, carrying me towards the ship, taking care as he walked up the gangplank, my Amethyst Talisman dangling out of his coat as we went.

'You're wearin' her Artefact now, are you?' Hyssop asked with a wan smile.

'My what?' What was he saying? My addled brain desperately tried to make sense of his words as Willow gingerly picked up Cwicsusl and followed us.

'This way, take her into the cabin,' Hyssop said, ushering us along.

Rian carried me into the cabin as Sage and Anise quickly collected up some cushions, and Willow removed Aldorbana from my back. Rian gently laid me on the cushions, Willow placing the Cursed Weapons against the cabin wall.

The colours around me suddenly brightened and swirled as Hyssop's words pierced my mind.

Artefact.

'Stay with me, Phire, don't leave me,' Rian said, stroking my hair and kissing my forehead.

What had Agate said about the Weapons?

They're made from a single diamond Artefact, totally indestructible.

But were they? Moonstone indicated the old Elemental Magic could defeat the Curse. Onyx had said something about some types of crystal not mixing – and then there was what Anise had said.

Sometimes you could use Artefact against Artefact, depending on the crystal.

Father's book had spoken of Quintessence Angle Spinners being the only ones who could break the Curse using Artefact against Artefact, but Anise had said he didn't think that was the case. You didn't have to be a Spinner.

I gasped.

Artefact against Artefact.

Amethyst against diamond.

Elemental Magic against Elemental Magic.

Maybe I had the answer in front of me all along.

CHAPTER TWENTY-FIVE

A flash of inspiration pierced the fog of my muddled brain.

'I know what to do,' I said, my voice trembling.

'What?' Rian asked as the others gathered around us.

'I know how to break the Curse,' I said, stronger this time.

'Are you sure?'

'I think so. I think I've finally worked it out.'

'Then how? How do we break it?' he asked, desperation filling his voice.

'Artefact against Artefact,' I said, reaching up to touch his anguished, fear-etched face. 'Their Elemental Magic against each other.'

'Will it work?' he asked, a catch to his voice.

'Amethyst is protective – it obstructs negative energy. Maybe the Magic in diamond isn't indestructible,' I said, struggling to sit up as the room swung before my eyes. 'Help me.'

'To do what?' he asked, reaching out to steady me.

'I need Cwicsusl,' I said, groping around for my shield. Where was the stupid thing when I needed it?

'It's here,' Willow said, grabbing the shield and holding it out towards me.

'What are you doing?' Rian asked, fear tingeing his voice.

'I need to use Artefact against Artefact,' I said.

'You mean Aldorbana against Cwicsusl?' Tarragon asked.

'No, we already tried that,' Anise said.

'It didn't work because they're both made from the same Artefact,' I said.

'Your Amethyst Talisman?' Hyssop asked from the door.

I nodded.

'You're sure it's an Artefact, Hyssop?' Rian asked, pulling the Talisman from his coat and looking at it in awe.

Hyssop nodded. 'I am.'

'Let's hope so, because this is my last chance,' I said as Rian pulled it off over his head.

I dragged myself into an upright sitting position and took hold of the shield, laying it on the floor in front of me. 'Give me the amethyst.'

'I'll do it,' Rian said.

'I don't think you can. The Curse has been placed on me, I have to do it,' I said, reaching out for the Talisman, my hand closing over the amethyst and Rian's clenched fist.

'But not yet. Stay with me while you can, even just for a few more moments, in case it doesn't work.'

'This is her only chance, Rian,' Willow said, helping me stay upright. 'It's this or nothing. Let her do it.'

Sage nodded. 'You have to help her, Rian. It's the only way you can possibly save her.'

Rian looked at me, his face tormented and troubled.

'I'm frightened,' I said. 'In case it doesn't work.'

'You can do this, Phire, we're right here with you,' Anise said.

'I-I can't lose you,' Rian murmured.

His hand still held the Talisman, and I placed my other hand on his, too. 'It'll be fine.'

'It better be.'

Tarragon glanced at the sword-tip. 'Bugger, you'd better do it quickly,' he said.

'But–' Rian's eyes were misty as he looked at me.

'It's the only way, Rian,' I said, tears glistening in my eyes. 'Please help me – please help me live. I want to be with you.'

Reluctantly, Rian let go of the Talisman. 'You're sure about this?'

I nodded. 'I'm sure. As sure of this as I am of my love for you.'

He leant forwards, kissing me gently, his velvet lips hot against my cold ones. I took a deep breath as he took over holding me from Willow. 'All right, I've got you,' he said, tears shimmering in his eyes.

'I love you,' I said as I held the amethyst, positioning the Talisman over Cwicsusl.

'I love you, too, my Samphire Amethyst,' he said brokenly, a tear running down his cheek. 'Always remember that.'

Life drained from me. A firestorm raged inside me, sucking my life away, tearing at my insides, setting fire to my mind. I swayed as a wave of dizziness passed over me.

Rian's breath hitched. 'I'll help you,' he whispered in my ear, placing his hand over mine on the amethyst.

Together we raised the Amethyst Talisman. Together we slammed the Artefact down onto Cwicsusl as the last red flecks in the sword and shield flickered and died.

Artefact against Artefact.

Amethyst against diamond.

Elemental Magic against Elemental Magic.

A bright flash of white light, brighter than any sun, filled the cabin.

Aldorbana and Cwicsusl screamed.

Pain streaked up through my hand, along my arm and into my chest. The voices of the Cursed Weapons intertwined and filled my head as their pain became mine as I, too, screamed in agony. The bright light twisted in front of me like a tornado, shimmered, and intensified with the pain, fracturing into all the colours of the rainbow, dancing like the sunlit water droplets of a fountain.

What was happening? Was it working?

'Phire? Phire!' Rian's voice punctured the screams. *I love you... always remember that.*

But the bright, fractured light remained, and I couldn't reply to him, couldn't voice anything except for the pain. The screams of Aldorbana and Cwicsusl slowly receded, as did the light, and, gradually, the pain. Only then did I stop screaming.

I gasped for air and opened my eyes, finding myself slumped in Rian's arms. He held me close, his arms around me, his head resting on my shoulder as he trembled. A bright purple glow filled the room, a light which made everyone shy away. When the glow faded, I realised it had come from Cwicsusl, discarded on the floor, and Aldorbana, propped against the wall, but neither were red or clear as they had been previously, but purple. A beautiful, deep, amethyst purple.

Rian drew back, his eyes wide. 'Are you all right?'

'I-I think so,' I said, my voice croaky from the screaming. 'I'm okay.'

'There was a bright light and then a purple glow,' he said, awe in his eyes. 'I thought I was going to lose you after all.'

'Is it broken?' Anise asked, leaning forward, and studying the purple weapons. 'Is the Curse truly broken?'

'It must be. I don't feel tired anymore. I feel – I feel fine. Great, even. Better than I have in weeks,' I said, grinning at Rian.

He grinned back and leant forward, kissing me so tenderly and with such relief and love it brought tears to my eyes. 'I love you,' he whispered in my ear.

Blood rushed to my face.

'So, diamond yields to amethyst? Interesting,' Anise said, raising an eyebrow.

'What do we do with these now the Curse is broken?' Sage asked, looking suspiciously at Cwicsusl and Aldorbana.

'Are they purple because of you, Phire?' Willow asked. 'Or the Talisman?'

'I don't know,' I said, reaching out and gingerly touching the shield. A welcoming warmth greeted my hand. 'But they'll need new names, now. I don't think "Life-destroyer" and "Living torment" are apt anymore. They're more like old friends – we've been through a lot together.'

'Something in old Aerban, perhaps?' Rian asked.

'It seems appropriate,' I said, grinning at him.

'Well, what about calling the sword Deorwine and the shield Glædwine?'

'Doesn't "wine" mean friend?' Tarragon asked, studying Cwicsusl.

Rian nodded. 'That's right, "deor" means dear and "glæd" means bright.'

'Dearfriend and Brightfriend?' Anise asked. 'Very suitable, all things considered.'

'Deorwine and Glædwine it is, then,' I said, satisfied with their new names.

'I assume everythin's fine now?' Hyssop asked.

'Yes, Hyssop, thanks to you,' I said, beaming at him.

A bemused look crossed Hyssop's face. 'I only said your Talisman was an Artefact.'

'Exactly.'

'You didn't know?'

I shook my head.

'I didn't know it could break the Curse, though,' Hyssop added.

'But how did you know that the amethyst was an Artefact and not just an ordinary talisman, Hyssop?' Anise asked.

''Cause my family originally came from Chroma, and these thin's were passed down through the years, just in case we needed to know one day, although a lot of it's been forgotten now,' Hyssop said. 'I was shown how to spot an Artefact, but that's all, nothin' more. Your Jade Amulet's one too, by the way.'

Anise's eyes widened as he instinctively clutched at his necklace. 'What?'

'Just sayin'.'

'Are you going to destroy them?' Tarragon asked. 'That's what the Chromians wanted to do after the Great Pestilence, y'know – destroy all the Artefacts.'

Hyssop shook his head. 'It was so they couldn't be used for Magical purposes, but Magic is dyin' out in people now, and though I might know what they look like, I don't know how to destroy them. That knowledge was lost long ago. Anyway, the last remnants of Magic are fadin'. Just look after them. They're still very valuable.'

Anise nodded, looking at his Jade Amulet with a renewed respect.

'Captain, we need to talk to you about passage,' Rian said.

'I'm due to set sail on the next tide about now, actually,' Hyssop said. 'But I'm headin' for Mere with a load of herbs, wood, and carvin's.'

'Can you take us with you?' Tarragon asked, scratching at his chin thoughtfully.

'You want to go to Mere?' Hyssop asked, his green eyes widening.

'We want to go anywhere but Aerba,' Rian said.

Hyssop raised an eyebrow. 'Are you in some sort of trouble?'

'You could say that,' Sage muttered, playing with his hair.

'I know you didn't say last time, but I worked out from your clothes you were Prince Valerian,' he said. 'You're all King's Warriors, except for Samphire. I know the old King is dead, and I heard the new King intended to have you executed, Your Highness.'

Rian nodded. 'It's all true.'

'Chervil wanted to get Valerian out of the way, so he made up charges against him so he could execute him, but we stopped him,' I said. 'Now Chervil wants us dead.'

'Well, you're all welcome and safe here – I'm sorry to say none of us on board have much love for King Chervil, if you don't mind me sayin', Your Highness,' Hyssop said.

'I don't,' Rian said. 'And don't call me "Your Highness" while we're on board – call me Rian.'

'Very well,' Hyssop nodded, smiling. 'I expect you'd like me to get underway as quickly as possible?'

'Yes, please, if you can – I imagine we've been followed,' I said.

'Stay here while we set sail. You can fill me in on all the details later,' he said, winking at me and gesturing to Deorwine and Glædwine.

'I will.' I nodded as Hyssop left the cabin and started shouting orders, rousing his men from their slumbers.

'We'll get our things from the horses,' Sage said, heading for the door, then paused. 'Samphire? Maybe there *is* such a thing as Magic.' He looked at me, his brown eyes sincere. 'I guess I was wrong.' He gave me a quick hug. 'I'm glad you're all right, by the way.'

'An apology?' Anise asked, feigning shock. 'You really believe in Magic now? Remember this day, Phire, it's unlikely to happen again.'

Sage scowled at Anise, then turned back, gave me a little half smile, and left the room with the others, Willow pausing on her way out to give me a hug.

'Are you sure you're all right?' Rian asked, helping me to my feet, holding my hand and looking at the gold ring with its tiny glittering diamonds that adorned it – the gold ring I'd now never take off. It already felt part of me; a part of him that was always with me.

I nodded. 'I am, now – thank you for trusting me,' I said. 'Here.' I passed him the Amethyst Talisman.

'Shouldn't you keep it?' he asked, uncertainty flashing in his eyes.

'No, it looks better on you,' I said, smiling.

He took it from me and placed it back over his head, glancing down at the purple stone as it glittered in the lamplight. 'I'll never remove this for as long as I live,' he said, holding it with one hand and studying it. 'With it on, you're always with me, just as you said.' He bent towards me, his hot lips brushing mine for an instant before pulling back. My heart thundered in my chest, hammering at my ribcage as I drowned in his eyes, gazing into his soul. 'Kiss me,' he murmured, moving closer.

I pulled him to me, my lips meeting his. He held me close, his hands resting on my back and waist as I slipped my fingers through his hair and around his neck while I tasted the sweetness of his warm mouth. Our kiss deepened until I floated on air, high in the sky with my love, sandalwood in the air around me. My heart thundered so loudly Rian had to be hearing it or, at the very least, feeling it through my chest.

He pulled away for a moment, smiling that lopsided smile. 'You're beautiful,' he said, bringing his hand to my face and gently stroking it, his voice slightly hoarse.

'I'm nothing special – Beryl was always the pretty one,' I said.

'You are to me, my Samphire Amethyst – the most beautiful, special and precious thing in all the world,' he said quite earnestly. 'And I love you more than ever, especially as I've almost lost you again. I'll never take you for granted.'

'Oh,' was all I could get out, my eyes widening at his words. No one had ever spoken to me like that before. I'd never been that special to anyone – Father and Mal, maybe, but I wasn't sure they really counted. To be special to someone, and for that someone to be Valerian, sent such warmth spiralling through me that I wasn't sure whether to laugh or cry with joy.

He looked into my eyes as blood rushed to my face and I slowly licked my lips, hoping for another kiss. He smiled, his pupils dilating as he chewed his bottom lip for a moment, then took hold of a loose curl hanging down the side of my head and started playing with it. 'Because you're my wife now–'

'Wife? It's not exactly legal, what we did.'

A flash of uncertainty crossed his face. 'It was the best we could do in the circumstances,' he said, a defensive note to his voice. 'And it's good enough for me, but if it's not what you want – I mean, if you don't want to be tied to me…'

'No, I don't want to be tied to you.'

He stopped twirling my curl around his fingers, his eyes clouding as he looked at me.

'I want to be bound to you forever,' I said. 'I meant everything I said in that dungeon, and I'll never take one word of it back again. I want to spend the rest of my life with you, husband.'

He relaxed, breathed, and smiled the sort of smile that goes from your lips across your face and lights up your eyes like stars, one that sent my heart racing. 'So do I, wife,' he said, his voice crackling with emotion, eyes full of wonder.

I smiled back.

I knew as far as the Blood Rule Decree was concerned, what we'd done didn't really count. Our vows to each other meant nothing. In our hearts, though, it was an entirely different matter. Those vows were more real to us, more sacred, than any ceremony in the Temple of Herbs or signed document ever could be.

He went back to twirling my hair around his fingers. 'You know what I really want to do now?'

'What's that?' I asked.

He leant towards me, his lips brushing mine, then paused, his mouth barely a hair's breadth from mine. 'I want to show you exactly how much I love you.'

I'd wondered when he might mention that. 'I'm not sure a hammock will make what you have in mind particularly easy – memorable, but not easy,' I said, my face burning.

'Are you sure you don't want to give it a go?' he asked, arching an eyebrow suggestively as he moved back a little.

'You're impossible,' I said, playfully punching his shoulder. He grabbed my hand and brought it to his face.

'I try,' he said grinning, before kissing my fingers with his hot lips.

'I think we should probably wait.'

He nodded. 'You're right. I want our first time to be special and unhurried – not in a hammock, worrying about whether someone's going to walk in on us,' he said.

'Or if we're going to fall out,' I said, giving him a long look.

'True. We'll just have to be patient and, for now, make do with this.' Rian leant towards me, my back resting against the cabin wall. His mouth met mine as he kissed me again, pressing his warm body against me as I wrapped my arms around him, his hands caressing my neck and side. A silken knot formed in my stomach at his tenderness.

As the kiss finished and we parted, I pulled him back towards me for a hug, and I couldn't help but kiss his neck, his sandalwood skin begging me to touch it. His breathing became heavier as I kissed his ear. He let out a moan, a kind of moan I'd never heard before, one that drew a shiver from me.

'Again,' he said, almost pleading, his voice like the warmest summer breeze. 'Do it again.' I did as he asked, once more gently kissing his ear. He pressed against me, letting out that soft moan again, and my heart leapt in my chest, sparks shooting to my fingers and toes, as I felt him respond to me. 'You'd better stop,' he said breathlessly, 'or I'll have to finish this, regardless of the hammock situation.'

He turned my face to his and we kissed again, for a while losing track of time.

Captain Hyssop soon had *The Sea Urchin* underway, and we all stayed below decks as the ship left the dock and slid out towards the open sea. As dawn stained the horizon, I peered out the cabin window to see a series of pitch torches making their way through Hops.

'Is that them?' I asked.

Rian came and stood beside me. 'Probably,' he said. 'Looks like we only just made it out in time.'

'They're unlikely to follow us once we leave Aerban waters, and certainly not all the way to Mere,' Sage said. 'After that speech, Chervil has his mind on waging war elsewhere.'

Anise nodded. 'We should be safe now,' he said, glancing at Sage, his eyes almost glowing as he slipped his hand into his boyfriend's. 'And free.'

'Free,' Willow said, standing on her tiptoes and kissing Tarragon gently on the lips.

He smiled at her, his cheeks flushing. 'I'm not sure what my father will think once he realises we've gone for good.'

'Or mine,' Sage said, tugging gently at his silver earring. 'But I'm not sure I care, now.'

'Chervil will go absolutely insane,' Willow said, smirking at Rian. 'Especially once he realises you've left Aerba.'

'I hope he does,' Rian said with a wry grin.

'You think anyone will notice if he does?' Anise asked.

'Probably not,' Sage said. 'It'll be business as usual for him.'

A little later, with Hops far behind us, Rian and I went out onto the deck. The sun rested high in the sky and we stood at the prow, watching the ship cut through the water, foam churning at its sides. The clear sky and keen wind made for a smooth voyage as the southern coastline of Aerba slipped past in the distance.

'Are you all right?' I asked.

Rian glanced at me. 'Yes, why?'

'Well, you know, your father and leaving your home.'

His eyes had a faraway look for a moment. 'Despite everything, I will miss Father, but I don't feel the loss I did when Mother died. As for leaving Aerba?' He sighed. 'I do wish things were different and we could stay, but, in the end, for me, home is wherever you are, so as long as you're with me, I'll be at home.'

'You do have a way with words, sometimes.'

'Do you think so?'

'I do.'

He shrugged. 'It's just the truth.'

I looped my arm through his and rested my head on his shoulder. 'What do you think happened to Priest Cardamon?' I asked, thinking of the old man.

Rian frowned. 'I don't know, but I don't think even Chervil would risk the wrath of the Herbs and the Priests by killing Cardamon. I think he's still alive somewhere.'

'Good,' I said, hoping he was right.

'You think the Coterie will still come after us?' Rian asked, looking out over the water.

'I don't know, but if we keep a low profile, we ought to be able to stay out of their reach, and besides, the archipelago isn't really somewhere they're interested in,' I said. 'There's no benefit for Juniper in doing anything there, and I'm not sure she'll want Beryl using up valuable resources coming after us when we're of no further consequence to Aerba or Iolite.'

'Well, let's hope they leave us alone,' Rian said, taking my hand

and intertwining his fingers with mine. 'At least we can be together now with no Curse hanging over our heads.'

I nodded. Deorwine and Glædwine still seemed intent on not letting me get very far from them, and they sat on the deck next to me, propped up against a barrel.

'We can be together, and so can the others,' I said.

Rian slipped his free hand around my waist, pulling me gently towards him. 'Free at last,' he said, letting go of my hand, caressing my cheek. 'Free forever.'

He gently kissed me as we stood holding each other, leaving the Aerban coast far behind as we embarked on our new future.

Together.

EPILOGUE

We sat around the captain's table enjoying an evening meal with Hyssop, freshly-caught fish the highlight of the menu. Sage looked sourly at the seafood, gnawing on a piece of bread.

'We need to put in at Scilla, in Flos,' I said. 'Rian and I have been talking, and we're going to look for Mal and the Fire Opal.'

Rian nodded.

'I thought Mal was dead?' Tarragon said, sitting up straight at the news.

'That's what Juniper wants everyone to believe,' I said. 'But Moonstone has heard that he's still alive, imprisoned by her somewhere. Onyx believes someone high up in the Flosian Royal Family knows where he is.'

'But what about the archipelago?' Sage asked.

'We'll meet you there later,' Rian said. 'But we must deal with this first.'

'You really think you'll find answers there?'

'That's what we're hoping for,' I said. 'I have cousins there who I can speak to. They might know something or know someone who does.'

'But what about the war? Chervil has already threatened Flos,' Willow said, a worried look in her eyes as she sipped on some of Anise's special tea. 'Aerbans won't be welcome in Flos.'

'We can use disguises,' Anise said, his eyes bright. 'Just like in Iolite.'

'We?' Rian asked, his eyes narrowing.

Sage sighed. 'We're hardly going to let you go on your little side quest alone, are we?'

'But–'

'Don't argue, Rian, we're coming too,' Tarragon said. 'We'd already discussed it amongst ourselves. We knew the two of you would probably be planning something like this to get the Fire Opal back, but we didn't know about Mal. It's just all the more reason to come.'

Rian looked at me. I shrugged and smiled. As much as I was happy to go alone with Rian, having the others with us would help, particularly if we got into a fight.

'As long as you think it's worth it,' Sage said, raising an eyebrow.

'I want to get the Fire Opal back. It's important to the whole of Aerba, but it's particularly important to me – you all know that.' Rian's amber eyes burnt with emotion. 'It's part of my heritage.'

'Ours, too,' Sage said, nodding. 'We don't have a choice really, do we?'

'No.'

'As long as we're not at sea, I don't care,' Willow said, sipping her tea.

'And I really need to find out what I can about Mal,' I said. 'See if I can discover where Juniper has him imprisoned.'

'I don't like to think of your brother languishing in prison somewhere,' Rian said.

I frowned a moment. 'Even though he…'

'Even though.' Rian nodded.

I smiled at Rian, so moved that he'd rescue my brother even after what he'd done to Rian's own sister.

'It would be nice to get the Fire Opal back,' Sage said.

Anise nodded and slipped his arm around his boyfriend's shoulders.

Tarragon nodded his agreement. 'I'd quite like to see Mal again, too, y'know?'

'So, we'll speak to Phire's family and see what we can find out about the Fire Opal and Mal's whereabouts. We'll find them both, then head for the archipelago, agreed?' Rian looked around the table.

Everyone nodded.

Rian reached out and took my hand. 'We will find your brother – your brother and the Fire Opal.'

I smiled at him, the warmth of his hand filling me with hope.

'Would you mind putting in at Scilla, Hyssop?' I asked.

Hyssop looked around at us, his eyes thoughtful. Throughout our discussion he'd remained silent. 'Not at all. In fact, I think you're right to hunt down the Fire Opal. It can't be left out there, its whereabouts unknown.'

'What makes you say that?' Rian asked, his head tilting slightly to one side as he raised an eyebrow.

'I know I said Magic was dyin' out in people, but it's not dead yet. There may still be Magic Spinners out there, and if the Fire Opal fell into the wrong hands, it could be used for hideous thin's we can't even imagine.'

A cold chill whistled through me at the prospect of Magic Spinners still living in the Five Lands today. Then a shard of ice pierced my chest as his words sank in. I looked at Rian, his eyes wide like mine. 'You mean it's a…?'

'The Fire Opal is an Artefact. Probably the most powerful one there's ever been.'

DRAMATIS PERSONAE AND GLOSSARY OF TERMS

LAND OF IOLITE

Agate – Librarian at the Iolite University.

Amethyst – An assassin. Daughter of the late Master of Iolite. Younger sister of Malachite and twin of Beryl. Legendary member of the Iolite Coterie of Assassins and known as Lady Merciless.

Beryl – Twin sister to Amethyst, and sister of Malachite.

Carnelian – A notorious assassin. Member of the Iolite Coterie of Assassins.

Citrine – An assassin. Sister to Carnelian. Member of the Iolite Coterie of Assassins.

Elm – Son of Juniper. Member of the Iolite Coterie of Assassins and involved in Coterie business.

Emerald – Dead Mistress of Iolite. First wife of Lord Peridot. Mother to Malachite, Amethyst and Beryl.

Feldspar – An assassin and member of the Iolite Coterie.

Flint – Chief Assassin of the Iolite Coterie of Assassins.

Juniper – Mistress of Iolite and Leader of the Iolite Coterie of Assassins. Mother of Elm. Widowed second wife of Lord Peridot and stepmother to Malachite, Amethyst and Beryl. Originally from the land of Trew.

Malachite (Mal) – An assassin. Older brother of Amethyst and Beryl. About to become Master of Iolite on his imminent twenty-first birthday. Member of the Iolite Coterie of Assassins.

Moonstone – Librarian at the Iolite University.

Onyx – An assassin and member of the Iolite Coterie. Best friend to Amethyst and Malachite.

Peridot – Dead Master of Iolite. Father to Malachite, Amethyst and Beryl.

Topaz – An assassin. Carnelian's girlfriend and member of the Coterie.

LAND OF AERBA

Angelica – Crown Princess of Aerba and heir to the throne. Eldest child of King Finule and Queen Myrtle. Older sister of Chervil and Valerian.

Anise – King's Warrior and Herbalist.

Bergamot – King Finule's cousin and Chief of the Military. Father of Sage and Sorrel.

Chervil – Prince of Aerba. Second child of King Finule and Queen Myrtle. Younger brother to Crown Princess Angelica, older brother to Valerian.

Finule – King of the Land of Aerba. Widowed husband of Queen Myrtle. Father of Angelica, Chervil and Valerian.

Hyssop – First mate of the ship *The Sea Urchin*.

Myrtle – Dead Queen of Aerba. Late wife of King Finule. Mother of Angelica, Chervil and Valerian.

Sage – Cousin to Valerian and King's Warrior. Younger brother to Sorrel.

Sorrel – Older brother of Sage, cousin to Valerian and King's Warrior.

Tarragon – Cousin and best friend to Valerian. King's Warrior.

Valerian (Rian) – Prince of Aerba. Third and youngest child of King Finule and Queen Myrtle. Head of the King's Warriors.

Willowherb (Willow) – King's Warrior-Attendant.

Wintergreen – King Finule's cousin and Chamberlain. Father of Tarragon.

Wormwood – Head of the Nightshade.

CAPITAL CITIES

Adamas – Capital city of Iolite.

Viridi – Capital city of Aerba.

CREATURES

Dryads – Creatures from the forests of Flos.

Powlers – Lake dwelling creatures, now seldom seen in Aerba.

Merean Blue Death Worms – Great worms that live out in the deserts of Mere.

Morgens – Creatures of the sea and lakes that take their victims down into the depths and drown them. Their beautiful song is as enchanting as it is dangerous.

Mynogres – Legendary creatures that once roamed the forests of Aerba.

TERMS

Artefacts – Crystals that could enhance the power of an Elemental Magic Spinner.

Blood Class System – Hierarchical system you are born into. Your Blood Class cannot be changed. Each Blood Class has particular rules and a dress code they must adhere to.

Blood Rule Decree – Laws governing the Blood Classes, including rules on relationships and naming of children.

Elemental Angle Spinners/Elemental Magic Spinners – Ancient High Bloods who could wield Elemental Magic.

High Bloods – The Royal Family and extended relations.

Iolite Coterie of Assassins – Order of Assassins led by Mistress Juniper and run from Iolite.

King's Warriors – King Finule's best Warriors.

Low Bloods – All citizens that do not fit into the High and Middle Blood Classes.

Magic Angle – The Element a Magic Spinner could wield: Air, Earth, Fire, Quintessence or Water.

Middle Bloods – Lesser nobles, high status citizens and priests.

The Nightshade – Aerba's spy network.

Thyme – Aerba's sacred herb.

ACKNOWLEDGEMENTS

Firstly, I want to thank Peter and Alison, aka Elsewhen Press, for rescuing Phire and Rian, and giving them a fantastic new home. You have my eternal gratitude, and I'm so glad you've loved their story as much as you have.

My biggest thanks go to my husband and daughter for their never-ending love, support, and supply of chocolate! To my sister who inspired me with the idea of Magic Angles and Spinning, I couldn't have done it without you.

To my original editor, Lauren Dooley, thank you for believing in me, Phire, and Rian – this amazing journey wouldn't have started without you. Editor Nicole Lindsay has travelled the entirety of the Six Lands with me, and my thanks go to you, too.

Two of my writer friends, Emma Bradley and Estelle Tudor, continue to offer great inspiration, and are amazing sounding boards when it comes to ideas and writing in general. Thank you both!

To everyone who has read and enjoyed Phire and Rian's story – THANK YOU! I hope you've had fun on their adventures, and with the various twists and turns along the way. If you want to know more about my writing and books, then please visit my website www.aerinapeltun.com and sign up to my newsletter!

Happy reading!

Aerin

Elsewhen Press

delivering outstanding new talents in speculative fiction

Visit the Elsewhen Press website at elsewhen.press for the latest information on all of our titles, authors and events; to read our blog; find out where to buy our books and ebooks; or to place an order.

Sign up for the Elsewhen Press InFlight Newsletter at elsewhen.press/newsletter

<u>CURSED WEAPONS TRILOGY BY AERIN APELTUN</u>

BOOK 1: THE AMETHYST TALISMAN

<u>ISBN: 9781917507332 (epub, kindle) / 9781917507233 (304pp paperback)</u>

BOOK 2: THE MALACHITE QUEST

Having escaped the land of Aerba, Samphire, Valerian, and their friends continue in their quest to find Samphire's brother, Malachite, and Aerba's legendary Fire Opal. But their travels are complicated by Aerba and Flos teetering on the edge of war.

Now knowing of the existence of Magic, and the Fire Opal's possible power, they continue on in the hope that they can recover the stolen Artefact, and Malachite – but hope is fading fast.

With a long journey ahead, and time against them, Samphire and Valerian find their love tested, and heartbreak before them. And when a friend from Samphire's past reappears and new tensions arise, can they not just overcome them, but also stay one step ahead of the assassins that dog their steps as they try to reach Malachite before they're out of time?

<u>ISBN: 9781917507349 (epub, kindle) / 9781917507240 (288pp paperback)</u>

BOOK 3: THE OPAL KING

ISBN: 9781917507356 (epub, kindle) / 9781917507257 (308pp paperback)

Visit bit.ly/TheCursedWeapons

THE WITCH'S JOURNEY

KEITH MILLER

A key may unlock more than just a door.

In a town beset by demons, from which the children are disappearing, redheaded Mira grows up wild and willful. When she's around, soups boil over and flowers catch fire, and one night in her sleep she unwittingly turns her house around.

The morning of her thirteenth birthday, Mira receives a gift from the river: a gold key. It will lead her on a journey, to seek the door her key will open.

The Witch's Journey is a dark fairytale embroidered with fairytales, full of sorrows and terrors, heartbreaks and delights, chocolates and mayhem and magic.

"A book to savor as you would fine chocolate: rich, dark, dreamlike, familiar as a fairytale, sweet as sin. I adored it."

– **Alix E. Harrow**, Hugo Award–winning
author of *The Once and Future Witches*

"Such a special story; the kind that steps into your dreams then wakes you with the taste of chocolate on your lips as a shadow in the corner walks away, and you are left remembering a place you've read about and a witch you suspect knows you've been there, and it all feels like the most delicious secret. I loved this book!"

– **Mary Rickert**, World Fantasy Award–winning
author of *The Memory Garden*

"This is rich and delicious magic for the bravest of readers."
– **William Alexander**, US National Book Award–winning
author of *Goblin Secrets*

ISBN: 9781915304933 (epub, kindle) / 9781915304834 (226pp paperback)

Visit bit.ly/TheWitchsJourney

The Forge & The Flood

Miles Nelson

When history itself seems written to keep them apart, can two radically different peoples really find it in their hearts to get along?

Sienna is an Ailura. His kind live on the lonely island of Veramilia, bound under traditions forged by countless generations.
Indigo is a Lutra. His kind goes with the flow, having lived as free as the ocean waves since the beginning of time.

When a great calamity strikes and the Ailura are forced to flee their island home, the Ailura and the Lutra come face to face for the first time in known history. In these turbulent times, it is Indigo and Sienna who are chosen to find a suitable habitat for the displaced tribe. One a princess destined to rule his kind, the other the only son of a would-be chief, the pair seem like a natural choice.

But as friendship blossoms into something more, and their journey takes them further and further from known lands, the wanderers begin to uncover secrets hidden among the ruins. Secrets which suggest the two species may not be as alien to one another as previously thought.

ISBN: 9781915304100 (epub, kindle) / 9781915304001 (184pp paperback)

Visit bit.ly/Forge&Flood

ABOUT AERIN APELTUN

Aerin Apeltun is an English writer based in the East of England. She started writing stories as a child, and has always loved reading about fantasy worlds. Aerin now loves to develop and write about her own worlds and mythologies.

Having been listed in a number of writing competitions, Aerin's Upper YA Romantasy, *Crystal Bloods,* was published by Elsewhen Press in February 2025, with a sequel to follow in 2026. Upper YA Fantasy Romance trilogy, *The Cursed Weapons*, out now, will be followed by a New Adult Historical Romantasy duology scheduled for 2026/7; she is always busy working on something!

A Second Class Archer, Aerin has had various careers in school/university administration and insurance, as well as a stint at the local library, but writing is her passion. She also loves to draw, and is a keen fantasy cartographer, designing maps for her worlds. Aerin enjoys travelling, taking inspiration from nature and landscapes for settings and characters in her books.